about the author

Chad Kultgen is the author of *The Average American Male*. He graduated from the USC School of Cinematic Arts, and lives in California.

the
lie

the
lie

a novel

chad
kultgen

HARPER ⬤ PERENNIAL

NEW YORK • LONDON • TORONTO • SYDNEY • NEW DELHI • AUCKLAND

HARPER ● PERENNIAL

HarperCollins books may be purchased for educational, business, or sales promotional use. For information please write: Special Markets Department, HarperCollins Publishers, 10 East 53rd Street, New York, NY 10022.

FIRST EDITION

Designed by Laura Kaeppel

Library of Congress Cataloging-in-Publication Data

Kultgen, Chad.
    The lie : a novel / Chad Kultgen.— 1st Harper Perennial ed.
      p. cm.
    ISBN 978-0-06-165730-6
    1. Triangles (Interpersonal relations)—Fiction. I. Title.
    PS3611.U48L54 2009
    813'.6—dc22

                                                    2008043425

09 10 11 12 13 OV/RRD 10 9 8 7 6 5 4 3 2 1

the
lie

kyle gibson

You're going to hate me. You're going to hate me more than most of the other people you've come to hate. Everybody else who hears this story does. Obviously, I wish things would have ended differently, but I don't have any regrets. I still stand by everything I did, but you're going to hate me. I just ask that, no matter how much it might seem like I'm the worst piece of shit who ever walked the planet and no matter how much it might seem like what I did is completely deplorable, you try to see it from my point of view. Try to remember the moment when all the stupid innocent things you thought about life and love, all the things you thought mattered, all the things you thought were true . . . try to remember when they all turned out to be lies.

heather andruss

I majored in elementary education. I never really wanted to be a teacher, but I always kind of figured that the stuff I learned would be great when I like have my first baby. Hopefully we'll start trying soon, which Kyle doesn't know about, but I'm sure it'll get back to him and when it does I hope he realizes that he's basically like the biggest dick I've ever met and I have a pretty much perfect life, just like I wanted, in spite of everything he did. I mean he completely tried to ruin my life. He was too pathetic to actually ruin it, but he literally tried to ruin my life. Seriously, what kind of asshole tries to ruin somebody else's life on purpose? Honestly I feel sorry for him now, but we all get what we deserve. I know I did.

brett keller

My father owns the second largest freight and shipping company in the southwest, Keller Shipping. My grandfather started the company, my father took it over when he retired, and now it seems I'll do the same when my father retires. The first time I had my dick sucked I was eleven. It was my babysitter. She was sixteen. Not that pretty, but nice tits. She smelled nice. She was also the first girl I fucked in the ass. I mention these events because, until very recently, I considered them to be among the most important moments of my life. I never thought anything Kyle and I were doing would lead to this, especially considering some of the more nefarious things I had done up to that point. I actually found it all to be quite amusing. I had little if any concern that it would have any further impact on my life beyond my previously stated amusement. I was clearly incorrect. The events that unfolded as a result of my involvement in all of this left me with little choice in the end. I couldn't risk the potential excommunication from my family had I acted on personal preference alone, so certain compromises were made to maintain my position within my family for obvious financial reasons.

part one
freshman year

I fucking loved her like no guy has ever loved a girl. I know every guy has thought that about some girl, and that's exactly why I'm saying it. I'm also saying it because it was true.

We met about two weeks into our freshman year at SMU. I was majoring in biological sciences with the intent of getting into a good med school and she was getting a bachelor's degree in elementary education—she wanted to be a teacher. That seemed so sweet to me at the time. She was actually going to college to learn how to be a good teacher. I had a few teachers I liked along the way, but I'll never forget overhearing Mr. Campbell, my high school history teacher, telling Mrs. Baude, my high school calculus teacher, that he started teaching because it was the only job he could get and twenty-five years later it was the only job he could keep. I always kind of figured that's how most teachers became teachers, but she was actively pursuing the career. It was almost noble.

Classes had just barely started. I got a few syllabi, but I still hadn't even gone to some first classes yet because the hadn't been held. I was sitting in my dorm room in McElvaney, talking to my roommate, Dave, about some stupid bullshit like how he couldn't wait to get back home for Christmas so he could get some of his mom's cooking or some other inconsequential crap. Actually, maybe he was talking about which frats he wanted to try to get into the following semester. I had no interest in joining a frat, which he tried to convince me was the biggest mistake I would ever make. Later I found out he was a born-again Christian, and when he found out I didn't go to church or subscribe to any religion he tried to convince me that burning in hell was almost as big a mistake as not getting into a frat. Anyway, whatever we were talking about got inter-rupted when we both heard a thud followed by some whimpering in the hallway outside our door. We went out to see what in the hell was going on and there was Heather. She was shit-faced beyond recognition.

Heather had apparently been too drunk to walk and had used her friend as a human crutch as they both stumbled back to McElvaney from whatever party they were at. Once they were in the hallway, her friend passed out, they both fell down, and Heather smashed her head against the wall. She had a small cut on her forehead and she was kind of crying or moaning—just making weird low noises, really. I remem-ber genuinely feeling bad for her.

I asked her if she was okay and she said, "I need to lay down, I think."

She was hot as hell, there's no question about that. But there was something about her, something beyond just looking good, that at-tracted me to her almost immediately. I had a few girlfriends in high school I thought were cute or whatever, but not like this. I know it's gay, but it was her eyes or something. I don't know. Maybe it was just seeing her completely out-of-control drunk, too. But there was some kind of immediate attraction that wasn't like anything I'd ever felt. So, seeing a hot chick in need of aid, I did what any normal guy would have done. Actually I did what any pussy-ass chump would have done. I helped her up and asked if I could take her back to her room, with no intention of making any kind of move on her.

She said, "What floor are we on?"

I said, "Third."

"I think my room is on two. I can't really walk anymore. Where's your room?"

I said, "Right here."

As Heather went into my room I tried to get her friend up off the floor, but when I reached down and touched her arm she started yelling, "Get your fucking hands off me, asshole." Then she launched a halfhearted punch at my balls that kind of glanced off my thigh. I looked back to Heather to see if she was going to offer me some help in wrangling her friend, but she was already in my room, on my bed. Not wanting to risk another nut-shot, I just left her friend there, assuming she'd sober up and find her way back to her room.

I essentially could have done anything I wanted to Heather that night, but it didn't even cross my mind. I took off her shoes, went down the hall and ran some warm water over a washrag in the bathroom, came back, cleaned the blood off her forehead, put a Band-Aid on the cut, pulled up the covers, and—get this shit—I went to sleep on the fucking floor so she'd be more comfortable.

I remember Dave just pretending to go to sleep. At the time I really didn't know why, but after I found out about how Christian he was I thought it might have had something to do with breaking some rule against God or something by having a girl in our room. Who knows? He was a weird guy.

The next morning was awkward at best. Heather woke up before I did. She nudged me and then we introduced ourselves.

She said something like, "Hi. I'm Heather."

I said something like, "I'm Kyle."

"Did we . . . I hate having to actually ask this, but did we have sex last night?"

"No."

"Oh, I thought we . . . Are you sure?"

"Yeah. Positive. I think I would have remembered."

"I thought we were both drunk, though. I just want to make sure in case we didn't use any protection, you know, so I can get a morning-after pill."

This was our first official conversation and she was basically telling me that she was so slutty that standard operations for her involved being unable to remember having sex with a guy five hours after his dick was in her followed by eating morning-after pills like they were daily vitamins and this didn't even tip me off at all that this chick was bad fucking news.

I said, "You were pretty out of it, but I was completely sober."

"Wait, you're not the guy I met at Tammy's party last night?"

"No."

"Oh."

Again, concrete confirmation that she was a fucking slut of the highest order. Again, completely fucking ignored by myself.

"So how did I get here exactly?"

"I heard you fall in the hall outside, so I went out to see if you were okay and then you just kind of came in my room and passed out in my bed."

She reached up and touched her head, felt the Band-Aid, then said, "Oh, oh my God. I'm so sorry."

"I tried to take you back to your room, but you asked to stay here. So I put a Band-Aid over your cut and let you have the bed."

"And you slept on the floor all night?"

"Yeah."

And it was right at that moment that she gave me this look. It's the only time a girl has ever looked at me like that. Kind of sad and sweet at the same time, like I had done something for her that no guy had ever even approached doing for her—almost like she expected me to have raped her or something, and because I didn't it made some deeper connection with her. At the time I thought the look was about all of those things, about her having some real feelings for me. But now, after all the shit that's happened, I realize that look, the look that essentially started all of this crap, was actually just pity. Nothing more. She thought I was pathetic because I didn't try to fuck her that night. And no matter what words were said and what things were done in the years that followed, she could never truly love me because she could never respect a guy who didn't take advantage of her.

After the look she said, "Oh my God, where's Annie?"

"Your friend?"

"Yeah, where is she?"

"She was passed out in the hall last time I saw her."

"Did you wake her up?"

"I tried but she was pretty drunk. She just asked me to leave her there so I did."

"Oh my God."

She got up out of my bed and opened my dorm room door to find Annie still passed out in the same spot, but now with some of her own puke dried on the front of her shirt.

She said, "Thank God she's okay."

"Yeah."

"Well, thanks for, you know, helping me last night."

I was too anxious to hold back. "Maybe we could go do something sometime."

"Yeah, I don't know. My roommate and I are just meeting a lot of people, you know, before we rush next semester, so . . . We'll probably be pretty busy, but I'm sure we'll run into each other again."

"Okay, cool."

"So . . . I guess I should probably be getting Annie back and everything, but really, thanks again."

And that was pretty much it. She left my room and scraped up Annie off the ground. I thought I might see her in passing or something, but I had already chalked up our encounter to what I hoped would be a long string of strange interactions with hot chicks in my dorm.

When she left I realized my roommate, Dave, was awake the whole time and was witness to my entire interaction with Heather. He said something like, "Good try, man. Just remember, if Christ wants something to happen it will, but it will happen in his time," which was my first real taste of the born-again-flavored shit pie he was going to force-feed down my throat every day of our freshman year.

chapter
two

Even though I was the one who hit my head on the wall and got injured, Annie was way worse than me. She didn't really wake up for like a long time and when I finally got her to stumble back to our room, she was still drunk. I had to call the RA because she was so bad. The RA looked at her and I guess he had seen this kind of thing before because he was like, "She has alcohol poisoning," without even batting an eye. Annie had to go to the hospital and everything and get her stomach pumped and an IV and it was just really bad, but she ended up being okay, I mean after her parents calmed down.

The entire time she was at the hospital I just stayed in our room, and I know it sounds really corny, but I just couldn't stop thinking about Kyle. I know he's a dick, but I didn't know it then and I mean how sweet was it that he took me into his room and put a Band-Aid on my cut? Seriously? I mean no guy does that. Or if they do it's because they're trying to sleep with you, or if they've already slept with you, it's because they're trying to have a threesome with you and your best friend or some weird thing like that. My first boyfriend in high school did things like that, but only because he didn't know any better, I think. As soon as we started having sex, he became a real prick. I got the feeling Kyle did it because he was like a really nice guy. It was kind of refreshing, I guess, at first anyway.

I mean, I figured we'd probably never go out or anything. Even from just that one night I could tell he was kind of a little nerdy and not like a good nerdy. Sometimes nerdy guys can be totally hot. He wasn't like that. He was like real nerdy—like the kind of nerdy that girls would laugh at if they knew we were dating. The kind of nerdy that might keep me out of my top sorority choices when I rushed the next semester.

I guess I can't say I remember much from the next few weeks because, honestly, I was completely trashed for most of it. It was just a lot of parties and a lot of hooking up with random guys who were going to be rushing—trying to figure out which ones might make good boyfriends, trying to figure out which ones might or might not make good fiancé material a few years down the road. Pretty basic, I guess.

There was actually one time, maybe like three days after the thing with Kyle, when I was at a party being thrown by Gabe Childress at his parents' house in Highland Park. Pretty much every guy there was sure he was going to rush SAE or Pike so it was fun and there was just so much coke and E that I couldn't really say no and I ended up in a bedroom with this complete asshole named Collin Davis. At the time I didn't know what an asshole he was and I was rolling, so Annie (fresh out of the hospital for alcohol poisoning) and me ended up giving him like a double blowjob. I regret doing it now, but at the time it was pretty fun. It wasn't the first time I had kissed a girl or anything but it was the first time I had done anything like that with a guy in the room.

Even before I really got to know Collin, I can remember thinking he was a loser. The whole time Annie and I were blowing him he kept saying, "Good girls, good girls," like we were fucking dogs or something. If I hadn't been on drugs I seriously would have like laughed in his face. The weirdest part about that thing with Collin is, I was thinking about Kyle the whole time I was doing it—you know, like wondering if Kyle would be saying, "Good girls, good girls." Then I remember thinking he probably hadn't even had a blowjob from one girl, let alone two. Then I started wondering what his high school girlfriend was like, or if he even had one. She was probably a band nerd if he did. Then I think I started thinking about his dick and what it might look like, and then Collin tried to cum on our faces, but totally missed and ended up just getting semen on his own pants. I wish Annie or me would have been together enough to say, "Good boy," back to him, but, like I said, we were really, really high so . . .

Now that I'm thinking about it, I actually did run into Kyle again pretty soon after we first met. I guess I didn't run into him, I just saw him walking between Boaz Hall and the Crow Building. The only reason I remember it is because he was walking with Brett Keller, and I was like, "How is that nerdy guy friends with Brett?"

Even though it was just a few weeks into our freshman year, pretty much every girl on campus knew who Brett Keller was. Probably one of the top ten hottest guys on campus and easily in the top five richest guys on campus, maybe the richest—he probably was. A lot of girls also said he had a huge dick, which was never my thing, but it did make him seem more important somehow—like if you hooked up with him, you were part of the "I had sex with Brett Keller and lived to tell about it" club.

As corny as it may sound, the fact that I saw Kyle hanging out with Brett made me think he might not be that bad. I mean if he was cool enough to be friends with Brett, then he was probably at least slightly cool himself. And even if he wasn't, I remember thinking that if we became friends or started hooking up or something, there might be a chance for me to hang out with Brett later and then maybe Brett would be into me.

I knew it was a long shot, but it did get me thinking that it might be worth my time to at least pretend to be interested in Kyle. Seriously, at the time I thought, worst-case scenario—I end up giving Kyle a few blowjobs before I find out I have no shot with Brett. Best-case scenario—I end up giving Kyle a few blowjobs before Brett realizes he wants to steal me from Kyle.

chapter
three

I've known Kyle since third grade. His father has worked for my father since that time as a regional manager at Keller Shipping. Although his family never had the money mine did, his father always made sure he went to the right private schools, associated with the right children of the men he worked for, fostered the right interest in personal and academic achievement, et cetera—all to give his son the best possible chance to ascend to the next rung on the economic ladder, the rung he himself would never see.

I think the reason we became friends so quickly has something to do with the fact that, although he was a member of the same social circles as me, he wasn't born into them. Even at nine or ten my boredom with the overprivileged kids of my father's friends had become palpable. Kyle was the only student at St. Mark's who had humility, an attitude that was so foreign to the rest of my peers that they quickly became disgusting to me. My understanding of the resource my family possessed wasn't immediate. It took the better part of my prepubescent years to realize I would essentially never have a real concern in my life. Any problematic situation I ever faced would be erased by the unwavering certainty that, whether the problem was solved or not, I could abandon it because my resource to create new situations was virtually unlimited. The rest of my social circle, Kyle excluded, didn't understand this, or if they did it was long after I had come to realize it. As a result they led what I found to be boring lives consumed with material and superficial concerns about new cars, clothes, who was fucking whom, where they were vacationing, and various other issues of false importance. My disdain for my friends, I quickly came to understand, had to be suppressed in order to calm my father, to make him believe I was just the next generation of Keller man who would socialize with the next generations of the other families that mine had socialized with in years past. I was just the next generation of Keller man who would run the company in exactly the same fashion my father had before me and his father had before him. I would exhibit no deviation, take no step outside the path that would assure my son would mimic all the same actions and have his own son who would do the same, so on and so on until the sun devours our planet. That is why I liked Kyle. He understood. It seems a simple reason for a friendship, but also potentially the only reason to maintain one.

Kyle was, very simply put, my only real friend. All the others existed, it seemed, in order to placate me and thus ensure that their families would remain aligned with mine for one more generation. Had they done anything to lose their connection to my family, they would have been the disgrace of their own. Coming from outside that pitiful world made Kyle immediately interesting to me. His first year at St. Mark's could have been very difficult were it not for me.

I was not unaware of the fact that, based on my family's vastly superior wealth, I was the de facto alpha male among the others. Nor was I ignorant or unappreciative of the benefits this afforded me, one being immediate acceptance into the group of whomever I deemed worthy, despite whatever other troubles such a person might have when attempting to enter the group as an outsider on his own. Kyle and I had been friends since early childhood, so his acceptance was never outright questioned, but there were always conversations held in his absence in which his place among us was challenged by the others. Another reason I came to despise my friends.

In the end, however, Kyle never knew that the others questioned him—nor do I think he would have cared had he known. But their outward acceptance, he knew, made his years at St. Mark's much easier than they otherwise would have been. For that he was grateful to me, I think. At least that's how our friendship started. As the years passed, I found him to be more intelligent and generally more interesting than almost anyone else. As we ventured into adolescence we shared many similar interests. We found that we both despised athletics, finding them an immense waste of time. While most of the other self-absorbed shits were at football practice, we would generally spend our time playing video games at my house after school. Despite my status I always felt my unwillingness to participate in sports was frowned upon by the others—which made no difference to me, but was worth noting. The hours we spent away from our classmates forged a friendship that I assume will last in some form until we are old men, despite the strain placed upon it by the current situation.

As we progressed in years our interests broadened to include girls. This was an area Kyle very quickly understood would be much easier for him to deal with as a result of being my friend. He would have been correct had he not squandered the resource he had in our friendship.

In high school he had two girlfriends whom I remember. The first was inconsequential other than the fact that she was the first girl he ever kissed. The second was inconsequential other than the fact that she was the first girl he ever fucked, and to my knowledge the only one before college. Neither were what I would consider attractive, but they were passable girls from Hockaday. The second one he actually met through me at a party where I fucked her older sister in their parents' bedroom, then pulled out and ejaculated on one of her parents' pillows, which amused me at the time. That is, of course, beside the point, which is that Kyle could have had virtually any girl he wanted because he was my friend. I say virtually because if I had wanted the same girl she would have been mine, but if I had been willing to pass, I would have only had to tell her that I thought they made a cute couple and the girl would have dated him if for no other reason than she was still trying to please me.

But Kyle's taste in women was simple and he was, for lack of a better term, romantic. I had come to a very early conclusion that being who I was gave me ample opportunity to fuck virtually any girl I chose in our small circle. So I did. College, of course, broadened that circle. I came to a similarly early conclusion that all women are vile whores and my hatred for them as a gender would most likely never be extinguished. My father's three wives, my biological mother included as the first of those three, sparked this hatred, but my own experiences kept the furnace burning. I also concluded that, although I would marry at some point to appease my family and to produce my successor, I would never love a woman and I would continue to fuck any girl I chose to. Furthermore, my wife, if she discovered my transgressions, would allow them rather than risk being disconnected from my family's money and local notoriety in Dallas.

All of this leads me to the point that when Kyle told me about Heather I wasn't that shocked. He had met her I think a week or two into our freshman year and over a lunch at RFoC he divulged to me that there was something about her, some illusory quality he couldn't stop thinking about. I tried to explain to him that we had just begun our freshman year and he shouldn't cut his dick off immediately—at least fuck a few girls before locking in on the one he was going to end his life with. He wouldn't hear it. He kept droning on about some look she gave him the morning she woke up in his bed that he was sure held some deeper meaning—some connection between them that was cemented in that look. The only look a girl has ever given me that has had even the most remote emotional impact is when her asshole is staring back at me just before I ram my dick into it, and this emotion is, of course, complacent satisfaction in knowing that very soon I will remove my dick from her throbbing asshole and put it in her mouth.

I even tried to persuade him by telling him that the night prior I had coaxed two sophomore girls back to my dorm room, where my father insisted I stay for the full freshman year just as he had, for a particularly athletic three-way ending with me forcing both girls to lick my semen out of each other's cunts. I further explained to Kyle that I didn't even know these girls' names, nor did I want to. Women are all evil whores bent on marrying a man and sucking his life away with dwindling sexuality, aging beauty, children, et cetera. This outcome is virtually unavoidable, but in the meantime a man should make use of as many women as he possibly can. I amended by explaining that this behavior is not the woman's fault. She has been lied to at every turn, told that marriage to a man of resource is valuable, that his resource, in fact, is more valuable than his substance. I don't fault women for what their gender has come to represent, but neither do I indulge it. And if this promise of resource is what drives them to submit to a man's will sexually, then I have all the empty promises they could ever want.

Kyle didn't share my sentiment. He claimed that he wasn't inter-ested in having sex with as many women as he could. He had never had a one-night stand and he didn't intend to ever have one. He claimed he wanted to find one girl who made him happy and be with her forever. He didn't outright claim he thought Heather was this girl, he just said he thought she was intriguing. Intriguing is the actual word he used, which I had to laugh at. The only thing intriguing I had ever noticed in a girl was a slightly overpronounced right nipple on Jennifer Dalton in the tenth grade.

Knowing after many years of friendship with Kyle that I would never change his mind, but never grow tired of the attempt, I told him I would do some investigating into who this girl was. Heather on the second floor of McElvaney. I knew she hadn't gone to Hockaday or Ur-suline, based on her absence from any of the prominent social circles at either of those places and the parties associated with them in our high school years. It was possible she'd gone to some lesser school, or even to public school. In any case I told Kyle I would help him in any way I could. Secretly I also hoped that he would land this girl and one of two things would happen: (1) She would genuinely make him happy for the rest of his life, or (2) she would ruin him and force him to understand women as I do—force him to see that there is no love, there is only the lie we tell ourselves that things are more important than they actually are, that our lives will have meaning beyond all the other lives that have come before us and been forgotten, that there is hope in any of this.

The rest of our conversation that day was about fraternities. I had no real choice in the matter. Although I had little to no interest in Greek life, my father and grandfather were both ATOs and so would I be in the spring. I expected more of the same type of entitled pricks I had gone to high school with, but potentially from different states. I urged Kyle to rush as well so that I might have one person in the whole ordeal who didn't make me want to swallow razor blades, but he had even less interest in all of it than I did.

I tried to convince him further by suggesting that Heather was most likely interested in joining a sorority, and if they were to be a couple he would surely have to change his mind or their relationship would be doomed from the start. He laughed it off. I couldn't tell if it was because he found the notion of having a relationship with this girl he barely knew to be absurd, or if he thought the idea that she could care about such things to be absurd. When he told me she had mentioned she was going to rush in the coming semester, I assumed it was the former.

chapter
four

A few weeks had passed. Class was actually starting to get interesting. In chemistry we were talking about mass relations in chemical reactions and reactions in aqueous solutions, which I wasn't fascinated by, but college chemistry wasn't as boring as I thought it would be. It wasn't as hard as I thought it would be either. We had one mini-exam in thermochemistry and I got the highest grade in the class.

I started to make a few friends in some of my classes. A guy named Carl Gill was doing pretty much the same thing I was—majoring in biology and then going to med school somewhere. He was a pretty smart guy and we ended up becoming lab partners in a few classes. His older brother had just finished the exact same set of classes two years before and was in his second year of med school at UCLA. Carl said he still had all of his brother's notes and everything, so that would be a pretty big help.

I also started my work-study job at Mac's, which was complete shit. My scholarship covered a decent amount of my tuition, and my dad helped me out, too, but I had to do work-study to cover the rest. I worked at a pizza place in high school, so I wasn't completely foreign to this type of work environment—I mean I was used to being the only person there who spoke English as a first language. I thought there might be one other student working with me who was also forced into work-study, but no, Mac's Place cafeteria was staffed with nine people per shift. There was some overlap but not much, so with a total of probably about sixteen to twenty employees whose first language was Spanish, I was forced to brush up on mine in a hurry. The lunch shift manager, Raulio, was probably the worst English speaker in the whole bunch. His favorite phrase was, "Now find trays and make them new." The "make them new" part didn't really bother me, but I always thought "Now find trays" was funny because it implied that the trays were hidden instead of being on tables or in the tray return bins, both in plain sight.

My job, by the way, was basically to wash the dishes during the lunch and dinner rushes and go get the tray stacks and return them to the front of the line where people first come in. The work itself wasn't bad, I guess, but being the douchebag in a hairnet that every hot chick in McElvaney would point and laugh at was about as bad an experience as I could have hoped for in a job. But I had no real choice. It was either that or not go to school, so I did it.

Anyway, even though I hadn't run into her at all, Heather was pretty much all I thought about over those next few weeks. I would go from being pissed at myself for not trying anything when she was in my bed to the more gay emotion of being sad that I would probably never see her again. I think I thought about her so much because all the chicks in my classes were either fat ugly pigs or they were so nerdy that they couldn't carry on a normal conversation. I remember telling Brett that and he said something like, "I've fucked a few nerds in my life and let me tell you this, they might seem unassuming, but in the sack they will peel your dick like a fucking carrot if you're not careful." I think I just laughed at him because I didn't really even know what that meant—if it was a good thing or not, having your dick peeled like a carrot.

The rest of my female interaction was at work, where I got acquainted with the only two coworkers who weren't men—Isabel and Monica—both of whom were around fifty and strangely missing teeth close enough to the front to notice every time they talked.

So, comparatively speaking, Heather was the single hottest chick I had interacted with the entire time I had been at school. Because of this, and because our next meeting happened by chance, I know I attached way too much meaning to it. Like most people, I think, I saw it as some kind of sign or predestined event—whatever you want to call it—even though I know all of that is a complete load of crap. I was in the laundry room at McElvaney getting my stuff out of the washing machine so I could put it in the dryer, but all the dryers were stopped, full of various assholes' crap that no one would come down to get for hours, making it impossible for other people to dry their clothes. So I picked the dryer closest to my washing machine and started taking the clothes out of it, piling them up on top.

I assumed the clothes belonged to a chick, based on the amount of thong underwear I was pulling out of the thing. And, as luck would have it, I, of course, was holding just such a pair of thong underwear, and imagining the ass it belonged to, when Heather walked in.

She said, "Oh, hey, Kyle, right?"

"Yeah." I pretended to vaguely remember her name, "Heather, wasn't it?"

"Yeah. Um . . . are you thinking about like stealing my underwear or . . ."

I realized I was still holding the underwear and I further realized it was hers. This is how completely retarded I was for this girl. At that exact moment I actually thought to myself that this would be a hilarious story to tell people later when we were married. If I could go back, I think I might just drop my pants and shit in her laundry. Instead, I said, "Oh, sorry, I was just, I was, you know, taking the stuff out of the dryer so I could use it."

She laughed. God, she was fucking cute. There she was, face-to-face with a guy who was basically a complete stranger holding a pair of her underwear, and she wasn't pissed or creeped out or anything. She just laughed and took her underwear out of my hand, put it with the rest of her stuff that I had piled up on the dryer, put it all in a little pink laundry basket, and said, "So how have your first few weeks been?"

I wanted to tell her I got the highest grade in my class on our thermochemistry mini-exam, but I held back. I couldn't let her think I was a nerd. So I said, "Pretty good. Just kind of getting used to all the classes and everything. You know, a little different than high school. How about you?"

"So far so good, I guess. Getting drunk way too much, as usual." She laughed.

I tried to make a joke, "Smash your skull into any more walls?" She stopped laughing and said, "Nope."

Then I said, "Cool." I was pretty sure at that exact moment that I would never fuck this girl in a million years of trying. This would be a conversation she would go back and tell her roommate about to illustrate how utterly retarded guys are when they're trying to pick up chicks. I was sure I was blowing it. But I wasn't. I think a lot about that day in the laundry room, wondering if there was anything I could have said to make her never talk to me again.

For some reason, far beyond my understanding at the time, she didn't leave. For some reason that became clear to me later, but that I was too naive to see at that moment, she kept the conversation going. "So what's your major? Have you figured it out yet?"

"Yeah, biology. I'm hoping to go to med school and biology seems to be a pretty good way to go. How about you?"

"Elementary education."

She could have told me she was majoring in shit-eating with a minor in injecting guys with AIDS blood while they slept, and I would have thought it was the greatest, most noble thing in the world.

I said, "That's really cool. This country needs more good teachers." Again, for reasons I couldn't quite place at the time, she stuck around, kept talking to me.

She said, "Yeah, I really think teaching is an important thing and, you're right, there just aren't enough teachers who really care about what they do in this country."

I should have fucking seen through her shit right then and there.

She fucking agreed with me. But the vagina has some pretty extraordinary powers. In this case it chose to exercise its powers by performing a nonsurgical lobotomy on me. I didn't care that she was lying to me—not literally lying to me, but faking that she had any interest in me at all. Not only did I not care, I didn't even notice. I couldn't separate what was really going on in that laundry room from the lies I was telling myself, which filled me with the overwhelming hope that this girl would somehow have sex with me, be my girlfriend . . . love me. She said, "How's your roommate?"

"Not bad. I found out he's a born-again Christian, which is kind of weird." Even as I was saying that, I remember hoping *she* wasn't a born-again Christian, not because I didn't want to offend her, but because if she was it would have been a deal-breaker for me. After all that's happened now, it makes it even worse to know that it all could have been avoided if that cunt would have had the same delusional belief in a god as 95 percent of the backwards assholes in the world. Oh wait—she fucking did, but she hid it from me until she had me wrapped around her finger.

She said, "Yeah, born-again Christians are about as weird as it gets." I, being a pretty rational guy, took her response to mean that she thought all Christians were off their rockers, that she was at least agnostic if not an outright atheist like myself. I found out later, much later, that neither of these things were true.

She said, "How'd you find out? Was he like praying over you at night and everything?"

"No. It was actually way worse than that. He asked me if I wanted to go to a Rangers game with him and some of his friends last week, and I had nothing better to do so I went. It turned out the friends were his prayer group or something like that and in the middle of the game this one chick who was with us stood up as everyone was trying to watch the game and started singing, 'God is good, he is the master of all creation' or some shit. Then all the other people, my roommate included, joined in. It was fucking terrible."

That was the first time I said fuck in front of her. It just slipped out, but I was kind of interested in seeing her reaction. I always thought it was a good way to tell certain things about a person, to see how they react the first time you say fuck around them. If they don't throw a shit or a crap or even a fuck of their own into the conversation after a few seconds, it seems like that person is probably a douchebag.

Her next three words were, "That fucking sucks." She was no douchebag.

She said, "Well, if you ever need some place to chill for a few hours when you've had enough born-again bullshit, you can always come down to me and Annie's room. We're in two-twelve."

I didn't want to sound too desperate or overexcited so I choked out, "Really?"

She said, "Yeah. If we're not out, we're usually in our room smoking or drinking some beers. Don't tell the RA." She laughed again. "So you should come by."

Again, not wanting to sound too overexcited I said, "When?"

She said, "What are you doing while your clothes dry?"

"I was just going to go back to my room and read some biology stuff."

"Screw biology. Put your clothes in the dryer and let's go smoke a bowl."

I had never smoked weed before in my life. It wasn't because I had any moral opposition to it—quite the opposite. I was and still am a big supporter of legalizing all victimless crimes. The only "drug" I had done at all up to that point was booze, though. I had been drunk a few times in high school, probably under ten total, but at that moment I would have injected two metric tons of black tar heroin into my fucking eyeball if it gave me even the most remote chance to have sex with Heather.

I said, "Okay, cool," tossed my clothes in the dryer, and followed her to her room.

I didn't really know what was going to happen once he came to my room. Annie was gone when I went to do my laundry, but I didn't know when she was coming back and, I mean, if she was there, probably nothing would happen. I couldn't see us doing a double blowjob on him or anything—especially without E, and even though we were getting to be pretty good friends, if she was studying or something it wouldn't have been cool to ask her to leave the room so I could try to have sex with Kyle. If Annie wasn't there, though, I had a pretty good idea what would probably happen, but you can never tell with some guys, the weird guys, I mean. And Kyle was pretty weird. I mean the first time we met he didn't even really have to put in any work to get me into his bed and he still didn't try to have sex with me. Which was nice, I guess, but also pretty weird. I assumed since I was inviting him to my room this time he wouldn't have whatever kind of mental hang-up he had that first time. But just in case, I'd get him high.

At that point I think I had actually had sex with five guys and had probably blown like around twenty-five or thirty or around there, like total, high school and college. I only had anal sex once and it was with my first boyfriend who I loved. I was pretty sure I'd never do it again because it wasn't really fun, it kind of hurt, and I thought I should keep something special about my first love that I would never do with any other guy. But I guess I'd probably do it with my husband every once in a while. So anal with my first love and then again with my true love.

Most of the guys I had sex with or blew definitely came back for seconds if I let them. So I was pretty sure that if I could get Kyle to make a move on me I could turn it into a thing that lasted for a few weeks or a month or whatever until I got to hang out with Kyle and Brett together.

Kyle was making weird, nervous jokes all the way back to my room and asking me if I played video games. I hate that video games have become so popular with guys now that I have to pretend to like them. I was like, "I play a few games, like *Guitar Hero*." I think he was surprised I even knew what *Guitar Hero* was. I was actually kind of surprised, too. I think I had played it once, maybe twice at this party. It sucked, but I remember some drunk guy screaming, "I am the *Guitar Hero* god and I will shove my guitar up your ass if you challenge me," over and over again while he played the game. That's how I remembered what it was called.

So once we got to my room, we walked in and Annie was gone. I couldn't find my pipe so I took Annie's and packed a bowl. I had no idea where mine was. That kind of bugged me. Then I offered Kyle the first hit. I could pretty much tell immediately that he had never smoked in his life just from the way he was holding it and everything. In some weird way that actually turned me on a little. Like he was so innocent or something and I was corrupting him a little bit. I had never been the more experienced person in any relationship when it came to drugs or sex or anything really. The guy had always been the one showing me how to do things, so it was kind of fun with Kyle.

So I was like, "Have you ever smoked before?"

He was like, "Honestly, not really all that much."

I was like, "Not really all that much or never?"

He was like, "Never, I guess."

So I took the pipe from him and showed him how to do it. Then he tried and, of course, had a minor coughing fit and almost puked. But then he got the hang of it and after a few tries he was pretty baked, which also turned me on a little. It was like I was introducing him to a whole new thing, which was pretty cool. I'll never forget the guy who smoked me out the first time. Greg Grubbs. He was kind of a chubby guy who was a few years older than me. He played football but didn't start, but was still a sweet guy. He took me and my best friend at the time out behind his house at this party our sophomore year and got us seriously high. He wanted one of us to have sex with him and my friend ended up making out with him, but that was all either one of us did with him. Then he ended up telling all of his friends on the football team that my friend gave him a blowjob and by the time it got back around to her so she could deny it, the whole school pretty much thought it was true. She was so pissed off.

But the weird thing that happened when Kyle got high is that all of his nervous nerdiness kind of melted away and he was actually pretty cute. I was also really high so that might have had something to do with it, but whatever. I was, at least right at that moment, actually into him.

He started talking about the nature of the universe and about M-theory or something or string theory. I don't really remember, it was some nerd science stuff. I was just watching his mouth. I hadn't noticed it until right then, but he had the slightest little snarl thing on the right side of his upper lip when he smiled. It was so subtle you had no chance of noticing it unless you really paid attention. But it was there and it made him even cuter to me for some reason. Like how sometimes a person's flaws can make them seem even more interesting.

So while he was talking about black holes or something I got up from Annie's bed and went over to my bed, where he was sitting. I sat down next to him and just leaned in and kissed him. I figured he was never going to make the move on me so I had to do it if I ever wanted it to happen. He would have been happy to keep talking about the nature of existence and whatever else until I passed out from boredom.

Going into this whole thing I was halfway convinced that Kyle had probably never kissed a girl in his entire life. But he was actually a really good kisser. Not too wet, just the right amount of tongue and pressure. He did this thing with his hand where he reached up and put it kind of on the side of my face, not behind my neck like most guys do, just right on the side of my face, just touching me while we kissed. It was nice, not great, not passionate, just really, really nice.

We made out for a while on my bed. I didn't know if it was because he was high or because he was kind of shy or what but he didn't try to take my clothes off or even feel my boobs or anything. He just lay there with me, kissing me. Again, it was really nice. I would have been perfectly content to just make out with him for a while then go get some food or something, but in the back of my mind I knew I needed to take it up a level if I was going to lock him in. And I was actually getting pretty horny from kissing him. So I sat up and took off my shirt and my bra.

I took one of his hands and put it on my boob, which he seemed to like. I've been told that I have really nice boobs. They're not huge—Bs—but most guys have told me they're just right and I don't think they'd have any reason to lie about it so I'm pretty sure I've got good boobs.

We made out like that for a few more minutes before I unzipped his pants and grabbed his dick. I remember that it was really, really hard. Like probably one of the hardest dicks I've ever felt. I know some guys have told me that weed gives them like super-boners. Maybe that was the case. I didn't know. But it was a nice surprise.

I jerked him a little and then moved down and started sucking his dick. He had a pretty nice one. Not too big, not too small, kind of right in the middle and not shaped weird or anything. It was clean, didn't smell like sweaty nuts or anything. It was perfectly straight. He could have used a trim on the pubes, but that was really my only complaint. And even for not trimming, it wasn't out of control, just slightly bushy.

My first boyfriend was really into blowjobs and he pretty much taught me everything I know as far as sucking dick goes. I've been told by most of the guys I give blowjobs to that I'm the best they've ever had. So I was pretty confident that it wouldn't take long to make Kyle cum. I was right. It was seriously like two minutes maybe. He really liked a little rub right under his balls. I did that and then reached up and put one of his hands on my boob and he came in like two seconds. I swallowed because I know guys love that, which I'll never really understand. I don't mind it, but, I mean, once you cum, who cares if I spit it out or not? I guess I can understand not having it spit back out on you, but if I spit it on the floor or into a towel or something . . . whatever. I swallowed and then came up next to Kyle.

He was like, "Oh my God, that was insane."

I was like, "Did you like that?"

He was like, "Um, yeah. A little bit."

I reached over to the little fridge that was next to my bed and got out a bottle of water. I swished it around to get the little strands of cum that were stuck to my back teeth to go down. I reached for my shirt and Kyle was like, "You don't need that yet," then he kind of pushed me down on my back, which I totally was not expecting, and started sucking on my boobs. While he was doing that, he reached down with one of his hands and unzipped my jeans.

I was more than surprised at this point. I really thought he was a timid nerd who I was going to have to make every move on. Now it was like he was taking what he wanted and it was right after I just gave him a blowjob. I had only ever had sex with one other guy who could go again and again like that. It was a little weird, but pretty hot, too.

He took off my pants and my underwear and I thought he was going to fuck me, but instead he went down on me, which I completely didn't see coming. I was already pretty wet from sucking his dick, which turned me on way more than I thought it would have, but when I realized he was going to eat me out, I could feel myself getting even wetter.

He started out kind of slow at first, making small circles around my whole pussy. It felt nice, but it wasn't what I wanted so I reached down and grabbed the back of his head and kind of pulled him right into my pussy. Once I did that, oh my God. As soon as he started licking my clit it was seriously one of the best sexual experiences of my life. He somehow knew how to get me so close to cumming and then back off. He did that like probably ten times and then finally used his fingers and his tongue at the same time to make me finish.

I probably almost broke his neck, my legs clamped down on him so hard. Then it was like I was in a coma or something. Waves of little aftershocks would go through me every few seconds for the next minute or two. I have to admit, he was really, really amazing at that.

I just lay there staring at the ceiling. He came up and lay down next to me. He kissed me on the cheek and I could smell my pussy on his face.

The next thing I remember was waking up, still naked, under my covers, with Kyle sleeping next to me. Annie still wasn't back from wherever she had gone and it was dark outside. I looked at Kyle for a few seconds, trying to figure out if I was feeling something for him, something real I mean. I think I probably was. I think that was the first time that I thought to myself he might actually be a cool guy. At the very least he was the best guy I'd ever had go down on me. If he hadn't been so good at it, none of this probably ever would have happened. A few other guys had been okay at it, but even my high school boyfriend never made me cum from just going down on me. I remember, as I was lying there, I wondered if Kyle was that good with his tongue because he was terrible at fucking or if his pussy-eating skills were just the tip of the iceberg—you know, like maybe he was just one of those guys who was naturally really good at everything that had to do with sex.

I definitely knew I wanted to keep this thing going to at least get him to go down on me a few more times and to test out how good he was at regular sex.

My stepmother had, once again, nagged my father into taking her to his Italian villa for the weekend, so I had our house essentially to myself, not counting the live-in maid who was new, her name unknown to me at the time. I invited a couple of girls from school to come over and indulge in some wine while sitting in the rooftop Jacuzzi, knowing that an invitation to the Keller mansion has literally never been declined by any girl I've issued it to. I also invited Kyle over, in the hopes that whatever strange hold Heather had over him would be sucked out of him by one of these whores along with a gallon of his deluded semen.

I don't know exactly what it was that compelled me to care so much about Kyle's well-being when it came to prematurely committing himself to women, but I was compelled nonetheless. Maybe there was something in me that recognized his inability to see that all women are worthless because his economic means didn't render women completely dispensable as mine did for me. Or maybe, and I've only come to give this theory any credence in the past few months, but maybe I was somehow jealous of Kyle's ability to see the good in women. As I've stated before, I see no good in any woman beyond her ability to aid me in ejaculating and, although I feel my outlook is correct and infallible, there is some part of me that wishes I could blind myself to their insignificance and believe in the lies of love and mutual respect—believe that each gender isn't using the other for selfish reasons.

I asked Kyle to come over thirty minutes earlier than I had told the girls to arrive. I assumed both parties would be on time—Kyle because he's never been late for anything in his life and the whores because they were just that, whores. And whores are never late where money is concerned. Although these whores weren't literal, that is I wasn't paying them to fuck me, they were whores nonetheless because they would fuck me and they would do this because they understood me to represent money that could potentially be theirs in various forms of gifts, dinners, et cetera. Furthermore, if one were lucky or skilled enough to sink her hooks in and eventually wed me, the money I would represent would be more than any common whore would make in ten thousand careers. They would not be late.

My reason for having Kyle come early was that I had acquired some information about Heather, and I hoped that it would make him see she was no better than the girls who would be coming over and that, in this realization, he would fuck the one I chose not to fuck and understand that this is what he should have been doing all along.

He arrived on time and, as predicted, we got into my father's scotch. I told him that some girls were coming by to fuck us, which elicited no visible excitement in him. And then I planned to reveal to him that, through the help of a private detective named Mr. Kenneman, whom my father had placed on retainer during his first divorce and whose services he had given me full access to for my eighteenth birthday, I had come to learn that Heather did not attend a private school. She graduated from Newman Smith High School in Carrollton, Texas—a suburb of moderate affluence, not as wealthy as Plano but not as pedestrian as Lewisville. She had had three publicly recognized boyfriends of more than six months apiece, all of whom attended Newman Smith with her. She had fucked at least five different guys, all three of her boyfriends and two others, one of the others while she was with boyfriend number two. She played no sports and maintained a very average grade point. It was by means of her mother's legacy that she found her application to SMU accepted. And it was by means of her father's upper-middle-class salary at the biggest utilities company in Texas, TXU, that she found her tuition paid. Her parents had been divorced for seven years but still remained friendly. The most telling detail of all, however, had nothing to do with her high school record or her family's past. In fact it was rumored to have happened less than a week into our freshman year at SMU, and it was information that found its way to me not through Mr. Kenneman, but through my own channels of social influence.

Collin Davis, whose father, Andrew Davis, recently won a large settlement that enabled him to collect one third of the inheritance his father had intended to give entirely to his two more responsible siblings, had in no uncertain terms claimed that he fucked both Heather and her roommate, Annie, simultaneously. This isn't condemning in and of itself, but Davis went on to say that after he was done with them, Annie left the room and several other male friends of his entered and proceeded to fuck Heather in all holes, then cum on her face. Although I question the validity of the story based on Collin Davis's reputation as an asshole and a liar, it's very similar to a girl claiming she's been raped. Whether she was or not, the accused is fucked for life. And whether Heather was defiled in the manner described by Collin Davis or not, the retelling of his story to Kyle would leave an image in his mind of Heather's face glazed in the semen of ten men that would never be erased. That image alone, I thought, would be sufficient to end his childish fantasies about her.

As I say, however, I only planned to reveal all this to him. Before I could, he told me that the day prior had seen Heather giving him the best blowjob of his life and him returning the favor by going down on her. He kept droning on and on about how amazing the day with her was and how they fell asleep in each other's arms and how her hair smelled so good as she lay next to him and how he didn't want to let her go when he had to leave, et cetera.

Logically I knew I should have told him the smell he liked so much in her hair was probably the aroma of ten drunken frat guys' semen, but I couldn't do it. For as long as I've known Kyle, he hasn't been what I would consider overly happy. He is very pragmatic, which is a quality I have the utmost respect for, but also a quality, I think, that removes any ability to blind yourself to the inherent flaws in any situation, no matter how perfect it might seem. The only aspect of his life in which he has been able to overlook the flaws, or I should say has been unable to see the flaws, has been with women. As someone who will never know happiness from any woman beyond seeing her with my semen or her tears or a mixture of both streaming down her face, there was something in his happiness I couldn't bring myself to destroy. Instead I shook my head, begged him to reconsider rushing into this thing with full force, and offered him another glass of my father's scotch in the hopes that he might get drunk enough to fuck one of the sluts who would be arriving momentarily, then feel enough guilt to tell Heather about it the following day and ultimately drive her away before any significant damage could be done. None of that happened.

Instead, the sluts arrived wearing bathing suits under their clothes and a child's fascination with shiny objects behind their eyes. Both were attractive enough to fuck, neither attractive enough to fuck in the vagina.

They came in, proceeded to get drunk in a matter of minutes, and both made a similar play for me. Their conversation was pointless and without intelligence, a kind of random pattern of talk that held no substance, value, or purpose other than to toss out a few lines of sexual innuendo here or there to let me know they were there to have sex with me, as if their presence alone wasn't indication enough of their willingness to allow me to defile them in any way I saw fit.

They virtually ignored Kyle, who seemed not to care—probably lost in the memory of the blowjob he got the day prior, or some fantasy of what his and Heather's children might look like, what their house might look like, what he would buy her on their first anniversary, et cetera. I pitied and envied him.

At some point in the Jacuzzi, both sluts were making fools of themselves in an argument about which of them could give the better blowjob and I submitted to the debate that each of them should suck Kyle's dick and let him be the judge. It was painfully obvious to see that they would have done anything I asked of them regardless of their own feelings about the request. To their delight, Kyle preemptively declined the blowjobs and they turned their attention back to me. One of them, Jordan I think her name was, explained that she had no gag reflex and maintained that this made her better at giving head than any other girl. The other's name was not Jordan but that's the only name of the two I remember so I'll call her Jordan as well. Jordan explained that she had some kind of anatomical abnormality involving her tongue and its ability to curl into a U-shape. This, she was convinced, gave her the ability to deliver a much more pleasurable experience while your dick was in her mouth.

I had no real interest in getting a blowjob from either of these whores unless it ended with one or both of them crying due to some humiliation that I was to initiate, which was not out of the realm of possibility but seemed like it might require more effort than I was willing to expend on that night. Kyle left the Jacuzzi to go inside, citing the fact that he had to make a phone call. I could only assume it was to Heather and it would be a long one. This would give me time to violate the Jordans in a manner far more entertaining than a mere blowjob/ejaculating in their eyes/laughing as they cried.

I told them both that I had had too many blowjobs to count. As a result I hated blowjobs. I despised them. It would be a miracle, I told them, if either of them could even get me hard by sucking my dick. Instead, what I really liked to do was watch two girls fuck each other. They laughed and thought I was joking. They asked me how they could possibly fuck each other. I explained that I had a strap-on dildo in my bedroom for such occasions. They looked at each other, neither wanting to actually do what I was asking, but I could see in each of their eyes an unspoken pact made at that exact moment that outlined their agreement to do to each other whatever I asked in the hopes that I might choose one to see again, to start a relationship with, to buy lavish gifts for, to marry, to make my princess, et cetera.

One of them challenged the claim that I actually owned such a piece of sexual paraphernalia by promising to let the other fuck her if I could produce the device. Throughout the course of my sexual adulthood, which I would argue began at eleven, I have owned every sexual aid that I have had the ability to purchase, for the simple reason that I like to challenge myself from time to time to see just how far I can push a whore, to see just how important my level of resource is to her. The strap-on dildo was easily one of the tamest weapons in my arsenal. I was fairly certain I had gauged these girls perfectly. The strap-on dildo was their initial upper limit. If they submitted to it as a first step, then I could potentially coax them into more depraved acts. But had I asked them to fuck my RealDoll, or to don schoolgirl costumes and shit on each other's chests as an opener to the night's activities, it would have been too much too soon.

As we walked back into the house, we passed Kyle, who was on the phone. I couldn't tell what he was saying but his general demeanor and gentle, hushed tone led me to believe he was talking to Heather. I thought about yanking the phone out of the wall and forcing him to watch what horrible magic I was about to conjure with the Jordans.

Instead, I left him to his folly and proceeded back to my bedroom where I forced the two sluts to take turns fucking each other with the strap-on dildo. It required little effort once the dildo was produced from a chest in the closet where I keep such things. Once they began, I found them, like all women, to be open to any whorish act I would suggest. Without even rinsing it off, they subjected themselves to inserting the dildo into each other's cunts, asses, and mouths while asking me if it was making me hot. After about half an hour of this I realized I wanted them to leave, so I fucked one in the ass, removed my dick, forced the other to jerk me off with her feet into the open mouth of the original, who was then commanded to spit my seed into a small cup of Listerine I had left sitting on my bedside table without using the night before. I was sure this final act of depravity would result in the Jordans making a quick exit, but that wasn't the case. The one who spit my semen into the Listerine actually asked me if I wanted her to fuck her friend some more. I had had enough. They had to leave. In a few quick seconds I devised my plan to force their exit—one final sexual act so foul their dignity would override their womanly lust for the resource I represented.

Once my seed had been swimming in the brine for a few seconds I commanded one whore to pour it into the other's open vagina. The unused Listerine, I reasoned, was a fortunate discovery and could become a future staple when dealing with semen-to-vagina contact, for a few reasons—the most obvious of which is the pain it causes when it comes into contact with the vaginal tissue. It also serves to choke the life from every sperm that swims in it, rendering my ejaculate incapable of producing any kind of offspring with the type of whore who is willing to let me or anyone else pour a cup of Listerine into her cunt. This, I felt, was a foolproof method of inciting enough outrage in both of them that I wouldn't be responsible for seeing them to the door. One thing I have learned throughout my years, however, is that as predictable as women are when it comes to pursuing material wealth, they are more than capable of producing genuine surprise when it comes to achieving new lows of self-respect in the service of that same pursuit.

After one of the Jordans held the Listerine in her vagina for around thirty seconds, she began to complain about the pain. I had to fight my astonishment at what I was witnessing enough to feign anger and tell her that she had ruined the whole mood and they both had to leave immediately. Finally the outrage I had hoped for emerged. The Jordan who had poured the Listerine was genuinely angry with her friend for ruining her own chance with me because she couldn't deal with the pain of four ounces of antiseptic mouthwash in her vagina. I wondered, if their roles had been reversed, how long the other Jordan would have been able to withstand the Listerine douche. It didn't matter. I commanded them, again, to leave at once.

As the Jordan whose vagina was full of Listerine and my dead semen rolled over, the concoction spilled out of her onto my bed. I would be sleeping in the guest room.

As they left, the Jordan whose vagina was not fresh and bacteria-free asked me when I would call them again. As a high school student, I used to take great pleasure in manufacturing elaborate lies about when I would call a whore and what we would do on our second meeting, and in purposely running into her at school or at a party after having failed to realize any of these promises so I could see the look on her face when I told her that the blame for me not calling her back was hers and hers alone because her pussy was too hairy, she was too whiny, her ass wasn't tight enough, et cetera. I was beyond that, though. I got more pleasure out of issuing outrageous sexual demands I knew would never be met as circumstances for our next meeting—or, if they did agree to meet them, even better. So I told them both that I would never call them again unless they would allow me to insert hard-boiled eggs into their asses and video them sucking the eggs out in a sideways sixty-nine position. As a finale to my film, they would gather all of the eggs they sucked out of each other's asses and have an egg-eating contest similar to the one in *Cool Hand Luke*. I thought about adding that I would have to shave my pubic hair with an electric razor while squatting over them as they ate the eggs. I decided against this addition, however, based on the fact that I didn't think either of them was worthy of my involvement in any of this.

Both reacted as I had predicted. They said something about what a bastard I was and one, the actual Jordan, I think, started crying. She claimed she'd allowed the false Jordan to pour Listerine in her vagina because she really liked me and she thought I might really like her, too, but now she saw me for what I really was, a complete asshole. I put my hands behind my head as they left my bedroom and breathed in deeply. The scent of their asses and cunts was still strong in my sheets, but not as strong as the Listerine.

When I left my bedroom for the guest room, Kyle was still on the phone. I told him he would have to sleep in one of the downstairs guest rooms because I was taking the only upstairs one that my most recent stepmother hadn't yet converted into a neglected art studio, a neglected yoga room, a neglected antique display room, et cetera. He nodded and then went back to whispering and cooing. As I lay in the guest room bed I thought back to my babysitter and the first time I had ever fucked. I tried to conjure some memory of emotion and, surprisingly, it did come.

I had felt something for this girl, who wasn't that attractive, that smart, that interesting. And all that I felt for her was erased when, after fucking me and sucking my dick for the better part of a month, she informed me that her birthday was approaching and there was a very expensive necklace she wanted. After that conversation I asked to fuck her in the ass, which she allowed. The next day I told my father that she stole a bottle of gin and she was fired.

chapter
seven

After the night she gave me the most incredible blowjob I'd ever had, I didn't actually see Heather for about four or five days, which killed me at the time. We talked on the phone a lot, but our class schedules never had us back at McElvaney at the same time and she was going to her mom's house a lot because her sister was visiting.

It was a Friday and I was sitting in my room reading up on cellular processes while my roommate, Dave, was reading his fucking Bible and trying to explain to me that even though I was an atheist he was praying for me so I could get into heaven. In the first few weeks of being his roommate, I had already exhausted myself with pointless attempts to get Dave to understand that believing in a Christian god is just as insane as being a suicide bomber for Allah. So when he started up with his self-righteous crap, I usually just went downstairs to the lobby to study, which is exactly what I was about to do when Heather called and said, "Hey, I'm downstairs in my room. You want to come down and see me?" I said, "Yeah," and probably pulled a hamstring running out the door.

I was so excited to see her, to hug her, to smell her, to just generally be in her presence again, that it never really even crossed my mind that there might be some awkwardness based on the fact that the last time we were in the same room we had each other's genitals in our mouths. Once I got down there, it was definitely awkward.

She opened her door and said, "Hi."

I said, "Hi."

Then we stared at each other for a few seconds. I didn't know if she wanted to just strip down and go at it or what. I didn't really even know if I wanted that. I genuinely liked her. I didn't want her to think I just wanted to fuck her, which we hadn't even done.

I said, "So how's your sister?"

She said, "She's back in Boston now, but it was fun to hang out with her."

"Cool. Cool."

"Yeah."

Then we stared at each other for another strange series of seconds until Heather said, "You want to go get something to eat or . . . I'm kind of hungry."

"Yeah. Sounds great." It actually did sound great to me. As gay as it might sound, and don't get me wrong, I did want to fuck her, but at that moment I really wanted to just hang out with her. I wanted to talk to her and see her smile and just spend time with her.

We ended up going to Big Al's and splitting a pizza. She saw some girl she knew there named Karin. When she introduced me to her she said, "This is my friend Kyle."

I knew we weren't dating or anything at that point, but it kind of felt shitty to be introduced as a friend, almost like she had no intention of us being anything more than that, even though technically we were already more than just friends.

After Karin left we talked about nothing in particular while we ate. I think she opened the conversation with, "So how're those biology classes going?"

I said, "Not bad. I'm getting good grades and we really haven't had to do anything too hard, yet. How're your classes?"

"I've been skipping some because they're so boring, but the ones I'm going to are kind of cool, I guess. I mean I'm not really all that into learning about child development and basic math and stuff, but I guess you need all of it to be a teacher, so . . ."

"Yeah."

Then we both just ate for a minute or so. It was weird. I think we both wanted to talk about the last time we were together, or at least I did, but I didn't want to bring it up and sound like an asshole who just wanted to fuck her.

She said, "So you're friends with Brett Keller?" out of fucking nowhere. I should have seen that moment for what it was. She was essentially telling me that she was only fucking around with me because she was interested in Brett, but I was so stupid I couldn't see it. Seriously, how did she know who Brett was or that I hung out with him, and on top of that, why did she even care? But, of course, this didn't tip me off in the slightest that she was a superficial, money-grubbing demon who didn't actually care at all about me.

I said, "Yeah, we've been friends for a while, since grade school."

"That's cool. Is he a cool guy?"

"Like I said, we've been friends for a long time and that probably wouldn't be the case if he was an asshole."

"Right." She kind of laughed. Then she didn't bring up Brett again for the rest of the night. She had gauged it just right. If she had said something else about him, I probably would have gotten a little suspicious—asked her why she was talking about him so much. But she didn't. She introduced the fact that she was interested in Brett without me feeling threatened or even really thinking about why she did it. I was basically in way over my head with her, but I didn't know it.

We finished our pizza and talked about other things of no real importance. She mentioned that her mom was getting a new car and her dad might be moving out of state because of a job offer. I think I might have told her a little about Carl, and maybe tried to explain to her how he completely fucked us over on our first chemistry lab exam with some shoddy titration techniques. Then I paid our tab and we went back to McElvaney.

As we got in the elevator and she pushed 2, I slowly raised my hand to push 3, hoping she'd stop me. She didn't. When we got to the second floor, though, she said, "If you don't have anything to study for, do you want to come hang out for a while?"

"Sure."

When we got to her room, Annie was gone again. We sat on her bed for a few minutes, still just talking about nothing. I wasn't sure if she was going to bust out the weed again, but I was ready to smoke it if I had to. I never knew if she had gotten us high that first night we were together because she thought it would loosen me up or if it was because she knew she had to be high to even entertain the idea of doing anything sexual with me. It was something that always kind of bothered me and I never got an answer to it.

I rationalized that she wouldn't have invited me back to her room if she didn't want me to make some kind of move on her, so I did. I leaned in and kissed her. She kissed me back. Then it was pretty similar to the last time we were together. We took off each other's clothes and I was expecting another blowjob, but instead she said, "Go down on me." I would have sucked a gallon of diarrhea out of her asshole if she had told me to. So I went down on her for about twenty minutes, then she said, "Fuck me."

I had a condom in my pocket that I had grabbed before leaving my dorm room just in case, but before I could even get it out she said, "There are some condoms in the nightstand." I figured there was no need for me to pull out my own then, and risk her thinking I had assumed we were going to fuck that night, so I went to the nightstand she was talking about and pulled open the drawer. There were probably two hundred condoms of all colors, sizes, and shapes. This is one of many signs I should have interpreted as an indication that Heather was a fucking slut. Yet, again, I didn't. I grabbed the one on top, no size indicated and with spermicidal lubricant, and got back in bed with her.

Up to that point I had only ever had sex with one other girl. Kaitlin

Harrold was my girlfriend from halfway through junior year to about halfway through senior year. She was pretty cute and on the debate team, which I found to be attractive also. We kind of eased into real sex after handjobs and blowjobs for the first few months we were a couple. I didn't know it when we first started dating, but the first time we actually had sex she told me that her doctor had put her on the pill for the past year to regulate her periods or some crap. So the fact that I didn't have a condom on me wasn't a deterrent at all in terms of us being able to take each other's virginity that night. I think I lasted about thirty seconds after I actually got my dick in. The more we had sex the better I got at it. Then she found out she got accepted at Harvard and would be moving out of Texas. So, rather than drag our relationship out over the last half of our senior year and then into our final summer together, she said something like, "Look, Kyle, I really like you. You're probably even my first love, which means I'll never forget you, but we have to be realistic about this. You're staying in Dallas—I'm not. It's pretty unlikely that we'd be able to keep this going through college, and even if we did, then what? We get married or something? That's even more unlikely, so instead of making it any harder than it has to be at the end of the summer, I think we should just break up now." And that was it. I think I did actually love her, if a senior in high school is really capable of love, but my whole point in all of this is that I had never had sex with a condom before.

I knew how to put one on, theoretically, but I had never done it. So I ripped open the package and before I even had the chance to see if I was capable, Heather took it and put it on for me, which felt pretty fucking good. And that was the last time my dick felt anything for the next half hour or so.

I got on top of her and she took my dick and kind of guided it into her. I couldn't feel if I was in or not, but the look on her face and the vague warmth around my dick made me pretty sure I was in. So I just kind of went through the motions, sucking on her tits and grabbing her ass a little more than I might have otherwise, just to make sure I kept my hard-on.

I fucked her for a while. She came once, but I wasn't even close because of the rubber. I hoped she thought it was because I was just really great in bed. To finish, I had to roll her over doggy style so I could actually look down and see my dick going into her. That was the only way I could get turned on enough to finish, because the condom pretty much rendered my dick numb. And the actual orgasm wasn't that great, because I had to work way too hard to get it. All of that being said, as I pulled out and lay down next to her, both of us sweating like pigs, I was happier than I'd ever been in my life.

I hugged her and kissed her. She said, "Jesus, that was great," and I'll never know if she meant it, but I believed her. And again, we fell asleep in each other's arms.

We woke up a few hours later, around one A.M., as Annie was coming in. We heard her unlocking the door in time to pull the covers up over ourselves and I realized I was still wearing the condom, which wasn't the most pleasant thing to realize. Annie walked in, looked over and saw me lying next to Heather, smiled, and said, "Hey, kids. You need a few minutes by yourselves?"

Before I could say anything, Heather said, "No, we're good," and got up out of bed completely naked, which elicited no reaction from Annie, and proceeded to pull on some underwear and a T-shirt. They were apparently okay with seeing each other naked. I, on the other hand, had no interest in having Annie see me naked, especially with a used condom on my dick, which had now become horribly shriveled due to the condom cutting off blood flow.

I stayed in the bed for a few minutes, trying to keep up in whatever the conversation was she and Heather were having. Finally Heather tossed me my boxers from off the ground, which I had to put on over the condom. Once my dick was covered from plain view I got out of bed, got the rest of my shit, and got dressed. I hugged Heather, kissed her, and told her I'd call her, then told Annie good-bye and got the fuck out.

I walked down the hall to the bathroom, went to a urinal, and ripped the condom off as fast as I possibly could. I took some toilet paper and kind of cleaned up the remnants of spermicidal lube and semen that were in my pubic hair. It was going to seriously suck if we had to use a condom every time, but it was worth it. That's what I told myself as I walked back to my room.

That night I listened to Dave pray as I stared at my ceiling thinking about Heather, wondering if she was on the floor below me thinking about me, talking about me with Annie, wondering if I was thinking about her. It hadn't taken very long and I didn't completely know it at the time, but I was falling in love with her.

chapter
eight

He was actually really good at sex. I kind of thought he might be after that first time he went down on me, but after we had sex for the first time there was no doubt. But what he was even better at than sex was after sex. All of the other guys I had slept with up to that point weren't very into doing anything after they came except like passing out. Kyle actually seemed to like hugging me and kissing me after we had sex. It was totally new to me and I liked it. I mean it was kind of like weird, like he was a little too feminine for my usual taste, you know. But it also seemed like he actually liked me, more than just as someone to fuck.

That first night after we had sex and Annie came back, I told her about how his arms felt and she laughed at me. She was like, "Uh-oh, somebody's falling for a nerd."

I was like, "No I'm not. He's just better than I thought he was in the beginning. That's all I'm saying."

She was like, "Whatever. You like this guy."

I was like, "Whatever."

She was like, "Whatever."

I was like, "You know he's friends with Brett Keller."

Annie was like, "Yeah, but you're having sex with him, not with Brett Keller."

I was like, "So?"

After that, I guess a few weeks or maybe like a month went by where Kyle and I were hanging out like three or four times a week and having a lot of sex. I remember one time we were right in the middle of it, I was riding him in his room, and his roommate walked in. He almost had a heart attack. It was pretty hilarious. He took one step inside, saw what was going on, then literally covered his eyes and ran out. I think that was probably why we mainly had sex in my room. If Annie ever caught us, she was pretty cool about it.

Anyways, after about a month or whatever, I had kind of forgotten that this whole thing was set up so I could meet Brett. At one point Kyle was going to set up a double date with us and Brett and some other girl and I kind of remembered why I started hanging out with Kyle in the first place, but it ended up not happening. Instead we went out with Carl and some other really nerdy girl from their biology lab class or something. But the weird thing was, I actually did like Kyle and it was fun to hang out with him. I looked forward to going out to eat with him or just to like sit around and watch TV or to do anything with him, really. He was a cool guy who was really good at sex and I guess I started to figure out that those things make a pretty good boyfriend, which he still officially wasn't. He had brought it up a few times, but I was always like, "Kyle, I'm going to be rushing next semester and I'm going to be way too busy to have a boyfriend." He didn't like that, but he accepted it I guess.

Then we were in NorthPark mall one day because there was a new Betsey Johnson store that I had to check out because she's my favorite designer of like all time, and I met Brett. He was up there to pick up some shoes from Cole Haan that they make custom for him and we bumped into him. He was seriously about as hot as a guy can get.

Kyle was like, "Hey man, what's up?"

Brett was like, "Not much, just picking up some shoes," then he looked at me and was like, "You must be Heather," which meant that Kyle had told him about me, which was cool for two reasons: One, Kyle was seriously into me if he was telling his best friend about me, and two, Brett had probably wondered about me at least a few times.

I shook his hand and was like, "Yeah, are you Brett?"

He laughed and was like, "Yeah, I'm Brett," like he knew that I already knew who he was. Then he was like, "So what are you kids doing in the most glorious mall in Dallas?"

Kyle was like, "She drug me up here to look at some Betsey Johnson store or something."

I was like, "She's my favorite designer."

Brett was like, "She's very good. Maybe we can meet up in the food court after you guys are done and grab some lunch."

Kyle was like, "Cool, man. See you in a few."

He shook my hand again and was like, "Nice meeting you."

I was like, "You too." And I'm not saying all the stuff I felt for Kyle disappeared right at that moment, but it did start to get harder to forget about why I went out with him in the first place.

Then we had lunch with Brett. Kyle wanted to get Chick-fil-A, but Brett was like, "Fuck Chick-fil-A. Are you a Neanderthal? Let's get McCormick and Schmick's."

While we ate, Brett and I had a really great conversation about fraternities and sororities, and Kyle wasn't even a part of it because he wasn't going to rush. I could totally tell that Brett and I were on the same wavelength and he would have seriously been a way better boyfriend for me than Kyle.

So we finished eating and Brett picked up the whole tab. When we were walking out he asked me what I thought of his shoes and I was like, "Those look really great on you," and they did. They looked like they were made for him, which I guess they were.

After we left the mall, we went back to Kyle's room and Dave was gone so we had sex. I thought about what Brett was like when he was having sex. Kyle really was the best guy I'd ever had sex with, but I was pretty sure Brett was probably better.

She was a cunt. There was absolutely no question in my mind that Heather was a complete and utter cunt in the truest American sense of the word. She was intellectually vacant and seemed to care only about herself, with necessary interest in the material status of those around her but only as it pertained to herself and how it might serve to elevate her own material status. I had only to eat lunch with her to become aware of her nature because I had been dealing with cunts like this for my entire life. Since the cunts I had known had been able to talk, they had been able to compliment me on my style and my material possessions, which is to say that they had been able to recognize my ability to potentially deliver the same material possessions to them. They disgusted me. Heather was different in no way except that she had the unique distinction of fucking my best friend.

She had mentioned at our lunch that she was going to rush after Christmas break and hoped to get into Pi Phi or Kappa. I didn't want to say it to her face—actually I wanted nothing more than to say it to her face, but not with Kyle sitting right there—that she wasn't of a refined enough caliber to even entertain the thought of belonging to either of those sororities. The truth was, however, that she would most likely become a Kappa due to that specific sorority's new reputation as a haven for girls who think they have means but, in actuality, have modest means or none. She would be able to pass herself off as a girl of high standing with other girls who were able to do the same. But she would have no chance of convincing the Pi Phis that she belonged in their world. The Pi Phis would smell her desperation and they would see all of the little unrefined nicks and dents Heather's *Us Weekly* etiquette training failed to buff out and, ultimately, they would dismiss her despite the fact that her innate instinct to cling to men of resource might have matched even their most ambitious members.

What would make her acceptance into Kappa Kappa Gamma all the more troublesome for me would be the fact that my fraternity would have regularly scheduled events with her and her sisters. The fact that she was a cunt did little to dissuade me from realizing that I would have several opportunities to put my dick in any hole of hers I chose and that she was attractive. The fact that Kyle seemed to be genuinely falling in love with her was the only thing that might keep me in check. On the other hand, I also rationalized that fucking her might be the best thing I could do for Kyle. Getting this whore out of his life would be a great favor. Seeing her for what she was made it very clear to me that he would never be able to give her the things she required for happiness, which is not to say that I agreed with the things she required for happiness. I didn't. But even if Kyle did achieve the financial means to make real her superficial dreams of material wealth, he would never succumb to her need for social status. This would ultimately drive her away from him, far down the road. She would seek a divorce if they made it to marriage, and she would take whatever home he had worked so hard to achieve, whatever children they might have spawned (despite Kyle being a better parent most likely), whatever family pets he might have grown attached to, half of his net worth (while never having made a cent of her own), et cetera. Or, still worse, Kyle might submit to her plans and become the unhappily kept man who attends all the social functions against his will. He might do it because he loved her, but soon that love would turn to unbridled hatred for the person forcing him to live a life he could not bear. In either case, Kyle's happiness was not a part of any life he would live with Heather.

And yet all of this was conjecture. Who actually knew what would happen—which sorority she would find herself in at the end of the year, whether she and Kyle would remain together through whatever the next years would bring? It was doubtful, I thought, but clearly my instincts were wrong.

I spent the better part of the day after meeting Heather for the first time attempting to make Kyle understand what a grave mistake it was to allow this whore to take up so much of his time. We were sitting near the fountain in front of Dallas Hall, and Kyle was complaining to me that he had asked Heather several times to be his girlfriend and she kept skirting the issue, citing the fact that she would be rushing a sorority and didn't know if she'd have time for a relationship. He wasn't taking it so well.

I tried to make him realize she was a cunt, but he wouldn't hear it. She had her hooks in and they were in deeper than I had previously imagined. I launched into what I thought was a very clean argument, and was right in the meat of what I thought was a very logical point— that on this planet there are certainly a finite number of women who are best suited for any given man, and on that scale a man can only hope to meet someone who is near the top. The odds of a man actually finding the number one best-suited woman for him on the face of the earth must be so astronomically close to zero that they aren't worth calculating. Furthering the point, I asked Kyle if he thought Heather was even in the top 50 percent of women suited for him, given that she seemed to be so completely interested in joining a sorority, which was something he not only had no interest in, but actively despises. Before he could answer, a girl approached us and made herself known.

She said something about having met me before and actually having been in my house. She asked me if I would like to go get some dinner with her at some point in the near future. I told her I had no interest in her and didn't think she had ever been to my house, even though she looked vaguely familiar. I've had far more than my fair share of girls pretending they know me from somewhere to feign a more meaningful acquaintance than actually exists. I turned back to Kyle to continue my point after dismissing her, but she wouldn't leave the conversation.

She became angry and raised her voice, loud enough, I'm convinced, for most of the other people by the fountain to hear as she proceeded to identify herself more clearly. She explained that she was one of the two girls who had come to my house some weeks prior and that she had been the one who had willingly allowed the other girl to pour Listerine into her vagina. She thought the least I could do to show that I wasn't a complete asshole was buy her dinner.

Although I did remember the incident when she brought it up—not because it was memorable but because it wasn't that long ago—I could not remember her name. When I asked her, it was all she could do to stop from punching me in the face as she spat out through gritted teeth that her name was Jordan.

I only asked her what her name was so I could more properly address her as I told her to fuck off. I further told her that any girl who would subject herself to a pussy full of Listerine in the hopes of impressing a man should probably do the world a favor and make her next meal a bullet.

She walked away in tears, just as she had the last time we talked. I expected to see Kyle laughing when I turned back to him, but he wasn't. Instead he was shaking his head. I tried to tell him that interactions like that with women could only be achieved if you had no connection to them, which would be impossible if he was to make Heather his girlfriend. He insisted that he had no interest in saying such horrible things to a woman, that he liked women.

I didn't laugh at him, but I must have smiled because he became slightly angry. I calmed him by pointing out that women will always be subordinate to men because in the sexual act—which is our only purpose as organisms, to repeat the sexual act—they are compromised, ruptured, penetrated, et cetera, by us. Because the very act that sustains us as a species so clearly forces our genders into the roles of dominant and submissive, no woman ever truly wants to be treated equally, not at her core. Subservience is literally programmed into their genes by eons of natural selection. Women have survived as a gender because they have adapted in order to naturally bend to the will of man. Being submissive is part of their biological identity as a gender. They crave to be treated as less than a man because in the sexual act they require a man to fill them, to give them worth, meaning, wholeness, et cetera.

By the end of this fruitless conversation, Kyle seemed to be in no better a place than he was when it began. He still asserted that he would remain with Heather in any capacity she would allow, be it boyfriend, fuck-buddy, one of one hundred guys who ejaculated on her face per week, et cetera. He had come to the conclusion that he was falling in love with her and was willing to accept their relationship on the terms she required.

Where before I had recognized envy in myself for his ability to feel this way for a woman, there was only pity now.

chapter
ten

She kept saying how bad she wanted to go to a homecoming party and I really couldn't have cared less. At SMU, homecoming was a major hassle. The campus didn't allow any alcohol at any of the tailgating parties, so if you wanted to drink you had to somehow get invited to one of the off-campus parties, which were usually thrown by frats. They'd have a bus come and pick everyone up and take them to wherever the party was. Heather had no way of getting into one of these parties, but Brett did and she knew it. She kept saying that going to one of these parties would give her a leg up on the other girls rushing in the coming semester because she'd get to meet girls who were already in sororities and all this other bullshit. Even though I really didn't want to ask Brett, I would have done anything for Heather, so I did.

I had to meet him over by Meadows because he was taking a painting class to fill a general elective. He told me he'd been planning to take music appreciation, but at the last minute he thought a painting class might give him a better opportunity to meet a very specific kind of girl. His plan was the usual—meet and abuse some poor girl—but he thought it might be more of a challenge if the girl thought she was above "the standard female interest in material wealth," so he said.

When I walked up to him, he was in a group of some other students, all painting what was supposed to be the tree they were gathered around. Brett's painting was more of a third-grade-style vagina, but he seemed to be enjoying himself. I asked him if he could get Heather and me into a homecoming party.

I remember he said something like, "Kyle, you're a fucking idiot. You're not thinking clearly because you think you're in love. The sad truth is that love doesn't exist."

I said, "I don't need the shit-talk, man. Can you get us into one of these parties or not? She really wants to go."

"Get you into one of these parties? I can *throw* the best one of these parties SMU has witnessed in the past decade if I want to. That's not a problem, and I'll do it because you're the best friend I've ever had and because a party thrown by myself at my father's house will have more whores with low self-worth whom I can emotionally crush into dust than any other party at SMU. But before I do any of that, I want to ask you something."

"Okay."

"Have you ever heard of the second of truth?"

"No."

"Then listen. It's different for all of us in terms of what we actually think during it, but its purpose is exactly the same for all guys. It's the second immediately following ejaculation when you see the world for what it is, see it bathed in truth. You know what I'm talking about?"

"No."

"Just after you fire off a load, your mind is cleared. It's like all of your worries, pains, fears, et cetera rode out of your body in that stream of semen. And it's in that single second after that release that the world appears to you as it truly is. It's in that second that you can actually think about things without being hindered by all the other shit in your life. For me, the second of truth holds an image that always repeats. As I ejaculate I imagine that, instead of semen, my dick shoots a giant plume of flames that incinerates the whore I'm fucking. I never have to see her, hear her, deal with her, et cetera. She's gone, turned to ash by the jet of molten fire being launched out of my cock. That's my second of truth. Do you know what it means?"

"That you're a fucking psychopath?"

"No. It means that when I see things clearly, for what they are, I don't want that woman anywhere near me. I'd rather see her dead than deal with her in any way other than sexually, and I bet your second of truth is probably pretty similar."

"Are you fucking insane? I have never in my life thought of my dick as a flamethrower."

"I misspoke. I didn't mean that you think of your dick shooting fire like me, but I bet that in your second of truth, if you look at it honestly, you'll see that you don't want Heather. I would bet that most guys, in fact, have similar seconds of truth, because we all know deep down that women are good for fucking and not much else."

"That's not how I think, man. I'm actually falling in love with Heather. After we have sex I actually like to fall asleep with her and to wake up with her and to talk to her about other things. I definitely don't want to melt her with my dick."

"All of the things you're mentioning have nothing to do with the second of truth. The cuddling and all that shit happens way after the second of truth. You only get a second before all of the concerns you're burdened with on a daily basis come back to you and lock you back in the cage of who the world thinks you are, not who you really are. And the world tells you that you love Heather, that you should want to cuddle with her, that you should want to stroke her hair, that you should want to make her happy, et cetera."

"Do you ever listen to yourself? You're fucking insane."

"You're the one who got tricked into thinking he's in love. Fuck, into even thinking love is fucking real and not a lie that women have tricked most poor bastards into believing."

"So are you going to throw a homecoming party or not?"

"If the next time you blow a load you remember to really focus on that second immediately after, really think about what you want, what you think about Heather, what you think about women in general during that second, then yes, I'll throw a party so you can fall deeper into a hopeless pit of self-delusion."

"You just told me you think your dick's a flamethrower. You have no room to talk about self-delusion."

"Do we have a deal? You'll think about what you really feel for Heather the next time you blow a load and I'll throw the party in return?"

"It's the most bizarre deal ever, but it's a deal."

After that conversation with Brett, I went back to McElvaney, to my room, and saw that Dave wasn't around. I had been thinking about the second of truth the entire time I walked back, and I didn't know where Brett heard about it or how he came up with it, and as insane as it sounded, I was curious. So I jerked off, and in the second after I came I really tried to think about Heather and how I felt. It was weird. Brett was right, everything did seem to make more sense, to be more clear. What I thought in that second was that I loved Heather more than any girl I had ever met or would meet. I didn't know it then, but I was completely fucked.

I got this text from Kyle saying he had something really important to tell me and I should come up to his room like as fast as possible. When I got up there he told me that he didn't just get us into a homecoming party, he got us into one that was being thrown by Brett. I almost passed out. Seriously, that was probably the closest to being in love with Kyle that I had ever been up to that point. So I was like, "I love you," but I wasn't really sure that I actually did. I was just really happy and I knew it was something that he probably wanted to hear. Then he was like, "I love you, too," and he really did mean it. I could tell. I knew he was going to want to talk about our relationship and being exclusive and everything if we both supposedly loved each other, but I didn't really want to get into all of that with him and his weird roommate was gone, so I just blew him right there before he could say anything. I let him finish in my mouth, and then I asked him if Annie could come to Brett's party and he said she could. I was so excited. I actually invited a few other girls from some of my classes who seemed cool and who had told me they were going to be rushing after Christmas. I figured Brett wouldn't care.

I don't even remember who SMU was playing or anything. I don't really like football and I don't see why anyone does really. Other than people talking about the game, the party was literally the best party I had ever been to, up to that point.

We got there like thirty minutes after it started because I didn't want us to be the first ones there, even though Kyle was like, "Brett's my best friend. It doesn't matter if we show up four hours early. He's not going to care." Whatever. Even though Brett was a freshman, he was still Brett Keller and that meant there could be sophomores or other upperclassmen at his party. I couldn't have other girls who were already Kappas or Pi Phis walking in and thinking I had been the first one there. Kyle just didn't get it.

Even though we got there half an hour after it started, we were still like some of the first people there, which wasn't actually as bad as I thought it was going to be. Kyle introduced me to Brett's dad, who was a total silver fox. Seriously, you could totally tell Brett was going to be a really hot older guy. His dad was really into talking about the football game with Kyle and everything, and I wanted him to like me, so I pretended to be really into whatever he was saying. I think he liked me.

Then I met Brett's stepmom. She was about as into the whole football thing as I was, and I think she could sense it, so she was like, "Heather, I know I'm bored out of my mind listening to this. Would you like a tour of the house?"

I was like, "Um, sure." I didn't want it to seem like I was way over-eager or anything, you know, so Brett's dad wouldn't be offended like I was bailing on his football conversation, but I did really want to see the house.

It was seriously insane. It was in Highland Park, of course. It was like the biggest house I've probably ever been inside of. I can't even tell you how many rooms it had or anything. It was that huge. And every room had really nice furniture and everything. I mean it was exactly what I expected his house to look like. I got to see Brett's room.

I imagined what it would be like to wake up in his room with him. Then I imagined what it would be like to be married to him and know that this huge house was half yours. As I was thinking that, I actually realized that I had never even been to Kyle's house or even really thought about what it might look like—not as nice as Brett's. That's for sure.

After Brett's stepmom gave me the tour, she took me back out into one of the living rooms where Kyle and Brett were talking. The party had started to fill out a little more. I saw that guy Collin Davis standing over by the fireplace and hoped he didn't remember me from the double blowjob with Annie—or, if he did remember me, I hoped he wouldn't like come up to me and say something shitty in front of Kyle or Brett.

There were a few girls wearing their sorority sweatshirts—a few Chi-Os, a few DGs, a few fat Alpha Chis. No Kappas and no Pi Phis that I could see at first, but it wasn't that big of a deal. I mean Brett was a freshman, so the fact that any girls who were already in sororities were there was pretty impressive.

Other than Collin Davis, there were a bunch of guys from different frats there, too. They all seemed to be waiting like vultures to talk to Brett's dad. I think they were mainly talking about the game, but sometimes I could hear them talking about their dads and business stuff that I could care less about. There were a few old guys there, too, who were wearing ATO stuff. I guess Brett's dad was an ATO when he went to SMU. I wondered if Brett was going to be an ATO, too, because of his dad. I mean they were still kind of cool, but probably not like they were when Brett's dad was in school. Brett seemed more like he belonged in Pike.

It was probably like a few hours into the party and I was seriously drunk. I kind of felt like I was going to puke, which I seriously did not want to do at Brett Keller's house, so I found Kyle and I was like, "Hey, is there a guest bedroom or something somewhere?"

He was like, "Yeah."

So he took me upstairs to a part of the house that I didn't really remember Brett's stepmom showing me, but it might have been because

I was so drunk I couldn't remember, I had no idea. He opened a door and we went into a room that was bigger than even my mom's bedroom in our house, and it was just a guest room.

Kyle was like, "Are you okay?"

I guess he could tell I was drunk but I didn't want him to know that I felt like I had to puke, because he might tell Brett and that would be fucking horrible. So I was just like, "Yeah, I just wanted to spend a little alone time with you."

I figured I could give him a quick blowjob or something and maybe he would pass out and I could pass out with him and hopefully not puke in my sleep.

So we started kissing and everything, and I don't know if it was because I was drunk or because I was in Brett Keller's house or what the deal was but all of a sudden I was seriously horny for Kyle. Maybe it had something to do with him getting me into the party or something. I don't know, but in that moment I think I really did love him.

So I was like, "Kyle, I love you."

And he was like, "I love you, too."

And again, I could tell he really meant it, like in a way that was like he would do anything for me. So instead of giving him a blowjob I took off my clothes and I took off his clothes and we had sex in Brett Keller's guest room bed.

And I guess he was kind of drunk, too, because he never even paused for a second to ask if we should be using a condom, which he usually does. I was seriously too drunk to even think about it, and in the moment I really was only thinking about how much I thought I loved him. And I also remember thinking that I was surprised at how good he was at sex. I know by that point we had had sex like a lot, and pretty much in every position you could think of, but I was seriously drunk. And usually when I'm that drunk I can't even make myself cum with a vibrator or anything. But he still could.

Then after he finished we just lay there and I didn't feel as drunk. I mean, I was drunk, but I didn't feel like I was going to puke anymore. I just kind of felt good all over. Then Kyle was like, "We didn't use anything."

And that was the first time I really thought about it. I was like, "It's fine. I'll go to the health center tomorrow morning and get the morning-after pill."

He was like, "That's all you need to do?"

I was like, "Uh, yeah." I've done it like a million times, but I didn't want to tell him that, so I didn't.

Then we just kind of fell asleep. It was really nice. We woke up maybe like an hour later, put our clothes back on, and went back down to the party. I saw Annie for the first time that night. She was being cornered by that guy Collin Davis. I don't know what I was thinking, but I went over to her to try and rescue her from the conversation.

Collin was like, "Hey, the other half of the dynamic duo."

And I was positive that he was going to say something about the double blowjob right in front of Kyle, whose hand I was still holding and who I just kind of realized I actually loved.

Then Collin noticed that I was holding his hand and he was like, "Now how in the hell did a chump like you land a dick-sucking machine like this?"

Kyle was like, "Excuse me?"

Collin was a total dick. He was like, "What's your name?"

Kyle was like, "Kyle."

Collin was like, "What are you doing at this party, Kyle?"

Kyle was like, "A friend of mine's throwing it."

Collin was like, "Oh really. You're friends with Brett Keller?"

And then, before Kyle could say anything, Brett came up behind him and put his arm around him and was like, "I'd say he's more like my best friend, douchebag. Now who in the fuck are you?"

Collin looked like a deer in headlights. It was seriously hilarious. He was like, "Oh hey, Brett, my name's Collin Davis."

And Brett was like, "I know your fucking name, asshole. The question was meant to be deeper. Who in the fuck are you, metaphorically speaking? Are you the asshole who sucks up to my father because he wants a job at his company after graduation? Are you the asshole who sucks up to me because he wants to keep getting invited to parties like this? Or are you the asshole who just insulted my best friend because he didn't know any better?"

Collin was like, "I'm sorry, Brett, I didn't know you guys were friends. I thought he was just some random guy."

Brett was like, "Well now that you know Kyle's my friend, I think you owe him an apology."

Collin was like, "Sorry, man."

Kyle was like, "Don't worry about it."

I liked that Kyle wasn't all agro and everything. It was a cool quality that he had. But I wished he would have been a little more like Brett and told Collin to fuck off or something.

So after all that, Annie actually ended up going back to Collin's place with him that night and letting him fuck her in the ass. But supposedly he couldn't stay hard long enough to finish. And supposedly he blamed it on how drunk he was, but I think it probably had something to with how Brett made him look like a retard.

Anyway, other than that minor thing, the rest of the party was really fun and I didn't end up as drunk as I thought I was going to be. After we left the party, Kyle slept with me in my room because his roommate was in his room and we saw Annie leave with Collin so I knew she wouldn't be back until the morning.

The next morning I woke up before Kyle and just kind of looked at him while he was sleeping. I really did love him. I snuggled up to him and just went back to sleep until he woke up at like noon or something and wanted to go get breakfast, which we did.

At breakfast I actually initiated the conversation with Kyle about us being exclusive. I know I had gotten into a relationship with him because I thought it might get me closer to Brett, which it did, but I was okay with us not seeing other people. I didn't want to have to deal with guys like Collin Davis anymore. Kyle was a good boyfriend and I guess I recognized that. He was about as happy as I've ever seen a guy. He leaned across the table over our eggs and pancakes and kissed me and told me he loved me.

I guess that conversation had both of us thinking about other things because we left breakfast and went back to my room and had sex again without a condom and it wasn't until the next morning that I remembered we had sex at Brett's party and I forgot to get the morning-after pill the next day, which is really out of character for me. I didn't tell Kyle because I didn't want him to worry and most likely I wasn't pregnant anyway—I mean, I had my period like the week before.

chapter
twelve

The morning after the homecoming party I was coerced into throwing by my supposed best friend, Kyle, the voices of my father and stepmother were audible enough to wake me up. My room overlooked one of our back patio areas, so I got out of bed and went to my balcony. They were having breakfast together, which was abnormal.

As I turned to go back into my room, thinking about joining them for breakfast, having some strange need to participate in this rare family moment, I raised my right hand close enough to my face to smell the asshole of the naked girl who was still passed out in my bed. Normally I would have made her get up, perform one last act of sexual humiliation, and then I would have introduced her to my stepmother as the "girl I filled with semen last night." But, again, I felt some strange need to be a part of this genuine family moment. So I recognized that this nameless whore was in such a deep state of unconsciousness that I could easily creep out of my room undetected and avoid dealing with her altogether, which is exactly what I did. I assumed she would wake up at some point in the next few hours, realize that my absence was her cue to exit as quickly as possible, gather her belongings, and leave.

When I got downstairs and out onto the patio I was almost happy about sitting down to breakfast with my father and stepmother. They rarely did anything together when they were both in Dallas simultaneously. Most often my father would be at work and my stepmother would be out wasting the money he was making.

I poured myself a glass of orange juice, realizing that I was actually too hungover to eat. My father started up a conversation with me about the game, which I had managed to miss every second of despite the fact that he had paid a large sum of money to be able to show a closed-circuit broadcast of the game at the party on ten seventy-inch televisions throughout the house. He also mentioned meeting several of my "friends" and went on to say that many of them seemed like they'd make great junior sales executives at Keller Shipping when they graduated. I was unsure if he was telling me this information because he was thinking of hiring them himself, or if he wanted my first task as an employee of Keller Shipping, upon my own graduation, to be the hiring of these douchebags.

I realized too late that sitting down was a mistake and that whatever semblance of family interaction might have drawn me into this was fleeting at best. My stepmother brought up how much she liked Kyle's girlfriend. It wasn't hard to see why she would have liked Heather. They were essentially the same person separated by twenty years— superficial money-grubbing sluts who would fuck any man they met if he offered the slightest possibility of elevating their material status. My stepmother further inquired as to why I let Kyle land "that girl" when I could have usurped her from him. When I told her I would never do that to my best friend, she said something about friendships coming and going but love lasting forever.

She went on to probe my relationship "situation" and assured me that although Kyle might have gotten that specific girl, there were probably others at SMU who were similar enough to make suitable wives. I wanted to tell the horrible cunt that I had found a girl who was every bit as nice and charming as Heather. I wanted to tell her that I couldn't remember the girl's name but I could remember that she gave a slightly better-than-average blowjob, and let me fuck her in the ass and then slap my dick across her face for five minutes before she jerked me off all over herself. I further wanted to tell her that this angel was sound asleep upstairs in my bedroom with my dried semen all over her face and tits. I also wanted to tell her that this nameless collection of holes allowed me to put my dick in every one of them because she knew it gave her a slight chance to acquire a piece of what my family had to offer, much the same way I was sure my stepmother had allowed my father to do all the same things to her for the same reason. I held back this information, though, and maintained that my special girl was out there somewhere, I just hadn't met her yet. I said this in some part because I knew my father was listening and it would placate him to know that I was following the grand pattern that had been laid out even before him by his own father. But more than that, I said it to successfully end the conversation.

I sat at the table sipping my orange juice for what must have been five more minutes or so. The next person to initiate conversation was the girl from my bedroom, who had found her way downstairs and onto the patio where we were having breakfast. She apologized for interrupting, which was considerate, and then thanked my father for throwing the party and thanked me for a "wonderful time last night." Her disheveled hair, incorrectly buttoned blouse, and general mauled appearance made it more than clear that I had done every vile thing imaginable to her the night before. I would also add that some of the specifics of the previous night's activities were most likely made obvious by her walk toward the table. Her gait was more than somewhat labored, appearing unusual to anyone who saw her walk, due to the amount of time I had my dick and fingers in her ass the night prior. My back was to her when she approached the table, but later when I actually saw her walking I noticed very clearly that significant discomfort, if not outright pain, was radiating from her asshole with every step.

The girl lingered for a moment, and I realized that she might have been too hungover to remember where the front door was, so I indicated its general direction with a head nod and told her I had her number and would call her later in the day, both of which were lies.

I was surprised at my stepmother's general lack of outrage in the situation. My father had witnessed more than his fair share of sluts I had discarded leaving the house the next morning. His acceptance of this whore's intrusion into our little family moment that morning was expected. I wouldn't say my stepmother had been blind to the fact that I indulged in treating girls with disregard, even contempt, and viewed them only as a means to sate my carnal impulses. However, she hadn't been face-to-face with one of the objects of my cock's momentary attention very often. The other two times I can remember, my stepmother literally looked the other way and pretended not to see the girls. In this case, she was forced to deal with the evidence of my disdain for her own gender because it was interrupting our breakfast.

Instead of being embarrassed or angry with the slut, both of which are reactions I would have expected, my stepmother was apparently angry at me for mistreating this whore. She stood up and insisted that I drive the slut back to campus immediately. Judging by my father's silent smile through this entire event, he was deriving some comic pleasure from the whole thing. Rather than put up any opposition to my stepmother's demand, which would only prolong the situation, I acquiesced, agreeing to take the girl home. At no time during this exchange was the girl's name ever inquired about, which seemed strange to me later. My stepmother would have been even more difficult to deal with had she discovered that I not only didn't remember the girl's name, but had probably never even learned it the night before.

I took a final sip of my orange juice and accompanied the girl out the front door to my car. When I got close enough to her, I could actually see some of my dried semen on her face. I wondered if my stepmother had detected it. I hoped she had.

The drive back to campus was uneventful. The whore tried to sucker me into going to breakfast with her and, no doubt, paying for it. I used the excuse that my hangover was too severe to even entertain the idea of eating, which wasn't entirely untrue. She had no choice but to accept my decision as I pulled onto campus.

Getting out of my car, she asked me what I had planned for the rest of the day. I told her I had a date, which was untrue but blunt enough that I hoped it would dissuade her from further conversation or desire for any interaction with me. This was not the case. She asked me who the date was with, and for some reason I was unable to concoct a lie in that moment, maybe because of the hangover. Instead I just told her that I had no date, that the date was a lie, and the truth was I just didn't want to see her again or have anything to do with her.

She didn't cry, at least not in my presence, but the look on her face, combined with an admittedly pleasant smell she had achieved through the application of some unique combination of perfumes, soaps, body sprays, et cetera, elicited in me a rare emotion. I actually felt like I had been unnecessarily harsh to this girl. I felt some kind of genuine sympathy for her and I apologized. This girl, whose name I would most likely never know, had through no intentional action reached something deep in me that I scarcely knew existed. I felt for a brief moment that I knew what Kyle must experience when he deals with girls. But the moment was, as I stated, brief. And a few seconds after my apology I again wanted nothing to do with this girl. She was the equivalent of a dirty sock I had blown a load in, a sock I didn't even care enough to wash, a sock I would rather throw away than wear again. I didn't tell her this. Instead I got back in my car and drove away, although I originally intended to spend some time on campus, find Kyle, see how the party went for him, et cetera. I watched the girl in the parking structure as I pulled away. I wondered if she had a boyfriend and I found myself, in another rare moment of compassion for the gender of whores, hoping that if she did, she would have the wherewithal to wash my semen off her face before seeing him.

The next month was probably one of the best in my life. Or maybe, looking back, it just seems that way because it was the last month or so before everything started getting really shitty. In either case, the month after the homecoming party was honestly one of the happiest times in my life.

I aced every one of my first finals, including chemistry, which was supposed to be some big deal. Professor Grant even told me after our last class that I had the highest scores on just about every test we took throughout the entire semester that he had ever seen a single student score. He knew my ultimate goal was to go pre-med, but he tried to convince me to at least think about some kind of professorial type job in chemistry.

School aside, the real reason that month was so incredible was Heather. We were a couple, an official couple. And it's obviously fucking ridiculous at this point, but the little gay things that she wouldn't do before Brett's party, like holding hands in public or introducing me to her friends as her boyfriend instead of just her friend—all those little stupid things that made me think she actually loved me added up, over the course of that month, to make me feel like I had the best life of anyone on the planet.

And of course we had a lot of sex. I know we were having sex before we became an official couple, but there was something different about it after the party. Again, I know this is about as gay as it can get, but Heather would look into my eyes more than she used to and squeeze my hands a little harder when she came. Shit like that goes a long way as far as making a guy think you're really in love with him.

I remember one time during that month we were in her room and Annie was there with two or three other girls. They were all talking about rushing in the next semester. One of them said to me, "So what frat do you want to get into?"

I said, "I don't really care about that stuff."

"That's a good attitude to have. Just, like, whichever one you get into, that's all that matters."

"No, I mean I'm not into the whole Greek scene."

That dropped all the jaws in the room except Heather's. One of the other girls, whom I had met a few times before but whose name I couldn't remember—just that her ass was strangely too small for her body—said, "Are you fucking for real right now? You're not even going to rush?"

I said, "No."

She said, "Seriously, are you for real?"

"Yeah."

"Are you some kind of big nerd or something? Everybody rushes."

And this is where Heather did something that was maybe the nicest thing she ever did for me. The bitchy chick in the room wasn't really bothering me. Heather knew that. But it seemed like the fact that this girl was giving me a hard time pissed her off in a weird protective kind of way.

Heather said, "Well, when you're thirty years old, twenty pounds overweight, wiping shit off your third kid's asshole and wondering why your shitbag husband, who you met at a frat, didn't come home the night before, remember this exact moment when you called my boy-friend a big nerd and know that when he's thirty he's going to be mak-ing shitloads of money as a doctor and you'll still be cleaning up shit."

Everyone in the room got kind of quiet and then started laughing. I don't know if I mentioned we were all high as hell, but we were. So there was no real animosity between anyone, but nonetheless she stood up for me. At least that's what I thought. After thinking about it I'm pretty sure she was actually standing up for herself. You know, defend-ing her choice in boyfriends to her friends. It had nothing to do with her sensing that I was being attacked. For Heather, it was more like she was being attacked and had to justify why she would ever date anyone who wasn't interested in being in a frat. Fucking cunt.

That month came and went and then we were on winter vacation. A lot of very important firsts happened on winter break. I met her mother for the first time, who seemed very nice, but in retrospect was too much like Heather to actually be nice. Heather met my parents for the first time. They seemed to like her, but in retrospect they were just trying to be supportive of my choice of a girlfriend. And a few days before Christmas—which my family celebrates even though none of us actu-ally believes Jesus was the son of God—in the Quiznos on Josey Lane by her mom's house, Heather told me she was pregnant for the first time. I never found it strange that she actually included the qualifica-tion of it being her first pregnancy. I guess I was just too shocked. But, obviously, I should have known she was lying.

She claimed she was a few weeks late on her period and she had taken a home pregnancy test that day and it was positive. She further claimed that she thought she got pregnant at Brett's party, based on timing and the fact that we didn't use a rubber and failed to get the morning-after pill the morning after. This is how fucked up and com-pletely in love I was: My first reaction wasn't to punch her in the stom-ach as hard as I could. I actually said, "Well, I know my parents will help us. I'm sure your mom will help us. I can even get a second job if I have to, but I think it's important we both stay in school. My parents won't care that we're not married, but if that's a big deal to your mom then I think we should get married. I love you and we can do this."

After saying all that, I swear to fucking God she laughed. I don't actually know if she did, but my memory of that moment always has her
laughing just before she says, "I'm not fucking having a baby."

And as much as that was obviously the best thing to do for both of
us, at the moment I was a little sad. There was some piece of me that
really wanted to start a family with her. Fucking insane, I know, but
true nonetheless.

I'm sure I said something like, "Are you sure? Have you thought
this through?"

She said, "Yeah. You don't have some problem with this, right?
You're not like pro-life or something, are you?"

"Me? Fuck no. But I just mean, this is kind of a big decision. Are
you sure you don't want to talk about it or anything?"

"Kyle, like we go back to school in two weeks and then in one more
week I'm going to be rushing. I can't be pregnant for that."

I don't know if it was the fact that the moment was kind of overwhelming or if I was just so in love with her that I had lost all sense
of reason or what the fucking deal was, but in that second her fucking
deranged and literally psychopathic reasoning made absolute sense to
me. She was rushing, she couldn't be pregnant. Of course not—what
in the fuck was I thinking even insinuating that she might want to take
a second to think before getting an abortion?

I said, "Do I need to help you make an appointment somewhere or
anything?"

She said, "No. I already did it. But I'll need a ride."

"Yeah. Of course. I'll help you through every step of it if you want
me to. I love you."

"I love you, too."

So we finished our turkey-and-Swisses and walked out holding
hands just like the conversation had never happened. It was strange to
think that a Quiznos turkey-and-Swiss would be one of the last meals
our unborn child would ever have.

When we got in my car Heather said, "Also, it costs three hundred
and fifty dollars."

"So how much more do you need?"

"Three hundred and fifty dollars."

"Shit. All the money I had from my work-study job I spent on books. You don't have any money at all?"

"No. My mom just gave me a thousand dollars for the month and I already spent it on some shirts and pants."

"Fuck."

"Can't you just ask Brett or something?"

I had never asked Brett for money in my life. The thought of that fucking disgusted me beyond belief. But after the hour or so it took to drive Heather back to her mom's house and then drive back to my parents' house it seemed like my only option. I didn't think of it at the time, but I'd be willing to bet anything Heather spent the thousand dollars she got from her mom after she knew she was pregnant, because she knew she could coerce me into asking Brett for the three hundred fifty. Fucking cunt.

So I called Brett and asked if I could come over. For some reason it seemed like this conversation should be done in person. He said, "Yeah, come on over. Dad and Stepmom are out of town. I have a few sluts here—"

Then in the background one of the sluts said, "We're not sluts."

Brett said, "You both just let me fuck you in the ass and you're both going to again because I live in a big house. You're right—you're actually whores. So you should take sluts as a compliment." Then he got back to me. "Yeah, I'm here. Just come over quick because at some point I will be fucking these whores again. Later."

When I got to his house, the girls in question were both lying on his couch in bikinis watching *Zack and Cody*. Brett was in the kitchen holding a cucumber and staring at an open refrigerator. He was in nothing but a robe, which was not tied.

I said, "Can you please cover your dick?"

He said, "You've seen it before, man."

"And I've asked you to cover it up every time."

"Lightweight," he said, and then closed the robe. "So what's up?"

I said, "It makes me fucking ill to have to do this, but I need to ask you for a favor."

"Why would that make you ill? I'm your best friend. If I can help you, you know I will."

"I know, but this is something that I feel really weird asking you for."

"It's not gay shit is it? Like you don't want me to fuck you in the ass a little or anything like that, do you?"

"No."

"You want me to get you a tranny whore or some weird shit like that? That I could actually probably do. And, of course, Heather will never know."

"No."

"You got me then, bud, what do you need?"

"Three hundred and fifty dollars."

"Money? That was what was making you ill? Fucking money? You know I'm rich, right? You know money is virtually meaningless to me? Asking me for money is like asking other people for, I don't know, their shit or something."

"I know, but I just feel weird asking. Like I'm just some other ass-hole trying to sponge off you."

"Kyle, you're my best friend. I know the other assholes are just try-ing to sponge off me and I know you're not. If you came here asking me for the money, you must really need it. What's it for?"

"I can't tell you."

"Oh shit, some intrigue. Well, you should have just made up a lie. You should have just said you want to buy your mom something nice for Christmas. Now I'm going to have to know what you need it for. I'm interested."

"It's pretty personal and I don't really think I want anyone knowing about it."

"I'm not going to tell anyone if you don't want me to, but you have to respect my position here. My best friend, whom I think I know pretty well, comes to me and asks me for money—something he has literally never done in the ten years or so we've known each other. Then he tells me he can't tell me what it's for. Well, that's some pretty interesting shit. What if it's for drugs or some shit? Are you strung out on fucking coke like the rest of the losers at SMU? You playing poker at a pickup game and owe some guy some money after a bad bet? I have to know why you need the money as a concerned friend who just wants to make sure you're okay."

"Fine. I need it for an abortion."

"Oh, shit. You know my stepmom's one of the chairs on the Dallas Pro-Life League's board of directors?"

"Yeah."

"That is some funny shit. Well, who's the lucky lady who gets her pussy torn apart and a dead baby sucked out? I hope this gets even better and it's some chick you banged behind Heather's back."

"No, it's Heather."

"Well, look, I have no problem telling you this. I would give you three hundred and fifty thousand dollars if it meant I was playing a part in ridding the world of the demon spawn that you would create with that whore."

"She's not a whore."

"Sorry. I'm just saying a kid would ruin your life right now, man, and as your friend I'd consider it an honor to pay for the murder of your unborn child."

"Jesus Christ."

"Come on. I know you don't have any moral hang-ups about this shit. So lighten up."

He reached into one of his robe pockets and pulled out a wad of hundred-dollar bills. He gave me five of them. I said, "You just keep hundreds in your robe?"

"Not usually, but the whores are here. I like making them feel like whores, even if they don't think they are, so I throw money at them when they do something especially demeaning."

"Also, I only need three hundred and fifty. Why'd you give me five hundred?"

"Because it's all the same to me and you'll probably want to buy her something besides an abortion for Christmas."

"Thanks, man."

Despite Brett's outward lack of consideration for the situation, I could tell that he actually did care and I was grateful to have him as a friend. I gave him a hug.

"Kyle, seriously. No need. I know you'd do the same for me or whatever the equivalent would be. Also, some advice—next time use a rubber. A slut might be able to have one abortion and come out okay in the head, but more than one and she's a fucking basket case."

"Will do. Thanks again."

As I left with the money I could hear Brett telling the girls that the first one to jam a whole cucumber up her ass would get two hundred dollars. I waited in my car for a minute or so to see if either of them would storm out of his house, insulted and outraged. Neither of them did.

My first abortion was in high school and it was fucking terrible. Like easily one of the worst experiences of my life. The guy was a baseball player at my high school named Gordon Hillhurst. It was just a one-time thing at this party where we were both really drunk and I was in between boyfriends and we didn't use a condom or anything, obviously, and I missed my first period after we had done it. I started getting morning sickness and everything and I seriously was like thinking about telling my mom, but I knew she'd make me have the baby and there was no way I was going to have a baby in high school.

At first I just kept it a secret and got like completely anorexic because I didn't want to start getting fat and have people notice. Plus I read online that if the mother has bad nutrition it can sometimes cause a miscarriage, which would have been the best thing in that scenario. I mean that's what I was hoping for. And of course it didn't happen, so like almost a month later I decided I was going to get an abortion. I didn't even tell Gordon I was pregnant and I didn't tell any of my friends so I didn't really have anyone to help me with money or anything. I just ended up telling my mom that there was a diamond necklace on sale for one week only and I really wanted it and it would be like an early birthday present and she gave me the money. Then I went out and bought a cubic zirconia version of the actual necklace and used the money to pay for my cab ride to McCarthy Family Planning Clinic, the abortion, and the cab ride to my friend Stacy's house. I had prearranged with Stacy to spend the night at her house. I didn't think I'd be able to look my mom in the face for at least a day after lying to her.

So I made the appointment during the day, skipped school, and got my first abortion. I guess I was sixteen. Yeah, it was like two months before I turned seventeen. And, like I said, it was seriously like one of the worst things I've ever gone through. I guess I didn't know what to expect—who does, right? I mean, everyone knows what an abortion is. They kill the baby in your uterus and pull it out. Up until that first one, that didn't sound so bad. Holy shit, though. It was awful.

With the first one, no one else was in the waiting room, thank God. And after I filled out my paperwork they took me back to what would be my room for the next half an hour and my doctor came in. His name was Dr. Staggert. He was seriously old. I remember thinking he was going to be the oldest guy to have ever looked at my pussy.

We didn't say much or anything. He was just like, "Because you've started your second trimester, we're going to have to use a procedure called dilation and evacuation. This means that the fetus has reached a size that will require your cervix to be dilated in order to safely remove it after the pregnancy is terminated."

I remember thinking that "safely" was a weird word to use, because the thing would be dead, but I guess he was talking about me.

He was like, "This is not going to be the most comfortable thing, but we're going to give you some local anesthetic that should help."

Then he put my legs up in the stirrups and a nurse hooked me up to an IV and he didn't say anything else except, "Okay, you're going to start to feel some discomfort."

No fucking shit. First he jammed a pair of forceps up my vag and

started stretching shit out like way up inside. He had given me something for the pain, but it still hurt pretty bad. Then he was like, "Okay,
I've dilated your cervix, now I'm going to terminate the pregnancy. Are
you doing okay?"

I was like, "Um, yeah, I guess." I mean, what are you supposed to
say at that point? Then he jammed the forceps up even further into my
vag and started twisting around on stuff. Thankfully that wasn't as bad
as the first part. But then he actually started pulling out chunks of stuff
and I could tell that he and the nurses were doing their best to keep me
from seeing anything, but I saw it. It was so bad.

On this tray that was sitting next to the doctor, I guess where he
was putting all the chunks he was digging out, there was a thing that
looked like a little piece of a leg with a foot that had no toes and there
was this other thing that kind of looked like a hand that was missing a
few fingers. I couldn't really tell what it was, but it looked so bad that I
just started crying when I saw it and I know that one of the nurses saw
me see it because she moved the little sheet thing that was supposed
to keep me from seeing it up a little higher. It was too late, though. I
saw it.

After that I just closed my eyes and cried while Dr. Staggert finished what he was doing. I really didn't think there would be hands and
legs. I thought that didn't happen until later. I thought the baby was
basically just a blob until like the last month. God, it was terrible.

After it was over I went to Stacy's house and waited for her to get out
of school about half an hour later. I was still crying when she got there
and I had to make up some story about Troy Perness calling me fat in
geometry, which she called me on because she knew I wasn't in school
all day. So I like had to make up another story about how he called
me fat the day before and I couldn't deal with seeing him so I skipped
school. She didn't hassle me about it. I always kind of thought she knew
what was going on.

That night I figured there might be like a lot of bleeding or something, so I brought like a whole box of tampons and pads, but it wasn't
too bad. It didn't even hurt, really. It just kind of felt generally sore, but
that was it. It was really like a kind of light period for a few days and

then everything was back to normal—except I always had to deal with my mom asking me why I never wore the necklace. I couldn't really tell her it would always remind me of my secret abortion and also it's a cheap piece of shit.

Anyway, that was all my first abortion. I hoped that, because I caught the second pregnancy way earlier, it wouldn't be as bad. I had heard somewhere that they could maybe even do it chemically and just make you have like a seriously heavy period that might have some chunks in it or something. I was going to wait until I got to the place to see what the options were.

Kyle picked me up and drove me there and made sure I had everything I wanted. He really was a good boyfriend, I mean the best I probably ever had at that point. Sometimes it really does suck to think about how everything turned out. But, whatever. So I made the appointment for the same place I got my first one—the McCarthy Family Planning Clinic. This time there was another girl in the waiting room. Kyle was there with me, but she didn't have anyone. She looked way younger than me and I hoped that if she ever had to come back here she'd have someone like Kyle with her.

So I filled out my paperwork for the second time and then, like twenty minutes or so later, they took me back to a room that was maybe even like the same exact one I was in the first time. It was a different doctor. It was a woman this time, Dr. Jiminez. That made me feel a little better about the whole thing for some reason.

She looked at my paper and was like, "Okay, so it looks like you're in your first trimester, toward the end of the first month. The procedure we're going to be using in this case is called suction-aspiration. It will involve inserting a suction tube through your cervix and into your uterus."

I was like, "Are you going to have to dilate me?" Because I remembered that being the worst part other than actually seeing chunks of the baby.

She was like, "Not much. Because you're still very early in the pregnancy I should be able to remove the tissue from the termination with not much dilating."

I was like, "Okay."

The nurses gave me the same IV and same anesthetic as they did the first time and then Dr. Jiminez was like, "Okay, try to relax."

Then she jammed this tube thing up my vag, and even though she said she didn't have to dilate me as much, I could totally feel the thing going in my cervix. It actually wasn't much different from the first time, except this time I didn't see any nasty chunks or baby parts or anything and I have to think it's because there weren't any. I mean I saw like red blood and everything getting sucked through the tube, but nothing recognizable. I guess because it was so early in the whole development of the baby and everything it probably really was just a blob this time. The whole thing was a little quicker than last time, too.

Kyle paid the bill and we left. He was really nice. He was like, "Do you want to talk about it? Are you okay?"

I was like, "We can talk about it if you want to. I'm fine, though." And I really was. This time didn't seem near as horrible as the first time and I think it had something to do with knowing that Kyle was there. He was kind of like normal life waiting for me out in the waiting room.

He was like, "I don't need to talk about it. I just want to make sure you're okay and you know I'm here for you if you want to talk or if you need anything. I'll do anything for you. You know that."

I did know it.

A few days later we celebrated Christmas. We did Christmas Eve with his mom and dad and we did Christmas morning with my mom. My sister stayed in Boston for the whole Christmas break. Some guy.

It was weird how much my mom liked Kyle. She never liked any of my boyfriends, but she really liked him. It was kind of funny—well, not funny, but like ironic or whatever that she liked him so much and was excited to have him over for Christmas and everything, and like three days before that he paid for my abortion.

chapter
fifteen

The last day of our winter vacation coincided with my nineteenth birthday—January 3. I hadn't heard much from Kyle since the abortion. He did call to thank me once again for loaning him the money, which I assured him was unnecessary. I explained that I despised children almost as much as women, and any opportunity to destroy one while causing the other pain was something well worth my investment. But larger than that was the opportunity to save Kyle from what would ultimately be a horrible existence. A child for Kyle in his freshman year of college would lead to him dropping out to support Heather, who would no doubt drop out as well. But instead of getting two jobs, like Kyle would, she would expect to be financially supported for the rest of her life.

I've always despised women who claim raising children is a "full-time job" and an important one at that. If indeed it is full-time, then why must the child's father participate in it part-time after his actual job ends each day and on the weekends? What of his actual full-time job, which he performs alone, with no help from anyone, least of all his wife? But as soon as he walks in the door from the job that actually pays money, he's expected to help his wife with the kids. She's been watching them all day long, with the aid of hired help, which her husband pays for, and now she needs a break. Well, whore, he's just fought traffic for an hour each way to perform a highly skilled function that you can't even begin to comprehend in order to purchase the home that you must consider your office if, indeed, watching the children he sired is truly your job. Heather has always struck me as this type of terrible whore.

At any rate, I was more than happy to help Kyle, as any friend would be, in a situation that could potentially change his life forever in the worst way possible. And it was with this happiness that I found myself on my nineteenth birthday. I've never been one to get overly excited for the coming of birthdays or any holidays, really, but my nineteenth birthday was also an anniversary of sorts for me. It was one year ago, on my eighteenth birthday, that, after passing through a few screening processes, I began donating sperm at the South Texas Fertility and Family Medical Center in the South Texas Medical Plaza.

I would have never even considered donating sperm had I not happened upon a random episode of *60 Minutes* a few years prior. Part of the episode contained a feature about a website called donorsibling registry.com. The Donor Sibling Registry was a resource for children who had been produced through sperm donors, their legal parents/guardians, and potentially for any donor who realized he wouldn't mind being contacted by any of his illegitimate progeny. On the program a doctor was interviewed who had sired half a dozen or so children through different women who had selected his sperm and had it surgically implanted in their wombs. The doctor, of course, had all the earmarks of a man these hopeless whores would want to be with if any man would have them. He made a good living, was intelligent enough to become a doctor, had generally desirable physical characteristics, et cetera.

The doctor claimed he donated sperm in college, if memory serves me correctly, and he had no intention of ever being contacted by his offspring. But once he found out about the website, and the possibility that he might have multiple carriers of his genetic legacy out in the world, he was less apprehensive about allowing his identity to be known to the various whores who bought his seed.

The idea of anonymously fathering children to whom I would owe nothing, to whom I would have no legal tie, was immediately intriguing for two main reasons and a third less important reason. One, I enjoyed knowing that somewhere in the Dallas area a desperate whore would be paying a doctor to inject my seed into her. Her life would be so hollow, so bereft of meaning, that she would believe ultimate happiness and fulfillment could come only from my seed. That, to me, was vastly entertaining. And two, through the website I could track my progeny and even make known to them who I was. I pictured a sea of children all knowing, along with their whore mothers, that their father was the heir to one of the largest fortunes in Texas, maybe even in the country, and that they couldn't touch it. They'd never see one penny. This entertained me as well. And lastly, I thought it actually might be interesting to track these children's progress through life, to see if there was some constant in them that would reflect an innate predisposition in my own genetic makeup. Would many of them seem to be drawn to similar things in life? Would none of them? Just how great a part would my semen play in the lives of these strangers?

I set up a fake account on the Donor Sibling Registry as soon as I saw the episode. I must have been sixteen or so. I practiced proper interactions between users, so when I was finally able to become a donor it wouldn't seem like I was making my identity accessible for any nefarious reasons. And the day I turned eighteen, I filled out the necessary paperwork, went through the necessary screening processes, was found to have "desirable genetic characteristics," and began masturbating weekly at the South Texas Fertility and Family Medical Center. I created an actual account on the Donor Sibling Registry and registered my donor number and location. I had no ability to contact any parents or offspring, but I opted to have my account eligible for contact from them should they feel the need. I surmised this wouldn't happen for some years, if ever. Despite allowing people to contact me, I was still anonymous. No one would know my identity or my net worth, so they would have no reason to contact me until the offspring was of an age to question his or her own identity. And even then, they would only seek me out if the parents were forthright about the child's creation and about the ability to contact me. And all of this was dependent on the parents or children being savvy enough to know about the Donor Sibling Registry.

The only people I would ever see who knew about my secret attempts at fathering children were the staff at the office where I masturbated. And they all knew who I was—who my father was, I mean. Several of the nurses made open advances on me based on what I correctly assumed was their interest in my status. One of them, a girl whose name might have been Sandy or Sandrine or something with an S, I actually did coax into letting me fuck her in the ass in my car in the South Texas Medical Plaza parking structure while she was on her lunch break. I would have fucked her in the pussy, but something in the back of my mind warned me that any woman who works at a sperm bank would probably keep the rubber and empty it into her own womb in order to produce a child to trap someone like me into being financially responsible not only for the offspring, but for her as well. I wasn't sure, but it seemed likely that once the semen commingled with any bacteria or other undesirable fluids in the anus it would be rendered ineffectual. There was another girl I found more attractive than the one I fucked in the ass, but I also found her to be more of a cunt. So the second time she asked me if I wanted to go get lunch with her sometime, I accepted, and further explained that the acceptance of her invitation was contingent on her thieving a vial of semen from the cryobank and swallowing all of its contents in front of me. For some reason this seemed like it would have been an amusing thing to witness. She, of course, declined and never asked me out to lunch thereafter.

Although I wasn't positive, I thought the odds likely that my father wouldn't find as much humor in the whole thing as I did, and I couldn't risk him finding out by telling any of my friends, including Kyle, which was difficult once I started siring children. Kyle, I knew, would find it interesting if not outright comical like I did.

My first child was born a little more than nine months after my first donation and cared for by a gay couple. One of the men involved coerced his sister into carrying my seed to full term and delivering the child naturally. My second genetic legacy was born a few months later to a woman whose husband had some type of deformity in his sperm. Mine had no such deformity, and as a result created a child with my genes that another, less virile man would have to financially support for at least eighteen years. Then a few weeks before my nineteenth birthday my third child was born in Spokane, Washington. This was strange to me, as the other two were local, in Dallas. I reasoned that I must have had some unique genetic marker that the parents, who counted my child as their second to be fathered by a sperm donor, found so desirable they were willing to scour the country for it.

And so on my nineteenth birthday, one day before the second semester of my freshman year in college, I drove to the South Texas Medical Plaza, parked my car, and went into the Fertility Center, suite 602, to masturbate into a cup while watching the best of the subpar pornography offered at the South Texas Fertility and Family Medical Center, a video entitled *Hot Teen Asses* that could be described as slightly more explicit than soft-core porn, so that some other whore might pay for my seed and raise my child.

chapter
sixteen

Our first week back at school was kind of weird. It was a lot like the first week of the first semester, in terms of classes at least. Some had started; some hadn't, really. But what I mean by the fact that it was weird is that Heather was really excited to be back, but kind of started to ignore our relationship even in that first week. I tried a few times to talk to her about the abortion—you know, to make sure she was doing okay and everything—and she just kind of ignored it. We hadn't had sex since the abortion, which I was fine with. She had a fucking abortion. That can't be an easy thing to go through and I'm sure sex is the last thing on your mind. So I was fine to just ride out the dry spell and not push the issue. I assumed she'd be the one to start it up again when she was ready.

I don't remember exactly how long it was from the time the second semester started up until the whole rush thing began, probably a week or two, but that was really the last time I had to spend with her that was just us. We both kind of knew it, too, I think. For me that meant trying to spend every waking moment with her, and for her I could tell that meant trying to distance herself, at least emotionally, so she'd be ready to see less of me when she started the whole sorority thing.

I guess it must have been just a few days before she started the rush process, and we were sitting in my dorm room watching TV. Dave still wasn't back from winter break, which I found kind of weird but chalked up to some crazy born-again Christian extended celebration or some shit. And even if it wasn't something like that, even if Dave got killed by a psychopathic murderer, I really wouldn't have given a shit. So I didn't think too much about it and was glad to have the room to myself.

So we were watching TV, something horrible and pointless like *Deal or No Deal* or something, and Heather kind of leaned over and put her head in my lap. I rubbed her head and it was one of the last moments we had together that I remember feeling like she really loved me. Or it might have just seemed like that, because after a few seconds she sat up and started a conversation that was one of the moments where I most felt like she didn't give a shit about me.

She said, "So I'm going to be rushing next week."

I said, "I know."

"And you know that means that like I won't be around as much and everything, right?"

"Yeah, I know."

"'Kay, I just don't want you to get freaked out that we won't be able to spend a lot of time together and I'm probably going to be seriously exhausted most of the time we can hang out."

"I assumed that would be the case."

"'Kay, I just want to make sure you're cool with it all and everything."

"Well, you know I think that shit is ridiculous and meaningless, but if it makes you happy then you should do it and I'll be fine. It's not like you're breaking up with me or anything, right?"

And I swear to fucking Dave's bullshit Christ that there was a hitch before she answered. Either she had to think about it, or she actually did want to break up with me—so she could suck as many frat-guy cocks as she wanted without having the guilt her over head during rush week—but didn't have the heart to can the guy who just helped her through a fucking abortion. I don't know which. But beyond the shadow of a doubt, that cunt paused just enough for my stomach to jump up into the back of my throat.

Then she said, "No. I love you. I don't want to break up," and she put her head back down in my lap and kind of squeezed me a little bit.

Instead of seeing that pause for what it was—an indicator of her hesitation to fully commit to our relationship, aka the first drizzle in a coming shitstorm—I just felt a tidal wave of relief at the fact that she claimed she didn't want to dump me. As long as she was mine I was okay, even if I still kind of felt like it was all teetering on the brink.

But before I could think about any of it for too long she said, "And I know things between us have been kind of like different a little bit and seriously, I want them to be like they were in the beginning before I rush."

I said, "Okay."

"So . . ."

Then she unbuttoned my pants and started sucking my dick. It was a strange blowjob. I was still a little shaken by the possibility that she might want to dump me, and I didn't really know how to take the blow-job. Was she doing it because she really did want to normalize things between us before she went off to all of these shitty sorority parties in the next few weeks, or was she doing it because she thought it would appease me? Or, worse yet, was she doing it because she just liked sucking cock, any cock, and during rush week some frat douchebags were going to be the recipients of the same insatiable hunger she had for cock? Once she took off her clothes and started riding me, I wasn't really able to think about any of that shit, and it's only in retrospect that I think she actually did want to feel like she did when we first started going out, before the abortion, before she rushed.

After we fucked it was probably like five or six in the afternoon and she just fell asleep. I know this is about as gay as it gets, but I really remember how the light, right at sunset, hit her face, and she was the most beautiful girl I had ever seen. I thought I had loved both of my girlfriends in high school, but right then, right at that moment, I knew

I really hadn't loved anyone until Heather. In retrospect I guess it was actually kind of fitting that the moment I really fell for her in a way that I would never be able to shake was at sunset. Instead of waking her up and going to get something to eat, I just sat there while she slept and looked at her, then I fell asleep next to her eventually.

Dave must have come back in the middle of the night, because he was there the next morning when we woke up and I'm pretty sure he jerked off while he was looking at Heather or something, because he was acting really weird.

chapter
seventeen

Rush week was seriously like one of the best weeks of my life. And Kyle was completely cool with it, which made it even more awesome. I mean I had always pictured myself being single during rush week, but Kyle was probably like the best boyfriend you could ask for in terms of being cool about it. I guess a boyfriend who was also rushing would be good, too, but for one who wasn't rushing Kyle was great.

So the first day was the eight-party day and you go to eight different houses for eight parties that are all like thirty minutes long or something to meet different girls and try to figure out which house you want to be in.

My first one was Theta. They were okay, but all of the girls seemed really slutty and everybody knows they're all drunk out of their minds like 90 percent of the time. I don't have anything against that, it's just like, not *all the time*, you know. Then I went to Chi-O, which was also kind of cool, but it seemed like the girls were a little too cliquish for me and some of them seemed really religious, too. Like this one girl, Brit Goreman, was like, "Praise Jesus," after everything she said. Like she was like, "And the Chi-O house is maintained by a cleaning staff who comes in once a week, praise Jesus." Seriously, don't get me wrong, I believe in Jesus and everything, but that's a little weird. So then my next party was Pi Phi.

Seriously, the Pi Phis were so awesome. I mean they were all so nice and I heard that one of the girls' dads was like Brett's dad's second-in-command at his company or something. And another girl's dad was friends with George Bush. That was kind of cool. Anyway, I know the party was only like thirty minutes or whatever, but I could totally tell that I wanted to be a Pi Phi in like the first ten seconds.

After the Pi Phis I went to the Kappas. They were pretty cool, too. All the girls in Kappa were from Texas, most of them from Dallas, so I fit in pretty well there. It didn't really seem like any of their parents did anything cool—well, not cool, but like hanging out with the president or anything. They were just more normal, I guess. Annie, who was rushing with me, was like, "I think they suit you better," and I was like, "Yeah, maybe."

Then I went to DG, which sucked, and Alpha Chi, which was like full of fat ugly girls. I really felt sorry for them and after about five seconds I left. And I can't remember the other two I went to, maybe Gamma or something. I don't know. It didn't matter. I was positive I was going to be a Pi Phi.

So after the parties there were a few after-parties that were like real parties. Annie and I ended up going to one of them and meeting a bunch of guys who were rushing, too. One of them was this cute guy named Brian Todd. He was hoping to be a Pike and he was totally into me. Annie even said so.

He was like, "So you know once we get in, we'll all be doing a lot of things together, parties and everything."

I was like, "Yeah, pretty cool."

He was like, "So are you guys single?"

Annie was like, "I am," and I just kind of nodded. I didn't really say I was or wasn't. I mean I wasn't going to cheat on Kyle or anything, I just didn't think it was a good idea to tell people I had a boyfriend who wasn't even rushing when I was trying to make new friends and everything who were, you know?

So we saw Brian here and there during the rest of the party, which was awesome, by the way. It was just fun to know that all the people at the party were going to be your friends and the people you did pretty much every social thing with over the next four years. Anyway as the party kind of wound down, Brian came up to me and he was like, "Can I walk you home?"

And even though I kind of wanted him to, I knew Kyle would be pissed if another guy walked me back home and he saw it. Also I was supposed to go by Kyle's room to tell him about how the first day of rush went. So I was like, "Thanks, but I'll be okay." So then he just turned to Annie and was like, "How about you? Need a walk home?" And fucking Annie was like, "Sure."

I mean, I know neither of us had dibs on him or anything, but what a bitch. He was clearly like way more into me. Anyway, I went back to McElvaney by myself and went up to Kyle's room. He was studying for some biology quiz or something.

I tried to tell him all about the eight parties and how much I liked the Pi Phis and everything and he was so cute at pretending to care. I knew he didn't, but it actually made me really happy that he faked it, and I kind of felt bad for some reason that I didn't tell Brian I had a boyfriend. Like I knew that if Kyle met some girl who was like, "Do you have a girlfriend?" he'd be like, "Yes and I love her very much." I was also drunk.

So I took him back down to my room because I assumed Annie would be out with Brian at his room or something and I fucked him. It turned out that my assumption was wrong, though, because Annie and Brian came into my room right when I was riding Kyle. I'm sure she was going to fuck Brian and didn't expect us to be there fucking, too. It was kind of funny I guess. So Kyle and I got dressed and all of us just stayed up talking—mainly Annie, Brian, and me talked about rushing and Kyle just kind of sat there. Brian was actually really cool about the whole thing, like he didn't bring up the fact that I had kind of led him to believe I didn't have a boyfriend or anything. And he didn't seem to care that he basically saw me getting fucked by Kyle.

So the next day of rush was the six-party day and it was like the eight-party day except you just didn't go to two of the places you went on the day before. Basically saying, *Okay, I know I don't like these two places.* And you just kind of got to know the girls in the six houses you did go to a little better. Pi Phi was still my number one choice and I didn't really see that changing or anything. And then that night there was another party and I saw Brian again. He was like, "Hey, are you with your roommate?"

I was like, "Yeah. I don't know where she is, though. Around here somewhere."

He was like, "Cool. Mind if I talk to you for a while until she gets back?"

I was like, "No. How was your second day?"

He was like, "Pretty good. How about yours?"

I was like, "Yeah, mine too. I think tomorrow is going to be really fun, though."

He was like, "You guys have craft day, right?"

I was like, "Yeah."

And then Annie came up and was like, "Hey, Brian, what's up?"

And I kind of stopped listening to them because I was already starting to get pissed at Annie. I mean seriously, I knew she was slutty, but fuck, I was in the middle of a conversation with him and she just came up and c-blocked me. Whatever.

That night I went back to Kyle's room and told him everything that I did that day, about the six sororities I visited and everything, and he pretended to be interested again, which wasn't as sweet as I thought it was the day before. Then he was like, "I really need to study for this biology quiz."

And I was like, "Okay, I'll just sit here and be quiet."

And he was like, "You're not going to go to your room?"

And I was like, "No, I haven't seen you all day, and I just want to hang out. So I'll sit here and wait until you're done studying," which wasn't totally true. I mean I really just didn't want to go downstairs to my room because I thought Annie would probably be in there fucking Brian and I didn't really want to see that. So I just sat there for like an hour until Kyle was finished, then we lay in his bed and watched TV for a while and he started to put his hand down my pants so I pretended to fall asleep. I just wasn't in the mood to do anything sexual.

Anyway, the next day was the four-party day where you went around to your four favorite sororities and each one of them had a craft project set up for you to do with some of the girls from the house so you could get to know them better. Theta's was seriously lame. They were baking cupcakes. I hate cooking and I didn't even really think cooking counted as a craft. So I baked some cupcakes with this girl named Francine Douglas, who was totally anorexic to the point of it being gross. She told me about how much she liked being a Theta and how cool the guys were in their brother frat and everything. It was all pretty normal, really. I mean I guess she was nice enough, but I didn't really think I would end up there.

Chi-O had this whole thing set up to make latch-hook rugs, which I thought was pretty weird. Like, I remember my great-grandmother doing latch-hook rugs when I was a little, little girl. I didn't even know they still made the stuff you need to do latch-hook, but the Chi-O's were like really into it, like they had brought latch-hook rug crafts back from the dead or something. And they were saying they were going to sell them and give the money to some AIDS charity. I was like, *Really? Who is buying your shitty latch-hook rugs?* I ended up making a rug that had a picture of a puppy on it with this girl named Amber Thomas. She basically said all the same crap Francine said at the Theta house. Chi-O was a fun place, nice girls, they hung out with hot, rich guys. And the girls were nice and everything, but I didn't think I'd end up there either.

Then I went to Pi Phi and they had a thing set up to make earrings that were really cute. One of the Pi Phis' dads was a jeweler, like a big-time one in Arizona I guess, and so he gave her all this stuff to make earrings with, like real stones and wire fittings and all of these jeweler's tools and everything. It was seriously cool. I made a pair of earrings with this girl named Kim Riley who graduated from R. L. Turner, my rival high school. We never knew each other or anything but we knew some of the same people. She had dated a guy who actually played football with one of my boyfriends. She was really cool and everyone there seemed awesome. I really liked the Pi Phis and I was pretty sure that was where I'd end up.

And then my last craft day party was at Kappa Kappa Gamma. Like every girl there was from Texas. Probably about half of them were from Dallas, mostly private schools, though. There was no one from my high school or even my school district. Wait—one girl was from Plano, I think. Anyway they had this thing set up to make wreaths that they were also going to sell to give the money to some AIDS charity. I wasn't too happy about making a wreath because Christmas had just passed and I was kind of over doing anything that had anything to do with Christmas. I knew that for at least a few years Christmas stuff was going to remind me of my abortion, which I was okay with, but not totally okay with yet.

I made a wreath with this girl named Kelly Marcus. She was really nice. Her mom and dad owned a car dealership in Houston and she went to private school down there. She ended up getting into a bunch of good schools like Stanford, which is where she really wanted to go, but both her parents graduated from SMU so that's where they made her go. I kind of felt sorry for her.

That night there wasn't a party so I went back to my room. Annie was there. She was like, "How was your craft day?"

I was like, "Pretty good. I think I'm going to end up being a Pi Phi. How about you?"

She was like, "I really like Chi-O and Theta."

I was like, "Cool. Have you talked to that guy today?"

She was like, "Who?"

I knew his name but I didn't want her to think that so I was like, "That guy from the party last night?"

She was like, "Brian?"

I was like, "Yeah."

She was like, "Not today."

I wanted to ask her if they fucked but I didn't. Kyle came by later and we went to Chick-fil-A. He bought me dinner and asked me about my day and still pretended to care about the things I told him about the different houses. He really was a good boyfriend before he became an asshole. I almost felt like I could tell him about Brian and about how I was like seriously getting jealous of Annie because I knew if she wasn't fucking him already she would be pretty soon. I didn't tell him, though.

After we ate I went back to his room and his roommate was gone so we fucked. He didn't go down on me, which I would have liked, but I remember it being a pretty good fuck. I thought about Brian during like one second of it, but I didn't feel bad about it. I'm sure Kyle thought about different girls when he was fucking me.

The next day of rush was the two-party day. You were supposed to go to your two favorite houses and sit down and talk with the girls and really get to know them and everything and then rank them as your first and second choices. I pretty much already knew Pi Phi was my first choice so I went there first. I heard that on this two-party day the girls in the houses try to make you feel attached to them by telling you some kind of really sad story about a parent or a sibling dying or something and then they tell you how their sisters helped them through it.

At Pi Phi this girl named Deirdre Wayne was like, "Last year was my first year as a Pi Phi and it was kind of a tough year for me. After rush I thought everything would be awesome, just a bunch of parties and everything and hanging out with my sisters, but I had something kind of terrible happen to me. I was walking back to the house from a party and I know you're always supposed to walk with a friend and if you can't find one call a campus car, but I had been drinking and I guess I just wasn't really thinking. So I just left by myself.

"I remember my phone rang and I stopped walking to get it out of my purse. I remember looking down into my purse and trying to find my phone and then the next thing I knew I woke up the next morning right there on the street where I had passed out."

I was like, *What the fuck?*

She was like, "I got up off the ground and I just started crying because I knew that I had narrowly escaped being raped. Someone had slipped a date rape drug into my drink at the party and I had blacked out. If I hadn't left the party, the rapist would have gotten me for sure. When I got back to the house, I told all my sisters and they were so supportive. I mean, it's hard to talk about even now. But knowing that I have the love and support of everyone here makes it easier. Thank you."

A couple of the girls clapped until they realized it was awkward. I just didn't get it. I mean she seriously set up the story to be like she was about to get raped or something, and then it just turned into her passing out because she drank too much. From what she said she probably didn't even get roofied. Seriously. I still wanted to be a Pi Phi, but that story was seriously lame.

So after the story we had to hang around and talk to the girls, try to find out who your big sister might end up being if you were a pledge, that kind of stuff, and I ended up talking to a girl named Karlie Hindenwagner. She seemed really cool and down-to-earth, so at one point I was like, "That story Deirdre told, wasn't that kind of retarded?"

She was like, "What do you mean?"

I was like, "I mean, nothing really happened to her. She just drank too much, right?"

She was like, "Well, yeah, she drank at the party, but what happened to her was very serious. She was almost raped."

I realized I shouldn't have said anything so I was just like, "Right. I know," and then I changed the subject to what the first Pi Phi party is after they make decisions on who their pledges are going to be. It was kind of an awkward conversation after that, but not too bad.

Then I went to Kappa Kappa Gamma. The Kappas said that every year on this night they ask all the sisters to go around and share something that no one in the house knows about them and no one can judge them for what they say. They just had to accept their sisters for who they were. They said they like to do it in front of the prospective pledges to make them feel closer, and the prospective pledges weren't allowed to share any of their own stuff, but if they became Kappas they'd be doing it next year. I thought it was kind of a cool idea.

So the first few girls said stuff like they cheated on their boyfriends or they smoked pot when they were thirteen or they stole money from their mom's wallet or any other kind of crappy little thing that no one really cared about. Then this girl named Andrea Corbin stood up and was like, "Okay, so what I'm about to tell you guys is something that no one other than me knows, not my family, not any of the boyfriends I've had, none of you guys. No one."

Then she took like this deep breath and she was like, "Over this past summer I, um—" Then it looked like she was about to cry and this other Kappa was like, "It's okay, Andrea, we're here."

So Andrea was like, "This was back home in Denver. It happened last summer. I met this guy. He was cool enough and everything and so we started going out and I told him from the beginning that it was just going to be a summer thing. I was coming back for my junior year and I knew that I really wanted to start dating guys like seriously, you know, looking for someone who might be a good husband and everything. And the guy was cool with that, so we just kept it casual. About a month before break was over, I found out that, um, I was pregnant. And as you can see now . . . I'm not because I, um, had an abortion before last semester started."

She started tearing up and all of the girls moved in and hugged her and then she totally lost it and started really crying. I looked around at some of the other girls who were rushing. None of us really knew what to do. Seriously, I didn't know why I did it at the time, but I stood up and walked over and joined in the group hug, too. And I couldn't help it, I started crying. I knew it was because I hadn't really dealt with what I did over Christmas break at all. I hadn't really had the time, with rush week happening so fast after the break ended and everything. So I just kind of let it all out and hoped they didn't think I was some kind of emotional basket case. Some of the other girls who were rushing got up and joined in, too, so I wasn't too worried about looking weird or anything.

After Andrea told everyone about her abortion, they just ended it. I think they knew after her story it would just be seriously in bad taste to keep going around and talking about stealing your parents' car to drive to your boyfriend's house. So we all kind of went off and talked to different girls.

I talked to Andrea. I didn't think I was going to, but once we started talking I told her about my abortion—well, my last one. She gave me a big hug and was like, "It feels good to tell somebody, doesn't it?"

I was like, "Yeah."

She was like, "I always thought that if I ever had to go through something like that, the guy would at least be around, you know, so you'd have someone to help you through it."

I realized she thought that I didn't have anyone with me through the whole thing, even though I never said anything to back that up. I couldn't really tell her otherwise at that point, though, so I was just like, "Yeah."

That night I went back to McElvaney and talked to Annie a little while about how her day was, but I was mainly thinking about Andrea and wondering how many other girls had had abortions. And I hadn't really thought about it until that night, but I wondered if both of the abortions I had were in heaven. I mean, I believe in God and everything, but I don't really think about him all that much. And I guess it was because I started thinking about how many girls have probably had abortions without anyone knowing, and then I started thinking about how many babies that is and where they all must go when they get aborted. I don't know. Kyle wanted to meet up but I told him I was really tired and just wanted to go to sleep, which was pretty much the truth.

The next day was the Pig Run, which is also bid day—you know, you find out which house accepted you. I was pretty sure I was going to get into Pi Phi, but I kept thinking about how Andrea told everyone she had an abortion and it really did make me feel a little more okay about being a Kappa if I didn't get my first choice.

So, basically, we all had to put on white shirts or sweaters and go down to the Hughes-Trigg Student Center. When we all got there they had a seating chart that was in alphabetical order. So I found my seat next to this kind of fat girl who was seriously going to be a Gamma Phi or an Alpha Chi. I kind of felt sorry for her. Anyway after we all sat down a Panhellenic spokeswoman came out and gave a speech for like twenty minutes and then told us that our bids were taped to the undersides of our chairs. Then they did like a ten-second countdown and we all opened them at the same time. I was pretty excited. I mean inside that envelope was going to be the place I lived for the next three years. So I opened it and it said that I had been invited to join the sisters of Kappa Kappa Gamma. I was kind of bummed that I wasn't going to be a Pi Phi, but like I said, Kappa wasn't bad or anything, it just wasn't my first choice.

So after we all found out which houses we were in, of course, we were all screaming like maniacs and then the Pig Run part came. Basically we all ran out of the student center screaming and everything and we kept running until we all got to whichever house we were now in down on the row. And all along the route we had to run there were frat guys with Super Soakers and water balloons and whatever. It sucked, because it was seriously cold. Luckily I didn't really get hit that bad, but the girl who was next to me for pretty much the whole Pig Run had giant boobs and the guys soaked her shirt as soon as she came out of the student center. I kind of felt sorry for her. I guess they call it the Pig Run because it used to be a lot worse than just water. Like the guys used to throw eggs, and there were some stories of a few different frats saving up their shit for like weeks on end and then bringing it in plastic bags and throwing it on the girls. But I guess the school kind of outlawed that at some point because we just had to deal with water.

Once we got to the row it was like one of the most awesome parties of all time. Every house had a DJ, and when I got to Kappa all of the sisters were there and everything and I saw Andrea and talked to her a little bit and it was just really cool. I didn't see Annie at all that day except in the very beginning of the Pig Run when we were in the student center. I can't remember what her first choice was but I found out later she got into DG, which was cool. Oh yeah, and I found out that Brian Todd got into Pi Kappa Alpha.

After the initial party kind of wound down we all went inside the house, which was awesome, and we got a full tour and everything. The rooms were really nice and I knew I would like living there my sophomore year.

After the tour they sat us down and this girl, Summer Flohr, gave a little speech to us about how we were the Kappa pledge class for that year, and then we found out who our big sisters were going to be. Mine was Andrea, which I figured would probably happen, and I was pretty happy about it. I felt like she and I could seriously become really good friends.

And that was basically it. I went back to the dorms that night and told Kyle everything—well, not that Andrea had an abortion, too, or anything like that, but that I had a cool big sister and that I liked the house and everything. He seemed like he was really happy for me. He tried to tell me about some biology quiz he did really well on or something but I think we both knew that his quiz was kind of unimportant in comparison to the stuff I had going on, so we didn't talk about it too much. I think he just wanted it to seem like he had things going on in his life that mattered too, or something.

I was pretty excited that night, like way too excited to even think about fucking, but Kyle wanted to pretty bad so we did. He went to sleep like almost immediately after and I just lay there for a while looking at the ceiling thinking about what it was going to be like to be a Kappa.

chapter
eighteen

Rush week, for me, was little more than a series of inconveniences I had no choice but to endure in order to appease my father. I ignored many of the mandatory events during rush week and chose to attend only those that had anything to do with Alpha Tau Omega. It was understood by all parties involved that I was to be a member of Alpha Tau Omega's pledge class with no possibility of alteration. Therefore, I saw no reason to partake in any other rush activities. And it barely mattered, I think, that I partook in the activities of Alpha Tau Omega.

So at the end of the rush week I was indeed inducted into the Alpha Tau Omega pledge class and introduced to my big brother, Greg Simmons. His father had worked for mine when I was in high school. I'm not certain what it was that his father did, but I remembered Greg from various company family functions that I was required to attend.

Greg was one year older than me and was in line for the presidency of Alpha Tau Omega his senior year. It was obvious that he was immediately threatened by my arrival. Upon his announcement that he was to be my big brother, he struck up a conversation in which he claimed to have heard that I was more than well-endowed. This was true. He thought of himself as having a larger-than-average cock. So, of course, he pulled his dick out and commanded me to do the same. Although mine was easily an inch or so larger, I refused his demand. This refusal of an upperclassman's direct command during your time as a pledge would have been enough to dismiss any other pledge from the house. But because I was my father's son, my dismissal was not up for consideration. Refusing Greg's demand and having no disciplinary action levied against me was more effective than if I had whipped out a three-foot-long dick and fucked him in the ass. He knew this.

As the rest of the Alpha Tau Omegas watched, waiting for Greg's re-action to my defiance, he took off his shirt. Greg was a douchebag with such an obscene lack of self-awareness that he was rumored to have allowed a fellow fraternity brother to tattoo a phrase across his shoulder blades with a homemade tattoo kit. This rumor's truth was confirmed when he showed me the tattoo and explained to me that we'd measure cocks later and he was "cool with me" as long as I, too, abided by the only credo he derived any value from in life. He pointed to his tattoo, which read, "Bros Before Hos."

As I stared at Greg's tattoo, wondering how I'd come to be asso-ciated with the most basic example of everything that is wrong with American youth, I became aware of a choice that somehow I never seemed to know existed before. I could reject this. I could tell my father I had no interest in becoming a member of his father's fraternity or in working at his father's company or in marrying a version of his father's wife, all things he had committed to blindly. And somehow the real-ization of this choice only made it easier to do nothing, to let events occur as though they were beyond my control. I alone had the ability to change my situation at any time, to end the lie. And somehow just understanding that the choice existed meant I knew the outcome. It was just a matter of time. Eventually I felt I would disassociate myself from all of this—not now, but eventually.

Very possibly my father's reaction to such a decision would entail the loss of many privileges to which I had become accustomed. So I did nothing. I let the lie play on and nodded my head in agreement with Greg when he demanded my allegiance to his tattoo, knowing that some day I would end this.

chapter
nineteen

I didn't see too much of Heather for the rest of the semester. We'd hang out once or twice a week, and fuck the same amount. I guess that actually is seeing each other pretty regularly, but it didn't seem like it after we'd spent basically every day together for most of the first semester. She was always busy with her sorority shit. She kept telling me it would get better once she was a full Kappa, that it was just really bad during the time she was a pledge.

When I did get the chance to spend a day with her during the week I'd never want her to leave. I felt myself getting a little clingy and I knew that was the worst thing I could do while she was having all of these new experiences and meeting new people. The last thing she'd want would be the boyfriend who was holding her back from "finding herself" and whatever other crap she saw on *Oprah*. I couldn't help it, though. I just wanted to spend time with her like we used to.

And the time we did spend together wasn't like it used to be either. I could tell we were starting to not have much to talk about. She'd tell me about all the stuff she was doing at her sorority, but I didn't really give a shit. I tried to fake it, but she could probably tell. I don't know how many times she thought I could listen to stories about one of her sorority sister's dad's being in the fashion industry and being able to get everyone she knows some kind of special Zac Posen bag or some shit.

I just focused on my classes mostly for the rest of that second semester. I thought buckling down and studying hard would help take my mind off missing Heather when I didn't see her for a few days at a time. When I wasn't studying I hung out with Brett a lot. He seemed to be hating all the shit he had to do for his fraternity, so he looked for every opportunity he could get to just hang out and do nothing with me. For the most part studying and listening to Brett complain about his fraternity worked.

I guess the thing that was the hardest for me to understand about the rest of that semester was why Heather didn't dump me. If she had, I think I would have been okay. It would have crushed me, but I would have been okay in the long run. I would have licked my wounds, gotten over her, and been okay. But she didn't dump me. Maybe it was because we only saw each other a few times a week and she didn't deal with me enough to realize she didn't like me anymore. I was easier to deal with in small doses. I don't know.

What I do know is that for the entire second semester we were still officially together, a couple, boyfriend and girlfriend, even if we didn't see each other all the time, and I think that's what fucked me up the most. I got used to the idea of us being us. Even if our relationship wasn't as good as it was in the beginning, that second semester gave me another four or five months to settle into the idea that Heather wasn't going to leave me, that she really loved me, which obviously wasn't true but it felt true. It was that second semester that made the end, when it finally came, so much worse than it would have been if she just would have dumped me.

I remember one night, when she was still a pledge, but right near the end of being a pledge, we went out to dinner. I didn't have too much money, but I had managed to save up a little bit from working at

Mac's Place, so I had a few hundred I could spend. She had been talking about how all of the girls in her sorority were rich, or their families were, and she was always going with them to the fancy restaurants and things, so I thought I'd try to compete with her sorority life by taking her out to a nice place. One of Brett's dad's favorite places to eat was a steak place called Nick and Sam's. I knew a bunch of the guys who worked for him would always eat there, and I thought there might even be some chance that one of the girls in Heather's sorority might be there with her parents or something. So I made us a reservation and told her I had a surprise for her.

She had some meeting to go to for her sorority that night and then she came back to McElvaney. She was actually pretty excited about the surprise, which I almost didn't expect. It seemed like the only thing that she got enthusiastic about at that point was her sorority.

When she walked in my room she sat down on my bed, closed her eyes, and said, "Okay, I've been waiting like all day for this. What's my surprise?"

I said, "I'm taking you out to dinner."

She opened her eyes, smiled, and said, "What's the occasion?"

"The occasion is I love you and I guess I've been missing you a little the past few months—"

"Because of Kappa?"

It was because of Kappa, but I didn't want her to think I didn't like her being in a sorority, even though I guess I actually didn't, so I said, "No. I know you love being a Kappa and I understand you have to spend time doing stuff. I didn't mean it like that. I just thought it'd be nice for us to go out like we used to and have a nice dinner."

"I agree. So where are you taking me? Big Al's?"

"Not quite. Got us a table at Nick and Sam's."

"Really?" And she lit up. She was genuinely happy, there was no mistaking it. It was just another in a long string of genuine reactions on her part that should have sent me running for the hills. If I had told her we were eating at Big Al's she wouldn't have given a shit, but Nick and Sam's, that's a different story. And it wasn't even about the food, it was about the money I was going to spend on it, that's what was behind her smile. It didn't matter to me then, though. All that mattered was that she was smiling because of something I did. She loved me.

We had a nice dinner that cost me every penny of the few hundred dollars I had saved. We talked about TV shows and movies and my parents and her sister and mom and about the summer camps we went to when we were kids. She didn't bring up her sorority once. I wanted to think it was because she was so involved in the moment that all she could think about was me and us but I know she was actually just showing a rare moment of consideration for me. I had shelled out the cash for her dinner, so the least she felt she could do in return was lay off talking about her boring sorority shit.

After dinner we went back to McElvaney. She grabbed my hand when we got out of my car and held it all the way from the parking structure to her room. I was already thinking about the blowjob I was about to get when she got a phone call. She looked down at the number and then said, "Sorry, hang on."

She opened the door to her room and we both walked in as she answered her phone. I sat on the bed and listened.

She said, "Hey. Yeah. Oh, okay. Sure. No, it's no problem. When? Yeah. Okay, sounds good. See you soon."

She hung up her phone and then turned toward me with a look that I already knew meant I wasn't fucking her tonight. As hard as I might have tried to have one night with Heather that was the way it used to be, I knew it would never happen again.

She said, "That was Andrea. They're having like an impromptu meeting right now about this quad party that Kappa is throwing with Pi Phi, Pike, and ATO. I kind of have to be there."

"Okay."

"I'm sorry."

"It's okay."

"Really?"

"Yeah. I have some studying to do anyway."

"If it doesn't go too late, I'll call you."

"Sounds good."

I stood up and she hugged me tighter than she usually did. I thought it was because she might have felt bad for bailing on me after I paid for dinner and everything, but I think she might have actually been doing the same thing I was that night, trying to hold on to something she used to love, something that used to be the best thing in her life. But no matter how tight she squeezed, it was gone. I think we both knew it that night. But, like I said, neither one of us did anything about it.

She left to go to her meeting and never called me back. I could only assume her "meeting" involved booze and probably some guys—not that I thought she was cheating on me or anything, but you never want to think your girlfriend is drunk hanging out with a bunch of douche-bag frat guys who are all waiting to drug her and rape her in the ass.

I mean, yeah, I felt bad about not calling Kyle back that night, but we just got really busy at this meeting and I couldn't really just step out to make a call or anything. Seriously, I was a pledge. I pretty much had to put my sisters and the needs of the sorority above everything else at that point. I knew Kyle understood.

I didn't really think too much about it, but I guess after that night me and Kyle just kind of slipped into a routine where we'd see each other a few times a week and wouldn't really do anything except watch TV together. We had sex I guess like probably two or three times a month, which I knew wasn't really enough for Kyle, but I was usually pretty exhausted from the pledge stuff I had to do all day, so when I finally did get to hang out with him I just wanted to sit there and do nothing, you know?

So Kyle and I just kind of maintained our relationship. I didn't really want to break up with him. I didn't even really have time to go through all of that and even though he was getting kind of needy, it wasn't bad.

And I know he didn't want to break up with me. I was pretty much the best thing that ever happened to him, and I knew he really did love me even if we were kind of starting to slip apart.

I guess the next big thing that happened for me that semester was my initiation. I pledged for around eight weeks, I think, maybe a little shorter, and I was glad to have it be over. We didn't really have to do anything horrible like the stories you hear and everything while we pledged. It was just mainly being at the house a lot and helping with party planning or cleaning the house sometimes and stuff like that. But we definitely didn't have the same status as the sisters. So it was really nice to finally be a real Kappa.

Our initiation ceremony was really cool. All of the other Kappas were there dressed in white robes and there were white candles and everything everywhere and we had to recite our oath and then we got our pins and it was honestly one of the best days of my life. I cried a little bit and Andrea did, too. We had had a few other conversations about our abortions and everything during the time I was a pledge so we had gotten pretty close and I could tell she was really happy for me and happy to have me as a sister.

Then once we got our pins we had like a week of parties and initiation activities. Some of the initiation stuff was supposed to be really nasty, but it wasn't. It was a pretty similar kind of experience to being a pledge really. I guess maybe the weirdest thing we had to do was steal a foosball table from the Pike house, which I guess used to be the initiation for the guys at KA, but in the past few years the frats and sororities all decided they were going to switch some of the initiation activities to make them more difficult. If anything, it made it even easier for us. A Kappa from my pledge class named Jennifer Halloway was fucking this Pike named Tommy Dresmeyer and I guess she was really good at deep-throating and she let him fuck her in the ass all the time, so he totally just let us take the foosball table without even having to sneak around or anything.

I mean I guess the rest of the semester was just filled with a lot of parties and everything, and it looked like going into the summer Kyle and I were going to be okay. I figured once the semester was over we would have the whole summer together and he would be happy to be able to see me more and I would be able to spend a bunch more time with him and figure out if I really wanted him to be my boyfriend as a sophomore. I knew that I'd still be partying a lot my sophomore year, and I did kind of think it might be important to be able to hook up with guys at parties and everything.

Anyway there was probably only like a month left in school and we got together with ATO and threw this Heaven and Hell party. It was a big end-of-the-year party that Kappa and ATO always threw together and you had to come dressed as an angel or a devil or something that had to do with heaven and hell. I was dressed like an angel. This one guy from ATO, Gary Johnson, came dressed like the Grim Reaper with a bunch of little fake aborted fetuses hanging off his belt. It was seriously disgusting and I almost started crying.

I was like, "Gary, that is fucking repulsive."

And he was like, "I would love to see you out of those wings."

I was like, "Fuck you."

Then I walked away. Seriously, what a fucking asshole. I found Andrea and asked her if she had seen Gary's costume yet and she had basically the same reaction I did. I wished Kyle would have been there with me. It was the first really big party I had helped plan and everything, and after seeing Gary I really just wanted to be with Kyle, have him hug me and everything. But obviously the party was fraternity and sorority only. For a little while I wasn't really feeling in the party type of mood, so I walked outside on the front lawn and found a spot kind of over by the back fence of the ATO house. As I was walking toward it, I ran into Brett. He didn't look like he was dressed up or anything. He was just wearing jeans and a T-shirt.

I was like, "Hey, Brett. Did you decide not to dress up?"

He was like, "Hey, no, I'm dressed up. I'm God. He made us in his own image, so he must look just like us, right?"

I was like, "I guess. How're things going for you now that you're not a pledge?"

He was like, "Fine."

I was like, "Yeah, me too. I love being a Kappa. The other Kappas are all so nice and it's just really cool, you know."

He was like, "Yeah, how're you and Kyle holding up through all of this bullshit?"

I was like, "Uh, we're doing fine. I think he misses me sometimes, but we're good."

He was like, "Sweet. Well, I'm off to get to know some of your sisters a little better. Have a good night."

I was like, "You too." And then he left to go back into the house. It was kind of weird that he called all the sorority and fraternity stuff bullshit, I thought. Anyway, I guess it really didn't matter. Talking to Brett kind of made me feel a little better about the party and everything and kind of forget Gary's terrible costume. I figured as long as I didn't run into him again, I'd be fine.

So I just kind of hung around the front of the house and I saw Annie. She actually looked pretty cute in this little kind of slutty girl-devil outfit. She was like, "Hey," and she gave me a big hug. I could tell she was already seriously trashed.

I was like, "How drunk are you right now?"

She was like, "Not drunk enough if I can understand what you're saying. Have you seen Brian?"

I was like, "Brian Todd? Are you guys dating or something?"

She was like, "No, not dating. But I would seriously love to fuck him tonight."

I was like, "I thought you guys already fucked."

She was like, "Yeah, we did a few times, but I'd really like to tonight, too."

I was like, "Oh. I haven't seen him."

She was like, "Okay, I'm gonna go look for him," then she left and went back into the house. I had seen Brian a few times while we were doing pledge stuff and a few times since at some random parties, but I hadn't really thought about him until Annie brought up the fact that she wanted to fuck him. I got kind of pissed off. I knew I still had Kyle and everything and I knew Annie had already fucked Brian, but I felt like I had first dibs on him and if I didn't have a boyfriend he'd be totally into me. Whatever.

So it was probably like fifteen minutes later or something, I was making myself a screwdriver and Brian walked into the kitchen.

He was like, "How have you been?" and he gave me a big hug. He had like really hard arms and everything, like I could totally tell he worked out. Kyle had a good body and everything, but not like that. Kyle didn't work out or anything.

So I was like, "Pretty good. How have you been?"

He was like, "Pretty good, too. Just trying to make sure I finish this semester without failing any classes or anything, you know."

I laughed and was like, "Yeah, seriously."

He was like, "So you still with, um, Kyle, right?"

I was like, "Yeah, but you know we're kind of in a rough spot. I don't know how much longer it's going to last." I have no idea why I said that, but it just seemed like something I should have said. Even as I was saying it I knew it wasn't really true, but it could be if I wanted it to be, you know. It was just like, here was this hot guy asking me if I was single basically and even if it was kind of a lie it was still probably the right thing to say. And now, after everything that's happened, I can see I should have just fucked Brian right then and there and emptied the used condom out on Kyle's pillow or something.

Anyway, Brian and I talked for like an hour or so about school and everything, and then as people started leaving the party we were like the only ones left in this little side room. We were both pretty drunk and we were sitting next to each other on this couch that kind of smelled like nut sweat and beer. I never liked how frat houses smelled. They all kind of smelled like nut sweat and beer, I guess. Anyway, he was like, "Well, we might not see each other until next semester so I should probably give you this now."

I was like, "Give me what?"

Then he leaned over and kissed me. This was a full-on make-out kiss and I was too drunk to really stop him and he was a really good kisser so I just kissed him back and we made out for like fifteen minutes or something. His back was so full of these little muscles I couldn't stop running my hands over it. Oh my God. I was so fucking wet and so fucking drunk. I really wasn't even thinking about Kyle, to tell you the truth. I was just lost in the moment and seriously fucking horny.

I started to pull up his shirt and reach down his pants. He stopped me and he was like, "For real, you have a boyfriend. We can't do this."

I was like, "I told you we're in a rough spot."

He was like, "Even if that's true, I can't do this while Kyle is your boyfriend."

I was like, "Why not?"

He was like, "Isn't Kyle best friends with Brett Keller?"

I was like, "So?"

He was like, "So fucking Brett Keller's best friend's girlfriend isn't a real smart thing to do."

I was like, "Then why'd you start kissing me?"

He was like, "I don't know. I'm drunk, I guess. I'd love to fuck you, but for real, I can't be messing around with Brett Keller's best friend."

I was like, "He won't ever know."

He was like, "If we fuck, we're going to want to fuck again and then we're going to want to do it again and again and eventually either your boyfriend or Brett is going to find out. Especially if we do it at this party. For real, that will suck."

I was like, "I thought all frat guys were like serial date rapists. Why do I have to make out with the one who won't fuck a girl who has a boyfriend?"

He laughed. He was like, "It's not that you have a boyfriend, it's that you have a boyfriend who is friends with Brett Keller. I wanted to have sex with you when I first met you and your roommate, but I found out you had a boyfriend and I found out he was friends with Brett. That's the only reason I ended up having sex with her instead."

I was like, "Seriously?"

He was like, "For real."

Then we made out for like a few minutes and he left. That night was seriously terrible. After the party I went back to the dorms and didn't even bother knocking on Kyle's door. I know it sounds weird, but I was actually kind of pissed off that he fucked up my chance with

Brian. I was so mad and horny that I just went in my room and fingered myself thinking about Brian, who was probably out fucking Annie because she never came home that night. After I came I kind of felt bad about being mad at Kyle, so I went up to his room and slept in his bed with him, but we didn't have sex.

chapter
twenty-one

A few months or so before the end of our first semester I came to a stunning realization while at a quad party thrown by two sororities and two fraternities, the names of which are irrelevant. I had just fucked a girl whose full name was Mandolin Jacobs, but she went by Mandy, of course. I should clarify. When I say I fucked her I mean that I fucked her in the ass for ten minutes as deep and as hard as I could, to ensure I got at least some fecal matter on my dick, and then I throat-fucked her until she could barely breathe before bringing my performance to a close by shooting my load all over her tear-streaked face. The realization came twenty or thirty minutes after the event I just described, when I walked into a bathroom only to find Mandolin "Mandy" Jacobs being throat-fucked by one of my fraternity brothers named Lee Marsdale. He gave me an enthusiastic thumbs-up in between thrusts and I closed the door.

As I meandered back through the party and looked for the next girl I could force into some act of sexual deviance, I became acutely aware of the fact that they were hardly worth the effort. As a girl named Daphne Gerber approached me, tongue-kissed me without provocation, and put her hand down my pants, I came to a greater understanding of my own nature. What I actually enjoyed about the demeaning sexual acts I had forced on various girls up to that point in my life was the fact that they allowed it because of my superficial material status. Once I became a member of this fraternity, however, the girls I demeaned allowed it for no reason other than they were sluts who would invite this type of behavior from any other member of any other fraternity. There was nothing unique about me to the girls whom I forced to eat vegetables that had only moments prior been jammed into their assholes with no lube. Once initiated into this strange social environment, these sluts would allow themselves to be debased by any of their male counterparts. It was simply the way things were.

As the second semester wore on I found myself hanging out with Kyle more and more, secluding myself from the activities of the Alpha Tau Omega house. I would attend only the mandatory functions and even then only for the minimum required amount of time. My lack of interest did not go unnoticed by the other members of the house, but there was little they could do to change this. They understood my membership to be exactly as it was—predetermined and immutable.

Every so often I would run into Kyle's girlfriend, whom I came to despise even more after actually seeing her as a mindless sorority whore, a role that upon our first meeting I knew she would naturally fall into. I wished Kyle could see her at one of these parties. I reasoned that if he could see her flitting around like the whore she was he would finally be done with her. And, after endless conversations with him about her increased absence in their relationship and the strain it was putting on him, I thought sneaking him into a party at which I knew she would be present might tip the scales. But despite my insistence that he attend one such party he argued that he had to maintain respect for Heather by allowing her to have her own experiences without him. If she had wanted him to come to the party she would have asked him.

With my best friend becoming a shell of himself—the core of his personality being sucked out by and wasted on worrying about this whore who at her own core could care less about him—and with the whores I myself was fucking offering me no true joy, I began to focus myself on the coming summer break. I had no obligations to the fraternity during the summer, and the sluts I would fuck would fuck me for my status again.

One week before the semester ended I went to Petco and purchased a collar-and-chain set meant for large dogs, with the intent of going out the night after our last finals, finding a willing slut, fucking her, and then chaining her to a tree near the gazebo in my family's backyard, where I would urinate on her repeatedly over the course of twenty-four hours, allowing her to eat and drink from dog bowls only. My father and his wife were going to be gone for almost the entire summer, vacationing in various places around Europe, making something like this very possible.

My father and his wife had invited me to join them on certain legs of their vacation but I declined, preferring to spend my time alone, with sluts who would hopefully be chained up in the backyard, or with Kyle, who I also knew had no vacation plans and would be staying in Dallas for the entirety of the summer, probably working at a meaningless job to save some money.

I envisioned myself inviting him over, taking him into the backyard to introduce him to a urine-covered whore who would be eating from a dog bowl, and explaining to him that his girlfriend was no different. I further wove the fantasy to include his actual girlfriend as the urine-covered whore. If such an act wouldn't have ruined our friendship I thought I would have had no trouble convincing Heather to bathe in my urine while eating out of a dog bowl with little more than a promise of us going on a few dates in the first semester of our sophomore year.

On the final day of our first year of college I checked donorsibling registry.com and found that I was the proud father of my fourth child, a son born to a man and woman who had had two natural children of their own in their youth but required the aid of a donor since the father had elected to have a vasectomy some years prior.

summer

I had worked every summer during high school at the AMC movie theater in Vista Ridge Mall near my parents' house. My first summer of college, I did the same thing. The job was easy; a lot of the same people came back every summer, and I had worked there long enough to at least be making more than minimum wage. I started the summer thinking I'd see a lot of Heather, but that wasn't really how things worked out.

My mom got like this child support settlement from my dad that she had been waiting on for almost a year and she took me and my sister on a trip to Europe for like almost two months. I know it kind of pissed off Kyle, but what was I supposed to do, not go? Seriously. I mean, we were together every day pretty much for like the first week of summer, and then I saw him once or twice a week when I got back for almost the entire last month of summer vacation. I sent him some postcards and everything. I didn't get why he was so pissed about the whole thing.

I had assumed Heather's absence for the majority of the summer would give Kyle ample time to realize he should move on, but it seemed quite the opposite was the case. He tacked every postcard she sent him to his bedroom wall and cherished them in the way a soldier's wife might cherish letters from her husband. I caught him sniffing one on a Sunday afternoon in late June. It seemed he was so consumed with her that he was bordering on insanity, at least from my perspective. Aside from that, my summer was actually quite pleasant. I never found a willing participant for my dog-collar-and-chain scenario, which was surprising, but in keeping with the canine theme of the summer I did manage to coax a twenty-year-old slut from the University of North Texas into sucking our fourteen-year-old pug Cleveland's dick with little more than the promise of a chance to eventually work her way up to sucking my dick. It wasn't as entertaining as I might have imagined.

part two
sophomore year

chapter
one

The first day of my second year at SMU was pretty much exactly the same as the first day of my first year. I got my job at Mac's Place again and had to fill out all the tax forms. I moved all my shit into a dorm room at McElvaney and met my new roommate. I knew most of the other sophomores had moved off campus, but I couldn't really afford it. So, yeah, I was back at McElvaney as the only sophomore I knew of on my floor, which seems like that would have made me pretty pathetic, but I really didn't give a shit. My roommate was a freshman named Russ Hammilman. Russ was from Grapevine, a little suburb of Dallas, and he was majoring in business or some bullshit and couldn't wait to rush in January. As soon as he moved in he grilled me for a solid half hour about what the frat parties are like. When he finally started to get the fact that I had no idea, he never really talked to me again. We just kind of had an unspoken deal to leave each other the fuck alone.

After I moved all my shit in, I called Heather to see if she wanted to get lunch or something. I think she said, "Oh, babe, I'd love to, but I'm like supposed to eat with Andrea and some other Kappas. Is that okay?"

I don't know why it pissed me off so much when she said, "Is that okay?" I guess it was like she was asking permission even though it didn't matter what the fuck I thought. She was going to do whatever she wanted to. I think I said something like, "Sure. How about dinner tonight then?"

And she said, "I can't commit now. I'm going to be pretty tired tonight after I move all of my stuff into the house. Can you believe I have my own room now?"

I said, "Yeah, that's great," even though I really didn't give a shit. I take that back. I actually did give a shit, because guys weren't allowed in the girls' rooms in the Kappa house, so if we wanted to fuck it was going to have to be in my shitty dorm room, and I knew that Heather would never actually want to stay in a dorm room at McElvaney over her own room in her sorority house. So when she did stay over, I knew it would only be for me and I was pretty sure she'd start to resent me because I'd be the only reason she had to leave her perfect sorority life. How did I not see what a fucking cunt she was? Every time I go back over it I'm still surprised by what a fucking idiot I was.

Anyway, that first day back I pretty much wrote off getting to see Heather. I had one class orientation I was actually kind of looking forward to—molecular genetics lab. I'd taken the pre-req my freshman year, instead of my sophomore like most people do, because I really wanted to take molecular genetics lab as soon as I could.

The orientation was pretty standard. The professor handed out the syllabus, tried to crack a few shitty science jokes, told us about the research he was doing, and then made us choose lab partners, saying this exactly: "Your lab partner will be the person you spend more time with than any other this semester. If you are married, if you have a boyfriend or girlfriend, if you have a pet or child, tonight you should tell them that you love them and you will see them again in five months. Your lab partner is going to be your new wife, your new husband, your new boyfriend/girlfriend, your new pet, your new child. I realize you are all complete strangers and I don't care. Whoever you choose today will be your lab partner until the semester ends or until one of you dies, period." I actually kind of regretted taking the class a year early at that point. My friend Carl, who was my lab partner for almost every class that required one my freshman year, ended up transferring to Arizona State, which sucked because we had become decent friends, we worked pretty well together, and we were essentially on the exact same track with our majors. So we effectively could have been lab partners in every class up until graduation. But since he was in Arizona, I was kind of stuck with the luck of the draw, just hoping I didn't get a complete douchebag.

Of course everybody paired up immediately, and I got stuck with the fat guy who smelled like dirty armpits and farts. His name was Reginald Fromme and I swear to fucking God he was wearing a Harry Potter T-shirt and he had the beginnings of a Jedi Padawan braid on the back of his head. I wanted to fucking kill myself. Once we paired off we had to go up and sign our names on a list and then it was set in stone. I told myself it wouldn't be that bad, even though I knew it was going to be.

Every once in a while, maybe five or six times in your whole life, something will happen that seems so lucky, so out of the blue, that you almost believe there's a god. This was one of those times for me. My fucking hand was on the pen and I was about to sign my name next to Reginald's when two people came into the room. One was another fat guy who probably also smelled like shit and was wearing a *Lord of the Rings* T-shirt, and the other was a girl who was pretty cute, not fat, and probably did not smell like shit.

As they came in the fat guy said, "Stop the press. Sorry I'm late. What'd I miss?" Reginald turned around, saw the guy, then turned back to me and, I shit you not, said, "My apologies, this lab partnership is terminated." Then he went and started yelling at the other fat guy for being late. He said something like, "You have to be more punctual. I almost ended up getting stuck with that guy," referring to me. "I would have never forgiven you."

So that left me with only one other choice for a lab partner—the cute chick, who I confirmed did not smell like shit. She said, "So I guess we're partners."

I said, "Guess so."

"I'm Erin."

"Kyle. Nice to meet you."

"You too."

We signed our names next to each other and that's how I met Erin Sullivan, who I admit I thought about that night while I jerked off because Heather opted to stay in her new room at the Kappa house.

chapter
two

I know it probably pissed Kyle off that I spent my first night of sopho-more year in the house, but what was I supposed to do, seriously? It wasn't like I was going to sleep in fucking McElvaney Hall with him my first night back when I had just moved into my own room and ev-erything. I made it up to him, though. The next night I stayed with him and had sex with him and let him finish in my mouth and he seemed to calm down a little and not be so high-strung, so it seemed like every-thing was getting back to normal. At least it did to me. I mean, at the end of our first year it was kind of getting strained because I couldn't see him as much as he wanted me to, but we made it through that, and then over the summer I think he thought we would see each other more than we did, but I had to go to Europe. So now we were back, and even though we didn't really see each other the first day, I let him cum in my mouth the second day. I figured I would see Kyle pretty much every other day and stay in his room maybe like two or three times a week and have sex with him one or two times a week and it would work out fine. Everything was fine.

I signed up for whatever classes my counselor told me I needed and none of them seemed too hard so I wasn't worried about that and I was just seriously excited to be living in the Kappa house for the most part.

We had our first big back-to-school party like in the first or second week back, and even though Kyle was seriously like the biggest asshole ever in all of this and pretty much all of it was his fault, I guess at that party I did kind of do something that I can at least understand him being mad at me for. I mean, I guess I just shouldn't have done it, but whatever, it still wasn't as bad as anything Kyle did to me.

I basically knew I was in for a long night before the party even started. The party was at Fiji, and a few of us went over to help them set up some stuff a few hours before it officially started. While we were setting up, this guy Cam Saunders, whose older brother Jim sometimes got coke and E for us, was like, "So my brother came through with some serious shit for this party," and he pulled out like seriously a trash bag full of weed, coke, E, oxys, and a bunch of other pills—I had no idea what they were. He was like, "For being such good girls and helping us set this shit up, you ladies get one of each," and he gave us all like half a gram of coke, some E, and some other stuff. Then he made us promise not to do them until the party started.

I wasn't like a big cokehead or anything. I had done it maybe like a dozen times or something at different parties my freshman year and it was pretty fun, so I didn't have a problem with it or anything, and I knew the stuff that Cam's brother got was like the best on campus.

After we set up, Andrea, Jill, and I went back to our house to get ready and everything. I was pretty sure I'd be way too fucked up to see Kyle after the party, so I called him and told him I was just going to stay at the Kappa house that night. I never told Kyle about any of the drugs I did. I knew he'd be weird about it if he found out. It was just easier not to deal with it, seriously. Honestly he really was a pretty good boyfriend when it came to giving me space and everything during that time. He never even asked questions when I would sleep for like twelve hours the next day.

So we got dressed back at our house and then walked down to the party with the stuff Cam had given us. When we got there, we all went to the bathroom together, did a few bumps, and took the E. Andrea took something else, too. I kind of drew the line at coke and E and obviously weed if it was around, but I tried to stay away from the really hard stuff. This coke was seriously the best I had had up to that point. I remember feeling so good and happy and just ready to dance. I could feel the music pumping through the bathroom door and I couldn't even stop myself. I just opened it and went out into the shitty Fiji living room where they had this crappy DJ that I thought was incredible because of the coke and I just started dancing. Andrea danced with me a little bit, but I could tell she was having a way different experience. She was kind of just staring at the ceiling and trying not to fall down mostly. Whatever that other pill was, it didn't seem like it went very well with the coke.

And then like fifteen or twenty minutes after I started dancing the E kicked in and I swear to fucking God I felt like I was made of light or something. I guess it must have been really good coke and really good E mixed together or something, but I seriously didn't even feel like I had a body. I just felt like I was the music or something. It was intense.

I think I saw Brett walking around at one point and I tried to give him a hug but he just walked away or something. So I grabbed Andrea and rubbed her shirt, which was kind of silky and smooth, for a few minutes. At that point I didn't really think I was going to do what I ended up doing. Then Brian showed up with Annie.

Annie was like, "Hey, you rolling?"

I was like, "Oh yeah."

She was like, "Where'd you get it?"

I was like, "Cam."

She was like, "How much?"

I was like, "He gave it to me for nothing so I don't know. Probably like thirty."

She was like, "I'm gonna go find him." Then she left.

Brian was like, "For real, are you okay?" And I guess I was kind of sweaty or something because he was like, "You need me to get you a towel?"

I was like, "No, I'm great. I've been dancing for a while is all."

He was like, "How was your summer?" I guess I hadn't seen him since we all came back.

I was like, "Awesome. I went to Europe with my mom and sister. How about you?"

He was like, "I actually couldn't stop thinking about you and about that last party at the end of last year, for real."

I was like, "Yeah, me too."

He was like, "Can we go somewhere that's not two feet from a speaker?"

I was like, "Okay."

He took me by the hand and led me off to some guy's bedroom that had the old beer and sweaty-nuts smell. We sat down on the guy's bed and Brian just leaned in and started kissing me, pretty much like right where we left off the year before. Oh my God, it felt so fucking good and I know it was because I was so fucked up from drinking and E—I'm pretty sure I was over the coke at that point, but the E was like hitting me right at its most intense point. I didn't know if Brian was high or anything, but he was definitely drunk because I had to suck his dick for like five minutes before it even got hard or before I even really realized what I was doing.

It just kind of happened in the heat of the moment type of thing, you know. We were making out, and then I was sucking his dick in some guy's room in the Fiji house. At some point he tried to push my head back to stop me and he was like, "Wait, what about your boyfriend?"

I was like, "Shut up," and just kept sucking his dick. I don't think he took a shower before the party, because his nuts were worse than the nut smell in the guy's room, but his dick was clean, it wasn't too salty or anything. And on E, sucking his dick was so fucking nice. At some point during it I think the guy whose room it was came in or something, because the door opened, but he must've seen what was going on and left because he shut the door and everything.

So I sucked his dick for like another five minutes after he got hard and he came in my mouth, which was also really hot on the E Cam had given me. He came a lot, too. It was like a huge amount, which was also kind of hot to me in a way it never had been when other guys had done it—like I had given him such a good blowjob that it emptied everything he had. I swallowed all of it that went in my mouth—some kind of dribbled out because there was so much—and then went up to kiss Brian. He turned his head, though, which wasn't a big deal. Some guys won't kiss you after you've sucked their dick. There have been times when it's close to my period and I'm not really into kissing a guy after he goes down on me. So I just lay next to him.

He was like, "Are you going to tell your boyfriend about this?"

I was like, "Uh, that would be pretty fucking stupid."

He was like, "For real."

Then he passed out and I just lay there thinking about Kyle for a few minutes. What I was doing hadn't even really dawned on me while I was doing it. I mean once you start sucking a guy's dick you really aren't thinking about much else, just hoping he cums before your jaw starts hurting. I wondered if Kyle would be able to tell. I still hadn't fucked anyone else since we started fucking, or since we were officially exclusive, I mean, so I hadn't really cheated on him. I just gave some guy a blowjob. I mean I knew he wouldn't be happy if he found out, but I thought I could hide it from him, like he wouldn't be able to tell what I had done just by looking at me or anything. For a split second I thought about breaking up with him. I was too fucked up to think straight, but like the next day or something I should have realized that if I was sucking some other guy's dick I probably didn't want to be with Kyle at that point, you know? But I didn't. As stupid as it might seem, when I was lying there on that guy's bed with Brian's cum still clinging to the back of my teeth, I kind of realized that I actually loved Kyle like a lot. I was too high to feel bad for what I just did, but I knew Kyle didn't deserve to be treated like that. Now I obviously totally wish I would have sucked a million dicks a day when Kyle and I were together, but then I thought he deserved better.

So I left Brian sleeping on the guy's bed and went back to the party. I made a deal with myself that if I didn't pass out somewhere at the party I would try to make it back to Kyle's room at the end of the night and fuck him, kind of so he wouldn't be suspicious, but also because I felt like I owed him that much. I ended up not making it, though.

chapter
three

The morning after the first big party of my sophomore year brought with it the worst hangover I'd incurred in some time. It also apparently brought with it the third black girl I had ever fucked, who was asleep in my bed. I was overwhelmingly certain I didn't meet her at the party as neither Kappa Kappa Gamma nor Chi Omega possessed any members who were anything other than Caucasian. My memory of the night was spotty at best and seemed to cut off at a certain point in the night that must have preceded my meeting of the black girl and the learning of her name, which remained elusive to me after several seconds of actively attempting to recall it.

She was positioned so my comforter covered one of her arms and the lower half of her legs, leaving her ass exposed. It was tight and muscular in a way only a black girl's ass can be. I slapped it. She woke up, semi-startled, and seemed to have a better memory of the prior night's events than did I, or at least she remembered or knew my name, because she called me by it.

My erection was obvious to her as I kind of rolled her over and tried to jam it into her asshole, which was a shade of purple only a black girl's can be. She laughed at my attempt and got out of bed, exposing her whole body to me. I wished I'd had any memory of what we did the night prior. I was too curious to care about offending her, so I asked how we met, where we met, what holes I put my dick in, et cetera. She was candid in her response, explaining that she'd met me as I was stumbling back to the Alpha Tau Omega house. I had asked her point-blank if she wanted to fuck and explained to her that I hadn't fucked a black chick in almost a year. She knew who I was and had heard that I had a big dick, which she complimented me on, so she figured why not? She further explained that we did not use a condom but, as the first person in her family to go to college, she had no intention of having a life-ruining child, so she let me cum in her asshole, which I wish I had some memory of.

She put on her clothes, explaining that she had a morning class she couldn't miss. I asked her what she was doing later in the day, my thirst for black ass still not slaked, and she explained to me that I was the first white boy she had ever fucked, and although it was kind of fun she would probably never do it again. Fair enough. She left without me ever knowing her name.

I remained in bed for no more than five minutes, sniffing the place where her pussy had been to try and trigger some memory of the night's events. This endeavor was fruitless. Then I took a shower and thought I would see what Kyle had planned for the day. We hadn't seen much of each other since coming back to school and I was curious to know if he and Heather were still doing well, hopeful that they weren't. And it was with one thought of Heather that a switch was thrown in my brain to start the slow release of memories from the prior night.

I was at the party. I drank to excess. I watched Greg show his tattoo to two girls and then do a keg stand. I had to piss so bad I almost did it in the Phi Gamma Delta living room. And then, like a ray of light parting the clouded mess of my mind, came the most crystal-clear and crucial memory of the night. I wandered into a room I thought was the bathroom and witnessed Heather sucking the dick of a guy from

Pi Kappa Alpha, who I think was named Brian Johns or something. I thought about it a second, third, and fourth time to ensure there were no missing moments in the memory, no errors in the identity of the parties involved, and there were none. I held in my mind a first-person account of Kyle's cunt of a whore girlfriend sucking another man's dick.

I have never sung in the shower in all of my life, but that morning I almost did. As I left the Alpha Tau Omega house and walked toward campus the sun seemed to shine a little brighter, the birds seemed to chirp a little sweeter, the sluts on campus seemed to be a little less whorish, et cetera. It was shaping up to be one of a handful of days in my life that filled me with the kind of anticipation and excitement that makes your anus tingle ever so slightly.

When I got to Kyle's room I found his roommate, whom I had not yet met. Clearly already knowing who I was, he introduced himself and was immediately forgettable. He explained that he didn't know where Kyle might have gone, offered me some marijuana, and told me I was more than welcome to stay in their room and wait for Kyle's return. I declined the pot and accepted the offer to wait for Kyle. This, it turns out, was a mistake. Whatever this douchebag-in-training's name was, he was one of the most annoying people I have ever met. In the ten minutes it took for Kyle to get back from wherever he had gone, his roommate was able to fire off no fewer than two hundred and fifty questions about fraternity life, in an unrelenting barrage of "dudes" and "bros" that made me want to kill him.

Luckily Kyle returned. He was curious to know why I was there and I was eager to tell him. I wasn't sure I wanted his roommate around when the information was divulged, not knowing what Kyle's reaction would be and not knowing how the leaking of such information might further affect Kyle if he chose to ignore my information—or, worse yet, to stay with Heather even after knowing of her infidelity. So we went outside.

There in the courtyard of McElvaney Hall, at some time approaching one P.M., I told Kyle in no uncertain terms that Heather, his whore of a girlfriend, had sucked another man's dick, possibly to completion—

of that I couldn't be sure—at a fraternity/sorority party the night prior. Understandably he required my recounting of every detail of the night to substantiate my claim, most of which I was able to deliver. After exhausting all of the possible alternate truths—it was just a girl who looked like Heather, she was just resting her head in his lap, the whole thing was a lie devised by me to trick Kyle, et cetera—Kyle eventually succumbed to what he knew was the truth. His girlfriend had sucked another man's dick, maybe to completion.

I asked him what his course of action would be and he explained he needed to think about it. I suggested immediately getting a slut to suck his dick, recording this event, explaining to Heather that he had made her a special video and wanted to show it to her in front of all her sorority sisters, and then doing just that. He was clearly too upset by the revelation to see the humor and justice in my plan. He thanked me for telling him and apologized for ever doubting me. Above all, he said that he valued the longstanding and honest nature of our friendship too much to have questioned me. He didn't know what his reaction would be, but it would happen soon. He said he needed to have some time alone to figure things out. I obliged.

I had only one class that day, a business management class that was to come later in the afternoon. I spent the few hours before that class sitting on a bench near the student center performing an experiment that I had come to be entertained by. I merely sat on the bench and waited for a slut to approach me based only on my identity. It took roughly twenty minutes for the first such slut to make her approach. She sat next to me and pretended to hold a conversation on her cell phone that contained as much laughing as possible and the admission to her imaginary friend that she was single. It was a rare approach but not unique. She let her fake conversation play out for a few minutes, then hung up, making sure I knew her imaginary friend was female by bidding farewell to a "Jennifer," not realizing this was the one piece of information that allowed me to conclude the conversation was disingenuous. How often do you use people's names when saying good-bye to them on the phone? The answer is never.

After hanging up, she turned to me and apologized for being so loud, then began the obligatory "Hey, aren't you Brett Keller? I saw you at a party last week, my dad knows your dad, you used to date my cousin," et cetera. Because I didn't want to be late for class I cut through her routine and explained to her that I knew she'd sat on the bench next to me because she wanted to fuck me, or rather because she wanted to believe that I wanted to fuck her, and that I was more than willing to reciprocate if indeed that was the case. Although she was slightly offended by my directness, she wasn't so offended that she denied my request to go to the nearest men's room and let me cum on her tits.

Once in the men's room I surprised her by pissing on her tits instead, which was more than difficult with an erection.

chapter
four

That feeling was fucking worse than anything. It was like the back
of my neck was on fire, like my whole face and head had been put
in a microwave and then my stomach was ripped out through my asshole. Brett telling me Heather sucked some frat guy's dick was easily
the worst feeling I had ever had. Little did I know that bitch would be
the cause of worse feelings yet to come. I'm surprised I didn't puke
or pass out; both seemed possible. That was the first time I had ever
been cheated on, that I knew of, and it was by a girl I loved more than
anything. The worst part was, I couldn't get the image out of my head
of her sucking some asshole's dick. I knew exactly what she looked like
when she sucked my dick, so it was very easy to just put the biggest
crooked-baseball-capped-frat-guy-douchebag I could muster on the receiving end. As luck would have it, that's exactly what my roommate
was, and I immediately told him to get the fuck out of our room when
he said, "Hey, bro, what's going down?" He could tell I was more than
a little pissed off, so he left without any hassle.

I just sat there staring at the fucking wall, spacing out. I went over everything I could possibly think of that might make her suck some other guy's dick. We hadn't been seeing as much of each other as we had our freshman year, but I thought we had worked out a decent schedule. She had time for her sorority bullshit and we still got to see each other a few times a week. I thought everything was fine. I really couldn't bring myself to think it had anything to do with our relationship, which meant it could only be one thing: Heather was a fucking slutty, cock-hungry whore who would suck a cock for shits and giggles, which is the absolute worst realization to come to about the girl you love.

And then of course there was the outrage. I had fucking humiliat-ingly borrowed money from my best friend to pay for an abortion for this cunt. I mean it was for me, too, but she wasn't asking anyone for money—she left that up to me. I helped her through it, I was okay with us not having sex for a long time after it, and she repaid me by sucking some other guy's cock. Would that asshole pay for her abortion?

I just kept going back and forth from overwhelmingly sad to over-whelmingly pissed off. Then I'd get mad at Brett. Why'd he have to tell me she was sucking dick specifically? Couldn't he have just said he caught her cheating on me? But that wouldn't have been enough. I would have forced him to tell me everything. He probably spared some horrible details about how she had one hand on his balls or some shit that she doesn't do when she sucks my dick.

And then the possibility that I'd never fuck Heather again set in. That was worse than all of the other shit—well, almost worse than thinking about her choking down a frat guy's load. She was the best sex I'd ever had and I didn't want that to end ever really. But what was I going to do, share her with every frat house at SMU?

Then, of course, I started wondering where she was at that exact mo-ment. It was sometime right after lunch, and all I could think about was Heather naked in some guy's shitty frat-house bedroom getting fucked in the ass or something, maybe even against her will, or worse yet actu-ally enjoying it. I thought at the very least she went home with the guy whose dick she sucked and was probably naked in his bed. Even if they weren't fucking, she was naked with him and they probably had fucked.

And I had no immediate recourse. I couldn't find her. Even if she was at her sorority house I couldn't go in her room. I tried calling her about fifty times and her phone was either purposely turned off or out of battery. So I just had to wait until she got around to calling me before I could do anything, which actually in retrospect was a good thing because it gave me a little time to cool down. Who knows, though—maybe it all would have worked out better in the long run if I had been enraged when I talked to her. Maybe I would have said something that would have made her never talk to me again and everything would have turned out different. It's all academic now, I guess.

So around five or six that night she finally called me. She said, "Hey babe, I got like fifty messages from you. What's going on? Is everything okay?"

It took every ounce of self-control I had not to call her a fucking whore over the phone. I said, "Yeah, I just, I was really missing you last night and when you didn't answer my first few calls today, I started to get worried."

"That's not like you."

"I just wanted to make sure you were okay."

"Yeah, I'm fine. We just had like this crazy party last night and I ended up getting seriously drunk. So I stayed at the house."

"Oh. You want to get something to eat or hang out or something?"

"Sure, when?"

"Right now, if you're up for it."

"Okay, let me take a shower and get dressed and I'll come over."

"Sounds good."

"Love you, babe."

It was so hard to fucking say, but I said it. "I love you, too."

I really had no plan when she showed up. Somewhere deep down there was a small part of me that just wanted to ignore it. Just pretend that I didn't know and keep the relationship that I had with her. But I couldn't. I did know. Over the course of that afternoon she had probably swallowed seventy gallons of frat-guy semen in the porno that kept playing over and over in my head. I couldn't ignore that. I couldn't be thinking that every night she didn't spend with me. It would have driven me insane and I knew that.

She knocked on my door. I let her in. She tried to kiss me. I pulled away, able only to think that the last thing her mouth touched was a frat guy's cock.

She said, "What's wrong?"

I said, "How was the party last night?"

I thought I could make her nervous or get some corroboration of Brett's accusation that was independent of me confronting her. I don't know why I wanted that, but for some reason I did.

She said, "It was pretty fun, but I was seriously like the most drunk I've probably ever been."

"Who was there?"

"Just the usual people. Andrea went, some other girls from my house. Why?"

"Any guys there that you might have known?"

"Yeah, there were a bunch. What are you doing?"

"Talking to my girlfriend about her night. What are you doing?"

"You're acting weird."

"I know you sucked some guy's dick."

And she froze.

chapter
five

Oh my God. Seriously, how did he find out? Was he at the party? Was Brett there? Did he see? Did fucking Brian tell him? Did Annie? The only way out of it was to deny everything, so that's pretty much like exactly what I did.

I was like, "What? What are you talking about?"

He was like, "Brett saw you sucking some guy's dick in a bedroom at the party last night."

I remember thinking that I was like seriously sad that it was Brett who saw me because I still kind of felt like somewhere down the road there might have been a chance for me and Brett to get together, but probably not if he saw me giving a blowjob to another guy.

I was like, "I don't think he saw me. Are you sure he saw me?"

He was like, "Heather, come on. I know you did it. Why are you pretending you didn't?"

I could tell he really did know. At first I thought maybe he heard something or had a suspicion and was just trying to get me to like give myself up by admitting it, but he knew. I could see it in his eyes. So I was like, "I'm sorry," and I just started crying. Kyle's face went white and he sat down on his bed and was like, "Holy fucking shit. I can't believe this. I loved you."

I was like, "I love you, too. I'm so sorry. I was drunk and high," which I didn't want to tell him but it kind of slipped out.

He was like, "High? So you were doing drugs and sucking cocks? How long have you been doing this? Was it just this one time or is that what you normally do at these fucking parties?"

I was like, "No. It was just one time."

He was like, "Jesus fucking Christ," and he was kind of getting mean. He was like, "How many other guys have you given blowjobs to or fucked?"

I was still crying pretty bad. I was like, "None, you asshole."

He was like, "Oh, I'm an asshole? You sucked a guy's fucking cock last night. I'm pretty sure that makes you the asshole here."

I tried to hug him and he stood up off his bed like he didn't want me to touch him. He was like, "So who is this fucking guy?"

I was like, "Just some guy. He's a Pike."

He was like, "I don't give a shit about what frat he's in. I meant how long have you known him? Has this been going on with him a long time? Do you want to date him?"

I was like, "I don't know. I guess I've known him since rush week last year."

He was like, "And have you ever done this before with him?"

I was like, "No."

He was like, "And do you want to go out with him or be in any kind of a relationship with him?"

I hadn't really thought about it until right then, how it might be pretty good to have Brian as a boyfriend. I mean, even though I really liked Kyle—I mean, I loved him, I guess—I did start dating him just to try to get to Brett, and that didn't really look like it was ever going to happen. So, seriously, having Brian as a boyfriend would be pretty cool. I was like, "I don't know. I don't think so."

Then Kyle sat down on his bed again and put his head in his hands.

I was still crying. I was like, "I'm so sorry. What are you going to do?"

He was like, "Heather, I love you more than anything. I can't believe you would do something like this, but I don't want to lose you."

I tried to hug him again but he stood back again like still he didn't want me to touch him.

He was like, "Here's what I think we should do. I think you should quit your sorority."

I stopped crying because that actually made me like get pretty mad. I was like, "What?"

He was like, "If we're going to stay together I'm not going to be able to handle you going twice a week to parties where I think you're sucking another guy's cock, especially if the guy whose cock you sucked is actually at those parties, which he will be."

I was like, "Well, I'm not quitting Kappa. I can't believe you'd even ask me to do that."

He was like, "What choice do I have? Should I just ignore this?"

I was seriously pissed off at this point. I mean, he supposedly loved me, but he just wanted me to throw away Kappa like it didn't mean anything to me. Honestly, it's like, did I really want to be with a guy who didn't understand what made me happy? And if I dumped Kyle, I could probably start dating Brian like immediately, so there really wouldn't be a time without a boyfriend. So I was like, "I'm not quitting Kappa. You're a fucking asshole for even trying to make me feel bad enough to do it, and I don't want to be with someone who doesn't care about me enough to know what makes me happy."

He was like, "Wait a minute. You sucked a dick and you're the one dumping me?"

I was like, "That's what it looks like. And I'm gonna suck his dick again, too. Probably tonight." I felt bad when I said that to him, like it was too much, but now I'm seriously glad I did say it, because he started crying.

He was like, "Wait. I'm sorry."

It was too late, though. I had already made up my mind. I kind of felt good, like a burden was lifted off me when I dumped Kyle. And as

I walked out of his room on that day I remember actually being excited about getting to fuck Brian. I could still hear Kyle crying on his bed as I walked down the hall toward the elevator in McElvaney. When I got outside, I called Brian and told him the good news. I went over to Pike that night and fucked him. He wasn't as good as Kyle was in bed, but his body made up for it, and the fact that he was a Pike was way better than Kyle not even being in a frat at all. So if we became a couple I was happy that overall he was an upgrade for sure.

chapter
six

To say Kyle was merely upset over his breakup with Heather would be similar to saying that I only occasionally derive a very minor amount of amusement from seeing a whore cry after being forced to swallow my semen from another whore's cunt. Kyle was barely recognizable as a fully functioning human being in the weeks after Heather was unfaithful to him and then initiated their relationship's end.

I became aware of how dire the situation was only after realizing that I hadn't heard from Kyle in several days, which was abnormal. After he failed to return any of my phone calls for the better part of a final day, I sought him out in person, arriving at McElvaney Hall sometime in the early evening to find him in his bed wallowing in very obvious self-pity—something I then had, and still have, little patience for. I have the capability to be understanding and possibly even sympathetic in situations that warrant it, and even in some that do not, like this one, but my patience was wearing more than thin. Kyle was free from what I knew to be the worst thing in his life. I understood that he didn't share my view, and therefore I entertained his sorrow for a few minutes upon my arrival. I tolerated a conversation that included Kyle's assumption that he would never love someone as much as he loved her, Kyle crying, Kyle admitting that he didn't care if she sucked a different man's dick every night as long as they were together, et cetera. It all became too pathetic for me to indulge.

After he told me that he hadn't left his room, not even to eat or conduct basic routines of hygiene, I failed to find inside me the sympathy I previously mentioned. I ripped him from his bed and forced him into the showers, dragging him under the running water without bothering to help him disrobe. This was something I had seen in countless movies and television shows and had always hoped for an opportunity to try myself. This, I reasoned, was that opportunity.

I valued Kyle as a friend and it was unbearable for me to see him, someone whom in many ways I considered my equal, reduced to what he had become. In retrospect I have wondered if I made an error in my actions on that day. If I had allowed Kyle to grieve properly over the loss of this relationship, perhaps he would have been more rational about Heather, and nothing that came to pass would have come to pass. I don't feel I've made many mistakes in this entire ordeal, but that was one of them. It was not the most heinous of my mistakes but it was definitely the first and possibly the one to which the others owe their existence.

As Kyle sat in the running water I explained to him that his new life was beginning that night. I gave him no choice in the matter, explaining that I would find some girls for us to fuck and insisting that he, in fact, fuck at least one of them. I concluded by saying that if he wanted to end his sorrow, the easiest and best way to accomplish that would be to move on, to forget about Heather. And, of course, the easiest way to do that would be to fuck another slut. I didn't call Heather a slut, though, even though she was one of the highest order.

I met with resistance from Kyle, which was expected, so I resorted to an appeal to two basic human desires, one decidedly more male in nature: revenge and carnal lust. I explained to Kyle that I knew he must be angry at Heather, that he must hate her for committing her act of infidelity, that he must want to return her favor at some level and make sure she found out about it. And I further explained that I would be able to provide for him any girl he could possibly want to help him in this plan for revenge. I suggested any girl from Heather's sorority.

As I spoke about my ability to convince any girl on campus to fuck him, something primal began to stir inside him. He told me that he did on some level desire revenge, and that "the sad truth," or so he called it, was that he hadn't had sex with anyone in almost two weeks, and since Heather's departure he had no prospect of changing that. His urge to fuck had returned to him, slowly creeping back through the malaise of emotional confusion and pain, a truth I found to be anything but sad. Kyle admitted that fucking a slut from Heather's sorority would give him pleasure beyond the carnal. Knowing that Heather would find out about it would give him closure much quicker, he thought, than wading through the mire of sadness and depression that he was just dipping his toes in at the time.

I helped him out of the shower and plans were made to meet back up that night at my place, where I assured him I would already have one of the most attractive girls from Heather's sorority waiting with her mouth open and ready for his cock. He laughed at this. I couldn't tell if his laugh was anticipatory or if he doubted my ability to make good on my promise. Either way, he would be fucking a slut who was not Heather and hopefully in so doing would return to his normal self once more.

I had had several dealings with most of the Kappa Kappa Gammas, and I was more than certain I would be able to coerce at least two of them back to my house for an evening of no-holds-barred sexual debasement.

I rang the doorbell of the Kappa Kappa Gamma house, unsure what to expect and having no premeditated plan. The girl who answered clearly knew who I was, greeting me by name, despite my having no idea who she was. I immediately valued her below my standards, and while she was easily attractive enough for Kyle to fuck I wanted to make this night better than what he was used to. I wanted him to fuck the second most attractive girl in the Kappa Kappa Gamma house (the most attractive to be fucked by me), who was clearly not the troll who had answered the door on that day.

Besides Heather, the only girl in the Kappa Kappa Gamma house whose name I knew was a slut named Gina DelMonte, who, at the time, I was unsure if I had ever fucked. She was highly attractive, with a slightly flat ass that was made up for by a pair of perfectly round and firm C-cup tits. I asked the troll to summon Gina, which she did without question.

Once at the door, Gina hugged me a little too readily, leading me to believe two things: (1) We had fucked at some point this semester, and (2) I, for some unknown reason, did nothing to demean her during that fucking. I told her I was having a few friends over, but trying to keep it very intimate. I extended an invitation to her and to one other of her sisters in the house, with the exception of any girls who were not as attractive or as willing to fuck as she was and, of course, Heather.

Her excitement disgusted me and made me look forward even more to taking a shit just prior to her arrival, wiping but not showering, and then commanding her to give me a thirty-minute rim job before jerking off into her face.

I guess part of me thought that it just wouldn't end up happening. When Brett brought it up and offered to make it happen, I was mad at Heather. I wanted to make her feel the way I felt when I found out she had sucked some guy's dick. And, as pathetic as it was, more than just making her feel like shit, I hoped she'd get jealous and realize she wanted to get back together. Also, I hadn't had sex in a while, so I was pretty horny, and it seemed like sex with one of Heather's sorority sisters was a pretty surefire two-birds-with-one-stone scenario. But I didn't really think it was going to happen. I thought I'd go over to Brett's house and we'd play *Rock Band* or something. I didn't even think he'd get any girls over on such short notice.

But when I got to his house I realized I was stupid to have ever questioned his powers. I don't really know why I would have questioned Brett being able to get two girls to his house who were pretty much there just to have sex with him. I had seen him do it a million times before. Nonetheless, when I showed up at his house and there were two really hot chicks in bikinis in his Jacuzzi, I was surprised.

He introduced me as his best friend, Kyle, and told me to throw on a bathing suit and join them, which I did. Once all four of us were in the Jacuzzi together it became pretty clear that Brett had already paired us off. I assumed he was going to take the brunette with the big tits by the way he was ramming his tongue down her throat and grabbing those previously mentioned tits. And I was going to get the other chick, who I personally found more attractive. Her name was Jenna and she was kind of pale. I thought I might have actually seen Heather hanging out with her at some point. I might have even met her, but when I asked her if we had met, she said, "You're not in a frat, right?"

I said, "No."

She said, "Then there's no way we could've ever met."

What happened next was just weird—weird for me, I mean. I'm sure Brett is very used to having sex with chicks who are essentially complete strangers, but it was going to be a first for me. I didn't really know if I should just lean in and start kissing her or what the deal was. I guess Brett could tell I wasn't really the best at getting things started, because he came up for air with the chick he was with and said, "Okay. What's your name again?"

Jenna said, "Jenna."

Brett said, "Jenna, this is Kyle. Remember how I told you he was my best friend?"

She said, "Yeah."

Brett said, "Well, I like to make sure my best friends are happy."

She said, "Okay."

Brett said, "And I'm pretty sure Kyle would be really happy if you let him suck on your titties."

Brett could always get chicks to do whatever he wanted. But I never knew it was literally as easy as issuing a command to them. In this case the command didn't even involve him and she still did exactly what he said. With a cute little smile she looked at me and said, "Do you want to suck on these?" And she untied her bikini top.

I looked at Brett and he said, "Why are you looking at me, faggot? There's a naked woman asking you to suck her titties."

I don't know why I was looking at him. He was right. There was something a little impersonal about sucking a girl's tits without kissing her first, so I kissed her for a few minutes and just grabbed her tits. Once I got a hard-on I started getting creeped out by being in the same water that Brett was going to be fucking his chick in so I said, "You want to take this to a bedroom?"

She said, "Okay."

We went to one of the downstairs guest rooms. Before I could even turn on the light and pull back the covers on the bed, she had taken off her bottoms so she was completely naked, and she jumped on top of me.

She said, "I want you to fuck me in this house."

I said, "Okay," even though that seemed a little weird. I knew she would rather be fucking Brett and was probably just going to fuck me because she thought it might eventually give her a chance to fuck Brett, but the fact that his house turned her on was strange to me.

She took off my shorts and started sucking my dick. She was pretty good. Not as good as Heather, didn't have the same lip strength, but pretty good. As she sucked my dick, I started thinking about Heather. I realized I wasn't mad at her anymore, I just wanted her back. I wanted this girl, Jenna, to be Heather. I was such a fucking retard. While this hot chick was sucking my cock I actually said, "Excuse me, can I ask you something?"

She stopped and said, "What?"

I said, "Do you know Heather Andruss?"

She said, "Yeah, why?"

"Is she dating anyone?"

"I don't know. Why are you asking this?"

"I'm her ex-boyfriend. I was just curious." I could feel my dick going limp. So could she.

She let go of it and said, "I know you're her ex-boyfriend, and as weird as this may sound, it's actually kind of sweet that you're asking about her while you're getting a blowjob from another girl." She came up from my dick region and kissed me on the cheek, then she lay down next to me.

She said, "I know you guys were a thing for a while, right—like a year or something?"

"Yeah."

"Heather told us about you guys breaking up. I'm sorry about that."

"Thanks. Um, is this weird for you at all? I mean having sex with one of your sorority sister's ex-boyfriends?"

"Are you kidding?"

"No. You don't think she'll be mad at you?"

"I'm fucking Brett Keller's best friend. Of all the people in our house she should be able to understand that."

And in that moment I had my first brief realization that the entire year we spent together might have just been because of Brett, but I ignored it.

I said, "She cheated on me, you know."

"Yeah. Not to put myself down or sound crude or anything, but she's in a sorority—it was bound to happen. That's why I don't have a boyfriend and I'm not going to have one until my junior year. Just not worth the headache. If I had a boyfriend, for example, I wouldn't be at Brett Keller's house trying to fuck his best friend."

She put her hand on my cock and started jerking it a little. I said, "The only reason you're doing this is because I'm Brett's friend, right?"

"The only reason you want to fuck me is to get back at Heather, right?"

"Well, you're also a really hot chick and, not to sound crude or anything, I kind of want to fuck you just because you're hot."

She laughed and then started sucking my dick again. I closed my eyes, trying not to think about Heather, but I couldn't get her out of my head. So I looked down at Jenna while she sucked my dick. She was incredibly hot and even though she wasn't as good at sucking dick as Heather was, her eyes made up for it while she was doing it. She looked like she really loved sucking dick, like a porn actress.

It was a weird time to be making any kind of decision, but in the few minutes she had her lips around my dick I had come to the conclusion that I had to fuck this girl. Brett was right—fucking her was something I needed to do to move on. So I reached over to the nightstand and opened the little drawer that I knew Brett always kept full of rubbers. I got one out and handed it down to her. She put it on with her fucking mouth. This was something she had obviously practiced.

Then she rolled off of me onto her back, spread her legs, and said, "Fuck me."

So I did. I fucked Jenna for around thirty minutes, in pretty much every position I could think of. I wanted it to be filthy and impersonal and everything sex with Heather wasn't. When we were fucking doggy style and I couldn't see her face, I pretended she was Heather and I fucked her harder than any girl I'd ever fucked. I think she came, but I wasn't really paying enough attention to be completely sure.

After we finished we lay there for a few minutes. I didn't want to talk. Having sex with Jenna didn't really offer me the closure with Heather that I thought it would. I felt slightly numb. It was weird, I almost felt like I had cheated on Heather even though we were broken up.

She said, "Heather was a dumb bitch to give that up. Jesus Christ."

I said nothing.

She said, "Thanks, seriously. I mean the girl who ends up with you is one lucky bitch."

I said nothing.

She said, "Do you mind if I go back outside in the Jacuzzi?"

I said nothing.

She said, "Okay, I'm going to go. Thanks again. Maybe I'll see you around school."

Jenna left and went outside to the Jacuzzi where I assumed Brett was fucking the other girl. I further assumed that Jenna must have known what was going on out there and her urgency to get back to the Jacuzzi was based on her hope to get in on a three-way before Brett blew his load. For a split second I think I felt what Brett must feel about women every moment of his life.

chapter
eight

I had just had some breakfast in the Kappa kitchen and I was about to go take a shower. I was walking through the living room when I saw Gina and Jenna sitting on the couch laughing and talking about something that they were like seriously excited about. I didn't give it much thought, but before I got out of the room I heard one of them say the word "Brett."

So I was like, "Are you guys talking about Brett Keller?"

Gina was like, "Um, yeah."

I was like, "What's the deal?"

Gina was like, "Well, you wanna tell her, Jenna?"

Jenna was like, "Last night he invited us to his house and hooked up with us."

I was like, "At the same time?"

Gina was like, "Well, first it was with just me, then it was both of us."

Jenna was like, "Yeah, his best friend was there and I had to hook up with him first."

I was like, "His best friend? Like my ex-boyfriend, Kyle?"

Jenna was like, "Yeah. And I have to say, I don't know why you got rid of him. I mean, I guess he's a little nerdy or whatever, but he is unbelievable in bed. Seriously, Brett had a bigger cock, but your ex-boyfriend was way better."

Seriously, I almost puked. I mean, I knew eventually Kyle would hook up with some other girl, and I thought I was okay with that, but I didn't expect him to ever be able to hook up with a girl in a sorority. Like, I could see him hooking up with a band chick or something—but seriously, another Kappa? I knew I wasn't supposed to be mad because I was like technically the one who cheated on him and then broke up with him, but I mean I wasn't very happy about it.

And then, to make it even worse, not only did Jenna hook up with Kyle, she also got to hook up with Brett. I guess Jenna could tell I looked a little mad or something, because she was like, "You're not mad, right? Like you're cool with this, aren't you? I mean I never would have done it if I thought you were going to be mad. But like, you were the one who dumped him I thought and everything, right?"

I had to be like, "Yeah. I'm cool with it," but I wasn't totally cool with it. I went to my room without taking a shower and called Brian. I was like, "Brian, I need to come over."

He was like, "For real?"

I was like, "Yes."

He was like, "Um, I guess. I have a class at two, though, so . . ."

I was like, "Okay. I'll come over now then."

So I went over to the Pike house and he let me in and we went back to his room. We weren't like an official couple or anything yet, but we hung out and hooked up like pretty much every other night. I wanted to tell him what was going on, but I knew I couldn't, so when he was like, "What's up?" I was like, "I just wanted to come over and see you. Is that cool?"

He was like, "Yeah, coolio."

I was like, "Okay, good."

Then we just sat there for a minute and he was like, "So, seriously, what's up? Do you want to fuck or . . . what's up?"

And I guess at that point I kind of figured out that it might have seemed weird that I was over there that early in the morning, and I didn't want Brian to think I was one of those girls who was always like a basket case or overly emotional or something. So I was like, "Okay."

He took off his pants and started jerking himself off to get hard and he was like, "I didn't brush my teeth yet. Is it cool if we don't kiss? My breath is nasty, for real."

I was like, "Yeah."

While we were fucking I could only think about Kyle. Brian was really fun to fuck because his body was so amazing, but he wasn't as good as Kyle. He just really didn't care about anything but getting himself off. Like Kyle would always reach around and play with my clit if we were fucking doggy style. Brian never did that. Or sometimes Kyle would just go down on me for like forty-five minutes before we ever even started actually fucking. I'd get off like two or three times from him eating me out, and then I'd get off again while we fucked. Brian had only gone down on me once, and it wasn't really even worth the time he spent. He just kind of tried to stick his tongue like in my actual vag. Like he never even went for the clit.

While Brian was fucking me in his room, doggy style, with me bent over the side of his bed, I like really missed Kyle for a split second. I kind of at least hoped at some point we could have sex one more time and I got kind of sad that I might never get to do it. Then I got kind of mad that Jenna was the last girl to have had sex with him. I mean, Jenna? I thought she probably just did it because of Brett, but still, she fucked Kyle. I didn't hate her for it or anything, but it was pretty shady.

I figured out I wasn't going to cum because I was thinking about all of this shit way too much. Brian pulled out, came on my back, and then kind of slapped his dick against my ass a few times, which he like did a lot. I thought it was kind of weird, but not weird enough to ever stop him from doing it. Then he was like, "I'm going to go to the bathroom. I'll be right back."

I was like, "Can I get a towel or something?"

He was like, "I only have one clean one left. I'll get you some toilet paper or something. Hang on."

So I stood there in Brian's room with his cum dripping down my back thinking about Kyle and wondering if Brian would want to snuggle in his bed until he had to go to class like Kyle did after we had sex. I figured I probably already kind of annoyed him just by inviting myself over so I didn't ask him to do it when he came back with a handful of toilet paper for me.

There was a spot of cum in the middle of my back I could feel but couldn't reach. I handed him the toilet paper and I was like, "Can you help me out?"

He took it and laughed and was like, "Sure."

He wiped the cum off my back and threw away the toilet paper. I turned him around and tried to kiss him but he was like, "I still didn't brush my teeth."

I was like, "I don't care."

He was like, "For real?"

I was like, "Yeah, for real."

When I kissed him I thought back to a time when Kyle and I were first dating, one of the first times I spent the night in his room. He actually got up in the early, early morning, when he thought I was still asleep, and I saw him take his toothbrush and mouthwash down the hall to the bathroom in McElvaney and then he came back and started kissing me. It wasn't even to try to fuck me; he just wanted to kiss me. Then I started thinking about Jenna fucking Kyle and I was glad I didn't ask her about the details. It was easy enough for me to think about what Kyle looked like when he was fucking me and then think of him fucking her instead. It would have been even worse if I had known the exact details.

After a few seconds of kissing Brian was like, "Okay, babe, I need to get some stuff done before this class. You want to hang out tonight?"

I was like, "Sure," and the fact that he asked me if I wanted to hang out that night made me happy. I put my clothes back on and Brian slapped my ass as I walked out of his bedroom, which also made me happy. I felt like he wanted me, and I guess it was like as long as I knew he wanted me, I could stop thinking about Kyle.

I admit I was surprised that Kyle was able to actually fuck one of the sluts I brought to my house that night, despite our initial agreement upon that being the very purpose for his attendance. I assumed the pride I felt for his actions was similar to what a father must feel for a son hitting a game-winning home run in Little League. I assumed that his old feelings for Heather hadn't completely dissolved, and more than that, I assumed his general attitude toward women had remained virtually the same. But I knew something slight in him must have changed. Up until that point, Kyle had never had meaningless sex, which is not to say it was meaningless for him. I should say that he had never had a one-night stand. Of course it had meaning for him, and I hoped that meaning was rooted in a step toward a deeper understanding of how all women should be regarded—as whores who exist primarily to slake our carnal thirsts and secondarily to carry children and aid in the propagation of our species.

These were the points I hoped to illuminate for Kyle when I took him to lunch the following afternoon. I had planned the event as a minor celebration and suggested we go somewhere worthy of the occasion, but he insisted on Chick-fil-A, his favorite place to eat. This had been his choice since we were children, and it was something that became very endearing to me. Anyone else, when presented with an offer by me to be taken to lunch anywhere in Dallas, would choose the most expensive restaurant imaginable. But Kyle never did. It was always Chick-fil-A.

This lunch conversation occurred on a Saturday. I remember this specifically because after getting our food I made sure to choose a seat next to two fat old women who were engaged in a conversation about the sermon that had been delivered in their church the previous Sunday. It had something to do with rationalizing the donation of more than 10 percent of your income to the church. The phrase "you get what you give" was thrown about several times, and both women seemed to agree that tomorrow they were going to up their contributions to the collection plate. This, of course, is all irrelevant.

In a voice I made sure was loud enough for the religious hogs sitting next to us to hear, I asked Kyle how he liked fucking the slut I coaxed to my house. I further inquired as to whether or not he fucked her in the ass, and finally asked him where he shot his load. My reason for wanting to know this final detail was that I had fucked the same girl only moments later in the Jacuzzi, and as I pulled her hair I thought I might have felt semen in it, but was too frenzied by the throat-fucking I had given her friend to stop and check.

He assured me he used a condom and all of his seed was contained within it, which led me to silently wonder what was in her hair. At this point the hogs, meals only half-eaten, chose to move to another table. As crowded as the Chick-fil-A was on that day, their table was quickly taken by a family with two young children. I pitied the children, knowing their mother had to be that certain kind of self-righteous, hypocritical, Christian, suburban Dallas cunt who would push her pedestrian and outmoded beliefs on them until they were fully indoctrinated, and they would repeat the cycle with their own children, and so on and so forth until the end of time.

I chose to keep my voice at a level of volume that would make me clearly audible to this family as I asked Kyle if he had gleaned any new understanding about the cold fact that he would, I was certain, ultimately come to realize as clearly as I did that all women are nothing more than collections of wet, warm dick-sized holes, the only variable being how tight those holes are on any given individual.

Before Kyle could answer, the father of the family cleared his throat and said something to me about there being children and women present. I pretended not to hear him and looked to Kyle for his response. He shook his head, presumably at my obvious attempt to offend the family, and explained, then thanked me for delivering the whore to him. He said going into the night he was unsure what his reaction would be, if he would even be able to fuck the slut, but once he started doing it he found it to be extremely cathartic. He made it clear that, while he was nowhere near the line of reasoning I employed when dealing with cunts, he had come to a more firm understanding of the fact that there can be sex without love, and he was sure that he was on the road to recovery from the breakup.

As a surprise, before we went to lunch I had called Gina at the Kappa house to learn of Heather's reaction when she was told about Kyle fucking the other slut whose name I must have known at some point. I relayed to Kyle that Heather seemed visibly upset, and almost immediately called Brian, the Pike whose dick I witnessed her sucking, and wasn't seen for the rest of the day after telling her big sister that she was going to see him.

This last bit of information, it turned out, should have been withheld. It seemed that Kyle enjoyed hearing about Heather's reaction up to the point that it drove her to the very man she cheated on him with. His questions about their official relationship status were unrelenting, despite my initial truthful admission that I had no idea about any of it. I tried to calm him, explaining that he would be better off without her, that he should focus on starting anew, that I could even arrange for him to fuck the same slut if he wanted, or a different slut, et cetera.

He calmed down at some point and agreed with me that it was best to put her out of his mind. Our lunch ended with Kyle telling me that he thought he was ready to turn a new page. I assumed that meant trying to fuck as many sluts as possible in the remaining three years he hadn't squandered at SMU. I was wrong.

It was only a few weeks after having sex with Jenna that I found myself in the molecular genetics lab passed out. I had been in there for probably five hours straight with Erin, working on our lab final. We had a few weeks to put the project together, but we were both pretty motivated to get it done as quickly as we could so we could get some feedback from the professor and change certain things here or there if we needed to.

So I was asleep, head down on the desk, when I felt hands start to give me a back rub. I woke up and found the hands were Erin's.

She said, "I'll do you, then you do me, then we'll work for thirty minutes."

We had actually become pretty good friends, but we never really hung out outside of class unless it was to study. She was an engineering student who was just interested in genetics, so she signed up for the class without ever taking the pre-req, which you could do if you got clearance from the professor. She said to get it he made her take some kind of a preliminary exam, which she got a 100 on, so the professor let her in. Yes, I found that attractive.

We'd spent a lot of time together, but the back rub was the first time she ever touched me beyond a brush of the hand here or there. It was weird. It seemed almost too forward, but it also kind of seemed like she had no sexual interest in me at all. It was clinical. Either way, it was nice; she had strong hands, and my back was really stiff from sitting at that desk for so long.

She said, "You seem really stressed out lately, like for the last month or so."

We had been lab partners for almost an entire semester, and she knew I had a girlfriend. But at that point I hadn't told her about how my ex-girlfriend was a dick-sucking whore or anything. Honestly, I was kind of embarrassed by it, and I didn't really think Erin would give a shit about it anyway. But for some reason I said, "Yeah, I uh . . . my girlfriend and I broke up."

She said, "Oh. That sucks."

I said, "Yeah."

She said, "What was the deal?"

"She's in a sorority and . . ."

"Say no more."

"What?"

"I already know what you're going to say. She did E at some party and had sex with another guy."

"Yeah, pretty much."

"That sucks. My sister was in a sorority when she went here, and she cheated on every boyfriend she had during college. So did every other girl in her sorority. I love my sister and everything, but she's a nasty skank."

She gave me one last squeeze on the back of the neck and said, "My turn," then sat down in the chair I'd been sitting in, and I started rubbing her back. Heather only gave me two back rubs in the history of our entire relationship, and they were both pretty shitty, as I remember, like she just didn't care about doing it. I always hated that.

As I rubbed Erin's back she said, "So you got any new prospects?"

I said, "None that I know of. If what you said about sorority chicks is true, then I might be up shit creek. Pretty much every girl at SMU is in a sorority."

"That's not true."

"It's around seventy-five percent, isn't it?"

"That leaves the top twenty-five percent of all girls at SMU for you to choose from. That's not so bad."

There was a time when a comment like that would have slightly pissed me off because it insulted Heather, but that time had passed. I thought she was out of my life forever. I hadn't heard from her in a long time, and I was ready to move on. I should have transferred to another school while my spirits were high. Instead I said, "I see. So you're putting yourself in the top twenty-five percent of all the girls here?"

She said, "Wouldn't you? Not to toot my own horn, but I'm going to be a literal rocket scientist at some point. And I'm not horrible to look at, right?"

She turned around and I looked at her. I'd thought Erin was cute from the first time I saw her—a little blonde with a round kind of face that made her look like she was always smiling even when she wasn't. She probably weighed all of one hundred pounds, and she had really nice legs. She ran three miles a day before class.

I said, "Not horrible at all."

She said, "You know, I don't have any prospects at the moment either."

I said, "I'm sure that's not true."

And at that moment I really had no idea what was about to happen. I guess I was always naive with girls, but Jesus fucking Christ, I probably could have been having sex with Erin a long time before we actually did, which wasn't that night but was pretty soon after. That night she said, "Well, you're right. It's not entirely true. The one guy I kind of liked for a while always had a girlfriend, but I just found out not too long ago that he's single. So I guess I kind of do have a prospect. But I don't really know if he likes me."

Again, I had no idea at that point that she was even remotely talking about me. I know, I was a fucking idiot.

I said, "Why don't you just ask him?"

She said, "Okay. Do you like me?"

And I don't know if it was because it was so late, or because I actually was suffering from some kind of a slight touch of Down syndrome, but I said, "Are you practicing on me, or am I the guy you're talking about?"

She said, "You're the guy, you retard."

I said, "Oh, really? Why didn't you say something sooner?"

She said, "Uh, you had a girlfriend."

I said, "Right."

She said, "So . . ."

And I thought about it with a little more depth than the occasional times I had jerked off while thinking about Erin. She was smart, pretty funny, very cute, not in a sorority; we shared a lot of similar interests.

I said, "Yeah, I think I do like you."

She smiled and said, "Then I think you're supposed to kiss me now."

I leaned in and kissed her. It started kind of slow. It was a weird experience to kiss Erin for the first time. We had been friends, and friends only, for so long that it seemed strange—not in a bad way. It was just very unexpected and the first few kisses were definitely feeling-out kisses, for me anyway. No tongue, just kind of seeing if this could actually work, and it did.

After the first few seconds, she put her hand on the back of my neck and pulled me down on top of her, right there in the molecular genetics lab. Heather had a good body, but not like Erin's. Erin was strong and athletic, which was something none of my other girlfriends were. Erin's entire body was tight.

We made out for fifteen minutes or so that first night and then she said, "Wait. Wait."

I pulled back a little and sat down in the chair in front of the table she was lying on.

She said, "I really do like you. I have for a while now. But I don't really want our first time to be in the molecular genetics lab. Is that okay?"

Honestly, I didn't really want that either. I didn't know then what would happen between us in the months to come, but I had a feeling there was a possibility for some kind of relationship to happen, and I did want our first time to be a little more special than it was shaping up to be.

I said, "How about this: Tomorrow night we go out to dinner, like a real date, and take it from there."

She said, "Okay," with her cute little smile.

I walked her back to her apartment, which was just a few blocks from campus, and we made out a little bit more on her front porch. Then I walked back to McElvaney, passing Heather's sorority house on the way home. I honestly didn't even give her a thought.

By the time homecoming came our sophomore year, Brian and I had already been like an actual couple for almost a full month. I guess if I'm being honest, there were a few things I missed about Kyle, but only a few. I missed how good he was in bed and how he really like actually seemed to love going down on me, which Brian didn't. And I guess every once in a while I missed how he liked to cuddle after sex, which Brian also didn't. But other than that, Brian was seriously like way better as a boyfriend. I mean just the fact that he was in a frat made it way easier to see him all the time, and I never felt like I was ignoring him like I did with Kyle sometimes, when I had to do Kappa stuff or go to a party that he couldn't come to.

For homecoming that year, one of Brian's friends, another Pike, got his older brother who was some kind of investment banker or something to book a bunch of us a ballroom at the Mansion on Turtle Creek, and then we all got a bunch of rooms too so we could just stay the night there. It was seriously the best party I had ever been to.

I had never actually been to the Mansion, but I had heard it was supposed to be insane. I mean I knew it was like one of the most expensive hotels in Dallas, but I had no idea how amazing it was. The whole hotel was like in this super-old mansion, which I guess is why it's called the Mansion. It was so pretty.

Brian and I got there right on time, like twenty minutes late, so we weren't the first ones there or anything but we didn't miss anything. As soon as we got there, we met up with Cam and Brian bought a few hundred dollars worth of coke. I wanted some E, too, but he only got coke, which kind of sucked but it wasn't that big of a deal. There were two open bars, and with the coke I knew I wouldn't have any real trouble getting fucked up. I just wished I would have had some E, you know.

Most of my sisters were at the party. Some of them ended up going to the ATO party instead, but not too many. It was supposed to be insane, too, at the Omni, but I knew Brett would probably be there and I had pretty much avoided him since breaking up with Kyle. I just really didn't want to talk to him about the whole thing, even though I guess he probably wouldn't have wanted to talk about it either. I mean I guess I just kind of put that whole part of my life behind me, and wanted to just focus on Brian and Kappa and move on, you know?

And also a lot of the guys from Pike were at the party. One guy who was really good friends with Brian, named Josh Paulson, was hammered before we even got there. So when we showed up he came over to us, like seriously barely able to stand up, and he was like, "Dude, some serious fucking skanks up in this bitch. None as hot as your skank, though."

Then they fist-pumped each other and Josh walked off. I was like, "Um . . . thanks? You didn't even stand up for me."

Brian was like, "For real, he was complimenting you. He said you were hot."

I was like, "He called me a skank."

Brian was like, "That's just what Josh calls all girls."

I was like, "I'm not a skank."

Brian was like, "I know."

His friend Josh was so gross, and for as long as I've known him he's always hit on me. I was having lunch with some of my sisters on campus and he came up to us and was like, "Heather, good to see you. How's shit going with my bro?"

I was like, "Good."

He was like, "Well, if things don't work out and you're looking for some hog on the side, let me know." He called his dick a hog. Seriously, he was so gross and for some reason he was way into me.

For the rest of the party I just danced and hung out with Brian. I talked to a few of my sisters about a party we were going to throw right at the end of the semester and also about rush week, which was only a couple of months away, and just about some other general Kappa things.

Then the party started winding down and I was seriously excited to see what the room Brian and I had looked like. I mean, I guess I should also say at this point that I was seriously drunk and seriously high. So we went up to our room and it was the nicest hotel room I've ever been in in my entire life. I mean, seriously.

It was so nice I wanted to have sex with Brian like immediately, to have like a really awesome memory of the night and everything. So I started taking off his shirt and he was like, "Hold up, babe. I think there might be some people coming by for a little after-party in our room."

That was cool with me. I was like, "Oh, cool. Who?"

He was like, "Just Josh and some people."

I was like, "Oh. Whatever."

He was like, "Babe, I know you don't like Josh, but he's a cool guy. You just have to get used to him, that's all."

I was like, "You know he told me if I wanted to cheat on you with him that I could have his hog."

Brian actually laughed and was like, "For real?"

I was like, "Yeah, for fucking real."

Brian was like, "That's just his way of joking."

I was like, "He wasn't joking. He's a gross asshole."

Brian was like, "Well, he's my friend and my bro, so you have to find some way to be cool with him from time to time, okay?"

I was like, "Okay."

Then there was a knock on the door and it was Josh, of course, and no one else. Josh was like, "Let's get this party started pronto," and he came in with two bottles of this vodka called Diaka or something that was supposed to be like the best in the world and that he said he stole from one of the open bars. And he also had some E, which I really wanted to do but didn't want to do around him, so I turned him down when he offered.

For pretty much the rest of the night we sat there, the three of us, watching pay-per-view porn because Josh put it on TV, and we drank. It wasn't terrible, I guess, but I wished someone else would have shown up like Brian said they were going to.

At some point I passed out and then was woken up by fucking Josh grabbing my ass. Brian was asleep across the room in a chair so I turned around and was like, "What in the fuck are you doing?"

Josh said, "Just checking out your goods."

I was like, "Get the fuck away from me."

He was like, "Sorry. I'm drunk. I'm high. Don't be pissed. Really, sorry. You're just super fucking hot and . . . I'm sorry."

It seemed like he really was sorry, and even though Josh was like seriously fucking disgusting I felt kind of bad for being mean to him. I mean it was kind of a compliment that he thought I was so hot he couldn't keep his hands off me I guess. He left after that and we found out the next morning he never made it to his own room but instead just passed out in the hall in front of our front door, where he also puked.

I woke Brian up and got him into bed with me and told him the whole story of Josh grabbing my ass while I was sleeping.

He was like, "That's just Josh. He didn't mean anything by it."

I was like, "I know. He apologized and I kind of felt bad for getting pissed at him."

Brian was like, "I'm sure he's cool with it if he even remembers anything tomorrow morning. We should fuck."

I was like, "Okay."

And then he rolled me over and fucked me from behind, not doggy style but like laying on top of me, which is usually one of my favorite positions but it only lasted for like four or five minutes and it was kind of violent, like Brian fucked me a lot harder than normal. The thing I remember most about it was staring at this painting of three birds sitting in a tree that was hanging over the bed. I was too fucked up from the alcohol and the coke to cum, which I knew going into the whole thing, so I was happy to just look at the birds and let Brian get off, which he did right before he passed out.

chapter
twelve

I was returning from a blood test that was mandatory every three months in order to continue to be a sperm donor the first time I met Erin. Kyle had called me the night prior to tell me that he had a new girlfriend whom he had been exclusive with for the better part of a week. She was his lab partner in a genetics class.

I can't say I was happy about the scenario. I had held on to the hope that Kyle would take the breakup with Heather and subsequent fucking of a meaningless slut in one of my guest bedrooms as the first step down a path that would lead him to the ultimate truth about whores. And it seemed to me at that time that he was very simply falling back into his old pattern, having gained no new knowledge from his first mistake, like a child who gets burned by the stove yet reaches to touch it again after the wound has healed.

Nonetheless, he was my friend and I was interested to meet any slut he chose to call his girlfriend. If she was no different than Heather, I felt fairly certain that I would be able to convince him of their similarity, see the error in his choice, end their relationship, and return him to his exploration of understanding the true nature of sluts with me as his tutor.

Of course we met at Chick-fil-A, which he claimed was his new girlfriend's favorite place to eat as well. I was unsure whether this was truth, a lie on her part, or a self-told lie on Kyle's part. In any case I found myself sitting across from Kyle and a cute blond girl, whom I personally found more attractive than Heather, as I ate nuggets.

Erin was interested in many of the same things Kyle was, which was a marked improvement from Heather as well. She seemed smarter than most sluts in both common sense and academic intellect, which was a much better match for Kyle than Heather, and she seemed to have a decent sense of humor that complemented her open acceptance of vulgarity in common conversation very well. All in all, upon my first impression, I actually liked this girl. I searched deep and found only a very mild, almost imperceptible desire to ejaculate in her open eyes— usually an overwhelming urge upon my first meeting with any slut. She seemed happy with Kyle and he returned the happiness in kind.

After lunch I invited them both back to my house. The invitation served a dual purpose for me, the first being the most obvious desire to spend time with my friend, and the second being to gauge Erin's reaction upon realizing that her boyfriend was best friends with an abundantly wealthy person, a fact she did not indicate being aware of during lunch. I had difficulty deciding if this ignorance of my identity, and of the means that identity afforded me, was genuine or put on for the purpose of disarming me.

Once at my house, Erin was very complimentary of many of the furnishings and the home itself, but not in the standard manner a regular slut would have been. She lacked the quality in her voice and demeanor that betrayed a secret envy to possess it all herself. Her compliments seemed honest, which was something I'd only witnessed in some of my father's friends who had amassed fortunes approaching the value of his own, people who were beyond envy because they possessed assets similar in value. I wondered if she was extremely wealthy but reasoned once again that Kyle would have mentioned it if she had been.

The only other alternative, one that seemed to be so unlikely it stood on the same ground as the existence of angels and God in my mind, was that she actually had no interest in wealth, in status, in material possessions, et cetera—that she existed with no pretense, with no trace of a lie.

In the backyard we sat in the enclosed gazebo near the pool because it was too cold to actually sit outside. In all honesty the conversation couldn't have been more boring for me. It consisted mainly of Kyle and Erin trying to explain the significance of nanotechnology as a technology that, along with robotics and genetics, would replace the current three most important technologies—atomic, chemical, and mechanical. These were things Kyle and I would talk about from time to time, but never in any great depth, and I realized in listening to their conversation that, in much the same way I had always viewed Kyle as being deficient or at least unable to share in one area of our friendship—sluts—I returned the inability to share in something that interested him on the same level. I was surprised at how well they seemed to complement each other, at least in that instance.

I knew from previous conversations with Kyle that, although he found her more than adequate at sucking dick and fucking, he couldn't help comparing her to Heather, and in that comparison she fell short— only slightly, but short nonetheless. It was a shame that had to be the case. It seemed to me that Erin and Kyle had more than just a regular college relationship. They actually appeared to be friends, something I had never bothered to achieve with a girl. And, knowing the nature of men, I knew their relationship was doomed from the beginning. In all ways Erin was Kyle's perfect woman, but she wasn't as good as Heather in bed.

I knew this would be a seed in Kyle's mind that wouldn't stop grow-ing until one day he found himself fantasizing about Heather sucking his dick every time Erin had her lips around his cock or fantasizing about fucking Heather every time he found his cock buried in Erin's cunt. This one thing would ruin his relationship with her.

After meeting Erin and witnessing how truly happy they seemed to-gether, I held back my prediction of their relationship's end from Kyle, hoping he would be able to overlook the only flaw he had ever admitted seeing in her. And I wondered what it was about the way Heather fucked that made her better than Erin. Beyond the very well-known errors a slut can make when sucking a man's dick—by using teeth or not taking as much of the shaft into her mouth as possible—the only thing I could think of was perhaps that Erin offered no enthusiasm when they fucked, that she lay perfectly still, forcing Kyle to do all the work. Or maybe her inexperience made her timid when Kyle favored an aggressive slut. Conjecture aside, the fact remained that as long as Kyle thought Heather was better at fucking, he would never be truly in love with Erin and that would lead to their demise.

When they left my house I gave their relationship one last thought and truly did want it to last. Then I called a whore I had fucked a few times but only in the ass and invited her over. When she arrived I let her suck my dick and then I fucked her in the pussy for the first time, trying to very accurately rate her on both her fucking and dick-sucking ability. She came in somewhere around a 6.5 on dick-sucking and a 6 on fucking. Those figures might have been arbitrary, but they seemed correct. I let her know where she ranked on my scale and then watched her run out of my house in tears.

chapter
thirteen

I was so fucking stupid. Everything with Erin was good, really good. I just could never see it as great, even though it actually was. We got the highest grade in our class on our lab final, and over that winter break she met my mom and dad the day before she left to go back to Florida, where her family lived. Both of my parents loved her and she seemed really comfortable around them. She was probably the closest thing to a perfect girl that could have existed for me at that point. The only problem was, at that point, I couldn't see it.

Our second semester started pretty much the same way they all did. First classes, syllabi, all the usual crap. We didn't have any classes together, but we saw each other pretty much every day. I almost never stayed at McElvaney, because she had her own apartment and it was a lot better than having to deal with my douchebag roommate.

I guess we were probably less than a month into our second semester when I woke up one morning in Erin's bed and she was staring at me. She said, "What do you want to do today?"

I said, "What is today?"

She said, "Sunday."

I said, "No classes. I don't know. What do you want to do?"

She said, "I'm pretty sure I want to tell you that I love you."

And that was the first time she ever said it to me. It was just a reflex for me. I had never thought about it. I didn't know if I actually did or not, but I said, "I love you, too," knowing that we had been together long enough that if I didn't say it back it would be weird and she'd start crying and everything.

She said, "I know," then started kissing me and then sucked my dick for a few minutes and then had sex with me twice before we ever got out of bed. She really was incredible but I couldn't see it. I had a girl that any other guy would fucking kill someone to have and she was completely in love with me and I couldn't see it. Everything that happened after it could have been avoided if I had just seen it.

Around noon that day I took a shower and we went to get something to eat. For the rest of the day I was in some kind of haze, thinking about Erin telling me she loved me and wondering if I really loved her. I guess there was just something about the entire relationship that seemed a little lackluster, even though it wasn't. I didn't ever directly think about Heather, but I knew that I had been through it all once before—been through the first kiss, the first fuck, the I love yous, been through all of it before, and the second time around it just wasn't as good. No, it's not that it wasn't as good, it was actually better, because it felt more real, more adult, even though it barely was. But I think that was the problem. After Heather I just couldn't give myself over to it the way I did the first time, and I didn't want it to be real or adult. I wanted it to be as all-consuming as it was with Heather, as it was the first time. What I never realized was that Erin offered a lot of firsts I just took for granted. She was the first girl I could actually have a meaningful conversation with about science or anything academic really. She was the first girl who made me laugh, really made me laugh. She was the first girl who I think actually really loved me. And somehow I overlooked all of that shit.

Our relationship went on without her knowing how I felt for months.

We would tell each other that we loved each other. She would mean it and I would only kind of mean it. We'd still spend virtually every night together. We had sex every day that we did spend together, and on the surface our relationship seemed pretty perfect. I even remember telling Brett at one point how I actually felt about the whole thing, that I had actually thought about breaking up with Erin a few times because I just wasn't as into it as I had wanted to be. I expected him to try to hook me up with some girl that he would force to have sex with me or something in order to get me out of the relationship, but he actually said something like, "Kyle, I can't believe I'm telling you this, but honestly Erin could be the one girl on planet Earth who is perfect for you. Now, I'm not saying you shouldn't cheat. It's a given at some point that you'll have to fuck someone else. But that's not the problem you're talking about here. I can't actually understand what you're saying about not being completely in love with her, because love is a lie created by women to trick men into believing they have to sacrifice their entire lives to marriage and family, but I will say you should give some serious consideration to your relationship and how lucky you are to have found someone like Erin."

I said something like, "Wow, I expected you to set me up with another girl in your Jacuzzi or something."

He said something like, "Heather was a cunt, Kyle. I would have hired a hit man to put a slug in her fucking skull if you would have wanted me to. Getting a sorority skank to fuck you after she dumped you was the least I could have done. Erin is not a cunt. She, in fact, is one of the rare women I've ever met who doesn't have an ounce of cunt in her. You know I don't advocate marriage, but I've always known you'd wind up in it for the long haul at some point with some slut."

I said, "Erin's not a slut."

He said, "Exactly my point. Think about what you'd be losing if you were to break up with Erin. You may not find another girl like her in your lifetime. She's rare, Kyle."

He was right, she was rare and I understood that. That understanding is what kept us together. Every time I'd start to feel bored or like everything Erin and I were doing I had done before and better, I'd just think back to that conversation with Brett and I'd go to sleep with Erin and still be with Erin when I'd wake up the next day. In time I realized that what I felt for her was actually love. I came to terms with the fact that it wasn't as strong or as passionate as what I had with Heather, but it was far more practical and that would eventually mean we would have much more reason to stay together for much longer.

Then it was somewhere around midterms that I saw Heather for the first time since we broke up. She was walking toward me across the lawn by Dallas Hall and we made eye contact. It was like a sledgehammer to the butthole. My stomach tied itself in a knot and I felt like I was going to vomit instantaneously. I got hot all over and my armpits started sweating. I assumed the feeling was identical to being sentenced to death.

We obviously saw each other and we were already on paths that would lead us to practically run into each other so it was inevitable. Neither of us veered off course or pretended not to see the other one so there, in front of Dallas Hall, I think a few days before midterms, Heather came up to me and gave me a hug, which I returned. She felt good, which pissed me off and made me sad at the same time. I was pissed off because it would have been much easier to deal with if she had gotten fat, and I was sad because I knew I wouldn't get to fuck her.

She said, "You look good. How have you been?"

I said, "Fine. You look good, too. And how have you been?"

She said, "Also fine."

I couldn't help it. I said, "You dating anyone?"

She said, "Yeah, yeah. You?"

I said, "Yeah, for a while now."

She said, "Cool. Very cool."

Then we just kind of stared at each other for a few seconds and she said, "Do you want to go get something with me, a coffee or something?"

I knew I shouldn't go. I knew it was a bad fucking idea, but she smelled so good and just hearing her voice again made me want to get as much of her as I could, to have something to hold on to. It was almost like she was recharging some battery that had been dead in me since we broke up and I wanted to get it as full as possible.

I said, "Yeah, sure," and we walked over to Java City in the Hughes-Trigg market. We got a couple of coffees and sat down and just talked to each other. It was amazingly civil. I wish she would have been a cunt or started talking about whoever her boyfriend was or something that would have made it easy for me to see why I was better off without her, but that didn't happen. She never mentioned her boyfriend and I never mentioned Erin. We just sat there and talked about TV shows and movies and my parents and her mom and her sister and we made each other laugh. It was comfortable in a way I hadn't expected, and after an hour or so she finally said, "Well, I should get going, but it was really good talking to you, Kyle. I guess I've missed you more than I thought."

I said, "Yeah. Me too."

She said, "Maybe we'll have to do this again sometime."

I said, "Yeah. That'd be nice."

She said, "Okay. See you later."

I said, "Bye," and she walked away.

I fucking hate myself every time I think back to that conversation. At one point I really fucking hated Heather. I guess that point was somewhere around the time I found out she was sucking some other guy's cock. I had held on to that hatred for a long time. Eventually, once I had been with Erin long enough, it just turned to a numbness, and I guess that's maybe what the problem was with me and Erin. I just couldn't feel as much as I did with Heather.

Anyway, that conversation took the numbness away. It didn't replace it with anything, but just sitting there talking to Heather made me realize I didn't hate her anymore and I felt like she was a good person again. That conversation actually made me entertain the idea of just being friends with her so I could have her in my life in some capacity. I was such a fucking retard.

She didn't say anything negative about me or about Erin like I semi-expected her to. After we broke up I had clung to this image of Heather as a horrible cunt, which, it turns out, she absolutely was. But after that conversation she wasn't anything to me other than a really nice person I used to love, and I was glad there was a chance she would be back in my life. What a fucking fag.

That night when I went back to Erin's apartment I didn't tell her that I had seen Heather. I wondered if Heather told her boyfriend about seeing me.

chapter
fourteen

I don't know why I never told Brian about seeing Kyle that day, but I didn't. I didn't really think he'd get jealous or anything. Brian wasn't really a jealous type of guy. I mean when Josh grabbed my ass when I was sleeping that one time, Brian didn't like even care at all. I guess I don't know why I didn't tell him about Kyle. Maybe I wanted to hold on to it for myself or something. I don't know. Whatever.

Before I saw Kyle that second semester was really fun, though. I got to help with all of the stuff for rush week, and it was seriously cool to see a new group of girls doing exactly what I had done the year before. When we had the two-party day Andrea told me she thought I should tell my abortion story like she did the year before, and I thought it was a good idea. It was like Andrea was the only one I had told up to that point, and it seemed like it would be really cool to share that with the rest of the Kappas on the two-party day. I didn't cry when I told the story, even though I thought I would. I guess at that point I was just over it, you know?

And everything with Brian was pretty good. Josh hung around a lot more and was always saying really nasty shit about me like how he wanted to fuck me—I mean, like the ways he would fuck me if he fucked me, like doggy style and shit. He was seriously nasty like right in front of Brian and whoever else happened to be in the room, and Brian would just laugh it off. It seriously grossed me out, but I got used to Josh's sense of humor eventually, and the three of us hung out a lot. Josh wasn't ever like my best friend or anything, but I guess I like learned to tolerate him for the most part.

I only saw Brett a few times here and there at parties and he always kept his distance. I never knew if he was mad at me for the whole thing with Kyle or if he just didn't care or what the deal was, but we never talked. And then at a certain point I found out that he had fucked like pretty much every girl in my house except me, and I was like seriously wondering if it was some kind of weird revenge thing with him or if he had just fucked like pretty much every girl on campus or something.

And then I saw Kyle. It was seriously weird seeing him and talking to him. It seemed like he was happy with whoever his new girlfriend was. We didn't really talk about either one of our significant others in that conversation, so I left it like wondering what she was like. I figured she was a band nerd or something like that, you know, right up Kyle's alley.

After our conversation it wasn't like I was thinking about Kyle every day or anything, but it did make me kind of miss him, you know like miss him being a part of my life. I didn't necessarily want to get back together or anything, but I thought about us being friends and if that would like work or if it would be really like weird. I mean I was glad he wasn't mad at me anymore, and he seemed cool with me, and I guess there was some part of me that just kind of missed hanging out with him and everything. And I admit, I did think about fucking him a few times and I missed that a little, too. All of that shit seems so stupid now that I know what an asshole he is. Whatever.

And that's kind of where I was in terms of like headspace and everything when Kappa and ATO threw our annual Heaven and Hell party kind of toward the end of our second semester, maybe like a month and a half left or something. Kappa and ATO had just done Sing-Song together, and we were like the best hands down, so we were really excited to throw the party. It had been cool the year before, but I thought I could make it much more awesome, so I like volunteered to be on the planning committee and everyone was cool with that because I was seriously an awesome party planner.

We turned the ATO basement into hell, with like red lights and dry ice and everything, and we turned their upstairs into heaven, with like white streamers and white pillows everywhere, and we turned the first floor into purgatory, with no decorations or anything. It was seriously amazing-looking when we finished everything. And then all the people we invited had to dress up like angels or demons or whatever, and this year we put a little thing on the invitations that said "please no offensive or insensitive costumes." I seriously did not want some guy to come dressed as like the Grim Reaper with aborted fetuses dangling from his belt again.

The party started out really good and everyone was complimenting me on the decorations and everything and Cam got his brother to hook up like pretty much anything you could possibly want for a party.

So I was dancing with Andrea out in the backyard by the kegs where there was a little open space and Brian came up and was like, "Open your mouth." So I did and he dropped some E in my mouth. He was like, "Cam gave it to me. Said it's really fucking good." Then he put one in his mouth, too, and kissed me.

He was like, "I'm gonna go grab another beer. I'll be right back," so I just kept dancing with Andrea and waiting for the E to kick in. And when it did . . . holy fucking shit. I don't know if Brian slid the E that he had in his mouth into my mouth or what, I mean I was pretty drunk already and had done a few lines in the bathroom upstairs, but it felt like I had been double-dosed or something. Seriously, I mean I either had to have done two tabs or the shit Cam's brother got was like pure chemical MDMA or something. I remember while I was dancing I started having like mild hallucinations and everything. Like when the bass would get really loud in a song I thought I could like see people and trees and everything rippling like waves in a pond from the sound.

It was seriously trippy. I had done E a bunch of times and I'd never had a reaction like that. It wasn't really that bad for like the first twenty or thirty minutes, but then I started feeling kind of sick.

Brian came back and he was like, "You don't look good, for real. Do you need to lie down or something?"

I was like, "Yeah, maybe."

He was like, "I'll walk you over to my house."

I was like, "Why? I can just find a couch here or something."

He was like, "Pike's just down the street and it'll be more quiet and everything. Once you start feeling better we'll come back. You really don't look good, babe. In case you have to puke or something we should probably not be in the middle of a party."

I was like, "Okay." I mean, everything he said made sense at the time, so I took his hand and we started walking out the front door of the ATO house and Josh came up to us and was like, "Where you kids going?"

Brian was like, "Heather's not feeling too good. We're gonna go back to our house."

Josh was like, "I'll come with you guys. I need to get some rubbers from my room. There's some skank who wants a piece of my hog upstairs."

I was like, "Gross."

As we were walking back to the Pike house I started feeling even more weird, like not just sick but really fucked up, like super fucking drunk. I was like, "Brian, this E is seriously fucking me up. Is it fucking you up?"

He was like, "No, babe, I feel really good."

Josh was like, "Maybe you got a bad tab or some shit or maybe you drank too much and the booze and the drugs are fucking you up. I've been there before."

I was like, "Yeah, that's probably it."

So we got back to the Pike house and Brian took me up to his room, put me in his bed, took off my clothes, and turned off the lights. He was like, "I'll go get you a glass of water."

I was like, "Okay," and closed my eyes. I don't know how much time had passed but I woke up to Brian laying on top of me and kissing me. I was still seriously out of it. Like it was so bad I kind of couldn't move right, like I was more drunk than I had ever been in my life, but I didn't feel drunk exactly. It was weird, but the E made his kisses feel really good so I kissed him back and he took off his clothes and was like, "Let's not go back to the party."

I was like, "Okay."

So we made out naked for a few minutes I think and then the door to his room kind of opened and Josh was like, "What's going on in here, kids?" And I remember when he opened the door I could hear one of Dane Cook's stand-up CDs playing in some room down the hall. He was talking about wanting to be a criminal or something when he was in high school and making his friend do like a home invasion.

I wanted to like cover myself up or something but I was so fucked up I just kind of rolled over on my stomach and didn't move or say anything. Brian was like, "Nothing, dude. What's up?"

Josh was like, "Nothing," then he came like all the way in the room. I was like, "I'm naked, Josh."

He was like, "I can see that," and then he started rubbing my leg. It actually felt kind of good, like in a very, very weird kind of way because of the E, but it was also kind of gross. I just felt so on the verge of a blackout that I really didn't do anything about it. I thought he would leave at some point, or that Brian would kick him out, but at some point I guess Brian had gotten out of bed and was standing kind of like next to where my head was at the edge of his bed. He reached down and put his hand behind my head and kind of pulled my face toward his dick and was like, "Come on, babe," then he like put his dick in my mouth. He had done that kind of thing before, just like kind of forcing me to suck his dick, which I didn't have a problem with. It was actually kind of a turn-on, like he was being really masculine and aggressive.

So I started sucking his dick and then I kind of came out of whatever drug coma I was in for a split second to realize that Josh had stopped rubbing my leg and was starting to finger me. It was hard to talk but I was like, "Josh, what are you doing?"

Josh didn't say anything but Brian was like, "It's cool, babe," then he grabbed the back of my neck again and put his cock back in my mouth. It was weird—from that point on it was almost like I was floating in the top of the room, just watching everything happen and not being able to do anything about it. I could still feel what was going on, but I couldn't really move or say anything.

Josh took off his pants but he left on his shirt, which was a red T-shirt because he was dressed like a devil for the Heaven and Hell party. Brian was basically face-fucking me at that point—not hard or anything, he was actually going kind of slow, but I mean I couldn't really move my head back and forth so he was doing all the work, holding my head up with his hands and just like sliding his dick in and out of my mouth.

Then Josh kind of like climbed on top of me and kneeled over me and started jerking off. Once he got hard he tried a few times to ram his dick into me, but I wasn't wet at all so he spit on his hand and rubbed it on his dick. Then he started fucking me while Brian kept sliding his dick in and out of my mouth.

It was weird—I completely knew what was going on and I didn't really want it to happen, but I was so fucked up from what I thought was the E that I just couldn't do anything. And it wasn't even like I was trapped inside my body or anything. I just kind of didn't really care what was going on. I could still hear Dane Cook.

Josh kept saying, "This is so fucking hot, dude." Every once in a while he would force his index finger into my asshole as he was fucking me. Brian never said anything. It took Josh maybe like five minutes to finish and then he was like, "That was fucking awesome. You going back to the party?"

Brian was like, "Maybe. I just want to make sure everything's okay before I leave."

Then Josh left and Brian got in bed with me. I was still pretty much incapacitated. Brian was like, "You're cool, right, babe?"

I couldn't even really talk. I think I might have said something like, "Cool." And then Brian was like, "That really turned me on, babe. You were so hot." Then he rolled me over on my back and started putting his dick in my ass. He was like, "You're cool?"

I still couldn't really talk, so I just lay there while Brian fucked me in the ass. After he came he was like, "I'm gonna go clean up real quick, babe. I'll be right back."

The next thing I remember was waking up in Brian's bed by myself and everything was sore. It was like two in the afternoon. I found my angel costume on the floor, got dressed, and walked out through the front door, which meant I had to go through the living room, which was full of all the Pike guys who were clapping and chanting shit like, "Walk of shame," and "Three o'clock slop." Brian and Josh weren't there.

I remembered everything that happened, and I didn't think Josh used a condom, so I went to the health center and got a morning-after pill. Then I went back to the Kappa house and took the longest shower of my life and I didn't cry until I got into my room and into my bed, but when I started crying I didn't stop for a few hours.

The Heaven and Hell party was, for me, an exercise in self-control. From a very young age I've found myself to be extremely mild-mannered in the face of conflict. Despite my deep hatred for most of my peers, I'm easily able to hold conversations with them and engage in casual friendly interaction. I've never known a person to have the ability to alter my natural demeanor. In the end, I suppose, I've realized that the resource available to me renders any potential situation of hostility completely meaningless. This was all true until the night of the Heaven and Hell party.

I despised costume parties. It wasn't because of the theme or the effort necessary to wear a costume; it was something deeper than that. The very idea of wearing a costume implies false importance surrounding the event that demands it, and the people who succumb to this demand seem weak to me. Nonetheless, the costume was mandatory so I wore a T-shirt with an image of Jesus Christ sucking a cock prominently displayed on the chest, which I purchased from cafepress.com after Googling "gay christ costume."

Most party attendees took the shirt in stride. Some were offended, yes, but they made no real effort to voice their distaste for my costume beyond a sarcastic "Nice shirt, asshole," or something similar. The only person whose indignation seemed genuine and problematic was my big brother, Greg Simmons, who was himself dressed as Judas with a sack of gold-foil-covered chocolate coins that he would hand out to anyone he passed while saying, "I'm rich, biatch." Even the most rudimentary research would have informed Greg that Judas' bribe was silver, not gold.

He had approached me near the beginning of the night and asked me to change my shirt due to its sacrilegious nature. I refused, citing the very same nature of his own costume. He countered by attempting to explain that Judas was a "Bible bad guy" and it was okay to make fun of him, but making fun of Jesus directly was a terrible thing to do. I told him I would change the shirt to avoid further conflict, having no real intention of ever changing it. My assumption was that by the next time I saw Greg he would be too drunk or too high to remember our initial interaction, or at least incoherent enough not to care.

I proceeded to drink to excess and futilely attempted to find a single whore at the party whose face hadn't already felt the slick warmth of my semen. At some point nearing two A.M., if memory serves, I came out of our kitchen, rounded a corner into the living room, and saw Greg with his shirt off forcing two Pi Phi pledges, whom I had not yet had the opportunity to debase, to pledge allegiance to his credo. Not thinking about my direct disobedience regarding the shirt I was wearing or what consequences it might bring I joined Greg, the sluts, and a tolerable member of Alpha Tau Omega named Jeff Rettinger.

The sluts were, of course, impressed by his tattoo and kneeled before it as per Greg's instruction as I joined the group. Greg greeted me and was amicable for seconds prior to noticing my shirt, at which point he became enraged almost instantaneously. What followed was a tirade in which Greg elucidated his true impression of me. With only a minor slurring of his words he claimed that he hated me from the first day I came into the Alpha Tau Omega house but could do nothing about it because of who I was. I remained silent as he spoke. He went on to explain that he was certain I viewed myself as superior to everyone there, based on my net worth, and I obviously didn't accept Jesus as my savior or I wouldn't have worn the shirt.

At this point I was too drunk, I suppose, to keep quiet. I informed Greg that he was only partially correct. I did view myself as better than at least one person in the room, and it wasn't based on the amount of money I had, it was based on the fact that I wasn't an ignorant douchebag. And I conceded the fact that I did not share his childish beliefs in talking snakes and imaginary friends who live in the sky.

Of all the insults based in truth I issued in that conversation, the attack on religion was strangely the one that sent him over the edge. He drew back his fist and punched a hole in the wall in my general vicinity. The sluts left immediately. I found myself wanting Greg to punch me for some reason. I knew I wouldn't fight back, but it seemed like an unchecked physical attack would cement in my mind that Greg was a living vessel of everything I hated in my peers. He was the purest version of the hypocritical self-absorbed asshole who truly believes he is correct in all things.

He didn't hit me, though. Instead he explained that he would love nothing more than to cave my head in, but he had secured a summer internship at my father's company and he didn't want to jeopardize it. For me, the revelation of this internship was more crystallizing than any physical attack could have been.

I had respect for my father. I just disagreed with much of what he stood for. This respect made it difficult for me to believe he would have knowingly agreed to allow a person like Greg Simmons within a thousand yards of his business. The only other explanation for the internship was even more horrifying to me. My father was so far removed from the business his father built that he had very little to do with the day-to-day operations, the quality of incoming employees, the basic ethics of anyone who worked for him, et cetera. My father must, I reasoned, have become a faceless name on the bottom of a check to all of his employees. In understanding this, I found some empathy for him. He, too, was possibly doing something only because he had been told to, and he had been doing it for so long that any alternative seemed impossible. His desire for me to follow his path was born only out of a lack of alternative possibilities in his own mind.

So it was there, standing in front of a seething Greg Simmons, his "Bros Before Hos" tattoo fully exposed, that I came to the conclusion my father had to know I did not desire the life he had led, that I had no intention of walking the same path two men had walked before me, that my future was uncertain, and that this uncertainty is what made me value it.

I wished Greg good luck at his internship, stumbled up the stairs to my room, and placed a call to my father. I reached his voice mail and left a message explaining that I had found out one of my fellow Alpha Tau Omega brothers had been granted a summer internship at Keller Shipping and that it had made me realize something very valuable. I asked that we discuss it later. And, strangely, I was compelled to end the call by telling my father that I loved him.

chapter
sixteen

There was still some time left until the end of the year, but Mac's Place was closing early to get started on summer renovations. So I went up there to clean out my locker, which didn't have much in it, just an old pair of tennis shoes I wore when I worked there. While I was there Raulio invited me to a barbecue. He said, "Kyle, you want a barbecue with me on weekend?"

I said, "Thanks, Raulio, but I have some stuff to do with my girlfriend this weekend."

He said, "Bring the woman. She get barbecue."

I said, "Thanks, Raulio, but I really can't."

Raulio had invited me to what must have been a dozen or so barbecues over the course of the two years I had worked with him. I had never gone to one. I always imagined his barbecues consisted of him and two other Mexican dudes sitting around a tiny charcoal barbecue in his front yard drinking beers and staring into the distance. In actuality they were probably really fun. I'd never know.

So I got my shoes and headed over to Erin's place. She was still at class but she had given me a key at some point, so I basically used her place as my own. I had more clothes at her place than at McElvaney, and she had a computer and Internet and everything so I didn't have to go to a computer lab to get online.

I was just about to get in the shower when my phone rang. I looked at the caller ID and saw it was Heather. I don't even know how to fucking describe my reaction. I had been thinking about her a lot at that point. It wasn't like anything was wrong or bad with Erin. It had just kind of reached a place for me where it was as good as it was going to get, and it wasn't the best I'd ever had. The fucking sweet irony of that is that it actually was the best I'd ever had and probably will ever fucking have for as long as I live. I mean she fucking made us dinner, gave me foot rubs, actually studied sex books and shit and would just whip out new positions and techniques every other week. And she didn't do all of that shit because she was into that shit, she did it because she was into me and she knew I liked that shit. It doesn't get better than that.

But I had been thinking about Heather a lot. It was probably a month or two after we saw each other by Dallas Hall and had our conversation and I wanted to call her but never did. I thought it would be a bad move. I thought if there was some chance to rekindle things, me making the first move would seem weak and it would turn her off immediately. So there it was—a call from Heather. I had no idea what she wanted, obviously, but no matter what it was, the call was another chance to talk to her. The fact that she was placing the call meant that she was taking the first step to be a part of my life again.

All of that is what I assume made me feel like I was about to puke, but in that good kind of excited way. I knew I was too nervous to talk to her so I just let the phone ring and waited for her to leave a message. I waited five minutes after the last ring to see if I got a new voice mail and I never did.

I was more pissed at myself for not answering than I had probably been for anything in my life. I would be much more pissed off at myself in the years to come, but that day, missing that phone call . . . I wanted to punch myself in the balls.

I got in the shower and went through all the possible reasons she could have called me and not left a message. The most likely, I assumed, was probably that it took her some amount of self-convincing to even make the call in the first place and then once she actually made it, she hadn't worked out in her head what she would leave on my voice mail if I didn't answer, so she just hung up. Before I arrived at that conclusion, though, there were some pretty good ones, like that she'd called just to offer me a three-way with her and the hot chick I fucked at Brett's house, but I had to have answered the phone to qualify, and because I didn't it was off the table forever. And there were some pretty bad ones, like that she'd called to tell me she was getting married to the douchebag she was dating and needed my address to send an invitation.

When I got out of the shower I went and looked at my phone hoping for a voice mail but there wasn't one. I must have spent half an hour staring at my phone wondering if I should call her back without a voice mail asking me to do just that, wondering if that would be just as weak in her eyes as calling her in the first place—or maybe even weaker, like I didn't have the balls to just call her but once I'd seen that she called me I could call her back.

Then I started thinking about the possibility that her call was for something completely innocent and not even worth leaving a message about. What if she'd called just to ask me what kind of cheese Mac's Place uses on its turkey-and-Swiss? I know it didn't make much sense, but it was possible.

After overthinking it to death, I decided I would call her. I picked up the phone, brought up my missed calls list, and was about to hit the call button when Erin came home. She tossed down her purse and jumped on top of me.

She said, "I missed you today."

I said, "I missed you, too."

She said, "You know what I was thinking about all day long?"

I said, "*Battlestar Galactica* being on tonight."

She said, "Yeah, that, but also about sucking your dick."

Then she unzipped my pants and gave me a blowjob. It wasn't the best blowjob, but I came in her mouth and she swallowed. The fucking horrible thing is the whole time she was giving me a blowjob, I was thinking about Heather. I'm amazed I'm still alive and haven't eaten a fucking bullet by this point. Erin was fucking incredible, but she wasn't Heather, and sadly that was all that mattered to me.

Erin cooked dinner, which we ate while we watched *Battlestar Galactica*, and then we had sex. During all of that the only thing I could think of was Heather. Where was she? Was she doing the exact same thing with her boyfriend, also lying awake thinking about me? I hoped that was the case. I waited until Erin fell asleep and looked at the clock. It was one-thirty in the morning. I thought returning a missed call that didn't leave a voice mail at one-thirty A.M. would seem pretty fucking pathetic and desperate, so I tried to go to sleep and succeeded at about five in the morning when fatigue finally overcame the fire that was burning in my brain.

I only talked to Brian one other time after the Heaven and Hell party. He called me the next day to see if I wanted to go get dinner and I said I wasn't hungry. Then he was like, "Okay, babe. Well, give me a call when you want to hang out," and I never called him again.

It was pretty weird. I mean, we were a couple and everything for like a pretty long time and he just never called me again. I seriously think he knew that he fucked up that night, letting Josh fuck me and everything. And the more I thought about how fucked up I was I realized he probably drugged me and had the whole thing planned or something. So I just decided to never talk to him again, and since he never called me it was like pretty easy to do.

It was maybe a few weeks after that when I called Kyle. I was just in my room thinking a lot about when we were together and what a good boyfriend he was and I guess I just like missed that, you know? After the thing with Brian I just wanted to be with someone who was like nice and wanted to cuddle and everything, and at that point Kyle wasn't a complete dick yet, so I thought he was the best candidate. I mean I guess I could have just tried to hook up with some other frat guy or something, but I didn't even really know if that was possible. Like I didn't know if Josh had already told every guy in Pike that he fucked me while I sucked Brian's dick, or if I could even really be into another frat guy after that. I mean if Brett would have been like, "Do you want to be my girlfriend?" or something, then yeah, of course, but I mean I didn't know if I could like start dating some other frat guy again. I know they weren't all like Brian and Josh, but they all had the same smell in their rooms and I didn't really want my next sexual experience to have anything to do with that smell and just the whole set of circumstances that always went with a frat guy.

So I was just in my bed one afternoon and I thought I should give Kyle a call. I really didn't know what I was going to say. I thought I might like ask him out for coffee again or something or maybe dinner. I mean I didn't even really know if I wanted to try to get back together with him or anything. I just kind of wanted to hang out with him and be with a guy who I knew actually cared about me and would listen to me and everything. But when I called him he didn't answer and I didn't want to sound retarded on a voice mail so I just didn't say anything. I hoped he'd see my caller ID and call back, but he didn't.

I waited a few days, and when he still didn't call I just guessed he was happy with whoever his girlfriend was and he didn't want anything to do with me. It kind of made sense. I mean at the time I did it, I wasn't really sorry for sucking Brian's dick and dumping Kyle, but as time went on I figured out that was a pretty shitty thing to do. Even now after I know what I know about Kyle I wish I wouldn't have done it. I mean I wish I would have just broken up with Kyle before I sucked Brian's dick.

Anyway, a few days had gone by and I had pretty much given up on ever talking to Kyle again. One afternoon Andrea called me up and asked if I wanted to go get some lunch down on Yale Boulevard at this new Mexican place. I don't remember the name, but they were having like a ninety-nine-cent margarita lunch special or something. So we went.

We got a table, sat down, and ordered some drinks. She was like, "So the reason I asked you to lunch is because I haven't seen you at any of the parties over the last couple weeks or so and you seem to like be kind of withdrawn and everything. You doing okay?"

I hadn't even really thought about going to parties or anything since the thing with Brian and Josh. But when Andrea mentioned it, I realized other people had probably noticed that I'd withdrawn from the whole thing a little bit, too.

I was like, "Yeah, I'm fine. Just been really tired. Some of my classes this semester are like kicking my ass."

She was like, "Oh, well, you know we're throwing a party with Pike next week and you did such an awesome job with the Heaven and Hell party . . . I was wondering if you'd want to help plan that one."

I was like, "I don't think so."

She was like, "I can tell something's wrong. We've become pretty good friends over the past year and a half. You know you can tell me."

I don't know why I didn't want to tell her. I guess I was ashamed that I let it happen. I also didn't want to get Brian in trouble. I didn't care as much about Josh. But Brian had been like a pretty good boyfriend up to that night. But I decided I should just tell her. I thought it might make me feel better about the whole thing.

I was like, "Okay. On the night of the Heaven and Hell party I went back to the Pike house with Brian and I was seriously fucked up and you know that guy Josh Paulson that always hangs out with Brian?"

She was like, "Yeah."

I was like, "Well, he and Brian did like a three-way with me."

She was like, "Gross—two guys?"

I was like, "Yeah."

She was like, "Was it fun?"

I was like, "No. I was like so fucked up that I couldn't move and they just kind of did it."

She was like, "Oh my God, Heather. Why didn't you tell someone?"

I was like, "I don't know. I guess it's not like that big of a deal. You have to promise not to say anything."

She was like, "I won't. I'll leave it up to you, but if those assholes raped—"

And then the waiter came and set down our drinks, which I started drinking like immediately.

When he left Andrea was like, "If those assholes raped you, you have to tell somebody."

I was like, "It wasn't rape—it wasn't like they tied me down or hit me or anything and I'm fine now so . . ."

She was like, "You said you were so fucked up you couldn't move. Are you sure you weren't drugged or something?"

I was like, "I was drugged. I drugged myself, Andrea. I took like E and was doing coke all night and was super fucking drunk."

She was like, "Yeah, but you've done that before and you weren't like paralyzed from it, right?"

I was like, "I guess."

She was like, "Like I said, I'm not going to say anything, but you know deep down if they like deserve to get called out for what they did then you have to be the one to call them out."

I was like, "Yeah."

She was like, "And I totally understand why you haven't been at any parties and why you don't want to help with the Pike party next week but eventually you're going to have to find some way to like look past this and start hanging out. Some of the other girls have been asking what the deal is with you, too."

I was like, "I know. I'll be okay. I just like need a little time to like not think about it every day, you know?"

She was like, "Yeah. Have you talked to Brian since it happened?"

I was like, "He asked me out to dinner once but I didn't go and I haven't talked to him since then. I don't think I'm like going to talk to him ever again."

She was like, "That's pretty fucking terrible."

I was like, "Seriously."

It felt good to tell her about it but I also knew what she was saying about like getting back into going to parties and everything was true. I pretty much knew I wasn't going to tell anyone else about it. Like I mean I knew I wasn't going to call them out or anything. It sucked, but it wasn't like it was violent or anything and I knew calling them out would probably be more trouble than it was worth in terms of staying in the Kappa house and having to go to parties and everything with people who were their friends. I figured I could just like find out which parties Brian and Josh were going to be at and not go or if I saw one of them I could just leave. Or I could just like ignore them or something.

I had like four margaritas at lunch and then Andrea drove us back to the house. I wasn't like super drunk but I wasn't sober. So I got out my phone and called Kyle again. This time he answered.

He was like, "Hey."

I was like, "Hi. How have you been?"

He was like, "Fine. How about you?"

I seriously had like no idea what to say. I was just drunk enough to not be able to talk very well and just sober enough to know that I should say as little as possible before I said something I would regret.

So I was like, "I don't know. I've actually been thinking about you a lot. Would you like want to go get dinner with me sometime or something? My treat?"

He was like, "Uh . . . yeah. Sure. I guess. Yeah."

I was like, "Cool. Tomorrow night?"

He was like, "Yeah, I can do that."

I was like, "Cool, I'll pick you up at seven."

He was like, "See you then."

I hung up the phone and felt happier than I'd been in a long time. I kind of thought we might talk about getting back together, but I wasn't sure. I mean I figured whoever he was dating he probably wasn't as into as he was with me when we were together, so I didn't think it would be hard to get him to choose me if he had to make a choice. I already knew which outfit I was going to wear. I had this shirt that really showed off my boobs from Forever 21 and this pair of Seven jeans that my ass looked seriously awesome in. Then for the first time since the thing with Brian I actually thought about sex and it was with Kyle.

chapter
eighteen

I was taking quite possibly the most foul shit of my lifetime, induced by hours of hard drinking the night prior, when my father called me. He rarely called me so I immediately wondered what the reason might be for that call. I then remembered my drunken decision to call him and inform him that I had decided to refuse the life laid out for me. I couldn't remember if I was that specific in the message I left but my question about how much I had actually divulged on his voice mail was answered when he asked what I had wanted to talk about.

Although I was more than certain that I ultimately could not follow the same path he had, once again I felt overwhelmed by calm, as if merely having made the decision made the telling of it to my father seem less pressing. I lied to my father and told him that I had been thinking about getting a new car, which wasn't entirely untrue, and sought his advice in the matter. His most recent purchase was a Range Rover, which he seemed to like, but he recommended that I live it up while I still had my youth. He reminded me that the semester was nearing its end and he asked me to delay the purchase of a new car because he was actually thinking of getting me one he thought I would like as a gift to let me know how proud he was of what I had acheived to date, which was little more than doing exactly what had been expected of me.

He ended the call by telling me that he loved me, which was more rare than receiving a phone call from him at all. I quickly remembered ending the voice mail I left him with a similar "I love you," which must have sparked some latent paternal emotion in him. My decision was unchanged, but it remained untold at the end of the conversation.

I hung up the phone and was preparing to wipe when I received another call, this one from Kyle seeking my advice. He explained that Heather had called him the day before and invited him to dinner. He questioned her motives, wondering if she could possibly want to get back together with him. The mention of this possibility brought an excitement to his voice that worried me. His basic question to me was how to conduct himself in order to make their reunion the most likely outcome. I finished my shit and sat on the toilet without wiping for the remainder of the conversation.

I asked him why he would ever have even the most remote interest in welcoming back a whore who sucked another man's dick while they were together. He seemed to think that enough time had passed since that event to allow for some fundamental change in Heather. I tried to explain to him that people don't change, they just have momentary steps outside of their true character, isolated actions contrary to their true nature. If she seemed like a changed person it was due to one of these moments. Kyle maintained that the dick she sucked might have been the isolated action and her true character was what he was see-ing now. I had no rebuttal. It was like arguing against the existence of God with a born-again Christian. If people are unwilling to see reason, there's not much that can be said to open their eyes.

Nonetheless I gave it my best attempt. I tried to take him back to the moment when he was made aware of Heather's transgression. I at-tempted to conjure those old feelings of betrayal and hatred that had made Kyle capable of fucking the whore I set him up with. It was a fruitless endeavor.

I then tried logic. I reminded Kyle that he currently had a girlfriend who was better suited for him in every way than Heather ever would be, maybe than any woman he would ever meet would be. Rationally speaking she was easily in the top 5 percent of the most compatible women in the world for Kyle. Surprisingly, Kyle couldn't argue this point. He agreed with me, but cited that Erin just didn't make him feel the same way Heather did.

When I brought to his attention that in order to become involved with Heather again he would have to smash Erin's heart into dust, he said it would be difficult but he would do what he had to do. I tried to make him understand how bad he would be hurting Erin, not because I cared about her but because I knew he did. I likened what she would have to go through emotionally to what he felt when Heather sucked another man's dick. He said he fully understood the emotional impact it would have on Erin but claimed it would be worse for her if he stayed with her never being able to be truly happy and always wondering what could have been with Heather.

I attempted one final line of reasoning by comparing Heather to the devil, which neither Kyle nor I believed in, but he understood the metaphor—pure evil, but an evil with a mind and motive behind its actions. I asked him if the devil asked him to dinner would he attend. He laughed but I pressed the point. If you were asked to dinner by someone you knew ultimately was a bad person or had hurt you in some way that was so profound you had become someone different, as I maintained Kyle had by citing the evidence of his newfound ability to have a one-night stand and his newfound inability to be happy with a girl who was perfect for him, would you ever want to give that person the opportunity to lay another trap for you? The answer seemed clear to me, but Kyle dismissed my analogy as ridiculous.

At that point I questioned why he called me at all if the advice he sought was so easily tossed aside. He told me he was nervous and he realized he really did want to get back together with Heather and had hoped for my blessing if that was to be the outcome of the night. I assured him that he would always be my friend, no matter what horrible cunt he ended up with. If he wanted my blessing in the matter of choosing a slut to end his life with, it would have to be Erin. I could not in good conscience tell him that I thought it was a good idea to be involved with Heather in any way.

I gave one final attempt at breathing some sanity into his clouded mind by asking him if he knew of her excessive drug use. He claimed he knew she used drugs recreationally but didn't think her use was excessive and he supposedly understood that some people in college have to go through such a phase of personal exploration and in his mind there was nothing wrong with it. I further reminded him that it might very well have been that so-called recreational drug use which led her to sucking another man's dick and quite possibly a whole host of other whorish activities that Kyle had no idea about.

I ended the conversation by wishing Kyle good luck, and explaining that that meant I hoped Heather was taking him to dinner to ask him to help her move or to tell him that she was pregnant with another man's child or that she was getting married, et cetera. I restated my final position on the matter, which was that Heather was the worst thing that had ever happened to Kyle's life since I'd known him, and I warned him to be careful above all else. If she did initiate some kind of conversation about reuniting, I asked that before he made a decision he give me an opportunity to talk to him one more time. He promised he would and he thanked me for talking with him.

I hung up the phone, wiped my ass, and thought for a few more moments about the possible outcomes of Kyle's dinner with Heather before going back into my bedroom and refucking the slut I had fucked the night before who was still in my bed. After I fucked her I tried to initiate a conversation with her about the nature of people and if they're capable of change, but she seemed uninterested so I made her suck my dick and tried to imagine what it would be like to truly love a woman as Kyle seemed to. I was unsuccessful.

For me, the lie of love, like so many other lies in which most people found false value—God, morality, the idea of right and wrong, et cetera—melted away in the flame of truth and reason.

chapter
nineteen

That night, in terms of making mistakes, was one of the worst ones in my entire fucking life, hands down, no-holds-barred, no questions asked. There were a few times in my relationship with Heather when I had the opportunity to just walk away and everything would have been fine. That dinner was absolutely one of them and, of course, I fucking didn't.

I had to tell Erin that I was going out with Brett. Brett and I hadn't hung out as much as we used to since I started spending virtually every night at Erin's place. I used that as the reason why he wanted to hang out. I also told her that we might end up getting drunk and I might end up staying at his place. I didn't even know why Heather wanted to go to dinner with me but I wanted to prepare for all possibilities. Erin was completely fine with it, suspecting nothing and completely trusting me. I really did love her. Fuck. I still can't believe I fucked that up as bad as I did.

Heather picked me up at McElvaney at seven, like she said she would, and took me to Nick and Sam's, the same place I took her once to try to show her how much I cared about her and that I was capable of doing something nice for her. I didn't know if her motives were the same or if she just liked the place or if she wasn't creative enough to figure out a place of her own or what the deal was. She looked fucking incredible. Her tits were pushed up and she looked like she might have even lost a little weight or something. She was wearing these tight jeans that made her ass look like you just wanted to take a fucking bite out of it. I liked having sex with Erin a lot, but I don't think I ever had the same kind of visceral, animalistic urge to just fuck her brains out that I had almost every time I looked at Heather and especially on that night. Despite all of her faults, that's one thing Heather knew how to do really well—look like she wanted you to fuck her.

The ride over was kind of weird. Neither of us said much. It was small talk mostly. She said, "How have you been?"

I said, "Fine. How about you?"

She said, "Pretty good. How is your girlfriend doing?" This was an interesting question. She brought it up fairly early in the night, which I thought could have meant one of two things: (1) She was trying to remind me that I had a girlfriend and this dinner had nothing to do with anything remotely approaching a romantic night out with her, or (2) she was hoping I didn't have a girlfriend so she could fuck my brains out, as her wardrobe indicated.

I said, "She's doing pretty good," with just enough hesitation to leave open the possibility for Heather to interpret what I said as indicating a hidden problem with the relationship.

I said, "How about you? How's the boyfriend?"

She said, "We haven't been together for a while now."

I said, "I'm sorry to hear that."

She said, "Don't be. It's all for the best. I kind of found out he was like a serious asshole in the end."

I said, "I see."

And then we didn't say much until we got to Nick and Sam's. Once we got there we were seated at the same table we ate at when I took her there. I wondered if that was coincidence or if she had called ahead and asked for the table specifically or something. She didn't mention anything about it so I assumed it was coincidence.

After we sat down and ordered there was a little more small talk. She asked me how my classes were going and pretended to care and I asked her how her sorority shit was going and pretended to care. I wanted to just flat-out ask her why she decided to take me to dinner out of the blue, but I knew that would probably make me seem desperate or overly anxious to her, which might turn her off, and then whatever chance I might have had to get her interested in me again would be blown. So I waited.

It was sometime just after we got our food and started eating that she started the conversation that would ultimately lead to everything going down the shitter. She said, "So, like, I know you're probably like, 'Why'd she take me to dinner?' and I don't know if you've been thinking about me at all since we saw each other and like had that conversation or anything, but I've been thinking about you like a lot."

I said, "I've thought about you, too."

"Really?"

"Yeah."

"Like, what have you thought about when you think about me?"

"You're the one who took me out to dinner. I think it's on you to tell me what you've been thinking about first."

"I don't know. I guess like I've just been thinking a lot about how things used to be when we first started going out and like I miss that, you know?"

"Yeah."

"So what have you been thinking?"

"The same thing pretty much. I miss how things were, how they used to be."

"And do you think that like we could ever have that again or . . ."

"Are you asking me to get back together with you?"

"I don't know. Is that what you want?"

"I'm asking you here. I never wanted us to be apart. You were the one who ended it. So now I'm asking you if you want to get back to-gether."

"What if I do?"

"Then that's another whole conversation, but if you're not absolutely sure this is what you want, it's not even worth starting that next conversation."

"Okay, I'm sure. It's what I want, Kyle. What do we do now?"

"And you're sure this isn't just because you and your boyfriend broke up and you're just lonely?"

"No, I don't think so."

"Well, if we're talking about me breaking up with Erin and us getting back together, you have to be more sure than that. I don't want to break her heart for you and then two months from now you're cheating on me with some other frat guy."

"I promise you that will never happen again. I know I never really said I was sorry for it, but I am. It's the worst thing I've ever done in my entire life and like if I could take it back, Kyle, I totally would."

"I know."

"So are we like a couple again or what? How does this work?"

I was surprised I was thinking rationally at that point at all. I wanted to take Heather back to my dorm room and kiss her and hug her and fuck her and wake up with her and fuck her again and just spend the whole day in bed with her and not think about anything else. But the situation demanded some practical thinking. I actually thought to myself that I might need some leverage if I was going to get back together with her. I actually planned out what I thought was a minor power play. I was so fucking stupid. Heather had me wrapped around her fucking finger and I thought I was gaining some kind of psychological advantage by saying, "So everything's out in the open now—how you feel, how I feel—but I'm not entirely sure this is what I want. I'm going to need some time to think about this, and if we are going to get back together, I'm obviously going to have to talk to Erin."

She said, "I know. I don't want to rush you or anything. You have to like be completely comfortable with this, too. So you do what you have to do."

We finished eating and talked a little more about the possibility of us getting back together. At one point she said, "I promise you if we get back together it's going to be the best makeup sex of your life." I'm pretty sure I got an immediate hard-on.

At the end of the night she drove me back to McElvaney and said, "Do you want me to come in?"

And I fucking wanted that more than anything, but I remembered how Heather made me feel when she cheated on me. And I realize it was all semantics if I was going to break up with Erin anyway, but I never wanted to make anyone feel like that, least of all her. And this didn't tip me off at all, by the way. I wouldn't fuck Heather because I remembered her making me feel like I wanted to die when she sucked some other guy's dick. That didn't even make me pause for a second and think about the fact that I was about to get right back into the shitstorm with her.

So Heather left. I told her I'd call her in the next few days after I had thought about everything and decided what I wanted to do. I sat on my bed for about thirty minutes, thinking alternately about fucking Heather and breaking up with Erin. My roommate wasn't around—I think he was rushing or pledging or something—so I took the opportunity to jerk off once to calm myself down. I was pretty worked up from thinking about having sex with Heather and I knew I needed to be rational.

It didn't take me that long to figure it out. Like a dipshit, I decided to get back together with Heather. I knew it was going to be one of the worst and most difficult things I had ever done, but I had to break up with Erin and be with Heather. For some sick fucking reason I thought that was the only way I could be really happy, like I was when Heather and I first started dating.

And once my decision was made, I started getting nervous and thought I might get scared and not be able to break up with Erin if I waited until the next morning, so I walked across campus to her apartment and rang the doorbell.

Erin answered it and said, "Hey. You and Brett called it early, huh? Weren't there any skanks for him to nail? Or did he already nail them all and call it a wrap?"

I walked in and sat down on the couch and said, "We have to talk about something," and that same feeling that seeped down my neck and into my gut when Heather told me she sucked another guy's dick came back. My face didn't get hot like it did with Heather, but my stomach felt horrible and I started sweating.

Erin said, "What's wrong? You look terrible. Are you okay?"

I said, "I don't know how to tell you this."

She said, "You know you can tell me anything. I'll love you no matter what."

There was a split second where I thought I wouldn't do it, a split second where I thought I could stay with Erin and be happy forever, a split second where I saw the mistake I was about to make and understood I didn't have to make it, but only a split second. It felt like I was jumping off a cliff as I said, "Erin, I love you, but I can't stay in this relationship anymore."

She couldn't even talk. She just sat down next to me on her couch. She didn't cry or ask any questions or anything. She just sat there. I felt like I had to explain myself and I felt like she deserved the truth.

I said, "I know this is really shitty, but I didn't go out with Brett tonight. I went to eat dinner with Heather. She wants to get back together."

Finally she said, "And you want to, too?"

I said, "Yeah."

She said, "Wow. After all the shit she put you through, ignoring you for her sorority, doing drugs behind your back, cheating on you, you're going to get back together with her?"

I said, "Yeah. I'm sorry."

She said, "Don't be sorry. You can't help how you feel. I just don't get it. I love you more than anything. I thought you loved me—"

I said, "I do."

She said, "Well, not enough to choose me over a cock-sucking sorority whore. I'm sorry. That was . . . I shouldn't have said that."

I said, "It's okay."

She said, "No, it's not. This is someone who's obviously very important to you, someone you love. I shouldn't have said it. I just want to ask you what it was about me that was never good enough. I could kind of feel it through our whole relationship. I didn't think it had anything to do with Heather, though. Was it always her?"

I said, "I don't know. I love you, Erin, I really do. You're an amazing person, it's just—I don't know, it's not the same."

She said, "The same as Heather, you mean?"

I said, "Yeah. I'm sorry."

And then she started crying and I wanted to crawl into a fucking hole and die. She had been nothing but loving and kind to me for our entire relationship and that's how I repaid her. Erin was really an amazing person and I'm sad she'll never be in my life again. That might be my biggest regret of all of this shit, that she hates me more than anyone else at this point.

As she cried she got up off the couch and went into her bedroom. Just before she shut the door she said, "I'm going to stay in here. Can you please just get whatever you have in my apartment and leave? I'll send you anything that's in the bedroom."

I said, "Yeah."

She shut the bedroom door and I got my toothbrush, an extra pair of tennis shoes I kept at her apartment, and my *Dune* collector's edition DVD. I went back to her bedroom door and said, "Erin, I'm sorry." I just heard her crying inside. She didn't say anything back so I left.

I walked back to McElvaney and over the course of the walk I went from feeling like a douchebag to feeling like a man reborn. It was surprising to me how quickly the guilt from dumping Erin subsided when I started thinking about Heather and getting excited about us being a couple again.

When I got back to McElvaney I took a shower and planned on going to sleep and waiting a few days to call Heather so I could maintain whatever power I thought I had over her in the situation, which was less than none. Instead, as soon as I got back to my room from the showers I called her. I said, "So I made my decision."

She said, "And . . ."

I said, "I think you should come over tonight and I'll tell you in person."

She said, "Seriously? Oh my God. I'm like so happy. I love you so much."

I said, "I love you, too. Now get over here as fast as you can. My roommate's gone. We got the whole shitty dorm room to ourselves."

She said, "Okay, I need to take a shower and then I'll be over."

I said, "Okay, I'll be waiting."

She said, "Kyle, I love you."

I said, "I love you, too," and despite all the things that were wrong with the relationship we were about to start up again the words felt right in a way they hadn't since I last said them to Heather.

chapter
twenty

I was like so excited. I mean a little part of me had a small amount of not like regret but almost like buyer's remorse or something, you know? Like I had thought about getting back together with Kyle and everything and it was definitely what I wanted but I just didn't like expect it to happen so fast. I mean I really thought after that dinner there would be a few days of him kind of thinking about it and a few days for me to kind of think about it even though I basically told him I wanted to get back together that night and everything, but he called me that night and was like, "I broke up with Erin and I want you to come over," so I pretty much had to. I couldn't really have been like, "Uh, hang on a second, I still thought I was going to get a few more days before we jumped back into things." I mean I was basically the one who initiated the whole thing. I wish I had said that to him now, but that night I guess I was just a little nervous to be getting right back into another relationship and really when you think about it, it was like the same relationship I was already in less than a year ago. But then the alternative was like hooking up with random frat guys, which didn't really seem all that appealing to me for obvious reasons.

I was kind of excited to have sex with Kyle that night. I mean he was still like the best sex I'd ever had and I knew he would go down on me. I didn't really for sure know if I was completely ready to have sex after the thing with Brian and Josh, but I didn't feel nervous about it when I was walking out of the Kappa house to go to McElvaney, so I thought that was like a pretty good sign.

When I got to his dorm, he let me in and gave me a big hug. I know it sounds stupid but it felt so good, like I could feel how much he loved me in that hug. I knew I had missed him because I was thinking about him so much in the weeks before we got back together, but I guess I didn't know how much I missed him until that hug. He kept on hugging me for like a minute, then he kind of pulled back and looked in my eyes and was like, "I love you, Heather."

I was like, "I love you, too." It felt good to say because I knew I really meant it.

He was like, "I don't ever want to have to lose you again. Promise me I won't lose you again."

When he said that I thought it was kind of weird, like a little too much too soon, you know? I mean I know we just got back together and everything and it wasn't like we were able to take anything slow or anything because we had already been a couple for like a year, so getting back together was pretty much starting where we left off, but he was basically saying he wanted to be together like forever. I loved him and everything, but we had literally been a couple again for like less than an hour and he was talking about never being apart again. It kind of freaked me out but not that much and I was just like, "I promise."

Then he kissed me and I remembered what a good kisser he was. It was like he actually liked to kiss. Brian never did, or if he did it was only to get me in the mood to fuck him. Kyle actually liked kissing and you could totally tell. We made out for like twenty minutes and then he started taking off my shirt. It was kind of weird at first—like I started thinking about that night with Brian and Josh—but I didn't really want to make Kyle think something was wrong. I mean it was our first night back together. I knew that we were going to have to have sex. So I just kind of tried to put it out of my mind and for the most part it wasn't that hard to do.

Once we were naked it actually got a lot better for me. Kyle was like really gentle and liked to cuddle and be like really intimate with how he would touch me and everything, which was like the exact opposite of Brian. So I wasn't really thinking about Brian. At one point I did start thinking about if Kyle wanted to fuck doggy style I didn't think I'd be able to do that. I mean any position really with a guy behind me was going to be a problem, you know? And I also was kind of thinking that giving a blowjob might be a problem, too. But after Kyle fingered me a little and I was like jerking him off a little I actually got really turned on by how into it Kyle was; like even more than his hugs and kisses and everything I could tell he really loved me by the way he touched me and that was a huge turn-on.

So I didn't really mind going down on him. And once I actually had his dick in my mouth it was so different from Brian that I was fine with it. Brian never really trimmed his pubes and he had like a pretty big bush that wasn't necessarily gross, but it wasn't all that appealing. I didn't know if Kyle ever trimmed his pubes, but he always seemed to be really neat and clean.

So after I sucked him off a little he went down on me, and at that point like any apprehension I had about having sex with Kyle was gone. I really had forgotten how good he was at going down on me and once he started I was seriously more horny than I had been in a long time and pretty much all I could think about was fucking him.

He was sitting up in his bed and I kind of sat in his lap so we were like face-to-face and I just rode him kind of slowly. He held me really tight and kissed me the whole time. He didn't even grab my boobs that much or anything. It was like he just wanted to get close to me and it made it really nice. I think that night probably more than any other with Kyle I really got to know what it felt like to be completely loved.

I didn't get off, but I didn't think that was a big deal. I mean given everything that had happened the last time I had sex. I figured at some point I would be able to again and feeling Kyle cum inside me was almost as good as if I had gotten off anyway. After we finished I lay down beside him and he kissed me on the forehead and then like rolled around behind me and spooned me.

Even after all the shit Kyle put me through and even though I know what a complete asshole he is now, I think I'll always remember that night, lying in his shitty bed in a shitty dorm room in McElvaney Hall, as one of the safest feelings I've had in my life.

The next morning I woke up in like exactly the same position I fell asleep in. Kyle still had his arms around me. I kind of turned over and watched him sleep for a few seconds before he woke up. It's weird to think about now, but I really did love him, like I mean a lot, you know?

We went and got breakfast that morning and then we went to NorthPark mall and just walked around. He went to Forever 21 with me and the Vera Wang store even though I knew he didn't want to and he didn't complain once and he held my hand the whole time, like he didn't want to let go of me. It was a really great feeling to have a guy who I knew loved me again. I was like seriously happy.

The information divulged to me by Kyle the day after his dinner date with Heather was not completely unexpected but was nonetheless shocking. He had escaped the jaws of death only to willingly place himself back within their bite.

My father had four courtside Mavericks season tickets that he rarely used, so I took Kyle to a Mavericks/Bulls game with the intent of getting the full story of his hellish reunion with Heather. Neither of us followed sports or ascribed to them any importance, but the courtside seats generally offered me the opportunity to find one or more whores whom I could easily defile that night. I was hoping the ease with which these whores could be acquired would convince Kyle of the mistake he had made.

Anecdotally, once at the game, Kyle and I found ourselves sitting a few seats away from Mark Cuban, who was in his standard entertaining form.

Kyle initiated the conversation about himself and Heather by trying to explain to me that love was real, despite my insistence on the opposite. I attempted all of my old arguments, and it became apparent very quickly that no headway would be made by either party. Kyle maintained that I had no real choice in the matter but to accept their relationship as legitimate and do my best to become Heather's friend, as she would no doubt be spending more and more time with him and, in turn, with me.

I asked Kyle if Heather was okay with the whore from her sorority that he fucked to spite her. He claimed that this event hadn't come up between them yet, but if it did he was certain she would have no choice but to be understanding in the face of her own sexual misconduct. His reasoning was sound, but in the face of a whore's logic, sound reasoning was virtually irrelevant—a fact Kyle still hadn't come to understand at that point.

After a brief lull in the conversation I turned his attention to two very attractive sluts sitting two sections above us. I attempted to appeal to his basic biological nature and posed to him a bet of sorts. I asked him if he would fuck one of the sluts indicated if I could get them to come down to us and share the other two seats. He claimed he wouldn't cheat on Heather. Even after I pointed out that either of the cunts was easily twice as attractive as Heather (which he incorrectly denied), Kyle was unwavering. Nonetheless at halftime I made my way to their seats and invited them to join us, which they, of course, did without hesitation.

Once in the seats I opened the discussion to them, forcing Kyle to fill them in on all the details of his relationship with Heather up to what was then its current status. I then asked the girls to give their meaningless opinions on whether or not it would be cheating if Kyle were to get in the Jacuzzi back at my mansion with either one of them. This statement was meant to serve two obvious purposes: (1) It informed the whores that I had a mansion, and (2) it allowed Kyle to see that sluts as attractive as these two could be interested in him (or at least could feign interest in order to see my mansion).

It was decided that sitting in a hot tub is nowhere near cheating, and since I, or my driver rather, was Kyle's ride, he had no choice but to come back to my house with these sluts. Once there his biological programming kicked in, and after several drinks he did indeed get in the Jacuzzi with myself and the two whores. I initiated the first sexual advance by informing the more attractive of the two sluts that she had two choices: remove her bathing suit or suck my dick. She agreed to the former with a drunken smile. Kyle was made visibly uncomfortable by this, so I commanded the other slut to comfort him. She made a legitimate attempt by moving in for a kiss, but Kyle shied away and got out of the Jacuzzi. He retreated somewhere inside my house and left me to fuck both of the whores myself. It was a very similar situation to the last time we were in the Jacuzzi with two sluts, except this time Kyle did not fuck one of them before I did.

After I was through with the whores I told them to take a cab back to whatever place they'd come from, then made my way inside to find Kyle. I found him asleep in a guest room, his phone next to his head. I looked through his recent calls to find that for the entire forty-two minutes I had been in the Jacuzzi fucking the sluts he had been engaged in conversation with Heather about what I could only assume was nothing of importance—probably wordless cooing and pet-name exchanging.

I left him to sleep without waking him up to revisit the conversation, knowing that I had more than likely lost my best friend forever. Heather had, by some means that remained unknown to me, stolen him once more, and this time her possession of him seemed so utterly complete that I feared the person Kyle used to be, the friend I used to have, would cease to exist soon after that night. The actuality of the transformation Kyle would undergo in the coming years was something far beyond anything I would have ever predicted.

I watched the sluts wait outside for a cab for a few minutes and then I got in my bed and thought of the days as children when Kyle and I used to spend hours playing *Mario Kart 64*. The game, despite its repetitive nature in a single-player format, never bored us when playing with each other. Sleep came easily that night once I reconciled the loss of my best friend to the very thing I hated most in the world.

summer

I finished up the rest of that year with really great grades and I honestly couldn't have been happier. Heather and I spent almost every day together or at least almost every night together and everything just felt right. I got my old job at the movie theater back, but didn't work quite as much, and Heather stayed in town, so we saw a lot of each other. My parents were actually really cool about letting her stay over every once in a while, too. Her mom wasn't so into that, though, so we had to kind of sneak around when we did it. The nights were the best. It would be hot as hell during the day, and it wouldn't really cool off much at night, but Heather and I would go out to this old swing set behind her house that she used to play on when she was a kid and eat Popsicles or drink this peach tea her mom always made and just talk. Every once in a while we'd fuck or she'd give me a blowjob, but mostly we'd just talk. It was probably the best summer of my life.

I hung out with Kyle like almost every day, which I actually really liked a lot. It was really good to like be with him away from all of the school crap. My old freshman-year roommate, Annie, was taking some summer courses so she actually stayed in town and I got to kind of hang out with her a pretty decent amount, too, which was cool because once we got in different sororities I didn't really see all that much of her. I didn't see a lot of Brett that year. I mean we hung out a few times, like me, him, and Kyle, you know? It was just a really relaxed, cool summer. Kyle and I got really close, like way closer than we were our freshman year, and we actually talked a few times about marriage. Not like we were going to get married that summer or anything, but about the idea of it and just kind of like if we might want to think about it.

Aside from being forced by Kyle to spend time with him when Heather was also present, the highlights of my summer were unremarkable, with one exception. I made a trip to my father's office on a day in mid-July, for reasons I can't recall, only to find Greg Simmons sitting in a cubicle outside the office of one of my father's vice presidents of sales. I, of course, was treated with respect by every employee of the company who crossed my path, because they all assumed that one day I would replace my father and be their employer. Greg, on the other hand, as the summer intern, was treated with slightly less respect, and my favorite moment of the visit to my father's office came when I had the opportunity to ask Greg to get me a cup of coffee with sugar in the presence of the vice president who served as his mentor. Under the watchful gaze of the man he one day hoped might give him a job, he had little choice but to obey my request and serve me a cup of coffee, which I left sitting on his cubicle desk untouched. His rage was obvious.

part three
junior year

Going into my third year at SMU, I couldn't have been happier.
My grandma, who I loved but really barely knew when I stopped to
think about it, died of old age toward the end of the summer and left
me seven thousand dollars, so I was finally able to get the fuck out of
McElvaney Hall. I got myself a little one-bedroom apartment a few
blocks from campus, which I was more than excited to have shitloads
of sex with Heather in. I signed up for all my classes, most of which
looked interesting and none of which looked too difficult except for
this applied physics class. For some reason physics always seemed
daunting to me, but I wasn't too concerned. I assumed I'd just have to
study a little harder.

But besides having my own place and a class load that seemed
pretty easy, I had Heather. I moved into my apartment a week before
our first classes and a few days before she had to do anything with her
sorority. She and my parents helped me get settled. My mom and dad
I don't think ever really liked Heather, and they liked her even less the

second time around, but they didn't say anything about it to me, which I always appreciated.

That first night, after everything was moved in, my mom and dad took us out to eat at Big Al's Pizza and they made a pretty decent effort to warm up to Heather. I guess they must have thought that if we were back together after all the shit we had been through, it was going to be for a while.

We got our food and sat down and my dad said, "So, Heather, you looking forward to some of your classes this year? You probably start some kind of student-teaching or something your junior year, right?"

Heather said, "Um, yeah, I guess. I don't like really know. I mean I know the first semester I don't think I have to student-teach yet. Maybe second semester."

My mom said, "Have you given any thought to what kind of a teacher you want to be yet?"

What she said next can just be thrown on the pile of statements that proved I had my head too far up her ass to hear clearly. She said, "I don't know. It doesn't really matter. I mean I want to focus on marriage and family and everything first and career second, so if I need to teach for like a year or something at an elementary school before I start my own family, then I guess I could be like an art teacher or something, you know?"

I love my mom. She said, "Oh, that sounds very fulfilling," in about as sarcastic a tone as she could muster, which wasn't very sarcastic at all. My dad and I got it, but Heather didn't.

The rest of the night was spent talking about nothing important. Back at my apartment just before my parents were about to leave, my dad peeled me off a hundred bucks and said, "Don't spend this on her. Use it to buy something for yourself," which I appreciated. I gave my mom and dad a hug good-bye and then it was just me and Heather alone for the first night in my very first apartment.

She said, "So we're all alone. What do you want to do now?"

I said, "I guess we should christen the place."

She said, "You mean we should both take dumps in the toilet?" And I remembered that occasionally Heather could actually be pretty funny. I hugged her and I kissed her and I said, "What I actually meant was that we could both take dumps in the shower," which got a laugh out of her and then we started kissing and didn't stop until we were fucking.

That night we fucked in almost every place you could possibly imagine in that apartment. The couch, the shower, the bed—and I guess that pretty much covers the entire place. It was pretty fucking small, but that made it better to me. It was like a little nest just for me and Heather, and it could have been even smaller, to be honest, and I would have been perfectly happy.

I remember that the next morning the whole place smelled like her. I can only assume that was because it was so small. After she left to go meet up with some of her sorority sisters I tried to clean some more stuff up, get some more stuff out of boxes, all the usual moving-in crap that no one likes to do, but I couldn't. Every time I would move in that place it would stir some little jet stream of air that would deliver a shot of her smell right to my nose and then I'd start thinking about us fucking the night before.

My shit stayed in boxes for a few weeks after moving in.

That first night back was like seriously the best. Kyle having his own place made it really seem like things were going to be different, you know, like they were going to be real or like more adult I guess. I mean when we first started dating and we lived at McElvaney it was like he was still a kid, kind of, but once he had his place it made everything just seem more legit, like we were getting further away from being high school kids and closer to being college graduates or something.

The next morning I went to the Kappa house to move some of my stuff back in and say hi to some of the other girls. We also had a meeting that afternoon that was like mandatory and everything. It was basically just to talk about like all of the new stuff we were going to be doing that year. They made the announcement that Andrea was going to be our new president, which was seriously exciting for her. I mean we all knew because the vote happened at the end of the year before, but we still had to have like the official ceremony and everything. I was really happy for her. I knew that meant that my chances might be a little better to be president when I was a senior, but I didn't really think I had a chance because of how I kind of didn't go to as many parties and everything right after the thing with Brian and Josh. That was cool with me. I never really wanted to be the Kappa president or anything, and honestly I was looking forward to spending time with Kyle that year more than I was even really thinking about doing anything for Kappa.

After the meeting we were all sitting around drinking wine and this senior named Harlow Gallerston came in and was like, "Sorry I was late for the meeting, guys, but I have a really good excuse."

We were all like, "Okay . . . what is it?"

And she whipped out her left hand and was like, "Garret proposed. I'm engaged."

We were all like going crazy. We gave her a huge hug and everything and she showed us her ring and it was really, really nice. It was like a three-and-a-half-carat princess cut in this really pretty platinum setting with two one-carat diamonds on either side of the middle one. All of the other seniors were seriously jealous. Kendra Thomas was like, "That's really pretty. Did you tell Garret what kind of ring to get you?"

Harlow was like, "Kind of, but he picked it out mainly by himself."

Kendra was like, "You should have been more specific. When Louis proposes to me this Christmas I told him he better not show up with anything less than four carats or he can find himself another fiancée." Then she laughed, but we all knew it wasn't even like close to being a joke for her.

Pretty much all the seniors had boyfriends and pretty much all of them knew they were going to get proposed to. The only girl who didn't know what was going to happen was this girl Casey Riddle. She had been dating the same guy since high school and all of the guys in his family had served in the military so he did, too. And he was in Iraq like right during her senior year so she had no idea if he was going to propose to her or even be able to make it back at all or anything. I felt so bad for her.

For the rest of the night we all just sat around and talked to the seniors about what they were going to do once they got engaged and then married and everything. Most of them were going to move back to wherever their future husbands were from originally. Some of their future husbands were from Dallas so they were going to start looking for houses and everything as soon as they got engaged. Most of them were pretty sure they were going to get proposed to over the Christmas break. Andrea had been dating this guy in Kappa Sig named Ron Thuron, who was like a really cool guy, but he was in Kappa Sig and he didn't really know what he wanted to do or anything and I kind of felt sorry for her, like she was settling. But it was like her senior year had already started. If she didn't end up with Ron, she was pretty much fucked. Like I don't even know how you would even try to find a husband if you don't have one pretty much locked in by the middle of your senior year.

I guess I hadn't really given it much serious thought, me and Kyle getting married, until that night, but I did think that Kyle would probably propose to me my senior year and I hoped he'd do it early so I could be like the first one, you know like Harlow, to show off my ring and everything. Like I wondered if I could get him to propose to me over the next summer break. I thought I could if I started laying in hints here and there. I just thought the ring might be a problem. I knew he had saved up some money from his summer job but he was spending it all on his apartment. I guess in the end I figured his parents would help him or he could get a loan or something. If he really loved me he'd figure it out and I knew he did really love me so I wasn't worried.

chapter
three

Year three of my mandatory and pointless four-year stay at SMU started much like any other—a trip to the South Texas Fertility and Family Medical Center to deposit my semen in a plastic cup, signing up for classes I had no interest in, and ending my first day back at school by ass-fucking someone—in this case Greg Simmons's younger sister, an eighteen-year-old freshman named Kennedy with a slight amount of hair around her asshole—in my bedroom at the Alpha Tau Omega house.

Alpha Tau Omega sponsored a family barbecue on the first day back to school. My father was to be a guest of honor of sorts but he was away on business. So his wife filled in, much to the dismay of virtually every member of Alpha Tau Omega and many of their fathers, all much too eager to kiss my father's ass and all much too aware that my father's wife presented far less than an adequate proxy.

It was at this barbecue that I met Greg's sister. She knew who I was immediately, which led me to the conclusion that my family was a constant topic of conversation for Greg's family—a fact I found amusing and personally satisfying. I leveraged the fact that I was known to her to lure her into my bedroom while the barbecue was still in full swing in the backyard of the house. Once in my bedroom, there was no real need to maintain the pleasantries. I told her simply that I wanted to ram my dick in her ass as hard as I could and I wanted to press her tits up against my window so the guests of the family barbecue, her parents included, could see what a nasty little slut she was. She agreed to the former but not the latter. And she was not given the chance to agree or disagree with my request to photograph us in the act because the request never existed. I simply took the photo and she never demanded it be erased so it wasn't.

She was attractive, aside from the sparse anal hairs I mentioned earlier. Had I not filled a plastic cup with semen shortly prior to the event, I'm sure she would have left my room and leaked semen out of her asshole for the next hour at least.

I fucked her in the ass for the obvious reason of merely enjoying firing a load into the anus of an eighteen-year-old, but I fucked her for more than that. My hatred for her older brother had become something different, more acute than the normal hatred I had for the rest of my peers. I think perhaps it was because, more than them, he was the most extreme and well-defined example of everything I thought was wrong with my peers, of everything I despised. For that reason, fucking his little sister in the ass calmed me in a way that was similar to a skilled masseuse massaging the one muscle that aches most in your body and hinders all movement of any other muscle. So, too, the knowledge that I possessed a photo of the act to publicly expose at will in a scenario that most called for it further put me at ease for the remainder of the barbecue.

After wiping my dick off with the bottom of Greg's sister's Marc Jacobs sundress and pulling my pants back up, I was able to mingle with the parents and siblings of each and every false piece of shit that I called my brother in Alpha Tau Omega without ever breaking my smile. I took particular pleasure in chatting with Greg's father, who couldn't have been more complimentary of my own father and of my clear potential as the future president of Keller Shipping. I agreed with all of his comments and listened intently to everything he had to say for the better part of fifteen minutes, each second of which was an exercise in self-control for me. My hand was gripped so tight around my phone in my left front pants pocket, ready to whip it out and force his father to gaze upon the image of my cock buried in his daughter's pliable teenage asshole, that I thought I might have been drawing blood.

As great a moment as it would have been, I thankfully had the wherewithal to realize that the photo was best used against Greg, not his father. For some reason there was in me a general feeling about my father's generation that made me pity them. I almost forgave their blind allegiance to the prior generation's will, or at least I certainly didn't have the venomous disdain for them that I did for my own generation, which did nothing more to garner that disdain than follow the exact same path. It seemed to me somehow that we had seen our fathers become their fathers and that experience should have given us some insight. Our fathers had no model to show them the pitfalls of becoming their fathers, but we were different. We saw exactly the slow transition that took place, the creeping loss of self that occurred in each of our own fathers once they started down the paths of our grandfathers. Our fathers saw it only after their lives had run their courses. We still had everything ahead of us. We should have known better. And yet for most of my peers the comfort of a life that had been lived twice or more already was all too inviting, and so they were eager to fall in line. I suppose that's what I despised most about them. Even after being granted the knowledge necessary to change, to strike out and accomplish something unique, my peers chose the same things as their fathers and their fathers' fathers before them.

I wasn't sure how a photo of my dick in Greg's sister's ass, with her smiling back over her shoulder at the camera, would play into liberating my peers from this psychological prison they all seemed so eager to lock themselves into, but I was glad I had it.

The barbecue lasted for a few more hours, and at its conclusion Greg's sister asked me for my phone number, which I gave her, calculating that I might be able to fuck her again and orchestrate a scenario in which Greg would walk in on us. Or at the very least I could take some photos of her with my semen all over her face.

chapter four

Of course I had thought about marrying Heather a few times. Or I guess I should say I just kind of expected that after we got back together that second time we'd eventually wind up together, married. What I had really never thought about were the steps required to get to that eventual outcome. I had never thought about a ring, the wedding itself, the honeymoon, where we'd live, how I'd pay for any of it, if we'd have kids, none of that shit. As it turned out, I was about to start thinking of at least one of those things pretty fucking quickly.

Heather wanted to go to Homebar because a bunch of her sorority sisters were going to get together for drinks. I had met quite a few of her sisters during our freshman year but I had never really hung out with them because I never went to any of the parties they threw. I kind of saw Heather wanting me to go to Homebar with her as her making an effort to include me in that part of her life. Even before we broke up, it wasn't a problem necessarily that she did her sorority thing and I wasn't really involved, but I was happy that she was trying to include me in that shit.

Andrea was the only other girl from Heather's sorority who was there when we showed up. I had met her probably a dozen or so times before that night and even hung out with her a few times freshman year before Heather and I broke up. I liked Andrea. She was always nice to me, while some of Heather's other sorority sisters could be complete cunts to me just because I wasn't in a frat.

As the other chicks started showing up, some of the cunts I mentioned were among them, which didn't bother me all that much. Honestly I felt like Heather and I were so close then that nothing else mattered. At one point, when one of her cunty sorority sisters started kind of picking on me for spending too much time studying and not enough partying or whatever in the fuck she thought was important, Heather actually jumped in and said, "Can you seriously like leave him alone? He's my boyfriend. If we're really supposed to be like sisters and everything, you should be cool with him," and it was one of those moments with Heather that, even after all the shit that led us to where we are now, I still think about sometimes, remembering why I loved her so much.

As the night wore on, a girl named Harlow showed up and all of the other Kappa Kappa Gammas kind of crowded in around her and were giving her hugs and generally acting like she was the Virgin Mary about to give birth to fucking Jesus or something. When I asked Heather what the deal was she said, "Harlow is the first senior to get proposed to."

I said, "Okay, why is everyone acting so crazy about it?"

She said, "Uh, are you kidding? She's like locked in already. That's like seriously a big deal. I mean look at her ring."

Then Heather made this girl come over and show me her ring. I didn't know anything about diamonds or rings or any of that shit, but even I could tell somebody dished out a truckload of cash for this thing. It was fucking insane. I remembered one of the things Heather had to do when she was a pledge our freshman year was this fund-raising event for homeless and displaced children and women in Africa. All I could think when I was looking at this girl's giant diamond ring was that the part of her brain that should have been registering the hypocrisy of the situation must not have existed. The diamond was probably worth enough to build houses for one hundred families in Africa, and what was even worse was that it was probably a fucking conflict diamond that led to the very families she was trying to help with her charity fund-raising being put out of their homes.

Harlow said, "I just had it cleaned. Supposedly it added like three percent more clarity."

Heather leaned in, looked at the ring, and said, "Oh yeah, you can totally tell."

I remember looking at Heather as she looked at that ring. Her eyes got big and took on a kind of creepy glint that was like fucking Gollum in *Lord of the Rings* looking at the One Ring. I saw that look in her eyes, but I was so in love with her that it didn't even register with me as a potential problem. I just got another beer and was happy to be hanging out with the girl I loved. In no part of my mind did I think that her almost literal salivation over a diamond would ever be a factor in our relationship. And that inability to see things that are right in front of my fucking face is what has led me to where I am now.

The rest of the night was pretty unremarkable until the last of Heather's sorority sisters decided to show up. Jenna, the girl I fucked at Brett's house, came in already pretty drunk.

I hadn't seen or talked to this girl since the night I fucked her at Brett's house. I knew Heather knew we fucked, but we never really talked about it because I got the feeling she didn't want to, just like we didn't really talk about much of what she did during the time we were apart because I didn't really want to know the details. But when Jenna walked in, that kind of unspoken moratorium we had put on shit like that went out the window pretty fast—through no fault of my own, I might add.

The drunken Jenna came up to us and said to me, "Hey. I like totally remember you."

I looked at Heather and she didn't look too happy about the conversation she already knew was inevitable.

Jenna continued on, "You were at Brett Keller's house that one night and we like totally fucked, didn't we?"

I said, "Yes."

Jenna said, "And it was right after you two broke up, right?"

I said, "Yes."

Jenna said, "But you're like back together or whatever, right?"

I said, "Yes."

Jenna said, "Oh, that sucks. Seriously I would fuck you again, you were pretty fucking good."

Heather, at that point, had had enough. She said, "Jenna, he's my fucking boyfriend. Can you like stop or something?"

Jenna said, "Sorry. Don't like be mad. He's a good fuck and you got him. Why are you like mad?"

Heather said, "I'm not mad. Can we just like not talk about you fucking my boyfriend, though? Would that be okay?"

Jenna said, "Fine. Sorry." And then she gave Heather a sloppy and drunk hug and kiss and wandered off into the small group of Kappa Kappa Gammas.

Heather turned to me and said, "You want to leave?"

I said, "Sure."

As we drove back to my apartment that night I remember thinking that I realized Heather actually never stopped loving me even when we were apart. If hearing Jenna talk about the one time we had sex bothered her so much, I thought Heather must have just been confused or something when we broke up. That night actually made me love her more, or at least feel like she loved me more than she did. Little did I know how completely fucking wrong I was.

I was on my way back from my first actual field exercise at a grade school in Flower Mound called Garden Ridge, where I basically just had to sit in this third grade classroom and like watch what the teacher did and how she handled the kids and everything, when I got this text from Brian. He was like, "What up? Haven't talked n a minute. Wondering how u been. Hit me back."

I ignored it at first because on the drive back to campus I was like seriously thinking about teaching and everything. After I watched that class I wasn't really that sure I wanted to be a teacher anymore. Or I guess it was more like I kind of figured out that I never really wanted to be a teacher and it just seemed like something that was really easy to major in, which it was, for sure, but actually seeing what I was going to be doing if I ended up doing that as a job seemed really shitty. But it was like pretty much way too late to be changing my major and everything. So I figured I'd just stick it out and hope that whoever I ended up marrying would make enough money that I wouldn't have to work. And then, as soon as I thought that, I started thinking that it was probably pretty likely I'd end up with Kyle. And then as soon as I thought that, I started thinking about if I really wanted to be with Kyle, because if he became a doctor he would probably make a pretty good amount of money and everything, but after college he would have to do medical school and all of that and a residency or whatever and that would take a long fucking time. It would be way easier just to get some guy who was already rich or who was going to have like some kind of business job making 100k right out of school or something. But as soon as I started thinking about any other guy besides Kyle I just couldn't see it, you know?

Obviously, I hate Kyle now. Or, no, actually I just kind of feel sorry for him. But on that drive home I remember really coming to the realization that like I wanted to be with him, even if it meant having to work for a few years while he was becoming a doctor. I knew I wouldn't like working, but I figured I could handle it for a little while, and then as soon as Kyle got a job as a surgeon or whatever I wouldn't ever have to work again.

When I got back to campus I went to the Kappa house and started trying to write my paper that was due the next day in field experience. I had to report on how the class observation went, and write about what I learned and crap like that. I didn't think it would take me too long, but then Brian started texting me again.

At first he was like, "U get my last text?"

And I just ignored it. Then he was like, "Plz dont ignore me. I just want to make sure ur ok."

I totally knew he was probably feeling guilty for that night and he either wanted to make sure I wasn't pissed so he could clear his conscience or what was actually probably way more likely was that he was scared I was going to tell somebody and he'd be fucked. I wanted to just keep ignoring him and let him wonder if I'd ever tell anyone about it, but I needed to write my paper and it didn't seem like he was going to stop texting me so I was like, "Everythings kewl. Bye."

Then he was like, "U think we could get together soon?"

I was like, "Why?"

He was like, "Bcuz I wanna talk."

I was like, "What about?"

He was like, "Just catch up."

I was like, "Not a good idea."

He was like, "Why?"

I was like, "I have a bf."

He was like, "I heard. So?"

I was like, "So, not a good idea."

He was like, "I miss you."

I was like, "Not a good idea. Bye."

He missed me? What in the fuck was that supposed to mean? Was it like he missed fucking me, or he missed drugging me and letting his gross friend fuck me, or he actually missed me? We didn't ever really do anything that wasn't like partying or fucking when we were a couple, so I didn't think he actually missed me. So he must have just been trying to fuck me again or something. Whatever.

He didn't text me again for the rest of the night, but it started me thinking about Kyle and about Brian and about pretty much everything that happened since freshman year with every guy I had done anything with. All the guys I gave head to and all the guys I fucked and Josh and even Brett and like how I wanted to fuck him when I started dating Kyle and everything. And as I thought about all of those guys I pretty much figured out that Kyle was like the best of all of them. I'd never fucked Brett or anything, but most of my sorority sisters had and I heard the stories and he sounded pretty nasty. Like he did really gross shit to them and everything. Kyle wasn't like that, and that night as I wrote my paper I was like pretty sure Kyle was exactly what I wanted. He wasn't mean or gross or a fucking asshole. He was like the best boyfriend I had ever had and after I finished my paper, I went to sleep that night really feeling good about the possibility that I would probably be his wife one day.

Kyle's apartment was nice enough. I didn't mind spending time there when I was driven from my own home by the presence of my father's wife and when I was coincidentally driven from my room in the Alpha Tau Omega house by the unbearable Wednesday pornography night, of course designed and overseen by Greg, in which each member of Alpha Tau Omega was required to bring and screen the most disgusting pornography he could find, most often involving homosexual or transsexual acts, all while Greg performed "boner checks." If a participant was discovered by Greg to be in a state of arousal at any point during the screening of the pornography, he would be singled out and required to masturbate to completion in front of everyone in a certain amount of time while being forced to watch a specific piece of pornography used specifically for this purpose. It was a four-minute clip referred to in the Alpha Tau Omega house as "Shitdick."

Although the moniker given to the clip by the members of Alpha Tau Omega is accurately descriptive, it by no means conveys the worst of what the clip has to offer. In the clip, three men are engaged in sexual activity. Two of them are performing oral sex on each other in a standard sixty-nine position. A third is fucking the man in the top position of the sixty-nine in his ass, occasionally removing his dick and forcing the man in the bottom position to perform fellatio on him. This continues for a solid two minutes until the third participant forces his dick back into the ass of the man in the top position at the same time the man in the top position's asshole expels a significant quantity of fecal material the consistency of a mashed banana. The feces coat the third man's cock, balls, and entire pubic region, which doesn't deter him in any way from continuing to fuck the man in the top position. As the third man's dick rams in and out of the man in the top position's asshole, the feces slide down onto the face of the man in the bottom position, into his mouth, eyes, nose, et cetera, which does nothing to deter him from continuing to suck the cock of the man in the top position. This continues for another minute or so until the third man pulls out and jerks off into the asshole of the man in the top position and into the face of the man in the bottom position. In the finale, all three of the men kiss one another and lick the semen and feces off each other's faces.

If the Alpha Tau Omega brother caught in a state of arousal was unable to reach orgasm by the end of "Shitdick" he was then forced to do a "Row Run," which required him to run the entire length of fraternity row naked. It seemed strange to me that no one ever opted to do the "Row Run" outright and avoid the clearly homosexual behavior that was masturbating in a room full of men.

At any rate, I found both my home and my room at the Alpha Tau Omega house to be uninhabitable at this time, and so I was at Kyle's apartment playing *Mario Kart* with him when Heather unlocked the door and walked in without knocking. This was the first time I came to learn that Kyle had obviously given her a key. It wasn't that disturbing to me, based only on the fact that I hadn't noticed a large number of her belongings in his apartment yet. While she had free access to his home, she had not, at that point, made it her own.

She was always strange around me throughout the second incarnation of her relationship with Kyle. I assumed it was because she feared that one day I would divulge to Kyle the details of some other depraved act I had witnessed her participating in at a Greek party, something beyond the dick-sucking, something maybe she didn't even remember doing. What she didn't know, however, was that Kyle was convinced he couldn't be without her. I felt, at that point, I could have shown Kyle a video of Heather being fucked by the entire SMU football team and he wouldn't have cared enough to break up with her.

When she came in she engaged me in brief conversation, attempting to seem interested in what I had to say about whatever matters she had brought up. It was clear she had some agenda in the conversation that she was waiting to engage, giving me time to speak so the transition to her topic would seem more natural, hoping that in random conversation I would deliver a segue that would make what she would say next seem prompted.

If my memory serves, I was in the middle of talking about cryogenics and how it seemed less than likely that any science would ever find a way to reanimate dead flesh, but that nonetheless even if the odds were less than one-tenth of one percent, those odds of cheating death were literally infinitely better than the absolute zero of burial and hoping for a spiritual afterlife that simply does not exist, when Heather chose her time to force a conversation about engagement rings.

Aside from clearly reminding me why I despise all women, the conversation served an even greater purpose. It illuminated the disturbing level of devotion Kyle had developed for Heather. I'm not suggesting that the game of *Mario Kart* had any importance in the grand scheme of life, but certainly it rivaled the conversation about the cut and clarity of stone Heather desired in whatever engagement ring she was to receive that Kyle abandoned the game for.

As I sat on his couch with the game paused I was forced to listen to Heather drone on and on and insist that her engagement ring needn't be overly expensive but that she really couldn't see herself wearing anything less than two and a half carats and the setting had to be platinum or white gold and she wanted a princess cut and a million other meaningless things that all faded into a general high-pitched whine as I stared at the pause screen.

The net result of this conversation between them was that Kyle was certainly more than willing to entertain the idea of buying her an engagement ring. I wondered how aware Heather could have possibly been of Kyle's financial status. I knew something about rings, only due to the fact that my father had purchased two during my lifetime, for his current wife and for the one prior. I knew the qualities Heather was demanding were by no means qualities possessed by the most expensive rings in the world, but neither were they possessed by any ring Kyle would be able to afford in the foreseeable future. I could only assume that Heather had no concerns about Kyle's ability to get the funds to purchase such a ring or what he might have to do to get said funds.

The most disturbing part of the conversation came when Heather opened her wallet and removed several pictures of engagement rings that she had cut out of magazines and catalogs. She had subsequently drawn diagrams on each of these pictures illustrating which qualities in each ring she would most want to be synthesized in her own ring. The attention Kyle paid to this was astounding.

At the conversation's end, Heather left the room, explaining that she didn't want to take up any more of our quality time. She left her diagrammed engagement ring pictures lying on Kyle's coffee table, as if to insinuate that she was leaving them for him in order to aid him in the purchase of her ring.

I was more than disgusted as Kyle unpaused the game and we continued to race.

I hadn't honestly ever given it much thought in my entire life. Buying an engagement ring seemed like a thing I'd do eventually, but it always seemed like that "eventually" was far off, way down the road. And yet, there I fucking was sitting in Robbins Bros. on Dallas Parkway showing the fucking pictures of rings Heather had diagrammed to some lady named Margaret. At that point I hadn't really decided when I was going to propose to her or anything, I was just interested to see how much money I was going to have to sock away to be able to afford the rock she wanted. Even now it's hard to believe how fucking brainwashed she had me.

Margaret looked the pictures over and said, "It's actually much easier to select a ring if a girl does something like this—you know, gives you an idea so you don't end up getting something she doesn't like. That's a girl's worst nightmare. I remember my first husband just went out and bought a ring without asking me what I wanted, and well . . . let's just say there's a reason he was my first husband and not my last."

From the way she laughed it seemed to me that she had probably done that exact joke five times a day for the last ten years. I played along and laughed, too, because I was a douchebag who didn't know any better then.

After around half an hour of looking at different rings and having shit like color and clarity explained to me, I was getting the idea that the kind of ring Heather would want was going to set me back somewhere in the neighborhood of seven to ten thousand dollars, which was money I had no chance of saving anytime in the foreseeable future. I made a little bit of money working at Mac's Place, but it was a very little. It was honestly just enough to cover going out to eat every once in a while with Heather or going to see a movie. The rest of the money I had saved up I knew I needed to cover my rent. I thought briefly about going back to the dorms to save money, but I liked having my own place too much, or I guess I should say that I liked having a place where I could fuck Heather without a roommate always being around.

I knew Heather wasn't really expecting me to propose until the following year, but after seeing how excited she got about that other girl in her sorority getting engaged, I knew it would be a big deal for her if she could be engaged before her senior year. It disgusts me how much of a fucking chump I was, but at the time I just wanted to make her happy. Maybe there was even some part of me that was afraid she'd suck another guy's dick or find some other reason to figure out that she didn't want to be with me. I wanted to lock her in. I wanted to make sure that what I went through when she broke up with me our sophomore year never happened again. On the drive back to campus I had pretty much made the decision that I was going to ask Heather to marry me before the end of our junior year, preferably even before winter break, which was around two months away at that point.

When I got back to campus I had to do some work in the advanced biology lab. As I was walking into the building Erin was walking out. We hadn't seen or really talked to each other since the night I broke up with her the previous spring. We both saw each other, so it couldn't be ignored.

She said, "Hey."

I said, "Hey."

She said, "You want to go grab a coffee or something?"

I said, "Sure."

And she led the way over to the Hughes-Trigg market and we got coffee at Java City, the exact same place Heather and I got coffee the first time we saw each other after we broke up. It was strange how similar it all felt, but despite the similarity in the scenario there was something missing with Erin. When I had this exact same interaction with Heather I remembered feeling a spark of hope. With Erin that just wasn't there, for me anyway.

We got our coffee, sat down, and she said, "So how have things been?"

I said, "Pretty good. You?"

"Pretty good, too. School's going well. Parents are doing good."

Then we just sat there for a minute or so and Erin said, "You and Heather still together?"

I said, "Yeah."

"And you're happy and everything?"

"Yeah, pretty happy." I didn't really care if Erin was dating anyone, but I thought it would have seemed like I was being a dick if I didn't ask her so I said, "You seeing anyone?"

She said, "No. Not really."

I didn't really know what to say to that. Despite everything that happened between me and Erin, I still liked her, still wanted her to be happy. The way she said she wasn't seeing anyone was almost like some kind of accusation that I was the reason she was single. It was weird.

She said, "Maybe I shouldn't be saying this, but I still love you, Kyle. It's been a long time since we broke up and I still love you. I know you have Heather and it seems like that's going well for you, but if anything ever happens between you guys or if you even just think you might have made a mistake with us, I just want you to know that you can always call me. The door's still open."

I was pretty blown away by how forthright she was, but Erin was always like that. It was one of the things I liked most about her when we were together. I didn't really know what to say in response. I said, "Okay, thanks."

She said, "And if you ever just wanted to go out to dinner or something like that one night and see how it went, I would be open to that, too."

I couldn't tell if she was offering to fuck me. I thought she was but then I wasn't sure if she was offering a onetime thing or if she was basically telling me she would have no problem having a full-on secret relationship with me. I thought about the last time we fucked and how good it was. It wasn't as good as Heather, but Erin's blowjobs were something I had to admit I missed. Then I started feeling guilty for even thinking about getting a blowjob from Erin. Less than half an hour earlier I was sitting in a jewelry store picking out Heather's engagement ring, and here I was entertaining the idea of cheating on her with an ex-girlfriend.

I said, "Okay, I guess I'll keep that in mind."

She said, "Kyle, I really miss you and I think we had something that's pretty tough to replace. I know you think you love Heather, but I really can't imagine what you have with her is better or even the same as what we had."

The sad thing is she was right. Erin was 100 percent correct, and instead of realizing that and taking her up on her offer, I got pissed off. In my mind she had basically insulted my relationship with Heather and I actually got mad at her for insinuating that what I had with Heather was anything less than perfect.

I said, "Erin, it was good to see you, but I think I should go before you say something that really offends me."

She said, "I'm sorry. I shouldn't have said that. I just wanted you to know how I feel about this whole thing. I've wanted to call you but I was afraid I would have been crossing some kind of boundary I wasn't supposed to, and then when we just ran into each other I thought I could sit down and have a normal conversation with you, but I can't. I just can't. I think we should be together and I think you think we should be, too. I get that you can't see it right now, but I don't want you to be mad at me for feeling this way. I just want you to know that this is how I feel and I don't see it changing anytime soon."

I should have forgotten about Heather, taken Erin back to her apartment, fucked the shit out of her, pledged my undying love to her, asked her to marry me even though I couldn't afford a ring, which she wouldn't have cared about anyway, and had a perfectly happy life. Instead I said, "It was nice seeing you. I think I should go."

And I left Erin sitting there by herself at Java City. I didn't turn around to see if she was still watching me walk away or to see if she was crying. I knew she was still sitting there, drinking her coffee, wondering how long it would take me to come to my senses, which pissed me off even more.

The fact that someone could outright question the relationship I had with Heather only made me want to be with her more. It wasn't necessarily to prove Erin wrong or anything like that. It was more to have something that I thought no one else understood. Whether it was Erin or Brett or even my parents every once in a while telling me that Heather and I seemed like a strange match, they all made me want to hold on to Heather and never let go.

Ironically, that conversation with Erin where she told me she'd always be waiting for me was the final straw in pushing me to decide that, no matter what, I was going to propose to Heather before junior year was over.

A bunch of us were like sitting around trying to plan a party we were going to be throwing in a few weeks with SAE when Andrea came into the kitchen like seriously bawling her fucking eyes out. We were all like, *What the fuck is going on?*

So I was like, "Andrea, are you like okay?"

She was like, "No."

I was like, "What's wrong?"

She was like, "Oh my God," and she sat down at the table with us and just like buried her head in her arms and kept sobbing. She seriously wouldn't tell us what was wrong. We were all like thinking that her mom died or something. And it turned out that it was even worse than that.

After she cried for like a solid minute without talking to any of us she kind of pulled it together a little bit and was like, "Okay, you guys, tonight is seriously like the worst night of my life and I really need some support."

I was like, "Of course, you know we're here for you."

She was like, "I just got back from eating dinner with Ron and he like dumped me." Then she started crying really bad again. We were all like asking her questions and trying to get the details but she cried for like another minute straight without responding to us. Then she kind of pulled herself together again and she was like, "I thought he was going to propose to me next week because it's going to be my birthday but instead tonight he told me that he's getting back together with Dianna." Then she started really crying even worse than before.

Dianna was Ron's freshman- and sophomore-year girlfriend. They were like totally an item and everything and pretty much no one thought anything could break them up. Ron was kind of a goofy guy and Dianna was like a little dumb. She was an Alpha Chi and it was always weird to me that Andrea would go out with a guy who had dated an Alpha Chi. But I guess the deal was Ron walked in on Dianna making out with some other guy at a party and he got all crazy and dumped her and they would like avoid each other at parties and everything after that.

Gina was like, "Did he tell you why he's like getting back together with her or anything?"

Andrea was like, "He said she called him and they had like this long conversation about how they never stopped loving each other and he told me that there was always just like something missing in our relationship that he felt like he had with her."

Then she started crying again and all I could think about was like how much I wanted to beat the shit out of that chick Dianna. I mean I guess she was a senior, too, and she probably needed to find a guy like ASAP so she could at least be engaged by the time she graduated, but seriously? Andrea had like been there to help Ron pick up the pieces and everything after he broke up with Dianna. Like that should have counted for something. And even besides that it was like Ron and Andrea were a way cuter and better couple than Ron and Dianna. I had only met Dianna a few times but I seriously hated her for this. I mean she basically completely fucked Andrea. And it didn't seem like it was something that Ron would have done on his own. Dianna had to have like instigated the whole thing. What a fucking bitch.

We only had a month or so left in the first semester. The senior guys were already starting to propose to girls in pretty much every sorority. The only guys who were still single were that way for a reason. There was some chance that Andrea would be able to find a guy who had a girlfriend but wasn't that happy with her. But usually something like that took at least a few months of groundwork to get him to dump his girlfriend and then close to a year of dating before he would actually propose. If she was really desperate, Andrea could try for like a junior boyfriend or something, but she probably wouldn't get the proposal until after she graduated, when the guy was a senior. It was a serious fucking nightmare and after I thought about it for a few minutes I like completely understood why she was crying so much. She had wasted two years with Ron that she could have been using to find another guy and lock him in to proposing. Her life was like basically over.

We were all thinking the same thing. I saw Harlow like put her hand in her pocket to hide her engagement ring, which was a nice thing to do I thought. Like the last thing Andrea probably wanted to see was a giant engagement ring reflecting back in her eyes after she just lost the best chance she had to get one.

Andrea stopped crying for a second and was like, "Okay, you're all my sisters and as sisters we all stick together. I'm going to ask all of you to come to me first if you hear of any guys dumping their girlfriends or if you hear of any guys getting cheated on or even if you hear of any guys who are looking to cheat or are even just like generally unhappy with the girl they're with. Okay?"

Everyone was like, "Okay," but we were all really like, *That is so desperate and I hope it doesn't happen to me.* Seriously, I bet we all would have reacted pretty much the same exact way.

I called Kyle that night and told him what happened. He was like, "Yeah, that sucks, but you have to look at it from—what's the guy's name?"

I was like, "Ron."

He was like, "Ron—look at it from Ron's point of view. If he didn't really love Andrea like he loved the other chick, then he's going to be much happier in the long run and ultimately so is Andrea. If the guy didn't really love her then that relationship would have suffered and eventually ended anyway."

I was like, "Yeah, but he could have proposed to her first and maybe even married her. Like he totally ruined the rest of her senior year."

Kyle was like, "I see."

I knew he wasn't on my side because he was a guy, but that night I went over to his house and sucked his dick like the best I've ever sucked it because I didn't want him thinking that he could dump me to get back together with that skank he dated when we were broken up instead of proposing to me.

chapter
nine

After a particularly boring business ethics lecture I returned to my room in the Alpha Tau Omega house and logged into my account on donorsiblingregistry.com to find that I was the proud father of my tenth child—a girl to be named Harriet who would grow up in the household of a single mother of thirty-eight who obviously hadn't found a man willing to impregnate her or, worse yet and possibly more likely, hadn't found a man even willing to fuck her at all.

I decided to celebrate by throwing an impromptu baby shower at my father's house in Highland Park, knowing that both he and his wife were out of town for the week. I called a girl I had met a few weeks prior at a party I couldn't remember. Her name was Bethany and she was the sister of a girl named Karlie who was a Pi Phi. Bethany didn't attend SMU, or any college for that matter, due to a certain level of academic ineptitude. I planned on using whatever insecurities she had about her intellectual inferiority to enhance the sexual degradation I would or-chestrate when she arrived at my home.

I also called Greg's sister and extended her an invitation. As much as I liked fucking her to somehow accentuate the feeling of dominance I already had over Greg, I found that I actually slightly enjoyed her company. She was a cunt to be sure. This was evidenced by her willingness to fuck me based solely on the fact that I was my father's son and maybe, I reasoned, partially to fulfill some pedestrian need to act out against her father. But there was something agreeable in her nature that I found far more pleasant to be around than I had expected. Whatever the case, she accepted, as did the moron.

After their arrival at my home it became apparent to me that, although Greg's sister had no problem with a three-way, the dunce seemed to have some lingering amount of self-respect that I hadn't anticipated. I assumed this had something to do with her general lack of knowledge in all categories, including the identities of the most wealthy families in Dallas. I gave one last push by telling her that if she wouldn't yield to at least sucking my dick while Greg's sister performed anilingus on her, then she'd have to go. Surprisingly she held fast to her sense of self-worth and walked out. It was mildly amusing only in that it was surprising to a degree and therefore novel.

I dismissed the event and took Greg's sister up to my room, hoping to use at least some of the items in my closet on her while photographing many of the night's events. I was inches away from Greg's sister's anus with a rubber fist when my doorbell rang. I wasn't expecting anyone but I thought it might have been the moron realizing her error. I reasoned that in such a case she would have to be willing to allow a more extreme defiling in order to gain admittance to my home once again. I told Greg's sister not to move—her ass in the air, dripping with saliva I had lathered it with only seconds before—then donned my robe and went to the front door still holding the rubber fist.

Standing there in my doorway was not the moron. It was, instead, Kyle, looking very nervous and sweaty. I was concerned as any friend would have been. He told me he had something very important to talk to me about and asked that I put the rubber fist away. I obliged his request.

I hadn't forgotten about Greg's sister. I just became far more interested in discovering the reason Kyle saw fit to show up at my front door unannounced, which was something he had never done at any point in our friendship. For this reason I understood that whatever he wanted to discuss with me had to be a matter of significance. Despite understanding this fact, I was in no way prepared to handle the issue he discussed with me that night.

After a deep breath, he explained to me that he intended to marry Heather. This was not news to me. I had come to accept that, at some point, Kyle would make the greatest mistake of his life and wed that cunt. This seemed so inevitable to me that I had stopped trying to dissuade him from it. This general feeling of inexorability informed my response to his announcement.

He went still further down this road of announcements by telling me that he planned to propose to Heather over the winter break. This admission elicited in me a reaction that even I was not prepared for. I had never been struck in the testicles so sharply that it caused me to vomit, but I assumed such a strike would feel similar to receiving the information Kyle had delivered in saying that his proposal to Heather would become concrete in less than two months.

I made the most coherent argument possible that he should wait at least until their senior year, that there was no harm in waiting, that there was no benefit in an early proposal, et cetera. None of this mattered to Kyle. He insisted that he loved her and he wanted to make her happy. He knew that nothing would make her happier than being proposed to during her junior year. He went on to explain to me that all of the cunts in the sororities at SMU viewed the date of their engagement as some kind of competition. Where I found this to be deplorable information bolstering my argument that Kyle should wait and gain certainty that Heather wouldn't accept his proposal just as a means to compete with the other cunts of the Kappa house, Kyle somehow found it endearing. He was lost. My best friend was lost and there was nothing I could do to find him again. In many ways that night was possibly the saddest of our friendship, despite the events that were yet to transpire.

What Kyle said to me next was at once laughable and horrifying.

Still nervous and almost shaking as he spoke, he asked me if he could borrow ten thousand dollars to buy Heather an engagement ring. He had asked me to borrow money one other time in our friendship and this request was accompanied by all of the same promises to repay me and all of the same apologies for having to ask for the money and all of the same assurances that if he had any other way to get the money he would have employed it.

In the first case of my lending money to Kyle, for Heather's abortion, he had indeed paid me back over the course of the next few months and I'd had no problem whatsoever loaning him the money. It was clear in that instance that Kyle would not have been able to raise the funds necessary to destroy the mistake in Heather's womb in any kind of timely fashion and furthermore the general purpose of the money in question was one I agreed with—the erasure of a mistake.

This was something wholly different. The amount Kyle was asking for was immaterial. Had he needed ten thousand or even a hundred thousand in order to pay for an abortion I still would have gladly given it. It was the purpose of the money in question in this instance that I couldn't bring myself to support. Not only was it a mistake in my opinion for Kyle to propose to and eventually marry Heather, it was a mistake to purchase a ring so soon.

In general I also despise the idea of engagement rings in that there is no male equivalent. Women seem to want everything to be equal in this world and yet they hope for an expensive engagement ring without ever even thinking of offering something of equal value to the man they marry. The double standard involved specifically with engagement rings repulses me. Beyond that the very idea of them transcends any logic I can identify with. I understand the symbolism of a ring, but why it has to be a diamond, and why that diamond has to be of a certain size to truly make a woman happy, is beyond me. It only further illustrates, in my mind, how foolish and childlike women are, in that they wait their entire lives for a man to give them a sparkling rock and only this can make them complete.

This view, of course, has nothing to do with Kyle's request for ten thousand dollars, which I flatly denied within seconds of his asking, citing many of the reasons I've already mentioned and trying again, in vain, to convince him not to propose to Heather.

He thanked me for listening, apologized for asking for the money, and told me as he left how much he valued our friendship and how much he hated having to ask me for the money. I assured him that it would affect our friendship in no way, and that although I didn't completely understand his point of view in all of this I could still respect him. I asked him what he thought he was going to do about getting her the ring and he said he didn't know but he would figure something out. I had no doubt he would.

As I returned to my bedroom—where Greg's sister hadn't moved an inch, with her ass still in the air—I realized I had left the rubber fist downstairs. I thought for one last time about Kyle and the mistake he was about to make. Throughout his and Heather's relationship there seemed to exist a small group of moments that signified Kyle's slipping away. I felt that this moment, this realization that he was going to ask her to be his wife was the final moment in the group, the one that ultimately meant he was finally gone. Any hope I had of retrieving my friend from the relationship that had swallowed him whole was gone, or so I thought at that moment.

I pitied Greg's sister in that moment, knowing that some of my frustration and some of my hatred for Heather and cunts like her would be channeled into whatever I chose to ram up her asshole. Luckily for her, Kyle's visit had taken the wind from my sails and I could only find the energy to use my dick. I took no photographs of the event.

I had been to probably every jewelry store in Dallas looking at rings, trying to find the best deal I could on a ring that managed to have at least half of the qualities Heather said she wanted. The best price I could come up with was $3,499. So my choices were: don't eat for the rest of junior year, take out another student loan and move back into the dorms so I could use the rent money I had saved up on her ring, or the most logical choice—don't get her a fucking ring. That, of course, was one choice I didn't even entertain.

I know at the time that I loved her and everything, and I really thought she loved me, too, but what in the fuck was I thinking? I could have waited to get her a ring until our senior year and she wouldn't have even cared. But I just couldn't get it out of my head that if I proposed to her during junior year it would make her so happy that she'd never leave me and all of her friends would be envious of her and I knew she wanted that so I wanted to give it to her. Also, as stupid as this is, somewhere deep down I knew that if I proposed to her as a junior it would validate me to her friends. I know it doesn't seem like that kind of a thing would have mattered to me, but it was kind of like icing on the cake of making Heather happy. It was almost like revenge in a way for me. A lot of the girls in her sorority were nasty bitches to me for the entire time I knew them. I knew that proposing to Heather would shut them up, and in many ways I would immediately rise to the top of their list of most desirable guys because none of their shitbag frat-guy boyfriends would have proposed to them yet. Petty, I know, but I couldn't help thinking about it.

So I had to come up with thirty-five hundred dollars and I had about a month to do it, because I wanted to propose to her the first day of our second semester. I was thinking about doing it over winter break, but Heather was talking about maybe going to see her grandparents in Florida with her mom so I didn't even know if she'd be in town, and besides that I kind of felt like I had to do it when school was in session so her cunty sorority sisters could be the first ones she went and told.

I thought about getting a second job, but with classes and the one job I already had there was no time during the day for me to do it, especially not if I wanted to see Heather at all. I thought about selling my car, which I probably couldn't even have gotten two thousand dollars for, let alone thirty-five hundred. I thought about signing up to do some of those medical research programs where they test drugs on people, but that didn't seem like it would get me enough money by Christmas break. I really had no fucking idea how I was going to get her this ring.

Then one night I was up late watching TV, waiting for Heather to come back from some party she was throwing with her sorority, and I saw something that made me almost shit my pants. On QVC they were selling a ring that I couldn't have designed more perfectly myself. It was the literal accumulation of each and every little thing that Heather had circled in the pictures of probably seven or eight different rings. It was exactly the ring she wanted. It was even better than the thirty-five-hundred-dollar ring I was thinking about getting her. And the best part—it was only $89.99. I was only confused for a second and then I realized it was a cubic zirconia—completely fake.

I remember staring at the TV with the phone in my hand, debating whether or not I should buy it. I didn't want to lie to Heather, and I knew engagement rings and shit like that were really important to her, but I also knew I wasn't going to be able to get the real version of the ring she wanted for a long fucking time. So I made the worst decision in the whole list of bad decisions I made where Heather was concerned. Actually, I take that back—it was a good decision, it just turned out bad. And when I say bad I mean it turned out *horrible*. And it ultimately led us all to where we are now.

I decided I was going to buy the fake from QVC, propose to her with it, and then eventually replace it without her knowing. I reasoned that, as long as she was happy, it didn't matter if the ring was real or fake or whatever. And, taking that delusion even further, I thought to myself that the ring was just a symbol anyway. For all intents and purposes it was the exact ring she told me she wanted. So what if it wasn't a diamond? It fucking looked just like one. Unless she was planning on using it to cut glass or something, she'd never know.

So I dialed the number, gave them my credit card info, guessed Heather's ring size, and prepared to wait the five to seven business days for the product of my poor judgment to arrive.

The next kind of big thing that happened that semester was, Cam's brother got arrested. The cops pulled him over for a DUI and he had like fifteen pounds of weed in his car. So we totally had like no one to get E or pot or anything from, and there were a bunch of parties coming up. So we asked Cam where his brother got his shit from, and Cam was like, "I'm actually going to meet with the guy tomorrow night if you guys want to come, too."

So I was like, "Yeah."

I tried to get Andrea to come with me but she was still way too fucked up from Ron dumping her and everything so I ended up getting Gina to go. We showed up at Cam's house at like around seven-thirty or something on whatever night it was. I remember it was a weeknight, but I don't remember which one, and then Cam drove us to this Valero gas station on Marsh Lane and it was kind of sketchy, but I knew Cam really well and I didn't think he was going to try anything and I figured if anything weird happened he would look out for us. It was like my first real drug deal, though. I mean I had bought weed and coke and E and whatever, but pretty much always through Cam on campus or through someone else who just happened to have it at a party or something. It was really weird actually doing it for real behind a gas station. I, of course, didn't tell Kyle what I was doing. He would have seriously flipped out.

So we got to the Valero and parked and I looked over at this car next to us and Annie was actually there parked in a car next to us. I hadn't seen her in a long time, so I was like, "Cam, is it cool if I go talk to the girl in that car over there? I know her." I didn't want to like break some kind of drug deal etiquette or whatever by getting out of the car.

He was like, "Yeah, it's cool. The dude we're meeting is driving around the neighborhood and I have to text him, so he won't be here for a few minutes anyway."

I was like, "Cool," and I got out and went over to Annie's car, knocked on the window, and got her to let me in. I got in on her passenger's side and saw that she was doing lines off a credit card.

I was like, "Did you just get that from a guy at this gas station?"

She was like, "Yeah, he has some pretty good stuff."

I was like, "Yeah, Cam took us over here to get some for this party at the end of the week. How have you been?"

She was like, "Really good. You know I started dating Jeff Gurddey."

I was like, "That senior Pike guy?"

She was like, "Yeah. I dated Brian for a while at the beginning of the year. I hope you're not mad."

I was like, "Not at all."

She was like, "I don't know if he was weird when you guys were dating, but he totally creeped me out, or I guess it was more like his friend Josh creeped me out. So I like broke up with him and then started dating Jeff."

Jeff Gurddey was actually a pretty good catch. He got arrested for public indecency after a crazy party that Pike threw our sophomore year, his junior year, but other than that he was supposedly like in a pretty rich family and everything. I was like, "That's great. How long have you guys been going out?"

She was like, "Just a couple of months. So I don't think he's going to propose or anything, but maybe by the end of the year or something. I don't know. How are you doing? I heard you and Kyle got back together."

I was like, "Yeah. At the end of last year we got back together and things have actually been like really, really good."

She was like, "He was always kind of a cool guy from what I remember. But he's still not in a frat or anything, right?"

I was like, "No. He's just studying hard and everything. He's going to be a doctor so he probably wouldn't have time to do the whole Greek thing anyway."

She was like, "Cool, cool."

I was like, "Do you come get stuff from this guy by yourself like a lot?"

She was like, "Not a lot, but since Cam's brother got arrested it's been like pretty tough to get anything good and this guy definitely has good stuff. So, you know?"

I was like, "Yeah."

Then the guy pulled up and I was like, "Well, I should probably get back to Cam's car and everything, so it was like really good seeing you, we should hang out some time. I feel like we never really do anymore."

She was like, "Yeah, give me a call."

I was like, "I will," then I got out of her car and I seriously knew that I was like never going to call her. I remember thinking how it's weird that you can like totally be really good friends with someone and then your lives take like different paths and not even like totally different paths, just like slightly different paths, and your friendship with them is just like not even the same anymore. I mean we were both in sororities. We were even at a lot of the same parties. But we just didn't hang out anymore.

So I got back in Cam's car and Cam was like, "Okay, you guys just want like a gram and how many tabs of E?"

Gina was like, "Ten or so. Whatever we can get for this," and Gina handed him the money we had collected from everyone back at the house.

Then Cam was like, "Okay, you guys stay here and I'll be right back." Then he got out of his car and went into the other guy's car.

Gina was like, "This is kind of sketchy, right?"

I was like, "Yeah, totally. I wish Cam would have just like bought a bunch and we could have bought it off him."

Gina was like, "I know, right?"

Then Cam came back and he had like everything we asked for and he drove us home and nothing happened. It was like my first real drug deal and it all went really smooth. In a weird way I was kind of proud.

chapter
twelve

There were only two days left in the first semester of our junior year and a significant amount of time had passed since Kyle's request to borrow ten thousand dollars. He had made no further mention of it or of his desire to propose to Heather in the subsequent times we had been in each other's company. I was certain he hadn't given up his dream of self-destruction, but I assumed he had put it on hold when he found that he was unable to procure the necessary funds. Like so many times in those four years, I was wrong.

Kyle and I had just completed the drum and lead guitar sections of Radiohead's "Creep" on Expert when he put his guitar down and told me that he wanted to show me something. He then proceeded to take a ring box out of his pocket and toss it to me. I didn't need to open the box to know what was inside, or hear him tell me that he planned to propose to Heather on the day our second semester began, but I was curious to see how much money he wasted on her, so I looked. The ring was clearly out of any price range that Kyle was capable of entertaining. I, of course, asked him where he got the money to pay for the ring, and he explained that the ring was fake. A cubic zirconia facsimile of the actual diamond ring Heather wanted.

At the outset it would seem that I would approve of something like this—tricking a cunt into thinking the worthless piece of shit on her finger was exactly what she wanted. And, at the outset, this was true, I did approve. But after a few seconds of scrutiny of the specifics of this scenario it became quite clear to me that this was a terrible idea.

Kyle insisted that Heather would never know, and eventually, when he had enough money to do it right, he would either replace the ring or give her an entirely new one that was even better. I attempted to bring him to his senses by explaining that Heather, by virtue of being a woman and therefore a horrible cunt concerned only with material gain, would be able to tell the ring was fake. I further explained that once Heather gained this awareness there were really only two possible outcomes. The first, and best in my opinion, would be that she would end the relationship. Kyle, of course, discounted this immediately, citing the fact that she loved him and the ring wouldn't really matter to her. Why, then, I asked, would she have so many demands about the type of ring she wanted? My logic was lost on him.

The second outcome, and the one I sadly thought was more likely, was that Heather would discover the true nature of the ring's make and hold this against Kyle for the rest of their relationship, which could be until he died. I reasoned that she would forever force him to buy her gifts and that he would have to display limitless tolerance for her every whim, all in order to apologize for the ring.

He discounted this immediately as well. When I asked him why he was showing me the ring, why he was involving me in any of this, he told me that when he and Heather actually got married he wanted me to be his best man. I had been in countless wedding parties for cousins throughout the years, so I was no stranger to the role, but this was different. I had never cared about anyone whose wedding I had been a part of in the past. If they wanted to ruin their lives, so be it. In this case, however, I was faced with a certain dilemma. Kyle was my best friend and as such I felt obligated to honor his request, and yet as his best friend I also felt a certain stronger obligation to stop him from making the mistake of marriage in the first place.

I, of course, told him I would be happy to be in his wedding party while I secretly hoped that the wedding would never happen. It was strange to me how badly Kyle desired a life that was repellent to me. Stranger still was the fact that the exact life Kyle desired—with a wife and children and a stable, uninteresting job—was readily available to me at any time I chose to accept it. And yet it was something Kyle had to work for, had to suffer to achieve. As I looked at his fake ring I thought about how strange life is and how easily things come to people who don't want them and how the opposite is also true.

That winter break, Heather ended up spending almost the entire three weeks in Florida with her mom, sister, and grandparents. I got to see her for only a week or so before she left, which actually worked out pretty well because it gave me a chance to figure out how I was going to pop the question. One of the things that pisses me off about how everything turned out is that she'll never fucking appreciate how much time and effort I put into trying to come up with the perfect way to propose to her. I don't know if any girl will every really understand that of any guy who asks her to marry him.

I thought about doing it at a really nice restaurant or something, but we didn't really have a place we considered "our" restaurant, and I wanted it to at least relate to our relationship in some way. I thought about doing it on the steps of her sorority, but that seemed cheesy as shit and, to be honest, I didn't really want to involve anyone from her sorority in a moment I felt should be about us and us only. I thought about a bunch of different places around campus where some of the more important moments in our relationship took place, but those all seemed stupid to me. I thought about just finding a nice place she would think was pretty, like the giant garden in Brett's backyard, but I knew he wouldn't let me do that. Then one night after I talked to Heather for almost an hour on the phone it came to me.

She was still going to be in Florida for another week when I decided what I was going to do, and I always thought it was a good sign that I had a little time to sit with it and I never second-guessed myself. She got back from Florida really late on January 4, and classes started up again on the fifth if I remember right.

That afternoon I called her up and told her I wanted to take her out to a nice dinner because we hadn't seen each other for a while. Then I told her I had a surprise for her.

She said something like, "Kyle, I'm so tired from the flight last night. Can we just do it tomorrow night?"

I said, "No, I think we should do it tonight."

She said, "I love you, babe, but like seriously, I'm so tired."

I said, "Well, I promise the surprise after dinner will make you a lot less tired."

She said, "Really? What is it?"

I said, "You'll see."

I could tell she was getting excited. She was just like a little fucking kid with surprises and presents and shit like that.

So I took her out to eat at Fogo de Chão, which was one of her favorite places to go, and all through dinner she kept asking me what the surprise was. To any person who wasn't half as retarded as I was with her, it would have become unbearably annoying. At the time, I actually thought her constant begging and inability to just enjoy a fucking surprise was cute. Every time I replay that dinner in my head, though, I want to eat a fucking bullet when I think about what an idiot I was.

Anyway, we ate and then got in my car and I made her put on a blindfold. I said, "Okay, now for the surprise. I'm going to take you somewhere and you can't see where it is until we get there."

She was so overly excited at the prospect of a surprise, I thought she might piss her pants. There was something in how childlike her reaction was that now disgusts me, but at the time I thought it was sweet and lovable and all the shit douchebags like me think about the horrible bitches they've been tricked into believing they're in love with.

So I drove from Fogo de Chão to the swing set behind her mom's house. The sun was going down, so it was getting a little colder. I got a blanket from my trunk and led her by the hand to the swing set. I cannot believe how fucking gay I was. At no point during this entire event did it ever dawn on me that I was being a complete fag.

I laid the blanket out and sat her down and then took off the blindfold. She looked around and it was clear that she was underwhelmed with the locale I chose to deliver her surprise in.

She said, "Oh, why are we here?"

I sat down next to her and prepared to puke out the little speech I had practiced thirty or forty times that morning. I said, "Last summer we spent a lot of time here, and that summer was probably the best one in my life. It just felt so easy and so natural to sit out here and talk with you about nothing all night long. This place is a place that I'll always remember as one where I felt like our love kind of started again. And I'm hoping it'll also be a place that I'll always remember as one where our love became something that would last forever."

I remember Heather looking at me like she didn't know what was going on, even though I thought it was pretty clear at that point. Nonetheless, I finished the rest of my little prepared act, got down on one knee, took the ring out, and said, "Heather, will you marry me?"

She was crying as soon as I got down on one knee, but she was bawling when the ring came out, and she was sobbing to the point of incoherence when she hugged me and said, "Yes. Yes. Yes. Oh my God. I'm engaged. I'm a junior and I'm engaged."

It took me a solid ten minutes of calming her down before she made any sense. The first thing she said that I could understand was, "Oh my God, Kyle, this ring is beautiful."

I noticed at that point that she hadn't looked at me since I put the ring on her finger. She was fucking transfixed by it. She said, "I just, I just like can't believe how amazing it is. How did you find it?"

What she actually meant to ask me was how could I afford it and how much did it cost, but she obviously couldn't cheapen the moment by asking something like that. So she kept the question veiled. So I did the same thing with the answer. I said, "I didn't want to get you anything other than exactly what you wanted, so I looked every day until I found it."

She held it out in front of her and tilted her hand back and forth in the light from a streetlamp that had just turned on. As it sparkled she said, "It's just incredible, Kyle. Really."

I said, "I'm glad you like it," then I kissed her on the cheek but she never stopped looking at that fucking ring. I honestly probably sat there looking at Heather for ten minutes while she stared at that fucking ring in a semi-catatonic state. She finally said, "Oh my God, I have to like tell all the Kappas. They're going to be like so jealous, seriously. Oh my God."

I said, "Can you wait until tomorrow to tell them? I think we should go back to my place and celebrate on our own."

She said, "Oh, for sure. I just kind of wanted to tell everyone, you know?"

I said, "Yeah, I know, but won't it be better if you wait until to-morrow morning when everyone's home? Right now they're all prob-ably out at parties. You should wait until pretty much everyone's in the house, don't you think?"

She said, "Yeah. I guess you're right."

I knew she wanted to show that ring off to her bitchy sorority sisters worse than anything, and I kind of wanted that, too. It was like I said earlier—there was something about Heather showing the bitchy girls in her house that ring that made me feel good, validated in some way, which is so fucking stupid. I can't deny it. Despite all of that, what I wanted more than validation from her sorority sisters was to take Heather back to my apartment and fuck her brains out. I said, "It'll be our first night together as an engaged couple."

She smiled, then gave me a big hug and a kiss and said something that I didn't expect. She said, "I know we started out kind of like rocky and everything our freshman year and part of it was my fault and I'm sorry for everything I did that was mean to you back then." Then she looked me in the eye for the first time since I proposed to her and said, "Kyle, I really do love you more than anything and tonight has made me realize that more than like I ever did. You know?"

I said, "I love you, too."

We kissed each other, got back in my car, and I drove her back to my apartment where I did indeed fuck her brains out. It was incredible. It was like somehow that ring gave her super fucking powers—and I don't mean "fucking" in the adjective form, I mean it in the verb form. She was super at fucking that night. We must have fucked for three or four hours straight and everything she did came with a level of genuine, or least what I perceived to be genuine, enthusiasm. She came three or four times. I did, too. It was probably the best single night of sex I had ever experienced in my life.

When we were too tired to fuck anymore, she curled up next to me and laid her head on my chest. She said, "Where will we live once we're married?"

I said, "Wherever you want," and she went to sleep. I stayed awake for a few more minutes thinking about the whole night, letting it sink in that I was engaged to a girl and every ounce of me was completely in love with her. I haven't felt that content and whole at any other moment in my life. I know it's fucking gay to say, but I went to sleep that night really knowing what it meant to be happy for the first time. As it turned out it was also the last time.

I like don't even know how to describe what it felt like that next morning after Kyle gave me the ring. I guess I remember waking up and he was already gone because he had an early class or something and there was like this little note on the pillow next to me that said like, *To my future wife—I get out of class at 5:30 tonight. Can't wait to hear all about how the other Kappas reacted. I love you. Love, Kyle.*

Seriously it was pretty sweet that he cared about what my sisters thought about me getting engaged and everything. I just like lay in his bed for half an hour or so looking at the ring. It was really pretty. It had like almost every little thing that I had showed him I wanted in a ring. I was completely impressed that he was able to get such a nice ring.

I took a shower and then headed over to the Kappa house hoping that pretty much everyone would be there, because it was early enough in the morning that I didn't think anyone would be at class or anything. When I walked in the living room Gina and Mandy were drinking coffee and checking their e-mail, so I put my hand in my pocket so they couldn't see the ring and I was like, "You guys, I have a seriously big announcement to make to like everyone in the house. Go see who you can get to come down."

They went upstairs and I could hear them waking people up and I was getting really excited. I mean the first time you get to tell all of your friends that you're engaged is like a seriously big deal. So I just kind of waited down at the bottom of the stairs in the main part of the living room and then Gina and Mandy brought down pretty much the entire house, with a few exceptions.

When I saw Andrea walking down the stairs I felt a little bad because I was like basically going to be rubbing it in her face that she had no hope of getting engaged, but it was my day and I knew she'd be happy for me even if she was like a little sad for herself. I waited until everyone was sitting down on the couches and everything and then I tried to get really serious and I was like, "Everyone, something happened to me last night that was like a life-changing event and I wanted to tell you guys first."

I could see a few girls were starting to look like worried. Like I bet they thought it was going to be something seriously bad like an OD or something. Then I pulled out my ring hand and held it up so they could all see and I was like, "I'm engaged!" Everybody seriously went fucking crazy. I was like easily the youngest girl in the house to be engaged and I could tell some of the girls were jealous but most of them were just happy for me. Andrea even came over and gave me a big hug and was like, "I'm so happy for you," and she was crying and everything. I think she was crying a little bit for herself, though. Whatever. It was still a nice gesture I guess.

Everyone wanted to know like how he did it and everything and I told them about how he blindfolded me and took me to the swing set behind my house and how sweet he was about it and everything. And then of course everyone was dying to see the ring. They were all really impressed. It wasn't like huge or anything but it wasn't small either and it was just so pretty.

When Harlow saw it she said, "Wow, that's really pretty. When are you getting it appraised?"

I was like, "You mean for insurance purposes?"

And we all laughed and then I was like, "Maybe later today if anyone wants to come with me."

Harlow was like, "Yeah, I'll go."

I was going to ask Andrea if she wanted to come, but I thought that might be like rubbing it in her face even more than I already had. So I figured if she wanted to go she would.

I set up an appraisal appointment and that afternoon I skipped my child behavior class and went to Robbins Bros. with Gina, Harlow, Mandy, and Sarah. The ride there was seriously like almost as much fun as actually getting proposed to. We were all like singing to Justin Timberlake and everything and it was just really fun for us all. And that ride in that car was pretty much like the very last thing I did while I was still in love with Kyle.

We went into the store and I found the lady I had talked to on the phone earlier that day and I showed her my ring. And it didn't even take her like two seconds of looking at it to be like, "Oh honey, I . . ."

I was like, "What?"

She was like, "Honey, that's . . . your ring isn't a diamond. It's a cubic zirconia."

I swear to fucking God, I wished a terrorist would have done a suicide bomb in that Robbins Bros. at that very moment.

I mean can you imagine? I was there with four of my sorority sisters, basically like my closest friends on the planet, on what was supposed to be like the happiest day of my life, and right in front of them and the whole store, which had like two other people in it, I found out that my engagement ring wasn't a diamond. I have never felt that mortified in my entire life and I'm sure I never will again because that's the worst thing that anyone has ever done to me or will ever do to me.

Seriously I would have rather had like one hundred abortions than to find out right in front of my sisters that my engagement ring wasn't real. I just started crying, like worse than I've ever cried in my life. Harlow and Gina and everyone were really supportive. They all hugged me and told me it was going to be okay. Gina was even like, "Maybe Kyle didn't know. Maybe he got ripped off," which didn't even really matter to me. The fact was still that my engagement ring was complete crap.

The woman at Robbins Bros. was like, "I can still appraise it if you'd like."

For fucking real?

I was like, "Uh . . . I don't think that'll be necessary."

We all got back in my car and it was the worst drive home from anyplace that I've ever had in my life. Nobody said anything. I looked at like Harlow and Mandy in the backseat a few times and they were staring out the windows. They couldn't even bring themselves to make eye contact with me in the rearview mirror.

When we got back to the house, I just went to my room and shut the door. Harlow, Gina, Mandy, and Sarah started telling everyone the bad news, and so I wouldn't have to deal with anyone else I asked them to tell everyone that I just wanted to be left alone for a little while.

Once I got to my room, I kind of figured out that I wasn't really sad anymore. Instead, I was like seriously fucking furious. I hated Kyle's guts more than anything. It was so weird that like the day right before that I had loved him more than anything in the world, but then it's like I found out my love was all based on a lie, on his lie, and everything I felt for him just disappeared. When I thought about him all I felt was rage. I wanted to tear his fucking head off.

chapter
fifteen

I hadn't heard from Kyle since the night of the actual proposal. He called to tell me she accepted and he was engaged. He told me I was the second call he made after his parents, who he admitted were less than thrilled, as was I, although I congratulated him. It was only one day after that phone call, so I assumed he and Heather were more than likely so enamored with each other at that point that they wouldn't be coming up for air anytime soon. Little did I, or anyone else for that matter, predict the hurricane of shit that was headed our way in the form of Heather's unbridled anger.

But one day before that hurricane of shit, I found myself at the Alpha Tau Omega house drinking to excess and listening to Greg talk about his postgraduation plans. He had interned at my father's company the summer prior and I was aware that his ultimate goal was to acquire a junior position at a company in Dallas that was of a certain size and level of prestige in the business world and would inflate his already bloated sense of self-worth. It wasn't until ten or fifteen minutes into his delivery of a monologue about how easy he assumed it would be to force anal sex on any female subordinate in the business world that he divulged he had acquired an offer for employment at my father's company.

Upon graduation he would be given the title of junior regional sales representative at Keller Shipping. I wasn't fully aware of what that title entailed, but I assumed it would come with minimal responsibility and moderate compensation. Neither of these assumptions bothered me. The unalterable fact that Greg would be an employee at my father's company, however, did more than just bother me. As I stood there drinking beer from a keg in the basement of the same frat house in which my father and his father before him had done the exact same thing, and watched Greg fist-bump the other members of Alpha Tau Omega whose fathers and fathers' fathers had all done the same thing, I knew the chain had to be broken. The dull hatred I had developed for this meaningless repetition of the same lives led by different generations, and all the people who gave in to it, sharpened to a fine point in that moment and I knew that there was something I could do to alter the course, even if that alteration was slight.

I could have withdrawn from it all. On that night I could have told my father that I wanted no part in the life he had manufactured for me from the plan of his father. I could have been done with it and never thought twice. But I felt some need to take firmer action as I watched Greg repeat what I was certain were the same actions of his predecessors—the shirtless chest-beating, the keg stands, the refusal even to entertain the idea of a unique experience, or worse yet the unyielding belief that each experience was unique, never even realizing he was merely mimicking those who had come before him. I could not sit by idly and watch it all happen again. I felt a need to destroy some piece of it all, was not content to just turn away. And on that night Greg was that piece.

I knew that proximity to me was all that was really required for Greg to initiate what would become his own undoing and I was prepared to make the sacrifice that I knew would come with this course of action. A small circle of Alpha Tau Omegas had gathered around

Greg, listening to his predictions of how fast he would rise through my father's company and then eventually form his own or, at the very least, jump to another company as a VP of sales in less than three years' time. They listened to him promise them all jobs under him at whatever company he chose to call his final home. They listened to him describe in detail all the cars he was going to own and where his first house would be located. I joined the circle and, as predicted, he filled me in on his new job, adding something in the phrasing that was subtly demeaning, something that let everyone in the room know he was technically my superior in Alpha Tau Omega and that, even after he graduated, he'd still hold some position over me, at least in his eyes, by being an employee of my father before I was. I failed to see the logic, but nonetheless set my plan in motion.

I conceded that Greg was indeed the president of Alpha Tau Omega, and that he would indeed be employed at my father's company at least a year before I would, and then I told him that there would be one thing I would always have over him. When he asked me what that was, I told him I meant the stink of his sister's asshole on my dick. Everyone laughed, thinking this was a joke, until I produced the pictures—causing Greg to lose control and punch me in the face three times before I fell down, whereupon he proceeded to punch me several more times.

No one had the wherewithal to know how to react, or—perhaps more disturbing—no one cared to intervene, not sure who in the situation held more power and therefore who should be supported in the conflict. I offered no defense in the fight, knowing that with each successive strike to my face Greg made a fate for himself that was more and more inescapable.

His rage subsided after a dozen or so strikes. I wasn't unconscious but certainly wasn't possessed of all my faculties. Even in that disconnected mental state I could tell that Greg had realized his error. He immediately began a flurry of apologies to me and begged me not to relay the events of the night to my father. I felt something so calm in that moment, so certain, that my only reaction to his begging was to promise him he was going to be better off, to tell him that he never really wanted to work for my father, that the life this event would eventually force him into living would be much more interesting and fulfilling. Then I got up off the ground and went to the bathroom to clean my face.

The sad thing about Greg's begging me not to tell my father was that he didn't realize I never even had to tell him. Word of Greg's attack on my person spread so fast, merely because I was my father's son, that it seemed as though the entire campus was aware of it by morning, and by mid-afternoon the fathers of everyone who worked with my father knew about it, and then so too did my father. Greg's prewritten future at Keller Shipping and consequently the connected events that would have been influenced by that position were all erased. This was my first step toward creating something for myself.

chapter sixteen

I knew something was up before Heather even came over that next morning. I tried to call her a few times the night before and she never called back. I thought that was pretty weird, considering we'd been engaged for less than forty-eight hours at that point, but I convinced myself that she'd probably been celebrating with her sorority sisters or something and was passed out drunk or just exhausted.

I was at my apartment already, and I knew she got out of class at four, so I took a shower and was hoping we could have sex as soon as she walked in the door. Instead I got the opposite of sex.

She walked in and said, "You fucking asshole. How could you?"

I honestly had no idea what she was talking about based on how enraged she seemed. In my mind the fact that her ring was a cubic zirconia wouldn't have warranted the reaction she was having.

I said, "What's wrong?"

Then I noticed she wasn't wearing the ring, and it really was like in the movies, when everything starts moving in slow motion because the main character realizes he's about to be in a world of shit. My head started throbbing, my heart pounded, I broke out in a cold sweat—the whole nine.

When she took the ring out of her pocket and said, "This is what's wrong, you piece of shit," then threw it at me, I thought it was best to just tell the truth. How mad could she be? Turns out, pretty fucking mad.

I said, "I didn't have enough money to get the real thing, but once I got the money I was going to replace it, or even get you a bigger one. I didn't think it was that big of a deal."

She said, "*Not that big of a deal?* Do you realize I went to have it appraised with four of my sisters? Do you know how embarrassing it was to sit there and have like this old lady tell me *my ring was fake?*"

I said, "You had it appraised? Why?"

She said, "For insurance purposes. It's like what you're supposed to do."

I said, "Really?"

She said, "Yes, you idiot. Maybe if you had known that you would have actually not been so cheap and gotten me a real ring."

I said, "So cheap? Heather, I have no money. It wasn't a matter of being cheap. More than anything I wanted to ask you to be my wife. What else was I supposed to do with no money?"

She said, "Uh . . . get a second job or something. I don't know. That's not my problem. My problem is that I'm basically like the laughingstock of the whole school."

I said, "But it's just a ring. I'm sure no one cares. It's just supposed to be a symbol anyway. Two nights ago, when I gave it to you, you were the happiest girl in the world."

She said, "That's when I thought it was a real diamond."

I said, "But that's what I'm saying to you, it doesn't matter if it's real or not. All that matters is that I gave it to you and it means that we're engaged. That's what made you happy, right? It wasn't the fact that you thought it was a real diamond, was it?"

She said, "It doesn't even matter what made me so happy. It's all completely fucked up now."

I said, "I really am sorry. I didn't know it was going to be such a big deal."

She said, "Such a big deal? Kyle, it's my fucking engagement ring. It's basically like the biggest deal in a girl's life and you turned it all into pure shit."

I tried to hug her but she pushed me away and said, "Don't touch me."

I said, "Come on, I'll get you a real ring if you want one. It's not going to be as big or as nice, and you might have to wait until next year sometime, but I'll save up and I'll get you one."

She said, "You don't get it, do you?"

I said, "I guess not. What's the deal?"

She said, "The deal is, asshole, we're through."

I actually thought I misheard her. The idea that she was dumping me—the guy who only two days before she had loved more than anything in the world—because I'd given her a cubic zirconia instead of an actual diamond was beyond insane to me. I really did believe that she loved me and that what would make her happy was being engaged to me. I thought that's all that mattered to her. But as I stood there looking at her eyes, so full of hate for me I could feel it, I realized she never really gave a shit about me through any of it.

I had once had a suspicion that she'd started dating me to get close to Brett. I got over that. When we got back together after the breakup, I assumed it was because she had real feelings for me, because she loved me. But in that moment when I looked at the ring I'd bought her lying on the floor at my feet, I knew she'd gotten back together with me because I was just the easiest means to a desirable end. She wasn't even crying.

Even if there's animosity between people when a relationship ends, it seems like if they had feelings for one another, actual feelings, there should be crying for the loss of something that was good for at least a little while. Heather didn't cry once that night. She just stared at me like I'd shat on her pillow.

I said, "You're breaking up with me over this?"

She said, "What else am I supposed to do?"

I said, "Marry me like you said you would two days ago."

She said, "Kyle, that ring—I mean, our entire relationship is based on that ring and the ring is a lie."

I said, "That ring has only been in our relationship for two fucking days. It's impossible for our relationship to be based on it."

She said, "No, Kyle, it's like that ring is what the entire relationship was about—you know like getting to the point where you would give it to me. And that point is fake, it's a lie. It's not like we can go on from this point and just pretend this didn't happen."

I said, "The ring doesn't fucking matter. We love each other."

She said—and this was the one that really fucking killed me—she said, "No, Kyle, I loved the guy who gave me a diamond ring. I hate the one who gave me a fucking cubic zirconia." Then she walked out.

I wanted to puke, shit my pants, stab myself in the heart with an ice pick, anything that would make me feel something different than what I was feeling. In my head I went through the entire sequence of events that had to happen to lead to Heather dumping me, and I blamed myself for making the wrong choice in every case. I should have listened to Brett when he said to wait. I should have just bought a cheap diamond ring. I should have asked my parents for help. I should have taken out a loan. There were so many things I could have done to keep her and I did none of them.

I sat on my couch and cried that night. I know it's more gay than anything I had done up to that point, but I fucking cried my eyes out. I really thought I was lucky enough to find the girl who was the one for me; then I was lucky enough to get her; then, even after we broke up, I was lucky enough to get her back. After all the shit we had been through I still felt like the luckiest guy on the planet. But after that night I was positive about two things. I realized the Heather I loved, the one I thought loved me, never really existed. She was always just putting up some kind of smoke screen. And, even worse, Heather was gone forever. And, even though I knew she wasn't the girl I thought she was, that was the worst feeling in the fucking world, so I cried.

I seriously went through like all the same stages a person goes through when somebody dies. At first I like denied that the ring was fake, then I like accepted it, and then I got seriously pissed off, and then I thought dumping Kyle would make me accept everything and move on, but it didn't.

The next morning after I broke up with him I came downstairs into the kitchen and pretty much all of my sisters were there. They all found out what happened and they were all actually really nice, Andrea especially. I guess because we were going through basically the exact same thing, except she didn't get humiliated in a Robbins Bros. But on the flip side I guess I was still a junior so I still had a little bit of time to try and find somebody. She only had a semester left. But it wasn't like the extra year was all that much. We all knew who the eligible guys were that were floating around the dating pool and they were all still eligible for a reason. They kind of like all sucked.

Anyway, everyone had made me a cake and gotten me cards and flowers and everything and they were all just really nice about the whole thing. Even Jenna was like, "I don't care how good he is in bed, I wouldn't fuck him now if he was the last guy on earth." I thought that was sweet.

We made mojitos and anyone who didn't have class stuck around for brunch and I started to feel a little better about the whole thing. You know, like my life wasn't completely over. Then Kyle called me. I shouldn't have taken the call, but I was curious to hear what he had to say. At that point I hadn't necessarily ruled out the possibility of getting back together with him if he could make things right. But he'd have to really make them right, like when that one basketball player anally raped that girl and then bought his wife a four-million-dollar ring— that kind of right.

So I went up to my room and took his call.

He was like, "Heather, I don't believe you really don't want to see me ever again. How can you go from loving someone to never wanting to see them again in twenty-four hours?"

I was like, "Twenty-four hours—it was more like twenty-four seconds as soon as I found out you lied to me about my ring."

He was like, "I never lied to you. I never said it was a real diamond."

I was like, "When you put it on my finger you implied it was real, you fucking asshole."

He was like, "Heather, I love you more than anything. I don't know how else to say it and I'm sorry and I know you still love me, too. This is all just ridiculous."

When he said that, I remember thinking to myself that he was wrong. I didn't love him anymore. I mean on that actual phone call I remember thinking about why I ever started dating him in the first place and it was like seriously easy for me to get back to that emotional state, you know like just completely not caring about him. And that was actually easier to deal with than the anger and like the hatred I felt for him when I thought about the fake ring and everything.

So I was like, "No, you know what's ridiculous is that you think this is ridiculous. Kyle, that ring might have been like a symbol or whatever to you and not that big of a deal, but it was really important to me, like the most important thing in our relationship, and if something that important to me doesn't even fucking matter to you, then there's no reason we should like stay together."

He was like, "That doesn't even make sense."

I was like, "Yeah, it does."

Then he didn't say anything for a while and then he was like, "I love you."

And I was like, "Bye," then I hung up on him. I thought he would try to call back, but he never did. I went downstairs and finished brunch with the girls who were there and as we were eating it started to sink in. I would probably never see Kyle again. He was a part of my life for like three years off and on and I really thought I would end up with him. Once I realized that I just started freaking out and crying.

Gina was like, "It's okay, you're going to find some other guy who's like a million times better for you and you'll be fine."

She didn't get it. I knew I was kind of under the gun a little bit to find a new guy and everything, but I was crying because I felt like I'd wasted all of that time with Kyle. I mean seriously, I only really dated two guys in college and they both turned out to be dicks. I mean they were dicks for different reasons, but they were both dicks. I gave some blowjobs here and there to other guys, but I should have been out there playing the field, finding like the best guy at SMU to marry, and instead I pretty much wasted my entire time there. That's why I was crying.

And then, also, like every guy at school pretty much was going to find out about why I was single if they didn't already know and none of them were going to want to like date me or anything. I mean, I really thought Kyle might have totally fucked me in terms of being able to find a new guy before graduation. I guess I was crying a little bit because of that, too. I just remember thinking that the first day of my freshman year there was no doubt in my mind that by the time I graduated I would have found a really great guy who was going to have a really great job who would propose to me with a real fucking ring, and it looked like none of that was even close to happening with like less than three semesters left in the whole thing.

I calmed down enough to drink like twenty more mojitos and pass out in the middle of the day. That's really the only choice I had.

chapter
eighteen

My wounds weren't significant enough to require any type of medical attention—no stitches, no salves, et cetera, but I was left with a black eye, which was a first for me. I enjoyed its novelty. It seemed to attract even more attention from the whores and cunts around campus.

I wasn't sure how any of the events of that night would affect Greg socially. I, of course, hoped for a social version of the same outcome he received from my father's company—a complete erasure of all connection and of any future prospect for any kind of involvement. My hopes were well met with the reality that followed. Greg had intermittently dated a girl named Michelle Rowanson for the majority of his four years at SMU. He had taken their brief times apart to fuck as many whores as he could until Michelle would ultimately come to the conclusion that she should forgive him for whatever transgression he may have been responsible for. In their time together Greg had been caught fucking one of Michelle's sorority sisters in a back room at Michelle's own birthday party, he had hidden her car keys in her vagina while she was nearly comatose from alcohol poisoning, and he had placed his own feces in the microwave at Michelle's sorority house and set the microwave to five hours before leaving, among other similar depraved acts. She forgave him for all of these things, but in the matter of his attack on me it seemed she wouldn't return a single phone call.

This type of treatment wasn't delivered to Greg by Michelle only. It seemed that within forty-eight hours of the event virtually every whore on campus had labeled him a pariah and so too had every guy. In his final semester as the president of Alpha Tau Omega and as a student at SMU Greg was crippled. I was pleased with the outcome.

I was sitting in my room at the Alpha Tau Omega house thinking about how masterfully I had destroyed him when our doorbell rang and I heard Alan Raggermore answer the door, followed by what I thought was Kyle's voice asking if I was present. I went downstairs to find that I was correct. Kyle stood in the doorway looking like he had just seen his mother and father murdered and had then been forced to fuck their corpses. Aside from the look on his face, I knew the situation to be dire based on his presence at the Alpha Tau Omega house. Kyle despised everything that had to do with the Greek system at SMU and would stop at nothing to be completely untainted by it. Appearing at the door of an actual fraternity house unannounced just to talk to a friend meant the world's end must have been close at hand for Kyle. Indeed it was.

I took him up to my room, where he proceeded to divulge to me all the details of the past forty-eight hours between him and Heather. I learned of the proposal and acceptance and I learned of the following day's events that led Heather to have the ring appraised—this, by the way, made me hate that cunt with more venom than I've ever conjured for anyone—and I learned of her subsequent decision to dissolve their relationship based on the pretense that she viewed their relationship to be too intertwined with falsehood to continue. If my father had ever employed a contract killer of whom I was aware, I would have given him a job opportunity then and there.

To see my best friend in shambles again, much worse than the first time, was almost too much to bear. I did feel genuine empathy for him.

I had gone through the cheering-up phase once before—the waiting for him to have a certain amount of time to grieve, the conversations assuring him that all would turn out just fine, the setting him up with a whore into whom he could spill his seed in order to ease his mind, et cetera. I knew that I would be able to tolerate all of that again.

As Kyle recounted the final moments of his and Heather's final conversation, I was fully prepared to not talk to Kyle for a month or so until he had worked through whatever horrible emotional bullshit he needed to. I was very pleasantly surprised, however, when at the conclusion of his description of their relationship's end he looked me in the eye, with no trace of tears or sorrow—with quite a chilling stare, actually—and proceeded to explain that he was done with it all. He claimed he was through with love and he wanted to fuck as many whores as me, never the same one twice. He refused to allow himself to go through this same terrible emotional experience that one girl had put him through twice. He reasoned that any relationship he might get into in the future would only yield the same outcome. To illustrate his point, he even used a line that I've always been fond of: "All things end."

I promised Kyle that I would fill his cup until it overflowed with cunts and whores of all shapes and sizes. I assured him that no matter how savage his thirst for nameless fucking I would eventually slake it. And if it could not be slaked then I would have a brother in arms until our dying days. I wanted to tell him that I knew this was a phase, a visceral reaction to the pain Heather made him feel. I wanted to tell him that after he fucked three or four whores, his old desire for love and stability would come back to him. I wanted to tell him these things, but I couldn't because I didn't believe they were true.

I remembered when he first asked me to set him up with a cunt to fuck without emotion a few semesters prior. Despite the fact that he went through with the act, there was still a spark in his eye, some glimmer of his true self both before and after he fucked the whore in my guest room. That glimmer was gone this time and in its place was something very familiar to me—a complete lack of caring for any being with a vagina. He didn't yet have the contempt, but he had no concern for them, no sense of equality or respect. It seemed as though he viewed them only as holes to put his dick in, which was, to my mind, the first step to true social enlightenment for any man.

I regretted not being able to help him on that night, as I had previously agreed to meet my father for dinner and talk to him about the events that had transpired with Greg. I ended up using that conversation to make certain Greg was blacklisted at a minimum of a dozen other Fortune 500 companies headquartered in Texas.

Instead, I assured Kyle, the following night I would help him celebrate his birth into true manhood by rounding up some willing whores. He seemed happy, as was I. Throughout the entirety of our friendship I had made countless attempts at changing Kyle's mind about whores. I had tried every technique I could think of to make him understand, as I did, the disposable nature of their entire gender. The irony was that, where I had failed in doing this, a cunt succeeded more supremely than I ever possibly could have.

chapter
nineteen

I guess I had never felt that empty before. Nothing mattered to me after Heather dumped me. I still went to my classes, but it was all robotic to me. I didn't retain much of what I was supposed to be learning. I just memorized, spit it out for a test, and then forgot it. I was used to making the best grade in every class I had taken up to that point, but I started to slip a little. I still made good enough grades to get by, but I wasn't the best in any of my classes by the end of that second semester.

I took the MCAT in April, which was the norm for everyone who intended to go to med school, and actually did really well. I should have also been volunteering at a hospital or something at some point in my junior year, but I just couldn't bring myself to give a shit. I applied to all the med schools in Texas through the AMCAS and even though I didn't have the extracurricular shit on my resume, my MCAT score was high enough to get into UT at Houston, which kind of surprised me. I knew I did well on the verbal reasoning and the essay and the biological science, but in the physical science specifically there were some inorganic chemistry questions that I really thought I fucked up. But I ended up pulling out a thirty-nine on the multiple choice parts—fourteen on verbal reasoning, twelve in physical science, and thirteen in organic science. And I got an R on the essay. So I didn't really have to worry that much about med school as long as I didn't flunk out my senior year. It seemed like that part of my life was all taken care of, which left me with a lot more time to hang out with Brett.

Brett was probably the worst friend I could have had around that time. He was there for me and everything and always hung out with me whenever I asked him to, so he was a great friend in that respect. But it was like I was a guy who said to his best friend, "Hey, my life really sucks, all I want to do is smoke crack," and the best friend was the biggest crack dealer on the face of the planet, with every kind of crack you can imagine and some kinds you can't, and that best friend said, "Lucky for you, I'll give you anything you want for free."

In the months after the breakup there were maybe three or four nights I didn't spend at Brett's house fucking some stupid girl who thought that by fucking me she could fuck Brett. The story of my fake diamond ring proposal had spread around campus, and almost every girl, at least every girl who was in a sorority, knew exactly who I was and what I had done. I almost became something of a strange pseudo-celebrity on campus. The more I hung out with Brett and adopted his lifestyle, the more this became the case, and the more I embraced it. I still wasn't matching Brett's numbers, but I do remember a girl who I had just fucked in Brett's downstairs kitchen saying, "I can't believe I just like had sex with you."

I said, "Why?"

She said, "You're like the guy who proposed with a fake ring. You're kind of like the ultimate bad boy or something, you know?"

I always thought that was funny. The worst thing these girls could think of a guy doing wasn't dealing drugs or raping somebody or even killing somebody—it was proposing to a girl with a fucking cubic zirconia.

I know it didn't really address all of the shit I was dealing with, but having sex with those girls just made it easy to coast and not feel and not think and that's really all I wanted to do. I purposely stayed away from any places where I knew I would have a higher probability of accidentally seeing Heather, and I got drunk with Brett a lot, and I had sex with the nameless girls he would set up for me. That's really all I did until the end of that semester. And I know it probably sounds like it was really fun, but it wasn't. And I know that by admitting that, I'm a fucking pussy.

I remember there was one moment toward the end of that semester when I almost pulled myself out of it all—just another one of those moments in this whole shitty story where everything could have turned around and the end could have been avoided, but that's not how it worked out. It was late, I was drunk, I had just had anal sex with some girl in Brett's hot tub because he said to her, "If you don't let my friend put his dick in your ass you have to hit the fucking road and I'm not paying for a cab." This poor girl clearly didn't want to do it. Don't get the wrong idea, it wasn't rape or anything—she just obviously didn't want to have anal sex. But she let me do it because of Brett and I did it because I just fucking hated everything and thought I could be Brett, at least in terms of how I looked at girls and relationships and everything, if I did the shit he did.

So anyway I had just had anal sex with that girl, and then she and probably three or four other girls stayed downstairs with Brett, and I think that night he made them eat slices of Velveeta out of each other's vaginas or something. That might not have been it, but it was something really disgusting like that. I went upstairs because I had gotten drunk enough to pass out and I just wanted to sleep. I did a lot of that, too—drinking myself to sleep, I mean.

I was in bed, the room was spinning, and I took out my cell phone and started looking through the contacts, not because I was thinking of calling anyone, but because for some reason staring at ordered text helps calm down the spins when I'm that drunk. So I was scrolling up and down through the contacts and I came to Erin. As soon as I saw her name I just hit the call button. It must have been three in the morning.

I had no idea what I was going to say, and even if I would have had an idea I was way too drunk for it to have mattered. Her phone went straight to voice mail, which meant she was probably asleep and had it turned off, but in my drunken state all I could think was that she was probably fucking some guy, which kind of made me mad, but then I rethought it. Erin wasn't the type of girl to just fuck random guys. I remember thinking she was probably asleep in bed with a guy she really loved, a guy who could have been me if I hadn't fucked everything up. It wasn't like I still loved her or anything; I didn't and I recognized that. But I felt like I could have if I'd given it a chance, or if I'd known what the outcome with Heather would have been. I felt like she was the girl I was supposed to end up with, but it was too far beyond repair to even entertain talking to her about it.

Again, I was drunk, so keep that in mind when I say that, as the beep went off and her voice mail started recording my message, all I could do was cry again. I know, I know. Even recounting that night now makes me feel like a pussy and I guess I was. Everything just seemed so hopeless and I guess Erin kind of represented the last bit of that hope fading away into nothing for me.

The next morning I woke up with a massive hangover, and as Brett and I were eating breakfast in his backyard Erin sent me a text message saying, "Got your message last night. Were you drunk?" I never responded and she never contacted me again. Again, I was a massive pussy.

I finished out that semester with okay grades in all my classes, and the overall number of girls I had had sex with was probably multiplied by twenty-five. I had achieved a level of numbness and apathy about virtually everything in my life that made it much easier to forget about how happy I was with Heather and how I would probably never be that happy again.

I know it was like seriously one of the most stupid things I could have done, but I was like seriously desperate once it got to the point of there being like only a month or so left in the semester. I mean, I had tried to hook up with like every single guy at every party I went to, but it was like they had all heard about the fake ring and they all like thought I was just looking for a guy to propose to me with a real diamond. So like pretty much every guy I hooked up with that semester just hooked up with me once and then never called me again. It was fucking miserable and it made me hate Kyle even more for forcing me to be in that situation.

I had no idea what I was going to do about finding a guy before the end of that year so I called up Brian and was like, "Hey, we haven't talked in a long time and I thought you might want to go get some lunch or something."

He was like, "For real?"

And I was like, "Yeah, for real."

I never really ate at Mac's Place, but I was still like seriously fucking furious at Kyle for giving me a fake ring, so I thought it would be a nice fuck-you to him if I showed up with Brian while he was working so he could see us together. But when we got there Kyle wasn't even working. Whatever.

So we sat down and Brian was like, "So what's up? How have you been and everything?"

I was like, "Fine. How about you?"

He was like, "Pretty good. You know, just getting geared up for finals."

I was like, "Yeah, me too," even though two out of my five classes didn't even have finals and one of the other three that did was my second field experience class, and the final was just getting the teacher whose class we sat in on for the whole semester to write an evaluation of how well we observed their class.

He was like, "Look, you know I'm really sorry for everything that went down between us, right?"

I was like, "I don't even care. It was no big deal."

He was like, "Oh, cool. For real, that's how I felt about it, but it seemed like you were kind of agro or something."

I was like, "Oh, weird. I wasn't."

He was like, "Then why did you never call me back?"

I was like, "I was just busy and everything and I thought it was better if we just kind of like cooled off for a little while and everything. I guess I just like didn't really want to be dating anybody at that point, you know?"

He was like, "But you got back together with your old ex-boyfriend."

I was like, "Yeah, it just happened that way I guess."

He was like, "Okay, but didn't he propose to you with a fake ring or something not that long ago?"

I was like, "It was like two and a half months ago. How did you hear about that?"

He was like, "Everybody heard about. It was like legendary. For real."

Then we just sat there for a few minutes like not even saying any-thing and finally he was like, "So, why'd you ask me out to lunch?"

I was like, "You know, I just haven't like seen you in a long time and I was just wondering how things were going. Really, I just like kind of wanted to catch up."

He was like, "For real? There's no other reason?"

I was like, "Well, are you like seeing anybody or anything?"

He was like, "Why are you asking me that?"

I was like, "I don't know. I just remember we had some pretty good times and everything and I was thinking maybe we could like give it another shot or something, you know?"

He was like, "You want to just jump back into it and be a couple and everything again, for real?"

It had been a while since the whole thing with him and Josh hap-pened, and if I thought about it too much it seriously made me ill, but the way I saw it I really had no other choice. If I didn't have a boyfriend, like a serious boyfriend, by the time senior year started, I'd end up like Andrea and be completely fucked by the time I graduated. Brian wasn't that bad of a guy except for that one night. I figured I could just get over it. But when he was like, "You want to just jump back into it and be a couple and everything again, for real?" I guess it was the first time I really thought about what that meant, you know, that I was basically putting all my eggs in that basket and hoping he would ask me to marry him at some point in our senior year.

I knew he'd wind up with a good job and he'd probably be a good husband and everything, but then I was like what if he still hangs out with Josh and one night they're drunk and they try to do that again and it was just beyond gross. Still, there were no other guys that would even entertain the idea of doing anything with me at that point except hooking up once and then never talking to me again, so he was a step up from that. And I figured worst-case scenario if something happened with Josh again or if Brian was just being a serious dick or whatever I could dump him and be no worse off than I already was.

So I was like, "Yeah, like we just pick up where we left off."

He was like, "Heather, I have a girlfriend."

I was like, "Who?"

He was like, "Annie."

I was like, "I just saw her not that long ago. She said you guys just dated for a little while and that was it."

He was like, "Yeah, but then a few months ago we started getting pretty serious."

I was like, "Like seriously?"

He was like, "For real."

I could not fucking believe it—even fucking Annie had someone. I'm not saying Annie was like a bad person or anything, but of all the girls who I thought might be okay with not having a guy going into their senior year I thought Annie would be that girl. She was always like so independent and never really cared too much about marriage, or at least never talked about it that much our freshman year, but I guess I didn't either. Whatever. As I sat there across from Brian in fucking Mac's Place, where Kyle wasn't even working, I started to think there was like no way I was going to find a guy who would propose to me, like with a real ring, by graduation the next year. It totally fucking sucked.

And then to make shit even like worse than I could have imagined, with about a month and a half left in the semester Andrea's ex-boyfriend's girlfriend died in this really shitty car crash with three Chi-Os. She was driving and was supposedly drunk and everything and it sucked but I didn't really know them that well so what sucked more for me was that Ron like immediately called up Andrea crying and everything and she helped him through it and within like two weeks he supposedly like realized how much he loved her and how important she was to him and everything and he fucking proposed to her on graduation day.

So I went from being the only junior in the house with an engagement ring to being like the only girl on campus who no guy would even consider marrying and Andrea went from having no chance at finding a guy to getting proposed to. It just didn't seem all that fair, you know? Needless to say I wasn't named the Kappa president.

The months that followed the demise of Kyle and Heather's relationship were strange for me. Kyle had been my friend for most of my life, and for the portion of that life in which we had taken an interest in cunts he had always been the one of the two of us to insist that there was meaning to be found in a relationship with a cunt beyond sexual gratification. He was always the one of the two of us to believe in the lie of love. Although I enjoyed the version of Kyle who was more in keeping with my own outlook on whores and their purpose in this world, it was slightly unsettling to witness the core identity of my best friend become so drastically altered.

I embraced it, though, and made it my goal to give to Kyle everything he had not allowed me to in the previous years of our friendship. Any and every kind of cunt he could imagine was his for the taking in the last half of that semester. The strange thing is that he didn't seem to enjoy it. Don't mistake that: He clearly enjoyed all of these cunts enough to maintain an erection and use it to its intended purpose on each of the cunts that I delivered to him. When I say that he didn't enjoy it, I mean that there was something missing from his interactions with these whores that I was used to in myself I suppose. Where I found amusement in these activities he seemed to find none.

His drinking escalated as well in those months. I had no real problem with this other than the previously stated drastic and slightly unsettling change that I was witnessing in my best friend. I did my fair share of drinking, but again where I found amusement he seemed to find none, which led me to question why he was doing any of these things at all. But I never questioned Kyle's new approach to life very thoroughly or for any extended period of time. I was, instead, thankful that he had finally come to accept the truest notion of what women were—meaningless whores, each one no different than any other, best used as tools for amusement and nothing more.

Other than my escapades with Kyle, the only other thing that happened to me of note during that semester, aside from the incident with Greg, of course, was my election into the seat of Alpha Tau Omega president. It was never really questioned by anyone in the fraternity that I would ultimately be named its president in my senior year, including myself I suppose. It was strange to me that the year before I had come to the decision to detach myself from the life my father had set out for me, to tell him how I felt about it and try to create something for myself in this life that was my own—and yet there I stood in the living room of the Alpha Tau Omega house being named the organization's new president just as my father had and just as his father had.

As Greg passed the torch begrudgingly on to me it seemed less difficult than it should have been for me to accept it all. Again, I felt comfortable in the fact that I had made the decision to end my participation in it all at some point—so comfortable that I was able to remain a willing participant. In retrospect, I don't know that I'll ever understand that reasoning again. It seems so foreign to me now.

As I was named the president, I made one final vow to myself—that by next year's end, sometime before I graduated, I would tell my father I could not work for his company.

summer

I didn't have the money to stay in my apartment over the summer, so I cut a deal with my landlord to sublet it until the next semester started up and then I'd come back. I got the same job at the same movie theater and I went out with Brett every night. My parents seemed to be worried about me. I guess they hadn't really seen me on a day-to-day basis since Heather dumped me and I probably didn't seem like myself to them. They cut me some slack, though, because of my MCAT score and my acceptance into UT Houston's med school. I ended up having sex that summer in one of the projection rooms with a girl who worked at the movie theater who was only seventeen. I didn't know it at the time, but when I found out I didn't really care. It was a fucking crime, a literal fucking crime, and I didn't care. That should have tipped me off to the fact that I was fucking losing it, but like I said, I just didn't care about that or about anything. I had one more year left. I thought if I could just get through that, graduate, and then start med school in Houston, I'd snap out of it and everything would be fine. That's what I thought.

My summer was seriously like the worst one I ever had in my entire life. I had like no one to do anything with. I hung out with my mom like almost every day and she was always like, "It's not the end of the world if you don't have a boyfriend." And I was always like, "If I graduate without one, how am I ever going to find a guy to marry?" And she was always like, "I think you'll be okay." She just like didn't get it at all. Andrea had like this huge engagement party that I went to and it was seriously hard to sit through. I was pretty much like the only girl there who wasn't engaged or already married and since most of the guests were Kappas or girls from other sororities they like all knew my story and everything. A couple of them who were like graduates from a few years before even knew about it. It was seriously horrible. I had like no idea what I was going to do going into senior year.

That summer for me included a discovery that would change my life forever. One night, while Kyle and I were relaxing at my house with some sluts from Brookhaven Community College, I happened across a website called cat69.com. It was run by a company called Viking's Resort, which sold packaged vacations to a private island in the Caribbean. This vacation, however, was unlike any other I was aware of. Their island was populated only by "escorts," or so the website touted. The island had a golf course and a five-star hotel and only a handful of men were ever allowed on the island at any given time. Different packages included the ability to be entertained by various numbers of "escorts" through your stay. That night I booked the first available opening for myself. I assumed Kyle would want to go, given his new outlook on whores, but when I extended the offer to him he refused, citing that he didn't know if he could bring himself to fuck an actual whore. This was proof to me that somewhere within him was a kernel of his old self.

part four
senior year

chapter one

I'd made it through so much shit with Heather and all I would have had to do was make it through one more fucking year and I would have been in the clear. I never would have had to see her or talk to her or think about her. I would have gone to med school, become a doctor, found a wife somewhere, had some kids, and lived the life I always wanted. But I wasn't thinking about any of that on my first day back at SMU.

I moved all of my shit back into my old apartment. The people my landlord sublet the place to over the summer must have had a dog, because there was dog hair everywhere and a spot in the kitchen by the microwave that smelled like dog piss for the rest of the year no matter what I did to get rid of it.

Classes hadn't started and I was restless. Brett was out of town on a vacation to some place he called Whore Island. He tried to get me to go, but even after I had pretty much become an emotional robot when it came to dealing with girls I still wasn't prepared to cross the line and have sex with an actual prostitute. I knew I'd probably had sex with a dozen girls over that previous semester who had banged more guys than any prostitute on Whore Island, but there was still something really dirty to me about having sex with a real prostitute.

Anyway, Brett was out of town for another few days and, like I said, I was restless. I drank about half a bottle of vodka and started thinking about Heather and thought about calling her, but I didn't. Instead I called Erin. The last time I called her I was also drunk, but this time I knew I wasn't going to cry.

She actually answered. She said, "Kyle?"

I said, "Yeah."

She said, "Hi."

I said, "Hi."

She said, "Did you call me back before the summer drunk or something and leave a really weird message?"

I said, "I don't think so."

She said, "Oh, so what's up? Why are you calling me?"

I didn't even know why I was calling her. I was bored. I was drunk. I was lonely. I had no one else to call or talk to. I guess I could have told her all of that. Instead I said, "I miss you."

She said, "You miss me?"

I said, "Yeah."

She said, "Kyle, what are you doing?"

I said, "Calling you because I miss you, I guess."

She said, "Are you fucking with me or something? I felt like after we had that conversation last year I didn't really mean all that much to you."

I was too drunk to even know what conversation she was talking about. I was such a fucking asshole, and I got even worse. I said, "You did, I just didn't know how to tell you that because . . ."

She said, "Because you were in a relationship with Heather?"

I said, "Exactly."

She said, "Why are you waiting to tell me this now? I thought you guys broke up right after winter break last year."

I said, "We did. I guess I just needed to work through some stuff. I don't know. I'm sorry."

I had no idea what I was doing in that conversation. I just wanted to keep talking to her because I knew that at one point she loved me. I thought she still might, and it wasn't that it felt particularly good to talk to her or anything, but it felt like something, and from the time Heather dumped me until that phone call I had done a very good job of feeling nothing.

It was probably around nine-thirty at night. She said, "Well, do you want to come over and talk about this face-to-face? I have a new apartment now, a little bigger."

I said, "Sure."

After she gave me the directions to her new place I realized she lived about two blocks from me and I stumbled to Erin's apartment.

When I showed up, she could tell I was drunk but I don't think she cared. She looked genuinely happy to see me. She gave me a big hug and then sat down next to me on her couch. Her new apartment was much nicer than her old one.

She said, "So you miss me."

I didn't really but it felt good to make her happy again so I said, "Yeah."

She leaned in and kissed me and it was a kiss that I hadn't felt in a long time. It was Erin, so specifically it was a kiss I hadn't felt in a long time, but I mean that all the girls I had sex with after Heather never kissed like that. It wasn't that they were cold or unfeeling or anything, but there was something in the way they kissed that was only carnal, there was no thought behind it, no real emotion, no real connection. With Erin there was. I wondered if she could tell that I wasn't returning the same thing in my kiss.

She said, "You want to see the rest of the place?"

I said, "Yeah."

Even though it was nicer than her last place, it was still just a one-bedroom apartment that a college student could afford. The grand tour ended at the bedroom, where she gave me another kiss and said, "I think you should stay over."

We hadn't talked about what that would mean to her or to me or to us in general. It all felt a little strange, like we were slipping right back into some kind of a relationship without even addressing it. Even as drunk as I was, I could tell it was weird. But I didn't care enough to stop it. I did want to have sex with her. The semester I spent having name-less sex with the girls Brett set me up with taught me that, no matter how weird it is, as soon as you put your penis in a vagina, it's not weird enough to make you take your penis out of that vagina.

She pulled me down on top of her and started taking off her clothes. I knew it was wrong but I didn't stop it from happening. She gave me a blowjob that reminded me how average she was at giving blowjobs. When I only had Heather to compare her to I always just thought that Erin was slightly worse than Heather, but since Heather dumped me I had had enough experience to create a hundred-point scale of blowjob skill, and Erin ranked somewhere in the thirty to forty range. Still, she was good enough.

When she lay back on her bed, I didn't even make an attempt to go down on her. I just rolled her over and started having sex with her from behind. After about two thrusts she said, "Wait. I'm not on the pill or anything."

I stopped and said, "Do you have any condoms?"

She said, "I just moved into this place two days ago, so if I do, I don't know where they are."

I wasn't mad or even really disappointed. I just got off her and went to pick up my underwear from the ground. Then she said, "Well, just be careful and make sure you don't finish inside."

Even drunk this seemed like a bad idea. I said, "Are you sure?"

She said, "Yeah. It'll be fine."

So I got back on top of her and started having sex with her again. I didn't enjoy it at all. Through the whole thing I just felt bad, like I was using her, like I was letting her feel something about me that wasn't true. I knew I didn't want to get back together with her under any cir-cumstance. And it wasn't because she wasn't great. She was. She was the best girlfriend I ever had. It was because I just didn't want to care about somebody again.

As I was having sex with her, she started moaning and she rolled over so she was facing me. She reached up and kissed me while I was on top of her. She still loved me. I kind of panicked. I wanted her to understand that I wasn't doing this because I felt anything for her. I wanted her to understand that I just needed to do this to prove to myself that I had no more feelings for anyone. I wanted her to understand that I wasn't the same person she used to love.

So I started thrusting a little harder at first and then really hard. She kind of winced in pain a few times, but I didn't stop. I kept going harder and harder. At one point I was thrusting into her so hard I actually hurt myself when my hip hit her leg. I just wanted her to see that the old Kyle was gone and I guess some part of me wanted to see that, too. I wanted to prove to myself that I could be there with the only girl who really loved me and not care at all about her.

Right before I was about to cum, I pulled out, and just to punctuate everything I was feeling in that moment I came in Erin's face. It was horrible. She kind of halfheartedly pretended to like it, but I could tell she was disgusted. I was, too. When she left to go clean her face off, I got dressed and left.

When I got back to my place, I finished the rest of the bottle of vodka and I started to notice something. Where before I had managed to maintain a level of numbness and apathy about everything, I now noticed something new coming to the surface. I couldn't get the image of Erin recoiling as my semen hit her in the face out of my head. I hated myself, and more than that I started to hate Heather for turning me into what I had become. Erin called me a few times that night but I never answered.

And so began the worst year of my fucking life.

chapter
two

The first day back was like seriously not fun. I ended up getting a new room at the house because I was a senior, but that was about the only thing good that happened that day. After I moved in I went downstairs and like pretty much every girl was talking about how their boyfriends proposed to them over the summer or how they were going to be proposed to in the first semester or at Christmas or whatever. I wanted to fucking jump off a cliff. And then they were all like, "There's a big party going on over at Pike, we're all going, you should go." So, of course, I went because I just wanted to get as drunk as possible and maybe do some coke and just not think about it anymore.

As soon as I got there, I did some E and started drinking and then like half an hour later I ran into Brian, of course. I should have fucking known that was going to happen. So I like tried to be nice and everything. I was like, "How was your summer?"

He was like, "Pretty good. Interned at Lairmoore and Grummin. Made some pretty decent contacts and everything. How about you?"

Despite the fact that it was seriously shitty, I was like, "It was pretty good, just relaxed. You know, chilled out a lot."

He was like, "Cool. Cool."

I was like, "So is Annie here?"

He was like, "No, she's not coming back until tomorrow. On some vacay with her mom."

I was like, "Oh."

He was like, "Yeah."

I was like, "Well, good seeing you. I think I'm going to get a drink."

Then I left and went toward the kitchen and he like seriously followed me in there. He was like, "For real, I'm sorry about that day we talked last semester. It was weird and I guess I'm just sorry if it was too weird, you know?"

I was like, "Yeah, it's fine."

He was like, "Okay. Cool. I just wanted to make sure."

I was like, "Yeah."

Then he gave me a hug and I let him and he did feel seriously good. I had forgotten how much Brian worked out and how hot his body was. I know it was probably the E but I couldn't like help it, I just kind of reached down and grabbed his butt. He had like those dents on the side of it, you know when a guy has like a really tight butt how it has those dents, his had those.

He was like, "Whoa, for real?"

I was like, "Sorry. I just— Sorry."

He was like, "Do you want to go to my room or something?"

I was like, "What about Annie?"

He was like, "She doesn't come back until tomorrow."

I was like, "Yeah, okay."

And he took me back into his room, which thank God wasn't the same room as the one he and Josh did what they did to me in. I don't know if I would have been able to handle it.

I don't really know what I was thinking or what I expected from having sex with Brian, but it was pretty much like every time we had sex when we were together. It was only doggy style and he did it a little too hard to actually feel good the whole time and he finished before I did and then didn't do anything to help me get off. The worst part of it was he kind of pushed on the back of my head at one point and like smashed my face in his pillow. I don't think he did it on purpose, but it made me feel like shit, like he was just using me to get off, and I guess he was, but it still made me feel like shit.

When he was done he got dressed like really quick and was like, "I'm gonna head back out to the party. Wait a few before you come out. Cool?"

I was like, "Yeah."

Then he left and I just stayed there in his bed for a few minutes thinking about the fact that he would be fucking Annie in the same bed in less than twenty-four hours probably. I don't know why I fucked him. I guess I thought that like there might be some way to get him back or that for a second I could at least feel like there was a guy who didn't just want to fuck me. For like half a second I thought about what Kyle was doing and wondered if I made the right decision by dumping him. But then I was like uh yeah I made the right decision. He gave me a fucking fake ring.

I heard Josh out in the hall. He wasn't coming in Brian's room or anything but I had literally not seen him since the whole thing happened and I didn't really want to so I just stayed there in Brian's bed for like another hour. He never came back to check on me and I didn't see him again for the rest of the night.

When I finally came out of his room, the party was seriously completely full of people and it was pretty easy to sneak out without seeing Brian or any of my sisters. I went back to the Kappa house and looked over my course schedule and started thinking about the fact that I was actually probably going to have to work when I graduated and that work was probably going to be teaching little kids all day long, seriously.

chapter
three

Viking's Resort was, in short, the greatest place on planet Earth. The resort was situated on a small island in the Caribbean and was populated by thirty to forty literal whores—prostitutes.

When selecting my vacation package from the Viking's Resort website I was given three choices ranging in price from four thousand dollars to twelve. The lowest end of the spectrum allowed for the choosing of just one prostitute who would remain by my side for all four days of my stay on the island. The next level up allowed for a new prostitute every twenty-four hours and the final level offered me unfettered free rein of all the prostitutes for my entire stay. I, of course, opted for this last package.

As soon as I arrived on the island I was greeted by the island's proprietor, or at least the woman whose job it was to serve as the face of Viking's Resort. She welcomed me and showed me to my room, which was a nice bungalow-style suite next to a pool. All the while prostitutes who were semi- or fully nude lounged around in the sun and generally attempted to make themselves known to me.

The proprietor made it clear that although tips were not necessary, the prostitutes would accept them and this meant that some of them were willing to work extra hard for these potential tips. She asked me if I had any questions and then wished me a good vacation and I never saw her again.

I put my bag down on the bed, put on a bathing suit, and headed to the pool. It was apparently already made known to the prostitutes that I had opted for the most decadent package because they flocked to me immediately, rubbing my back, kissing me—one even started to manually stimulate me, all before I had uttered a word. In some way it was almost like a more streamlined version of SMU.

The first prostitute I fucked while at Viking's Resort was a girl who gave her name as Natasha. She had a thick Slavic accent. I never asked the specifics of her origin because after I blew a load in her eyes just twenty minutes after my arrival on the island I found small talk to be pointless. And beyond that she seemed to care as little about the pretense of false interest in one another as I did. It was novel.

The first day I was there I fucked six different girls, most of them in all of their holes. One escaped having my dick in her ass because she was so adept at riding my dick with her cunt that I was unable to hold back an orgasm before I could get my full money's worth out of her. Each of the prostitutes had the same lack of interest in pretense that the first one did. As I slept that first night, virtually spent from a full ten hours of fucking, I became aware of the fact that I would have to visit this island at least twice a year. I felt a calm that was previously unknown to me, a certain contentment that I reasoned I would never experience when dealing with women who were anything but actual prostitutes.

The next morning is when I first encountered Tim Garlin, the only other man on the island during my stay. I met him on my way to one of the pools that I hadn't yet seen. He had two naked prostitutes with him, both black. He nodded to me and made some comment about us being the only two guys on the island. Then he gave me a fist bump.

I had breakfast, face-fucked a prostitute on the fourth hole of the golf course, and then returned to the pool as I had no real interest in golf beyond face-fucking a prostitute on the course. Back at the pool I ran into Tim again, and it was this second encounter that yielded a conversation about his profession, which revealed that he knew who my father was and had done some business with his company. He asked me if I was next in line to run Keller Shipping. I told him I was, and chose not to tell him that I had decided to reject the position and the life that came with it. I didn't want to waste any time on the island thinking about my life back home and the inevitable conversation that I was going to have to have with my father very soon.

That night I had a four-way with prostitutes who were Asian, Indian, and one who looked like she was fourteen. I didn't ask her age and instead chose to assume that the island would have only employed prostitutes of consenting age. In any case, after I came in the face of the prostitute who looked fourteen, I watched the Asian eat the Indian's asshole for a few minutes and as I did my thoughts turned to Kyle briefly. I wondered if he would have enjoyed the trip to Viking's Resort. I hoped he wasn't reverting back to his old obsession with Heather in my absence and was slightly anxious to get back home and make sure he wasn't. But I still had two more days on the island.

The third day brought with it my strangest moment on the island when I woke up from a thirty-minute afternoon nap to find Annika, a prostitute from the Eastern Bloc whom I had fucked on day one of my vacation, sitting in a chair in my room. I left the doors not only unlocked but open in order to enjoy the mild weather, but had yet to have a prostitute enter my room uninvited, let alone while I was sleeping. It wasn't alarming, but I was slightly unsettled. She proceeded to tell me that it was her dream to come to America. She further explained that it was against the rules of the island to talk to me about such things but she didn't care. I seemed like a nice guy to her and she thought she could trust me. She told me that she would essentially be my sex slave in America as long as I could pay for her living expenses. There was something so candid in what she said to me, so bereft of any of the lies I was used to dealing with back in Dallas, that I found myself feeling something bordering on respect for this girl. Although I admired the forthrightness of her offer, I had to decline, which led her to tears immediately.

It was strange, but I felt some actual sympathy for this prostitute. I assumed she had probably used this same story on every guy she had fucked on the island, which I'm sure was a number too high to calculate. Her only goal in all of the fucking she did was to come to America—not to marry a rich man, or to have a giant diamond ring, or to trap a man into marriage by having his child, just to come to America, and it would never happen for her. Despite the fact that I didn't need to subscribe to the philosophy in my own life, I always admired the people who lived by the credo that through hard work you can achieve anything. And there sitting in front of me was living proof that the philosophy was inaccurate. I fucked her against my bedroom wall, but in the middle of the act felt I should take her to the bed. She continued to cry a little as we fucked, which prompted me to fuck her missionary style, which was something I almost never did, as I had grown tired of it at a young age. While on top of her, I couldn't help but look into her eyes and see the extreme sorrow that could only have been accumulated through years of being a prostitute. I found myself stroking her hair and telling her that everything would be fine. As I did this I lost the desire to fuck her. I pulled out and lay beside her instead. It was strange what I felt for this girl. I assumed it was similar to what most men feel for their girlfriends or wives. It clearly wasn't anything approaching the lie of love, but I did have a certain admiration for her ability to exist without the pretense that all the other women I was used to had come to brandish in every moment of their lives. She stayed with me that night. Eventually she stopped crying and fell asleep next to me. I continued to stroke her hair as a novelty, knowing I would never have the inclination to do such a thing to another slut once I returned home.

On my final day on the island I found myself so sated from the prior three days of fucking prostitutes, and slightly disoriented from the previous night's platonic interaction with Annika, that I had little desire to continue. But like an obese person at an all-you-can-eat buffet I was determined to get every ounce of value from the trip that I could. I arranged, that final afternoon, to have ten prostitutes sent to my room, where I planned to engage in as many acts of demoralization as I could until my time was up.

I planned to go far beyond regular sex. I wished to piss on several of them, to shit on one or more of them, to place foreign objects like pencils and lotion bottles in their cunts, to put one or more of their faces in the toilet and flush it while fucking her doggy style, et cetera. But when the whores arrived in my room it became obvious to me that none of these plans would come to fruition. Instead I found myself wanting to see Annika one final time.

I ordered the other whores to leave and replaced them with Annika. We had a conversation about how long she had been on the island and about what led her to become a prostitute. She had been there for one year and it was only because she felt it gave her the greatest possible opportunity to find a way to America. She explained that most of the girls on the island would just come for a few weeks at a time, then return home after having made some money only to come back a few months later. They treated it almost like a part-time job. Annika, however, explained that she could never return home, not even for a brief stay. Her home was worse than hell, or so she claimed, and although she did not particularly enjoy being a prostitute it was better than the horrors she would no doubt be made to endure in her hometown.

The problems she had seemed real to me and of consequence. Annika seemed real to me, far more real than the ciphers I had dealt with all my life. This stirred something in me. I kissed Annika gently and laid her down on the bed. I began fucking her in the missionary position again. As insane as this sounds, I felt I could trust her, because her honesty, up to that point, had been absolute. For this reason I failed to wear a condom.

In my head there were many good reasons for doing this. Annika was the only girl on the island I fucked without a condom. She probably wouldn't get pregnant because on the fourth and final day of my stay my ability to produce sperm was likely so muted I would be incapable of fathering a child. If she did get pregnant she would most likely abort it. Even if she didn't there would be no way the child could be traced back to me. Even if it was traced back to me it would be amusing in some way to have a child with a prostitute. But beyond the practical reasons, I just wanted to feel as close to her as I could, just to experience that with a woman once.

I woke up the next morning to find Annika still asleep in my bed. I had experienced something with her, with this prostitute, that I had never experienced with any other girl. I left the island knowing that I would think about her often and hoping that I might see her again on my next trip to Viking's Resort.

The flight back was uneventful. There was a girl sitting next to me who obviously had no idea who I was, and I thought about striking up a conversation with her about where she was going and where she was coming from just so I could tell her about my stay at Viking's Resort. Instead I slept like a baby all the way back to DFW.

After what I did to Erin, something changed in me. I felt ashamed of
what I had done to her and I despised myself for being capable of doing
something like that. But I couldn't change it. I thought about Heather
a lot and about how I used to think about relationships and love and I
started to think that I finally knew what Brett was talking about. I hated
that I couldn't go back to believing in love and believing in the possibility of there being a girl out there who could make me happy.

I felt like I'd found that girl, and she turned out to be exactly what
Brett always said she was, a fucking cunt who only cared about money
and status and all of that shit. And every girl I walked past on campus
made me think that somewhere there was a guy who she'd dump if he
ever gave her a cubic zirconia. I just couldn't get it out of my mind that
they were all the same. And I think in retrospect that's probably why I
treated Erin so badly. She represented the one girl who clearly wasn't
like Heather, the one girl who actually did love me through it all and
knowing that was the case was stopping me from feeling the absolute

hatred for all women I needed to feel to get over Heather. I was so fucked up, and I hated Heather for doing it to me.

I was glad Brett was back from his trip to Whore Island. I thought if I hung out with him it might take the edge off how shitty I was feeling about everything, maybe lessen the contempt I was feeling for pretty much every woman on the planet.

The day he came back, I met him at the fountain outside Dallas Hall as one of his classes was getting out and we sat down so he could tell me all the twisted details of his vacation. It was a pretty insane story. He kept insisting that I would have loved it. I kept telling him that I didn't think I would have because it seemed disgusting to me—not the idea of whores, but knowing that a million other dicks have been where you're putting yours. Once he got through all of the stories of the different girls he'd had sex with he said, "So on the last day, man, I actually did something really fucking stupid."

I said, "What?"

He said, "I was drunk and not thinking and I nailed this whore bareback."

I said, "Are you fucking serious?"

He said, "Yeah, I know. Stupid, right?"

I said, "Yeah, really stupid, man."

He said, "I know, I know. I'm pretty sure I'm in the clear, though. I've been over it a million times in my head. If she's pregnant I don't think there'd be any way to trace it back to me. With the number of guys she probably fucks it's pretty unlikely they'd call up every guy who's been to the island over the past month and make them submit to paternity tests, right?"

I said, "Pregnancy is the least of your problems, man. What about fucking AIDS?"

He said, "These whores were clean."

I said, "You realize you just said, 'These whores were clean'? Whores, man. They're whores."

He said, "Yeah, yeah, yeah. I'm getting tested tomorrow. I'm sure I'm fine, but I know you're right and I'm getting tested."

I said, "Jesus Christ, good luck."

He said, "Thanks. So what'd you do while I was getting AIDS?"

I said, "I fucked Erin."

He said, "Oh fucking shit. You're getting back together with her, aren't you, you asshole?"

I said, "No."

He said, "You just hit it and quit it?"

I said, "It was weird. I went over there a few nights ago, drunk."

He said, "Nice."

I said, "And I told her what she wanted to hear just so I could fuck her basically."

He said, "Welcome to being a man, finally."

I said, "It wasn't because I was horny or anything, though. I just wanted to do something vile to her because she was the last girl who really loved me, I guess, and I wanted to ruin that."

He said, "Who in the fuck are you?"

I said, "I'm being serious, man."

He said, "So am I. That's some bold shit. So after you fucked her, did you just leave or did you stick around?"

I said, "I came in her face and then left before she came out of the bathroom. She called me a few times but I never answered or called her back."

He said, "And the student becomes the master."

I said, "I think I finally get what you've been saying about girls all along."

He said, "Kyle, I know this is going to seem like I want to fuck you or something, but I don't. Your cathartic rebirth into the age of reason should excite me but it's actually kind of weird, man. I don't know how I feel about the new you. I get that you got dumped by Heather, but you might be taking this whole thing a little far. I don't know how well it suits you."

I said, "I don't give a shit if it suits me. I just want to hurt any girl I can before she does it to me, I guess."

He said, "Okay. Okay. That's valid, I suppose. I guess I just question what's behind all this. I know I'm not one to be talking here. I've done more foul shit to bitches than anyone, but before you sink down to my level make sure it's what you want. I always kind of liked the fact that you believed in love and all that stupid shit, and let me tell you something, there is a point of no return in this. You can only treat women like pure shit so many times before that's all you can do."

I said, "That's all I want to do."

He said, "Okay," whipped out his cell phone and dialed a number, then said, "Maybe you can watch me give this stupid cunt AIDS in my Jacuzzi."

It was a few days after I had sex with Brian that I was walking by Dallas Hall, which I like rarely did but they made some error on my course schedule and I had to go to the registration office and deal with this stupid bullshit. So I was walking by Dallas Hall when I saw Kyle for the first time since we had broken up. I got like cold sweats and I got jittery and I just felt like really weird. I didn't think I would have had that kind of a reaction to seeing him. I would have thought it would have been more like pure rage and like I'd want to go over and kick him in the balls for being such an asshole, but it wasn't like that.

He was sitting by the fountain talking to Brett, who I also hadn't seen in a long time. I thought he was going to be at the party that I had sex with Brian at, but I don't think he ever showed up. I heard that he was the new ATO president, which was cool. I thought about stopping by and saying hi to Brett and just like totally ignoring Kyle but that seemed like it would be bitchy. And also I wasn't sure if Kyle was like mad at me or what his deal was. I mean, I knew he was like having sex with all of like the grossest skanks from every sorority on campus, but I didn't really know what his deal was in terms of how he felt about me. So I just kept walking.

I tried to walk close enough to hear what they were talking about without them seeing me, but that was too hard so I just walked by without hearing what they were saying.

When I got to the registration office I had to wait for like forty-five minutes because I guess there were a lot of people in the elementary education program who had this same class screwed up on their schedules. So I had to sit in the waiting room for a long time.

I thought a lot about Kyle and about how when I saw him again I remembered that he was kind of cute and he was a pretty nice guy. I wondered if he would want to get back together, not that I would actually ask him or anything, but I just wondered if he would ever even think about doing it. I figured if I still hadn't found a new boyfriend by the time there was like two or three weeks left that year I would just call him up and be like, "Hey, I'm sorry, we should totally get back together," and I would just have to deal with the fake ring until he could get me a real one. I mean I wanted a real ring and everything, but once we graduated it probably wouldn't be that big of a deal. Like I probably wouldn't be dealing with any of my sisters or anything after graduation so nobody that I would be seeing on a daily basis would know it was fake or anything. Whatever. I was basically just killing time by thinking about stupid shit I guess.

I wondered what would have happened to me if I had never seen Kyle talking to Brett that one day our freshman year. Like if I would have ended up with some other guy who was really cool or something. Then I started thinking about all of the guys in the different frats and there weren't really any guys who were better than Kyle in terms of personality. They all had like way more money and were cooler and everything but they were all kind of assholes who cheated on their girlfriends or did weird shit like Brian did. Kyle actually wasn't a bad boyfriend at all and he would probably have even been a good husband, but he gave me a fucking fake ring. It's like, how do you even get around that? I think I would probably dump Johnny Depp if he gave me a fake ring, unless he like made it himself or something weird like that, which I could totally see him doing.

The more I thought about it, the more it seriously pissed me off. Like Kyle and I could have been totally happy together. Up until the ring I really did love him. Why did he have to give me a fake fucking ring? Even if he would have just gotten me a smaller ring and said he was going to replace it later, that would have been a lot easier to deal with than a fake ring he was going to lie to me about for the rest of our relationship. What a fucking idiot.

Anyway, whatever. Everything turned out like it turned out and now I'm much better off, but I remember sitting in that registration office just wishing he hadn't fucked everything up so bad.

Every six weeks I was required to take a blood test in order to remain a viable candidate for sperm donation. As luck would have it, the end of one of my six-week intervals coincided with my return from Viking's Resort. Two days after my return, in fact, I was tested, and roughly a week later I was scheduled to visit the South Texas Fertility and Family Medical Center to donate. I had received no notification from them to indicate that I shouldn't come in so I assumed my test results had yielded a clean bill of health.

I arrived at the Fertility Center, entered suite 602 just as I had done dozens of times before, and noticed there was a new woman behind the desk in addition to the one who had been there since I started my donations three years prior. I said my hellos and signed in. I waited the ten minutes or so I usually waited for someone to tell me which of the donation rooms I'd be in, and instead a nurse came out whom I had never met and told me that a Dr. Greene would now see me. I obviously became aware of the fact that something was not good. I hoped I was not HIV-positive, despite my jokes about AIDS.

Dr. Greene, it seemed, was one of two actual MDs who worked daily in the Family Medical Center, more specifically in the sperm donation portion of the center. He explained to me many things that I already knew. He explained that they are required to do mandatory blood tests every six weeks for recurring donors. He explained to me that this ensures the health of any children born using a donor's sperm. He explained to me that engaging in high-risk behavior is not something the South Texas Fertility and Family Medical Center recommends for current or prospective sperm donors. And then he explained something to me that I was not yet aware of.

My blood test had come back positive for herpes simplex virus type 2, more commonly known as genital herpes. Dr. Greene further explained to me that although the South Texas Fertility and Family Medical Center was grateful to me for all I had done in order to help people who desperately wanted children but were unable to produce their own, they would no longer be able to accept my services in the future due to the results of my latest blood test. He thanked me for my time and gave me a pamphlet entitled "Take Charge: Don't Let Genital Herpes Stop You from Living Your Fullest Life," which featured a man and a woman on the cover lying in the grass next to each other smiling as though they were having the best time of their lives even though the implication was that one or both of them had genital herpes. Dr. Greene shook my hand and explained to me that there was a number on the back of the pamphlet I could call if I had any questions or needed anyone to talk to. Then he stood up from his desk and showed me out.

I sat in my car flipping through the pamphlet for a few minutes. I was surprised at my own reaction to this development. I was aware that herpes did nothing to you physically; that is, it posed no real health risk in terms of a disease. Of the sexually transmitted diseases that were incurable it was easily the best to get. The others all resulted in malfunctioning genitals, blindness, death, et cetera. Herpes, though, wasn't actually that bad. The pamphlet I read claimed that one in four people had it. I was unsure if this statistic was drastically inflated to make the readers of such a pamphlet feel better about their situation or if it was true. In either case I found I didn't really care all that much about my brand-new case of herpes. I was disappointed, of course, to learn that I could never donate sperm again, but I had done well in my three-plus years of donation. I had seventeen known offspring who had been registered on the Donor Sibling Registry, and I'm sure there were others who were unaware of the website. I could take pride in the numbers I had already accumulated.

Furthermore, as I drove back to the Alpha Tau Omega house I realized that I had an entirely new weapon in my arsenal against whores. Gone were the days when the most degrading act I could force a whore to perform involved eating her own feces or eating my feces. A whole new era had dawned for me. Now any act that involved unprotected sex with me delivered with it a chance to be infected with genital herpes. I would make this fact known to every girl who wanted to fuck me, and it was my prediction that this would stop none of them from going through with whatever act I demanded of them. Even if I were in the middle of the most heinous outbreak in history with herpes blisters covering every inch of my cock, I surmised that the whores at SMU would suck my dick, take it in their asses, and even let me blow a load in their cunts, because herpes or not I was still my father's son.

When I got back to campus, I called Kyle. He had expressed concern about the results of my test. I told him that I had herpes but that it wasn't as dire as it might seem. He placed far greater weight on the scenario than was warranted. I assured him that I was fine and that it would not impact our friendship or my life.

After Kyle, my next call was to a girl I had fucked once before who had been in the same sorority as Heather her freshman year but then dropped out of Greek life after having a bad experience with ecstasy and alcohol that left her hospitalized for twenty-four hours. I remember her specifically telling me that she had read many articles about my father and about my family and thought we were the equivalent of Dallas royalty. Her name was Kaitlin. I asked her to come over and she obliged.

Once she arrived, I took her to my room and made the necessary small talk for the necessary amount of time and then started kissing her. She offered no resistance so I took off all of her clothes and all of mine. I stood before her wishing to display a cock that was covered in red blisters, but I had yet to suffer my first outbreak. I wondered briefly what that experience would be like. Then I explained to Kaitlin that I had contracted genital herpes. I further told her that I refused to use a condom and that I wanted to fuck her in the ass.

She bargained with me, which was unexpected. She claimed that if she was willing to risk getting herpes then I should risk getting her pregnant so she could potentially at least have a chance to be the mother of my child. Her ultimate offer included her allowing me to fuck her without a condom in any and all holes I wanted, but I had to cum in her cunt.

I laughed at her and told her to leave my room. Unprepared for my hardball tactics she acquiesced and allowed me to fuck her in the ass unprotected and then shoot my load on her tits and face. As she was getting dressed she asked me if I really had herpes. I told her I did. She claimed she thought it was just some weird role-play thing I was doing. I assured her it was not.

As she left she asked me if she could get herpes even though I wasn't in the middle of an outbreak. She claimed to have read something that indicated the virus was not transmittable unless the carrier was in the midst of a full-blown outbreak. I told her that I thought her information was correct, that she most likely hadn't contracted herpes from me, but, of course, I hoped she had.

Before she went I made her a deal that when I was experiencing my first full-blown outbreak, I would call her and I would fuck her in the cunt if she still desired such an act. I was careful with my wording of this deal, to leave room for myself to still pull out and blow a load in her face, but she seemed satisfied with the terms and told me to call her when I got my first visible outbreak.

It was almost unreal to me how far these whores were willing to go in order to have a chance to be a part of my family, to be a part of what my father's father had created. Not that any woman has ever had the same drive or industriousness as a man, but it was shocking to me on that day how blatant the female desire to achieve material wealth without working for it was.

I wondered if my father would care that I had herpes.

Brett was the first person I knew who had any kind of STD. It was kind of gross, I guess, but it was obviously a lot better than AIDS or syphilis or something like that. Brett actually kind of thought it was funny. I wasn't prepared to go that far, but I was glad that he wasn't taking it too hard.

In the few days that followed Brett finding out he had herpes I was all consumed with thinking about Heather and the life I could have been living with her if she wasn't such an enormous cunt. I thought about Erin a few times, too, and I even started to convince myself that she got what she deserved because if I had gotten back together with her she'd eventually have done the same thing to me that Heather did. I was pretty fucked up.

I went over to Brett's house the night after he told me about his herpes because he had claimed that his new STD wouldn't slow him down one step in terms of getting laid. I didn't really believe him, so he invited me over along with a few girls, which was a scenario I was pretty familiar with at that point. He invited everyone into the Jacuzzi. I didn't get in. I know I wouldn't have caught his herpes from the Jacuzzi, but it was still a little disgusting to me so I just sat on the side and made out with one of the chicks who came over. I think they were from Brookhaven or something. I forget how Brett even knew them. I want to say one of them had interned at his dad's company or something and Brett had met her when he was up there talking to his dad. I don't remember.

Anyway, the point is, after everyone had a few beers in them Brett stood up in the Jacuzzi, pulled down his pants so his dick was completely exposed to these girls, and said, "Ladies, does my cock strike you as strange in any way?"

They all said, "No."

He said, "Look closely."

One of them leaned in and he said, "Don't get too close, though, unless you want to get herpes."

They all laughed and he said, "This isn't a joke. I have herpes, girls, and I just want you to know that before you do anything with my dick tonight."

One of the girls said, "Really?"

He said, "Yes, really."

One of the other girls said, "It doesn't look like you have herpes, though."

Brett said, "That, my dipshit, is because I'm not experiencing an outbreak right now, which does minimize your chances of contracting the virus, but does not eliminate them. Are there any questions?"

One of the girls said, "Does it taste different?" and then started sucking his cock right in front of everyone. He looked at me with one of those looks that basically said, "I told you it wouldn't make a bit of fucking difference," and he was right.

I ended up fucking the girl I was making out with in his parents' wine cellar, which I had never done. It was kind of weird. I actually wondered if Brett had ever done it in there.

After I fucked her I drank a half bottle of scotch and wandered upstairs into a guest room to pass out, but instead I just lay awake thinking about the girls who were still fucking Brett. I wondered if they just didn't care that they were putting themselves at risk of contracting herpes, or if they really thought they were okay because he wasn't in the middle of an outbreak. Either way, it was pretty mind-blowing. I guessed that for somebody like Brett herpes really didn't matter. His money was enough to make a girl basically do anything in order to catch his interest. But those girls . . . I didn't feel sorry for them at all, but I couldn't stop myself from thinking that if they got herpes, their lives were basically over. I knew they were all the types of girls who wanted to find rich husbands and never work again or they wouldn't be fucking Brett, and if they got herpes they were done. No guy would ever fuck them again, they would be stuck going on herpes dating sites, and that would be their lives forever.

And then the worst idea I've ever had in my life popped into my head, though at the time I thought it was the greatest. I got out of Brett's guest bed and stumbled down to the Jacuzzi, where Brett was balls deep in the ass of the girl who had been sucking his dick in front of us an hour or so earlier.

Brett said, "Hey, what's up?" without slowing his pace. The girl didn't say anything.

I said, "I have a proposition for you."

Brett said, "What is it?"

I said, "It's private."

Brett said, "It's not some gay shit, is it?"

I said, "No. It just shouldn't be discussed in mixed company."

Brett said, "Oh, hang on."

And I shit you not, almost on cue, Brett gave that girl three more hard thrusts, came in her ass, and then said, "There's no toilet paper in the bathroom by the kitchen, so get a paper towel or something if you're going to use the one by the living room, so you don't drip my seed on the carpet while you're walking."

And again I shit you not, she said, "Okay. Thanks." Yes, she fucking thanked him for the tip about the paper towels.

Anyway, once she left it was just me and Brett. The other girls must have been asleep somewhere inside.

Brett said, "So what's the deal?"

I said, "I think I came up with an idea that you're going to love."

Brett said, "I just want you to take a moment and drink this in. What was it, less than a year ago you were head over heels for some whore? And now you're banging a different whore every night and you're coming up with weird devious plans and shit. I like the new you. It scares me, but I like it. Shoot."

I said, "Okay, it involves Heather."

Brett said, "I'm not helping you get her back in any way, no matter how great your plan is."

I said, "I don't want to get her back, I want to fucking destroy her."

Brett said, "As I said, it scares me, but I like it."

I said, "You know she'd probably love to date you and marry you and all of that shit, right?"

Brett said, "Not specifically, I don't think, but she's just like every other whore on campus, sure."

I said, "I think maybe even specifically. There was a time after we first broke up that I thought she just went out with me so she could hang out with you."

Brett said, "What a fucking cunt."

I said, "I know. So here's the deal. Whether it's specific or not, she would do pretty much anything you said. I was thinking that it probably wouldn't be that hard for you to start actually dating her, get her to fuck you when you have a massive outbreak, and give her herpes. She'd be done. No guy would ever want to fuck her again."

Brett said, "Except guys with herpes."

I said, "Right."

Brett said, "Shit, man, is that illegal, to not disclose that you have an STD to chicks before you fuck them?"

I said, "I think only if the STD can kill them. It's like manslaughter or attempted murder or something. But herpes just gives you red spots on your junk. I don't think you have to tell anyone about that before you fuck them."

Brett said, "If that's the case, I'm fucking in. It's been a while since I felt like I had anything interesting to do. It'll be like a fun little project.

But before we do this, you have to be totally cool with me fucking her. I don't want to do this and then you get all weird about me having fucked your ex-girlfriend and love of your life or some shit."

I said, "I wouldn't have brought this up to you if I had cared, man. She's fucking dead to me. I just want to see her ruined like she ruined me."

Brett said, "Okay, calm down, man. Don't be so creepy about this. It's going to be fun, not weird and psychopathic."

I said, "Okay. When should we start?"

Brett said, "Tomorrow."

I had just spent like two hours looking through pretty much every guy on my Facebook to see who was single. I was even looking at guys I went to high school with who didn't even go to SMU. Some of them didn't even go to college at all. I was seriously about as desperate as I've ever been in my life. And then my phone rang. The caller ID said it was Brett. I was like, what?

So I answered it and Brett was like, "Heather?"

I was like, "Yeah, how are you?"

He was like, "This is Brett Keller."

I was like, "Yeah, I know, how are you?"

He was like, "I'm fine. How are you?"

I was like, "Doing pretty good I guess. What's up? You guys throwing a party or something?"

He was like, "We are actually, I think, next week, but that's not why I'm calling."

I was like, "Oh, so what's up then?"

He was like, "Would you like to go out and get dinner sometime with me?"

I didn't know if he was asking me on a date or if it was some weird thing where like Kyle was going to be there, too, or what the deal was, but it was Brett Keller asking me out to dinner. There was pretty much no way I was going to say no to him.

So I was like, "Yeah, I'd love to go to dinner with you."

He was like, "Great. I'll pick you up at eight."

I was like, "Tonight?"

He was like, "Yeah, if that's okay."

I was like, "Yeah, that's fine. See you then."

He was like, "See you then."

I wanted to run downstairs and be like, "Hey, everyone, I'm going on a date with Brett Keller." It was kind of a big deal. I mean, there were plenty of girls who had fucked Brett or been to his house or whatever, but I don't think I ever heard anyone talk about having gone on a date with him. But I didn't even know if it was a date or anything yet, so I just kept it to myself and started looking for what I was going to wear and figuring out my hair and everything. I decided on a nice skirt that I got at Forever 21 and a tight Donna Karan shirt that made my boobs look as big as they possibly could be. I didn't know if he was going to be taking me out somewhere like ultrafancy or just a normal place. Either way, I was pretty sure the outfit would be appropriate and make me look really good.

I took a shower at about six-thirty and made sure to wash my vag like really good. I didn't think I would have sex with him on the first date, necessarily, but I thought it was better to make sure I had the capability if I needed to. I did my makeup and got dressed and like right at eight the doorbell rang. I still hadn't told anybody what was going on. Gina answered the door and I was listening to the whole thing from upstairs.

She was like, "Brett, how's it going?"

He was like, "I'm here to pick up Heather."

She was like, "Really?"

He was like, "Yes, is she home?"

She was like, "Hang on, like let me see."

Then Gina came up into my room and saw that I was kind of dressed up and was like, "Are you going on a date with Brett Keller?"

I was like, "What do you think?"

She was like, "I think it looks like you're going on a date with Brett Keller."

I was like, "Don't wait up," and went downstairs.

Brett was fucking hot. I mean seriously fucking hot. He was wearing like a black blazer over a really nice shirt with pants that matched the blazer, and his shirt had the top three buttons undone, and his hair was kind of messy. He always had that look of like a guy who doesn't even have to try because he just doesn't care but he's still really hot no matter how little effort he puts into it.

He was like, "You ready?"

I was like, "Yeah, where are we going?"

He stuck his arm out for me to take it like it was some kind of old-school prom or something. It might seem corny, but it was actually kind of romantic.

He was like, "That's a surprise."

As he walked me out to his Land Rover I seriously knew that Gina was telling everybody in the house that I was going on a date with Brett Keller. It was awesome.

On the ride to wherever he was taking me I was like, "So why'd you ask me out?"

He was like, "If you want to know the truth I always thought you were really cool when you were dating Kyle, but I never made a move because he's my best friend. You guys haven't been an item for a while now and so I thought it would be okay to take you out."

I could seriously like not believe what I was hearing. Brett was basically saying that my whole plan to date Kyle so Brett would notice me actually worked. I was excited that Brett was taking me out, but I was also kind of pissed that he never made his move sooner. I mean, if he had done something like our freshman year, I would have never had to go through that stupid shit with Kyle and the fake ring.

I was like, "You liked me freshman year?"

He was like, "Like I said, I thought you seemed really cool and you're obviously attractive."

Again, I was pretty much in shock. Brett Keller was telling me he thought I was attractive. I was like, "Oh, thanks."

He was like, "No problem."

Then I was like, "Does Kyle know we're going out?"

He was like, "Would you rather he know or not know?"

I was like, "Why? Does he know already?"

He was like, "He doesn't know. I was going to tell him tonight . . . or tomorrow depending on how the date goes, but I won't if you don't want me to."

Um, okay, so Brett was basically saying he was going to try to fuck me after dinner or whatever, and he was also basically telling me he would lie to Kyle if I wanted him to. Seriously, it was like one of the best nights of my life. I didn't know what I should tell him. I kind of liked the fact that I could get Brett to keep a secret from Kyle, but I also kind of wanted Kyle to know that I was going out with Brett. I figured that would seriously piss him off. But then I also thought Brett might be testing me or something. So I was like, "I think you should do whatever you want to. He's your friend. If you want to tell him, go ahead."

He was like, "Okay."

We drove around a little more and then he pulled into the parking lot of Abacus, on McKinney. Seriously, like one of the best restaurants in Dallas. I had never been but I always wanted to go. When we walked in the door the guy was like, "Good evening, Mr. Keller. Would you like a table by the window or the bar?"

Brett was like, "The window will be fine, thanks."

I was pretty sure going on a date with Brett was pretty much the same as going on a date with like a celebrity or something, at least in terms of how he was treated in this restaurant. Even after we sat down, the waiter was like at our table in less than a minute and also called Brett "Mr. Keller." It was really cool to be with someone who was treated like that. It made him like a hundred times hotter to me.

Brett ordered lobster for both of us and like a four-hundred-dollar bottle of wine. I don't even really like lobster all that much but it was seriously the best lobster I've ever had. The whole night was just really incredible. We talked mainly about how our senior years were going and what we thought we were going to do after we graduated.

I was like, "I'm supposed to start student-teaching next semester and then I guess I'll try to get a teaching job at an elementary school somewhere when I graduate."

Brett was like, "It doesn't sound like that's what you want to do."

I was like, "Well, it's what I'm majoring in, so I figured I might as well try to use it for something. What about you?"

He was like, "I'm not sure. My father wants me to go to work for his company and ultimately take over for him when he retires in seven or eight years. It seems like that's what's been laid out for me since I was a kid, but I'm not real sure that's what I want to do."

I was like, "What else would you do?"

He was like, "Anything would be more interesting to me than that. Who knows?"

That part of the conversation was kind of weird, I thought. I mean it wasn't like I knew Brett like as well as Kyle or anything, but I knew him pretty well just from hanging out with him over the years and I never even thought it might be a possibility for him to not run Keller Shipping. I wondered if that would mean that he wouldn't make as much money or if his dad would like cut him out of the family money or something. That would seriously suck.

After dinner we had another bottle of wine and I was pretty drunk. Brett paid the bill and as we were walking back out to his car he was like, "So do you want to come back to my house and maybe take a dip in the Jacuzzi?"

I almost said yes. It would have been so easy to say yes, but as soon as he said the word "Jacuzzi" all I could hear in my head was like every girl I knew talking about how they got fucked in that Jacuzzi. That was like the place where Brett always fucked girls, and even as drunk as I was I knew that if I let him fuck me in that Jacuzzi I would just be another one of them to him. So I decided to take a pretty big risk. I was like, "I don't think I can tonight. I actually have some stuff I need to study for so I should probably just go home."

I could tell he was pretty surprised and I hoped it wasn't a bad kind of surprise that would make him never call me again or anything. I just didn't want Brett to be like the next guy in a string of guys who just fucked me and then never talked to me again. I would have rather just not fucked him at all if that was going to be the case.

He drove me home, and we did make out a little in his car before he walked me to the door, which I asked him to do mainly so everyone in my house could see us together. After he pulled away I remember wondering if I had been pretty much the first girl to ever tell him no.

chapter
nine

I explained to Kyle that Heather was the first girl in recent memory to tell me no. He didn't find it quite as amusing as I did. His lack of levity in those months was unsettling to me. He had, in a very short period of time, come to embody all of my own most misogynistic characteristics, without the benefit of tempering them with an overall carefree attitude. It was strange: Where I found amusement in the things we did to whores, it seemed he found nothing but a stronger desire to repeat the actions. He rarely smiled. Even when the absurdity of a situation was undeniable, such as forcing a whore to eat peanut butter off our cocks and then eat jelly out of her friend's pussy, Kyle's scowl and general discontent were ever-present.

It wasn't that I minded the new sinister version of Kyle, but anytime the core qualities of a person change so drastically it usually is symptomatic of some deep-rooted problem that must be solved. I found myself more and more wishing for the return of my old friend. And perhaps all I would have had to do to facilitate this would have been to end the game we had begun to play with Heather, but I couldn't. It was one of the greatest schemes I had ever been aware of, so exact in its justice. It amused me to no end and so I continued on.

No more apparent was this new version of Kyle than on the night after my first date with Heather. After our conversation about it, and after Kyle's assurances that she would fuck me eventually if I persisted, Kyle insisted that I invite some whores to my house for us to demean. I obliged him.

I reasoned that because our scheme involved the wooing of Heather it probably wasn't wise to invite over any whore from her sorority, or any whore from the entire student body for that matter. Kyle agreed. I knew a fair number of girls from other social circles, but I had exhausted many of my relationships with them through various acts of unforgivable sexual deviance. As it happened, on that night the first whore to favorably respond to my invitation was one of my stepmother's personal trainers. Her name was Emily Charter. She was twenty-six and her body was of the sort that was more muscle than anything else. She wasn't mannish in any way but neither was she as feminine as the average woman might be. She was novel and I had never actually fucked her. I had attempted to once before while my stepmother was upstairs taking a shower after a workout, but Emily was unwilling to jeopardize her professional arrangement. I assumed my stepmother gave a more-than-generous tip of my father's money after each training session. Despite the fact that I wasn't able to fuck her on that day, it was made quite clear that anytime I wanted to, I could phone her for meaningless sex. I did not tell her Kyle would be joining us, reasoning that it would be less difficult to ease her into the idea of a threesome once she was in my father's living room drinking his wine. This strategy turned out to be successful.

I invited a single woman with no friends also as a sort of test I would administer to Kyle. Up to that point we had never engaged in fucking the same whore simultaneously. I had fucked many whores whom only moments prior he had fucked, but never had our cocks been in the same whore at the same time. I recalled several conversations Kyle and I had engaged in over the years in which he claimed this act of two men simultaneously penetrating the same whore represented in his mind the worst degradation a woman could undergo. I felt that if he was willing to engage in the act, then I would know with absolute certainty that he had become the very darkest parts of my own psyche and in many ways the very thing he used to claim he was the exact opposite of.

Emily arrived at my house in a dress. I had only ever seen her in some kind of athletic apparel. The dress was backless, revealing her every overly defined muscle from the back of her neck to the top of her ass. I introduced her to Kyle, whom she was surprised to see. I thought I was going to have to do much more coercing than I actually did in order to get her into the Jacuzzi.

The Jacuzzi was another test of mine. I had never seen Kyle fuck a whore in the Jacuzzi. Maybe it had something to do with the number of whores he had seen me fuck there, I can't be sure, but for some reason he had, to my knowledge, never fucked a girl in the Jacuzzi. I reasoned that if he would fuck a whore at the same time I was while in the Jacuzzi then all traces of his old self had been erased.

Emily claimed she had no suit. This claim was, of course, met with the standard and mandatory counter that we could just all go naked, which she agreed to. When she disrobed I was stunned at the lack of fat on her body. I hated fat whores more than regular whores, but I came to realize all too quickly that overly muscular whores were the worst of all three. Her breasts were small and the striations of muscle beneath them were visible. It was strange. Not strange enough to deny fucking, but strange.

Once in the Jacuzzi we had a conversation that lasted no more than thirty seconds before I suggested that Emily kiss Kyle, which she did. I moved around behind her as she kissed him and started to rub her back, just testing the water in terms of discovering if she would allow the impromptu threesome. Not only would she allow it, but she herself reached back with one of her hands and grabbed my cock. I looked at Kyle to see what his reaction was to the event that was about to unfold, waiting for him to become uncomfortable and leave the Jacuzzi. The reaction never came.

As Emily pulled back from Kyle and started to kiss me, he actually raised her ass up out of the water and started to finger her from behind without hesitation. Her moans were evidence of her acceptance of what was about to happen.

I stood from the water and forced my cock into her mouth at the same time Kyle stood from the water, grabbed a condom from a small basket I kept by the Jacuzzi, jerked himself off to erection, put the condom on, and thrust himself into her so hard that I felt her teeth graze the base of my cock.

I looked down at Emily with my cock in her mouth and smiled. It was amusing to me. I looked across at Kyle and saw his face twisted in labored anger, a bead of sweat running down his temple as he fucked her like you might imagine a man might rape another man in a prison shower. There was no joy in this for him; there wasn't even a release of any of his pent-up rage. It seemed that as he fucked her it only served to recycle and purify his anger.

In an effort to lighten his mood I reached across Emily's back and held up my open hand, offering to give him a high-five while my dick was in her mouth and his was in her cunt. Instead of a high-five, he looked up and gave me a closed-fist punch to the hand, unable to enjoy the absurdity of how easy it was to demean this whore. It was more like he felt obligated in some way to return my high-five in a manner that would expend as little energy as possible so he could focus it all back into the rage he felt while fucking her. In all honesty, I was slightly scared that Kyle might accidentally slip into a psychology that would make him capable of a criminal sexual act that very night.

Thankfully he blew his load a few seconds later, pulled out, and vacated the Jacuzzi immediately. I remained and fucked Emily in the ass, accidentally causing her to bleed slightly. She was surprisingly a good sport about it, claimed that she had never done a threesome with two guys before, and maintained that she enjoyed herself. I couldn't have cared less.

After Emily left I found Kyle in an upstairs guest bedroom watching an old UFC that was still on the TiVo. I tried to engage him in conversation about the night's events, but he was uninterested. I wanted to confront him about his change in personality, make sure he was doing okay, ask if he needed any of my help, et cetera, but it seemed pointless. Instead we planned the next date I would have with Heather.

I got the first F of my entire life a few days after I had my first three-way with Brett and his mom's trainer. It was on a midterm in genomics and bioinformatics, a class I didn't even need to graduate. I was actually interested in it and I still failed the fucking midterm. And it wasn't even a difficult exam. It covered the basic standard technology used in most molecular genetics labs around the country. It was fucking memorization. I rationalized getting the F by telling myself it didn't matter, I was already accepted at a pretty good med school, and the class wasn't even mandatory for my major. Instead I should have seen it as an indicator that I was seriously fucking up my life and needed to snap out of it. But I didn't. Instead I told myself I would make it up somewhere down the road on the next exam and end up pulling out a passing grade.

My professor even called me into a mandatory meeting to talk about my failing grade, because he fucking saw that it was a symptom of a bigger problem, but I didn't. He offered me extra-credit opportunities and told me I could retake the exam if I wanted to, on a graduated scale so the highest grade I could get was a 75, but it was still a chance to bring up my score from the 52 I got. I told him I'd just study harder for the final and pull my overall grade up in the end. He actually told me he thought I was one of the smartest students he had seen in the biology department in a long time and he knew the reason I failed the exam wasn't that I didn't get the material. He was a cool guy and now I wish I would have listened to him.

Instead I left his office and went to Homebar by my fucking self at three in the afternoon and proceeded to get drunk. I knew Heather and her sorority sisters hung out there and it was my plan to keep drinking until the place closed just to see if one of them showed up. My plan failed when I passed out at the bar at around seven or eight and they carried me out into the street and put me in a cab. I got home and puked on my floor and didn't even bother cleaning it up or brushing my teeth or taking a shower. I just got in bed and thought about Brett fucking Heather doggy style until he gave her herpes. Then I passed out.

I woke up to my phone ringing. It was Brett. I guess there were some guys from his frat at Homebar who had witnessed my binge drinking the night before and told him about it. He said he was concerned and thought I needed to take it down a notch. I told him to fuck off and went back to sleep.

I had to go to my parents' house that day for a barbecue that my dad always did just before Thanksgiving. Some of my cousins would come over, and some guys my dad worked with, and he'd cook a bunch of shit and they'd all watch football games and drink beer. I got there an hour late, which my parents weren't thrilled about, and proceeded to drink myself stupid fairly immediately. I'd say I pounded six or seven beers over the course of the first forty-five minutes I was there. I was almost too drunk to stand up, let alone carry on a conversation with anyone, and my mom and dad kept forcing me to talk to all of their friends, telling them how proud they were of me and what a great student I was. I had always been good at disguising my level of intoxication, but it was beyond me how they weren't even the slightest bit suspicious. I don't even know what I said to those people, but I'm sure it was gibberish. I'm sure my parents were really proud.

Then it got even worse when I got myself a plate of barbecued ribs and tried making my way into the living room to sit down for a while because shit was starting to spin. Instead I tripped over my own feet basically and threw the ribs all over my mom's white carpet, spilled beer all over the same carpet, then fell down and puked on the same carpet. It was your basic record-scratch moment.

I should have been embarrassed by the whole thing but I wasn't. Any normal human being would have wanted to die in that moment but I didn't fucking care at all. I almost enjoyed it, the fact that I had ruined something. I stood up, puke still dribbling down my chin, picked up the half can of Bud Light that didn't spill out when I dropped it, and took a fucking swig right there in front of the entire party.

My mom, I fucking love my mom, she came over to me and cracked a joke about having too much to drink and about how everyone's been there, and then she took me upstairs, sat me in the bathtub, and started crying. I made my mom fucking cry and this meant nothing to me. I was twenty-one years old and my crying mother was cleaning puke off me in the bathtub and I felt nothing, no guilt, no shame, no sadness, absolutely nothing. That's not true. I did feel something, but by that point it was the only thing I had felt for so long that it was almost like it wasn't there. I felt rage. As I sat there in the bathtub letting my mother clean me and trying not to puke again I felt like I wanted to punch everyone in the face who was downstairs at the party. It was like no one got it. No one seemed to realize what a sham everything was. Marriage, love, trying to make someone happy and thinking they care if you're happy . . . it was all a fucking lie and everyone believed it—everyone but me.

My mom cleaned me up, dried me off, and laid me down in my old childhood bed. She was still crying. She told me that she would love me no matter what and that I could tell her anything. Then she asked what was going on with me and I told her that I had just had a little too much to drink. She told me that ever since Heather and I had broken up she had noticed something different in me and it had gotten worse over the past few months. I told her not to worry about it. She gave me a hug and told me to go to sleep and I did.

I had been out with Brett on like three dates, like where it was just me and him, and I had hung out with him once with some other guys from ATO and some of my sisters at Homebar. It was like probably a week before winter break and I still hadn't fucked him and it seemed like my plan was working. Like the last time we went out he basically invited me to stay over at his house, so I knew he really wanted to fuck me bad. It was like basically impossible for me to keep from fucking him, too. He was so hot and he was Brett fucking Keller. So I was pretty proud of myself for coming up with a plan and sticking to it.

Anyway, that night he picked me up and he was like, "Tonight I thought we'd do something at my house. Is that okay?"

I pretty much already knew I had dragged out the no-fucking thing for as long as I could before he was going to lose interest so I was planning on fucking him that night. I was like, "Yeah, sounds good."

When we got to his house he was like, "Come here, I want to show you something," and he took me out in his backyard. It was kind of cold outside, so I hoped that whatever he was planning wasn't going to keep us out there long, but I was curious. When we got out in his backyard, it was seriously like the most romantic thing I had ever seen. There were heat lamps, like the kind at restaurants, going from the back door all the way out to the gazebo. In the gazebo there was a little table with some candles on it and it was set up for us to have dinner. And to make it even more insane, Brett had like a few of the maids from his house out there to serve us. It was unreal. I almost couldn't believe it was happening to me. There were a lot of girls who had been to Brett's house just to fuck him and everything, but I had never heard of any of them getting this kind of treatment. I really thought my plan to like not fuck him for the first few dates was paying off. I mean why would he have gone to that much trouble if he just wanted to fuck me, you know? That's what I thought anyway.

So we ate dinner and I don't even remember what we talked about really. I think I was like, "Where are your parents?"

And he was like, "My father's in Canada dealing with some business and his wife is in Florence with her sister."

I was like, "Oh."

I'm sure we talked about other stuff, but even as we were talking about it, I was forgetting it. I mean I was just so blown away by everything he did to make that night like seriously special.

So when we finished dinner we just left the gazebo and walked back inside. We just left everything on the table and his maids cleaned it up. It was so amazing. Back inside we had some wine and sat by this fireplace that was in a room I had actually never seen before. I mean I hadn't like been to Brett's house as much as Kyle had or anything, but I had definitely been over there at least a dozen or so times if you think about all the times I was there with Kyle when we were dating and everything. This room was really cool, though. It was like some kind of a study or something, but it was way bigger and Brett had set up candles everywhere, so the only light in the room was coming from the candles and the fireplace.

It only took like five minutes or so before he leaned in and kissed me and then we started making out and then he was like taking off my clothes. Honestly at that point I don't think I could have held out if I had wanted to. It was like the hottest night I had ever had with a guy.

Once we were completely naked he laid me down on this rug that was like some kind of animal skin or something. It was really soft and fuzzy and right by the fireplace. It was seriously like straight out of a movie. Then he started fingering me and I was so wet I was almost embarrassed but I couldn't help it I was so turned on by the whole thing. I was about to fuck Brett Keller.

I kind of got my bearings for a second and realized that I should probably be going down on him. I didn't want him to think that I didn't like doing blowjobs because I didn't want him to have any reason to ever want to stop seeing me. So I reached down and started jerking him a little bit and then started kissing him on the neck and the chest and the stomach and then moved down to his dick.

Ever since my first blowjob I had always given a guy's dick a quick once-over. It wasn't like I was checking to see if it was clean or anything. I guess I just like to look at it, you know, to check it out and see what it looked like. Some dicks look really weird, some look really hot. So I looked at Brett's and I noticed something that would definitely have been in the weird category. There were some red spots, like closer to the nuts than the head, on the shaft of his dick. I didn't want to say anything. I mean, it was Brett Keller and this was the first time I was going to have sex with him. But there were these two red spots on his dick.

I put my mouth on the head of it for like one second and then I couldn't help myself. I was like, "Brett?"

He looked down at me while my face was like an inch from his dick and he was like, "Yeah?"

I was like, "Um . . . I know this is kind of a weird question, but you have two like red spots on, you know . . ."

He was like, "Really?"

I was like, "Yeah, is it like cool for us to be doing this?"

He grabbed his dick and checked it out himself for a few seconds, found the red spots, and pointed at them. He was like, "You mean these?"

I was like, "Yeah."

He started laughing and he was like, "This is kind of embarrassing but I guess I'll tell you. The past few weeks that we've been going out, I haven't really had any sex with anyone else. I guess I just felt like that would have been wrong so I needed to kind of, uh, take care of myself if you know what I mean."

I was like, "Jerking off?"

He was like, "Yeah. And I kind of did it a lot and, uh, rubbed myself raw in a few spots."

I was like, "Oh, really? It's from jerking off?"

He was like, "Yeah. I know it's really gross, but . . ."

I was like, "What were you thinking about when you jerked off?"

He was like, "You, mostly."

That was about the hottest thing I had ever heard in my life. Brett Keller was thinking about me and jerking off so much that he rubbed raw spots on his dick. I gave him the best blowjob I've ever given a guy, and just before he was about to cum I stopped and got on top of him. I didn't even ask if he had a condom or anything and he never stopped me to ask for one either, so I just assumed he was cool with it. At one point he was like, "Are you on the pill?"

I was like, "No."

Then he was like, "Then we can't finish like this."

I was like, "You can do whatever you want."

So he flipped me over and fucked me doggy style for a few minutes and then pulled out and I thought he was going to jerk off on my back, but instead he rubbed the tip of his dick around the rim of like my butthole and he was like, "I want to finish in your ass."

I had never really been a fan of anal, and I kind of wished that my first time with Brett would have finished like in missionary or something so we could look at each other or whatever, but it was so fucking hot I really didn't care. I was like, "Okay."

He put it in pretty slow so it didn't hurt that much but once he got going it hurt pretty bad. Luckily it only took him like a minute or two until he came. When he finished he pulled out and sat down on the rug. He was like, "There's a bathroom over that way if you need it."

I could feel his cum dripping out of my asshole, which was kind of gross, but I didn't want to leave him. So I kind of snuggled up next to him and was like, "I'm okay."

I didn't really even come close to having an orgasm in anything we did that night, but I thought it was the hottest sex I had ever had. I was like, "Oh my God, that was incredible."

He was like, "Yeah. Do you want to stay over tonight?"

I almost started crying I was so happy. I was like, "Yeah, I'd love to."

We went up to his room and got in his bed. I mean I went to the bathroom in between and got as much of his cum out of my ass as I could, but then we went and got in his bed. He fucked me like five or six more times that night and into the next morning. And there were a few times that we didn't even fuck, but he would just rub his limp dick like all around my pussy. We never used a condom and I never came. Like, in retrospect I should have paid a little more attention to those details I guess.

chapter
twelve

It was with great pride that I found myself knocking on the front door of Kyle's apartment on the afternoon following the first night I fucked Heather. Several knocks were required until a disheveled and clearly hungover Kyle answered his door. I had seen countless fraternity drunks on the morning that followed an all-night bender. Kyle was far beyond that. He more closely resembled a sixty-year-old career alcoholic—dead eyes, without even an inkling of joy derived from the night that had produced such a hangover, just pain and annoyance at the world that wouldn't let him sleep—than did he a binge-drinking undergraduate student. I hoped my news of our plan's success would change his mood.

I informed Kyle that after much posturing I had been able to engage in unprotected sex with Heather during a visible outbreak at least half a dozen times, with some added attempts to rub my open sores on and around her cunt. I further informed him that I never came inside her in any orifice that could produce an offspring, opting instead to spread my seed over as much of her body as I possibly could, also taking these opportunities to rub my exposed blisters on her flesh wherever possible. I wasn't positive that she had contracted my virus, but it seemed highly likely.

Kyle's reaction was a smile and an invitation to go get lunch, which I accepted. It was good to see him excited about anything, and he was excited. He insisted that we go to Chick-fil-A, his favorite. I took this as a sign that perhaps my old friend was returning—perhaps the completion of his revenge on Heather had ended the horrible cycle he had begun almost a year ago.

At lunch he begged for every detail, which I found strange. It wasn't that I had any respect for whores or for the sexual act as anything more than an opportunity to express dominance over a whore and to expel semen, but it was somehow strange to me that he would want the images in his mind of me debasing the whore he used to claim to love. Nonetheless I obliged. His favorite moment in the recounting of the prior night's events seemed to be when I made Heather use the tip of my dick like she would a tube of ChapStick and apply my semen to her lips. It was good to see him smile again.

After the initial retelling of the story Kyle was curious to know when I would next see Heather. I explained that I would likely never see her again. Kyle entreated me to see and fuck her as many times as I possibly could in order to maximize the chances that she would contract my virus. I observed that if the prior night's activities were not enough for her to contract the virus, then she must have the world's most resilient immunity to it. I was in the middle of a visible outbreak and my unsheathed cock had swabbed virtually every inch of her body including her genitals and mouth. He seemed content with this, but required a promise from me to inform him when and if I ever became aware of Heather's positive herpes status. This went without saying in my mind.

The conversation then turned to an outcome neither of us had previously anticipated. What if Heather contracted the virus but kept this information hidden from everyone? We might never know if our plan had worked. And it was on the basis of this possibility that Kyle insisted I continue to date her. Even if she wouldn't divulge the information, surely I could bear witness to an outbreak when it occurred once she had contracted the virus. Despite the fact that I had become overwhelmingly tired of dealing with Heather and pretending to be interested in her at all, I could do nothing but agree with Kyle. To see our plan to its end required obtaining conclusive evidence of our success.

Winter break was fast approaching, and I had scheduled another trip to Viking's Resort, among other trips that would have me out of the country for virtually the entire month. Kyle and I both reasoned that this would do little to dampen Heather's interest in me so long as I explained to her that I was interested in having an exclusive relationship with her. We agreed that this was the best plan of action and that I would fuck her once a week during this false relationship and then dump her as soon as the evidence we required was produced.

Happy with our plan, we finished lunch and I returned to the Alpha Tau Omega house, where I encountered Gordon Hallern, a sophomore who was so similar to Greg in virtually every respect that I wished him dead. He served as an undeniable reminder to me that, despite any attempt I could possibly make to change the unfaltering path upon which we were all set, the path would right itself. I might have been able to stop Greg from becoming the cog in the wheel he was destined to become, but the machine itself would create another Greg to take his place. It was disheartening.

It seemed Gordon had just returned from Deep Ellum, where he'd gotten his first tattoo, and he felt the need to display it for anyone who would view it. When I saw what it was, the futility of everything became so crystal clear it was painful.

Across his stomach, in a style and lettering similar to Tupac Shakur's "Thug Life" tattoo, Gordon had the words "Bitches Ain't Shit . . ." It was clearly a reference to Dr. Dre's seminal masterpiece "Bitches Ain't Shit" from 1992's *The Chronic*, but it was in the style of Tupac. I wondered if this was done on purpose, done by mistake, or, more likely, done with only a minor knowledge of the origin of the phrase and a misplaced respect for its overuse in the suburban white culture Gordon had no doubt grown up in. I wondered what my father would think if he knew that Gordon had this tattoo when he hired him for his first job, which I was certain was inevitable. I was one step closer to having the conversation with my father about rejecting the life he would have me lead. I wondered if exposing the fact that I had herpes would make that conversation easier, possibly giving my father something else to place his disappointment in rather than just my own decision to reject what was essentially his own life.

After getting the good news from Brett about Heather, something changed for me. I started actually being able to think about other things. I still didn't know if the whole plan had worked, but I felt like there was already some closure on the whole situation and I guess that's what I really wanted the whole time, just to know that someone as horrible as her couldn't just get away with completely fucking somebody over like she did me.

The first thing I did was to e-mail my genomics professor and tell him that I was interested in retaking my midterm if the offer was still open. The semester was really close to being over and our finals were happening the next week, but he was nice enough to cut me some slack. The only shitty thing was that I would have to take the midterm retest on the same day I would take the final. It wasn't fun but I did it.

I got the highest grade in the class on both of the exams. The retest, of course, was on a 75-point scale, so even though I got a 99 percent on it I was only given a 74. And I got a 98 percent on the final. So I ended up pulling out a high B overall that semester in genomics and bioinformatics, which wasn't bad. It was my first B, but I could live with it. It wasn't anything that would really raise any eyebrows on the admissions board at UT Houston and that's all that actually mattered.

I went home to visit my parents on the weekend before our winter break started and apologized to them for the party I ruined. The morning after that party I had just kind of left without telling them and I hadn't really said much to them since. I didn't know how to say what I wanted to. But after my conversation with Brett I felt good enough about everything that it wasn't that big of a deal to talk to them about it because I really felt like that was in the past.

I told them that breaking up with Heather had really screwed me up but that I was over it and I was glad to have them as parents and I thanked them for putting up with me while I was such an asshole. They were happy to have me apologize and told me that they loved me no matter what but that they were a little scared for me there a few times, the party being the most scared they'd ever been. I felt bad about that, really bad, but like I said, it really felt like all of that shit was behind me.

I didn't get to see Brett like at all over the winter break. He was off on a bunch of trips out of the country with his parents and everything, which was like not that big of a deal I guess. But before he left he took me out to dinner and he was like, "Heather, I think we should be an exclusive couple. What do you think?"

I seriously like literally almost crapped in my pants. I mean like at the beginning of the year I was totally fucked, and then by winter break I had Brett fucking Keller asking me to be his girlfriend.

I was like, "I think that sounds seriously awesome."

He was like, "Me too."

I was like, "Oh my God, this is so exciting. What should we do to celebrate?"

He was like, "We should finish eating dinner and then we should go back to my house and fuck."

We did a lot of fucking. Not like every day or anything—I mean we actually only saw each other like once a week because Brett was always busy doing stuff—but when we would get together it was like he would fuck me like five or six times in a night and rub his dick all over me. I thought it was kind of weird, but it wasn't any weirder than like Brian forcing me into a three-way with Josh. I just thought like every guy had his thing and Brett's thing was rubbing his dick on me. I guess I should have thought about that a little more.

So I wasn't having sex with any other guys and like probably a month after our second semester started I was in the shower shaving my pubes and I noticed a little red spot right on the outside of my left lip. And then I noticed one on the inside of the right lip. I was like, "What the fuck?"

I went to the health center to get it checked out and the guy looked in my vag and everything and he was like, "Are you sexually active?"

I was like, "Yeah."

He was like, "Do you engage in unprotected sexual activity with multiple partners?"

I was like, "I just have one partner at the moment."

He was like, "Well, you're going to want to tell your partner that you have herpes simplex 2."

I was like, "What? Is that like the cold sore one?"

He was like, "It's genital herpes." Then he handed me a pamphlet that was all about dealing with getting herpes. I was so fucking pissed and panicked I had no idea what to do.

The guy was like, "One in four people have herpes simplex 2, so it's not the end of the world. There are many medications available now that can suppress outbreaks so you get them as infrequently as once every few years. That pamphlet covers most of it and directs you to a few websites that should answer any questions you might have. If you feel you still have questions please don't hesitate to contact us here at the health center."

Then the guy took off his rubber gloves and was like, "You can get dressed now," and left.

I just sat there with no pants on and my vag hanging out for like five minutes. I felt so fucking gross, like I was basically ruined for the rest of my life. I had fucking herpes—like how in the hell did I get herpes?

I started going through the whole list of guys I had fucked without a condom and I didn't think anyone had herpes. But from the end of our junior year and kind of into the first part of our senior year there were like a lot of guys that I fucked because I thought they were into me, and any one of them could have had herpes.

I never thought it was Brett. I mean we had just started dating like exclusively and everything was going so well and he really seemed to like me. I just never thought it was him. And on top of that I actually felt bad that I might have given him herpes. We never used condoms and we had had a lot of sex. I felt like such shit. More than feeling bad for him, though, I felt bad for myself. I had basically landed the best guy in school and now I was going to have to tell him I had herpes.

Then I started thinking about if I was going to have to tell my mom about it and that was fucking gross to me. Like what was I going to say? "Hey, mom, nice to see you. Your skanky daughter fucked some guy without a rubber and now she has herpes. I love you."?

Then I started thinking about who I was going to date. I almost thought I wouldn't tell Brett, would just keep it a secret and hope he never got herpes from me. If I did tell him, I hoped he'd be understanding enough to stay with me. I knew that was pretty unlikely, though. I started thinking that there were probably like dating sites dedicated to people who had herpes. That's where I was probably going to have to find my husband—on fucking eHarmony.com but for herpes.

Seriously, my life was fucking over.

I was perusing the personal ads at a website called prescription4love
.com, which I came to after searching "herpes dating site." I had assumed two things: (1) A herpes dating website must exist, and (2) any
whore desperate enough to list her profile on such a site would be willing to engage in sexual acts so degrading they might put a normal
whore to shame. What I found on prescription4love.com was nothing
less than mind-blowing.

Not only was there an entire member's section devoted solely to
helping people with herpes meet one another, there were sections of
the site devoted to people with AIDS, cancer, obesity, deafness, diabe-
tes, IBS, impotence, allergies, hepatitis, alcoholism, epilepsy, arthritis,
dwarfism, MS, para- and quadriplegia, Parkinson's, burns, lupus, HPV,
ADD, Asperger's, autism, breathing disorders, psychiatric disorders,
blindness, heart disease, cerebral palsy, dyslexia, Tourette's, chronic
fatigue syndrome, anxiety disorders, skin problems, et cetera. In short,
I learned that the Internet was a treasure trove of horribly desperate

whores who already had such amazing doubt about their own self-worth that they could easily be exploited into any act I chose.

I was midway through writing my descriptive paragraph for a profile to appear in the burn victim section of the site when my doorbell rang. I let the maid answer the door and heard Heather's voice. An unannounced visit was strange. I assumed she had discovered a herpes lesion on her cunt and was standing in my doorway to confront me and unleash her anger on me for having given her the virus. I was only partially correct.

She sat down with me in one of two living rooms near the front of the house, put her hand on my hand, adopted a wistful gaze, and blathered on for several minutes about how important I was to her and how much our relationship meant and how in the time we had spent together she had come to realize that she had found someone with whom she thought she could spend much of her life, et cetera. It was difficult to keep from laughing, but I wanted her to go through her entire process. I wanted her to speak every word that I knew she had rehearsed in her bedroom multiple times before finally delivering her performance. I wanted her to put all of her effort into this last attempt to keep me and then I wanted to destroy her.

So I waited. I waited through several more minutes of her listing some of the moments in our short relationship that she had come to value as precious memories. I listened to her recount the first time we met when she was still dating Kyle. I listened to her explain that she had told her mother about me and her mother was apparently very excited to meet me.

And when the first half of her performance was over, she turned somber and claimed that there was something she had to tell me. As I was a person she had the utmost respect and admiration for, she felt it wasn't right to keep such a thing a secret from me. She went on to say that she didn't know from whom she had contracted the virus, but she had conclusive proof that she was a carrier of herpes simplex 2, genital herpes.

She had become conscious of her herpes infection during a recent trip to the student health center, shortly after discovering some red blisters in and around her cunt in the shower. She had not, however, even contemplated finding fault with me for her new status as an STD carrier. This was something I had hoped would happen but was less than certain of.

As soon as the final word, "herpes," fell from her lips, I jerked my hand out from under hers, conjured the finest fake attitude of outrage I had ever mustered, and began a tirade so excessively angry that I thought Heather must have assumed I meant to do her physical harm.

I hit every insulting point I could in my monologue, whether I knew the insults to be true or not. I called her a whore and told her that only the most irresponsible and intellectually stunted people on earth allowed themselves to contract herpes. I accused her of cheating on me while we were an official couple over the winter break. I accused her of being aware of her status before we ever started fucking and keeping it from me so I wouldn't dismiss her. I accused her of only being interested in my money, which, of all the insults, was probably the most accurate. I ended by telling her that if she gave me herpes I would tell not only the entire student body of SMU but the entire city of Dallas, Texas. She, of course, broke down sobbing, her herpes-laden tears falling into the ten-thousand-dollar fabric of my stepmother's favorite couch. I momentarily thought of my stepmother sitting on the couch naked and contracting herpes from Heather's tears, no matter how unlikely it seemed.

After I had my fill of watching her cry, I commanded Heather to get out of my house and told her never to call me again. She tried to give me a hug and I refused. She cried some more, and the maids were watching, so I finally gave her one in the hopes that she would be appeased and leave peacefully. As we embraced, I whispered into her ear that if she just would have stuck with Kyle none of this would have happened. I thought this final twisting of the blade would keep her awake at night, and I knew it would be a welcome addition and punctuation to the story I would be telling Kyle the following day.

As I watched Heather drive away from my home that day, sobbing so violently it appeared that she was convulsing, I could only feel pride for Kyle and myself. We had created a plan and carried it through to fruition. In some way I'm sure my father would have been proud of me. This thought led me to realize the time was fast approaching to have what would be his most disappointing conversation with me. I set the date in my mind for this conversation to take place on my graduation day. It seemed a good time to make the break from both my academic life and my father simultaneously.

chapter
sixteen

I felt like the Incredible Hulk immediately after he was the gray Hulk and then got transformed back into the green Hulk, but had all of Bruce Banner's intellect. Maybe the analogy is a bad one, but after Brett told me the good news I felt like my old self again, except that I also understood there was value in having meaningless sex with as many different girls as possible. I felt like I had come out of a coma or something. It was good to care about shit again and not feel like I wanted everyone to die. It was almost like in a movie—at the very end, after the good guys take out the bad guys, there's always one last scene with the good guys sitting around saying to each other, "Wow, that was some crazy shit, but it's all over now." That's what it felt like for about a week—until the extra scene that's not in any movie happened, the one where the good guys fuck everything up and ruin their lives.

After coming out on the other side of the whole thing I had a new outlook on frats and sororities in general. It was obviously too late to rush or anything—we only had a few months left of school—and honestly I don't think I would have rushed anyway. I just mean that I didn't think the guys in frats were as douchey as I once had thought, and I saw the benefit of being able to get drunk and have sex with different girls every night in a way I never had before.

Brett's frat was throwing a big party with Heather's sorority and he told me I should show up. It wasn't very normal for someone not in a frat to be at one of these parties, but an invitation from Brett was about as good as it got in terms of preapproval by everyone at the party, even for an outsider.

I was never really coherent enough, nor did I really ever care enough, during my drinking-and-fucking binge to realize that I guess I had kind of developed a reputation among the girls of the Greek system. In retrospect it seems like that reputation would have been a bad one, because I basically got drunk, stayed at Brett's house a lot, and had sex with any girls he brought over, including a fair number of the ones at that party. Instead, though, every girl I saw said hello to me; some even gave me a kiss when they saw me. At the beginning of this party I felt like I was getting to see what it was like to live in Brett's shoes for a little bit. Then I really got to see what it was like when every girl who said hi to me started asking me if I could take her to Brett's house. Before the thing with Heather was resolved that would have pissed me off and I would have wanted to fuck any chick who asked me that, shoot a load in her face, and tell her to fuck off. But at that party I actually found it all kind of amusing.

I ended up making out with a few random girls here and there. I was half-expecting Heather to show up, but since it was a party thrown by Brett's frat I guess it made sense that she wouldn't be there, given the events that went down a few weeks earlier. All in all it was a pretty good night until the party started winding down.

At about three in the morning I found myself standing with Brett and three other guys from his frat. One of the guys was named Gordon. Gordon had his shirt off so everyone could see a tattoo he had across his stomach that said, "Bitches ain't shit . . ." It was pretty obvious Brett hated his fucking guts. The fact that Gordon had already openly questioned my attendance at the party didn't help.

Gordon said, "So I took this bitch's head and totally shoved it down toward my crotch and I was like, 'Bitch, suck that dick.' And she was like, 'Okay, but don't cum in my mouth,' and I go, 'Okay.' So this bitch starts sucking and about fuckin' five minutes later I'm ready to nut all over her. So instead of telling this bitch, 'Get ready for my load,' I just don't say anything and spray a rope down her throat. She fuckin' tries to jerk her head back but I hold this bitch's dome down with both hands until she swallows my shit." Then he punched me in the shoulder and said, "You ever done some gangster shit like that, dude?"

I didn't know how drunk Brett was or how much he actually hated this kid, but I guess the levels of both things were off the fucking charts because Brett proceeded to say, "Gordon, you're a fucking moron. You think you have it all figured out and you think you're a real fucking badass, but you're a fucking punk piece of shit who will have punk-piece-of-shit babies who will do the same and so on and so forth until this whole world is populated by pieces of shit just like you. You want to know about some real gangster shit, Gordon, take a look at my friend Kyle here. Take a look at the guy you don't even think should be at this party."

He put his arm around me and said, "Kyle isn't in a fucking frat. He doesn't have a shitty Tupac tattoo on his stomach. But you know what he did, Gordon, that you'll never ever do in your life?"

Gordon said, "What, bro?"

Brett said, "He loved a girl so much that when she fucked him over, he fucking ruined her life forever."

Gordon said, "What? Dude, what the fuck are you talking about?"

I said, "Brett, it's cool. You probably actually shouldn't say anything."

Brett said, "No, Kyle, this fucking shit-eater needs to know who he's standing across from and show some fucking respect."

I said, "Really, it's fine, Brett."

Brett said, "My friend Kyle here concocted a scheme to give a whore herpes and it fucking worked."

I could tell Gordon was actually impressed. He said, "No fucking way, dude," and he put out his fist for me to punch, which I did in an attempt to try and end the situation before Brett said anything else. It didn't work.

Brett said, "You all know this whore. Heather Andruss."

Gordon said, "Holy shit, yeah, you were the dude she dumped for giving her a fake ring or some shit, right? And you gave her the fuckin' herp for that shit? How'd you get the herp?"

I said, "I don't know what Brett's talking about."

Gordon said, "Wait, though. I thought *you* were dating that biatch for a minute, Brett."

Brett tapped Gordon on the forehead. "And the gears do turn in that little machine, don't they?"

Gordon said, "Holy shit, dude—you gave her the herp, Brett!"

Brett said, "The lord giveth and the lord taketh."

Then Brett puked right in the middle of our little circle and stumbled off somewhere in the house.

Without reacting to the puke at all, Gordon said, "Dude, you had your friend fuck your ex-girlfriend to give her herpes? That is some sick-ass shit, bro. One love." Then he hugged me and said, "Seriously, dude, that is some shit of legend. I'm glad I got to meet you tonight. But what the fuck, so Brett has fuckin' herpes? Who gave him fuckin' herpes?"

All I could say was, "I don't know," before I found my way out of the party and back to my apartment. That night I wondered if Gordon or the other two guys would tell anyone. I wondered if anyone would believe it if they did.

chapter
seventeen

I was like, "Uh . . . are you fucking kidding me?" Seriously, I thought Gina was fucking high on meth or something. I was like, "Who told you this?"

She was like, "Kim Darcey."

I was like, "And where in the fuck did she like hear it from again?"

She was like, "She was fucking that sophomore guy in ATO with the tattoo, Gordon or whatever, and he was like trying to have anal with her and she didn't want to and he supposedly was like, 'Don't make me give you herpes like Brett did to that one slut in Kappa,' and she was like, 'What are you talking about?' and he told her the whole thing, like that Brett and Kyle totally made a plan to give you herpes."

I was like, "Can you please leave me alone for a few minutes?"

She gave me a hug and was like, "Let me know if you need anything. I'll be downstairs."

I just sat in my room like a statue for like half an hour. I seriously don't even think I was like breathing. It was like, did Kyle think he didn't ruin my life enough when he tried to get me to marry him with a fake ring? He had to give me fucking herpes, too? And then Brett . . . what the fuck? He like made me think I got it from someone else and then dumped me just to be a fucking asshole. Ever since Brett dumped me I had basically just like sat in my room all day wishing I would die. But after Gina told me that shit, I was beyond mad. I seriously thought about getting a gun and shooting someone. I thought if it went to court or something and I like shot Brett's and Kyle's dicks off, I would probably not end up going to jail. The jury would totally understand where I was coming from.

But instead of killing anyone I just sat there. Gina came back up with some vodka and we started drinking. And I was like, "I don't know what to do."

Gina was like, "You should totally get even with them."

I was like, "How?"

Gina was like, "I don't know, like give Kyle herpes or something or accuse them of rape or something. That would fuck them up for sure."

I was like, "But if I accuse them of rape, like I'm going to have to get checked by a doctor and everything and they'll find out it's a lie."

Gina was like, "Not if you actually have sex with them."

I was like, "Brett will never even talk to me again, let alone like actually have sex with me."

Gina was like, "So get Kyle to do it and say it was Brett or something."

Then we just got drunk as hell and I passed out. The next morning I remembered all the stuff Gina and I had talked about, but it all seemed a little crazy, so I just kind of blew it off. Then I got out of bed and took a shower. In the shower all I could do was stare at the little red spots around my vag, and seriously like doing that for ten minutes straight made me want to kill Kyle and Brett again. But I got out of the shower and just tried not to think about it.

Then that night I was at a party, it wasn't an ATO party or anything, but Brett was there anyway. And it was seriously like everyone in the place was staring at me and like laughing and shit. So I think pretty much everyone knew by that point everything that had happened. I was so fucking pissed. So I just did as many drugs as I could find at the party, which wasn't actually a bunch, just some coke and E, pretty standard I guess. I guess I kind of wanted to leave the party, but something in me was like, no, you should stay and prove to these assholes, to Brett, that you deserve to be here just as much as anyone else. And it turns out that it was a good thing that I stayed because I didn't really know how I was going to get even with Brett and Kyle until later that night. And honestly it wasn't even my idea.

I had just come out of the bathroom where I made myself puke because I was starting to feel way too drunk and I stumbled into a bedroom where there was like a full-blown orgy happening. At first I was like gross, but then I realized what was actually going on. Brett was fucking like four girls. I knew three of them and then there was just some other random chick. The lights were out and I could only really tell who it was from the light coming off a neon Dos Equis thing that was hanging on the wall in the room. I was about to leave and then Brett was like, "Why don't you join us?" He obviously didn't know it was me, but as soon as he said it, I knew exactly what I was going to do.

So I like took off my clothes and hoped the three girls I knew were too fucked up to notice it was me, or maybe just too fucked up to like care it was me, which they were. And it seemed like Brett was even more fucked up. And there were five girls in bed with him and it was dark. I was pretty sure he like wouldn't figure out it was me. I had never done anything like that before and I didn't really like it or anything, but I guess because I had like a specific goal in mind as I was doing it, it wasn't that bad.

I made sure to not do any of the things that I did with him when we slept together before, like not use any of the same techniques or anything, in case he might recognize me. I guess it was because he was drunk or something but it took like a long time for him to cum. He fucked like every girl in the room, including me, which I thought for sure would make him recognize me, but it didn't. And then finally he came. When he did, I took the condom and went in the bathroom. I probably wouldn't have done this if I wasn't super drunk and high, but whatever. I turned it inside out and stuck it up my vag and kind of moved it around to get as much of his semen inside me as possible. I didn't think it had any spermicide on it, but even if it did and like the baby was retarded or something it didn't really matter. I just needed to get pregnant. Then I went home.

I waited like three weeks, which was a week after I missed my first period, and took a home pregnancy test. I was pregnant. I honestly didn't think smearing his semen in my vag would work and I kind of assumed that I would really never do anything to get revenge on Kyle and Brett. Like I said, I was seriously fucked up at that party and it was just like kind of something I did. But then once I found out it actually worked I guess I like got back in that mind-set of finishing the job, you know? Like I had to now carry out the rest of the plan.

So I was like fuck it. I put on some makeup and a shirt that really showed my boobs off and I went over to Kyle's house. He was there and he was fucking seriously surprised to see me. He was like, "Hey, what are you doing here?" He looked scared, too, like he probably knew that I knew everything, which is what made him even more pathetic than I already thought he was for what I was able to get him to do.

I was like, "I know we've had our differences and everything, but there's only a few months left in school and I just wanted to come over to like say that I'm sorry for everything and I guess I just like wanted you to know that."

I could see him starting to feel seriously guilty for making Brett give me herpes. He was like, "Oh, yeah, I'm sorry for everything, too."

Then I was like, "And I guess I also wanted you to know that through all of this stuff I guess I realized that like I never stopped loving you, you know?"

He was like, "Really?"

I put my arms around him and I was like, "Yeah. I mean I know getting back together would probably be a long shot, but I thought maybe we could have like one more time together before we graduate."

He was like, "Really?"

I kissed him and I was like, "I miss you," then I reached down and felt his dick through his pants. He was already hard. Fucking pathetic.

Seriously that's all it took. I'm not lying at all. That's how easy it was to get Kyle to fuck me again after all the shit we went through. All I had to do was like show up at his house, tell him I still loved him, and say I wanted to fuck him. What a fucking idiot.

But before we started he was like, "We should use a condom."

I was like, "Why? I'm on the pill."

He was like, "I know but since we broke up I've been with some different people and I'm sure you have too. We should just be safe."

I couldn't get around that one. It would have like been nice to have given him herpes too, but that wasn't why I was there so I was just like whatever and let him use a condom. While we fucked I was like, "Fuck me harder, come on, harder," which I know got him going, but it also served a purpose in my overall plan. He finished in like one second and then he was like, "We should go get dinner or something."

I was like, "I don't think that's a good idea. I mean, I just wanted one last time, you know?"

And he actually looked sad when I left. I seriously fucking hated him. I mean I guess I still do. Whatever.

So after that I went over to Brett's house. His maid let me in and he was pretty surprised to see me, too. I knew I probably wouldn't be able to get him to fuck me but I tried anyway.

He was like, "What are you doing here?"

I was like, "I have some stuff to talk about with you."

He was like, "Well, I don't want to talk to you. So leave."

I knew there was no point in beating around the bush so I was just like, "I know you and Kyle gave me herpes."

I thought he would have been more surprised but he was just like, "Okay, and now what?"

I was like, "Now Kyle is completely fucked, but you still have like a chance to avoid having your life ruined."

He was like, "Get to it."

I was like, "I just came from Kyle's place. He fucked me."

He was like, "No he didn't."

I was like, "He did. All I had to do was tell him I still like loved him and he caved."

He was like, "No, Kyle. Why?"

I was like, "I'm going to the health center immediately after leaving here and telling them I was raped."

He was like, "Did he fuck you without a condom? He knows you have herpes."

I was like, "No, he used a condom, but like date rape has a lot of gray area, you know? He's fucked. He's getting accused of rape and that's it for him."

He was like, "You can't really be this malicious."

I was like, "You fucking assholes gave me herpes. My life is fucking ruined. Do you get that?"

He was like, "I guess. So am I getting accused of rape too?"

I was like, "Not even close. You're going to be a daddy."

He was like, "I'm pretty sure I have to fuck you to be the father of any child and that will never happen again as long as I live because you're a fucking whore."

I was like, "A fucking whore who is pregnant with your child right now."

He was like, "First of all, that's impossible. Second—"

I was like, "Let me just like stop you at first of all, because first of all you did fuck me. Last month you were fucking like five girls at the same time. I was one of them and you got me pregnant."

He was like, "I remember that specific incident. I used a condom."

I was like, "Well, they're not like a hundred percent effective."

He was like, "You've got to be kidding me. You're not pregnant."

I was like, "I took the pregnancy test this morning and you're more than welcome to have it verified by a doctor if you want. And you're like the only guy who could even be the father, so if you want to do a DNA test, I'm down for that too."

He was like, "Is this even possible?"

I was like, "Yeah, totally possible."

He was like, "You know I have no obligation beyond financial to you if you have this child. I will never be a part of its life and I will never be a part of yours."

I was like, "Somehow I think that like when I tell your dad that he's going to be a grandfather, he'll make sure you're a part of your kid's life."

He just stood there for a few seconds, then he was like, "And so . . ."

I was like, "And so what?"

He was like, "And so . . . what's my out? You're obviously here to offer me some way out of this."

I was like, "I guess so. So like here's what I was thinking. I'll have an abortion, which you have to pay for, if you propose to me and marry me."

He was like, "Out of the question."

I was like, "Then I have the baby and tell your dad that I'm pregnant with it today."

He was like, "Wait. All I have to do is propose to you?"

I was like, "And actually marry me. With no prenup."

He laughed and was like, "You can conjure up all the babies you want for my father—there's no way around the prenup. Even he'll tell you that."

I was like, "Fine. You have to marry me and we have to stay married for at least like a year and you have to propose to me publicly in front of my sorority house. And if I get the abortion and you don't propose I tell your dad everything, and your stepmom especially, how you made me murder their grandchild."

He thought about it and then he was like, "And if I agree to this, will you spare Kyle?"

I was like, "You can't stop Kyle from being fucked. You're the only one who can potentially save yourself."

He was like, "Why are you doing this? Are you fucking insane?"

I was like, "Not at all. I was like thinking about getting a gun and blowing both your dicks off. That was insane. This is totally sane."

He was like, "And what happens at the end of a year?"

I was like, "We take it from there."

He was like, "But I can divorce you and you'll never tell anyone of this?"

I was like, "Yeah."

He was like, "This is not fucking happening."

I was like, "Yeah, it actually is. So like figure out what you're going to do."

He was like, "Well, it's kind of a big fucking decision so you're going to have to give me a little more time."

I was like, "Okay, you have until Friday. By then you'll probably already start to see how Kyle's life is falling apart. Maybe that'll help you make your decision."

Then I left and went to the health center. I worked up some tears and went through the front door and I was like, "Excuse me, I um, I was just like date-raped I think and I want to make sure I'm okay," and then I just broke down crying.

The lady at the desk was like, "Oh honey, I'm so sorry," and she took me back to a room where a doctor examined me and found like "signs of forced vaginal penetration," which is what he wrote in his little report. I had to keep crying but I wanted to like do a fucking dance I was so happy that Kyle's life was over.

chapter
eighteen

I called Kyle immediately after she left to confirm her report that he had, in fact, fucked her. He confirmed it. When I asked him why in the name of anything he held sacred he would have done such a thing, his only response was to tell me that through it all, even through engineering the plan that was meant to bring about her demise, he had always known that she was the one girl he would ever truly love. And to have her, even if it was just for one last time, was too tempting an offer for him to refuse. He said he wanted to feel like he did when they first met. It was the worst thing he ever said to me. I explained to him the dilemma I was faced with. He explained that he thought we could just go to someone and reveal her scheme, but she could counter with her knowledge of our own scheme to give her herpes, which there were witnesses to corroborate. We were the only people who knew about her plan. She could deny it and it would be her word against ours.

The person Kyle had grown into in those last months was one I would have never suspected capable of such a horrible relapse. But I will never understand this lie of love and its hold over people like Kyle. I told him about the conversation I had with Heather. He held strong to the notion that somewhere within herself she actually did still love him, that the sex she had with him wasn't all an act, that somewhere deep down they would always have a connection, and he reasoned that this connection would keep her from levying the accusation of rape against him. He was incorrect, and in spite of all that was to follow for Kyle I still believe it was the shattering of this hope he had—that she still cared for him—that hurt him the most.

After my phone call with Kyle I sat down and thought seriously about all of my options. I had a cousin who had impregnated a whore several years prior at Boston College, did not marry the girl, and ignored the child except for his financial obligation. He had been on track to go to work for my father's company and he was very well liked, not only by my father but by virtually everyone in our family. But once the child was born and he failed to marry its mother or pay it any attention, my father and most of the rest of the family quickly severed ties with him, effectively ruining his life financially. I could very easily see that treatment being mimicked in my case.

I remembered a specific conversation I had with my father at roughly the time of the birth of my cousin's child, in which he explained to me that we would not be attending my cousin's birthday party because the most valuable thing we have is our family's name and our cousin had tarnished that name. For that my father would never forgive him. I was young at the time, but my father's words landed with significant impact. I remembered him saying to me that my cousin was essentially dead, a member of the family to be forgotten.

With that said I essentially could expect one of two outcomes if I chose not to propose to Heather. The first would be that my father would see me just as he saw my cousin and excommunicate me from the family, severing all of my ties to anyone in the family, to any hope of being part of his business, and to any claim to the resource my family possessed. The second would be that my father would be severely disappointed, but because I was his son and not his nephew he would take more pity on me than he did my cousin, and after many years of repairing our relationship and doing anything and everything he said to do with my life I would be allowed all of the original privileges that came with being my father's son. With this second outcome I also assumed that I would be required to be a part of the child's life, even if I was not a part of its mother's. I knew my father would not stand for a blood member of his family, let alone his own grandchild, being neglected. The former seemed more likely to me, and the latter seemed a prospect that was almost worse.

My other option was to marry Heather. In truth I enjoyed fucking her. I had had far better, but I had had far worse as well. As a person she was clearly deplorable and her personality was vacant and uninteresting, but so too were the personalities of virtually every whore I had ever met. And marriage was the path my father had chosen for me to begin with. He would be more than proud if I was engaged upon my graduation and I would start work for him a few weeks after. These were the things I had already decided to deny in whatever life I might lead. But their comfort seemed appealing, much more appealing than the alternatives.

There was no good decision available to me so I made a bad one. I took Heather to the McCarthy Family Planning Clinic, where for the second time I paid for her to have an abortion.

chapter nineteen

I couldn't believe she actually did it. As she sat across from me at the disciplinary hearing she never even showed one sign of remorse or regret that she was ruining my life. It was unbelievable to me that she could be so callous.

Luckily there wasn't enough evidence to bring criminal charges. It was basically her word against mine. But it turns out that it didn't really matter that there was no criminal case. The disciplinary committee was enough to totally fuck me over.

I remember the guy who was in charge of it said, "Just because this case had no criminal evidence, it doesn't mean we don't take it very seriously. Our job as administrators is to make sure every student here feels that this is an environment which is safe and conducive to learning. If a student feels threatened and that threat is found by us to be real then we are required to take some form of action. With that said, we'd now like to hear from each of you."

Heather was already crying fake tears. What a fucking cunt.

She took her seat in front of the three members of the committee and said, "This is hard for me."

The guy running it said, "I know. Take your time, but please be as detailed as possible in your retelling of the events that took place so we can get an accurate picture."

She said, "I went over to his house because like it's our senior year and everything and we did really used to care about each other and I like wanted to have like one last conversation with him about everything and put all of the bad stuff that happened between us like in the past, you know?"

It was un-fucking-real to me how good she was at this. I wondered if she was just naturally talented or if her hatred of me boosted her performance up to the Oscar-winning level I was witnessing.

She said, "After we talked a little bit he leaned in and kissed me and I like totally admit that I didn't mind the kiss. It was actually kind of nice, you know? And then he started getting a little more aggressive and I started to feel uncomfortable a little bit, but I just kind of let it happen anyway. And then he started taking off my clothes and I got a little more uncomfortable and I like told him I was uncomfortable and he was like, 'No you're not. Just let it happen.'"

There was no way for me to object during this or I would have. I don't think I've ever told a girl, "Just let it happen," in my life. I don't think anyone outside of a bad after-school special about date rape has ever even used that fucking phrase.

She said, "He got out a condom, thank God, and then he started having sex with me. He was on top. As soon as he like . . . penetrated me I was like, 'Stop, I do not want to do this.'"

And then she really brought on the waterworks. I don't even know how to describe it. She was really good at what she was doing. I'll give her that.

She said, "I tried to get him off me but he held me down and after like a minute of struggling I just kind of went limp, you know, like my mind just shut off and I was like seeing everything like I was floating outside my body. I just wanted it to be over as soon as possible."

One of the people on this committee was a woman. She actually fucking came out from behind the desk she was sitting at, hugged Heather, and shot me a "fuck you, asshole" look. I didn't even have to tell my side of the story to know I was fucked with this bitch, but I did it anyway. My story was the real version, the true version. But of course everyone believed the lie.

I had to wait for forty-eight hours for the official decision after the committee's deliberation. I got a letter delivered to my apartment. Not a phone call, nothing in person, just a fucking letter that read:

Dear Kyle Gibson,

After careful examination of the evidence in your case, we must inform you of our decision to initiate immediate expulsion for your involvement in what we feel is a gross violation of student conduct.

If you have any questions please contact the Office of Student Conduct.

And that's how I got fucking expelled with about a month and a half left in my senior year. I was so pissed at Heather I wanted to give her fucking herpes again, or AIDS or something. But there was no fucking recourse for me whatsoever. Once the disciplinary committee made a ruling, there was no appeal process. It was absolute. I looked back at every little step along the way with her, from the night we met all the way up through getting expelled, and I just couldn't believe that that's how everything was going to end for me.

I, of course, had to tell my parents. They weren't too fucking happy. I never really knew if they believed me, either, that Heather cooked this shit up just to fuck me over. I think my dad might have, but I think my mom actually thought I raped Heather.

Word traveled pretty fucking fast to UT Houston and I got a pretty similar letter from them about a week later telling me that my acceptance into their medical program had been revoked after hearing about my recent expulsion and involvement in an act of student misconduct.

I moved back in with my parents while everyone else was graduating and tried to start figuring out how to pick up the pieces.

I like knew it was going to happen so it wasn't really a surprise or anything but it was still the best moment of my life like hands down, even though it was kind of fucked up. It was just after graduation and I was going back to the Kappa house where we were going to have like a graduation party with all of our families and everything. When I got closer to the house I saw Brett in a suit standing on the front porch. My mom and my sister were both with me and like pretty much most of my sorority sisters.

I was like, "Hey, Brett. What's up?"

He got down on one knee and flipped open this ring box, and I went from being so happy, because up to that point he was doing everything just like he said he would, to being ready to kick him in the balls. The ring in the fucking box was the exact same one Kyle gave me. It was the same fucking cubic zirconia.

I couldn't be like, "You fucking asshole," in front of everyone, so

I just had to be like, "Oh my God," and act all surprised and everything, and of course I accepted. He hugged me and kissed me in front
of my mom just like I told him he had to do and I tried to put it out
of my mind that the ring was a fake. I knew I could make him get me
a real one later. But it did kind of take something from the day, that
like I had to show pretty much everyone that ring and pretend it was
real, and I know there were some of my sisters who had seen the one
Kyle gave me who could totally tell it was the same ring. But nobody
said anything.

Later when Brett and I were alone, I was like, "You're a fucking asshole. Why'd you give me that ring?"

He was like, "Fuck you."

I was like, "You can't be all pissy through this whole thing."

He was like, "I can be however I want to be."

I was like, "But you're going to get me a real ring at some point,
right?"

He was like, "What do you mean by real? Can you touch it? Then it's
fucking real. That's the only fucking ring you're ever getting from me."

I was like, "I can't like believe you went on QVC and bought the
same fucking ring."

He was like, "I didn't. That's the exact ring Kyle gave you. He kept
it and I convinced him to let me give it back to you."

I was like, "What an asshole. Not you—Kyle."

He was like, "Why do you want to be married to a guy who fucking
despises you?"

I was like, "You don't really despise me."

He was like, "I despise you more than any human being on the
planet. You ruined my best friend's life and you're currently in the process of ruining mine."

I was like, "I'm not going to ruin your life. You'll see. It like won't
be that bad."

He was like, "You know I'm going to fuck other whores and never
be around and never spend any time with you, right?"

I was like, "Yeah you will."

He was like, "Why would I?"

I was like, "Because no other girl is going to fuck you when they find out you have herpes."

He was like, "That hasn't stopped any of them so far."

I was like, "Well then when they find out you're married and have herpes maybe that'll stop them."

He was like, "I can guarantee the wedding ring will make whores want to fuck me more. And I'm going to do it right in front of you, too. This is not going to be fun for you."

He seemed like he was really telling the truth and I started to think about like if this whole thing was a good idea or not. Like I knew the prenup would have something in there that would let Brett fuck like as many girls as he wanted and I wouldn't be able to get any money if we got divorced. That seemed like it would really suck. But then I like also knew that I would never have to work or do anything I didn't want to do really, so it seemed like a pretty fair trade-off. The only thing that I thought would kind of suck would be if Brett refused to have sex with me. Then I'd have to like cheat on him and if he ever caught me I'm sure he could divorce me and I wouldn't get anything in that case either. I just figured he was a guy and it wouldn't be that hard to get him to fuck me once in a while.

I looked at my ring. It really was a pretty ring, and as long as people thought it was real I guess it wasn't that big of a deal. And it wasn't like Brett lied to me when he gave it to me like Kyle did. I was pretty sure I could deal with that ring being my ring while we were married. It did kind of suck that it was from Kyle, but whatever.

chapter
twenty-one

And so on my graduation day, instead of having a conversation with my father about my need to be free to pursue my own path in life, I took my first step down the one he had walked before me.

After spending a few hours at Heather's sorority house, I was forced by her to attend a celebratory dinner with her mother, her sister, my father, and my father's wife. My nausea during the entire event was extreme. The smiles on the faces of each person present, mine included, betrayed the actuality of the circumstance. I wondered who my next wife would be.

At some point in the evening my father took me aside and told me that he was extremely proud of me and that he hadn't even known that Heather and I had been serious for long enough to think about marriage. He told me that he couldn't wait for his first grandchild, and he hoped it would be a boy who would run the company when I got too old to do it—which brought him to what he considered to be further cause for celebration. He told me that one of the positions of junior vice president of regional sales had just opened up and I was to begin work at the company headquarters in Las Colinas as soon as I wanted to. He impressed upon me that there was no real rush and hoped that I would spend some time with Heather in order to relax and enjoy life a little bit, maybe go to Europe, but when I was ready in a month or so the position was mine. He claimed to be excited to work side by side with me.

I told myself there would always be time to change my life, to have the conversation with my father that I should have been having with him on that day, to find my own path in the world. But I knew that was a lie.

kyle gibson

I worked at the movie theater full time until I got enough money to move out of my parents' house and into my own apartment. I remain one semester's worth of credits short of graduating and I haven't really given much thought to trying to finish undergrad. I'm going to reapply to some different out-of-state med schools next year. I think my MCAT scores and my grades in the pre-req classes should be good enough to get me in. But any school I apply to is going to ask why I got expelled from SMU as an undergrad, and they'll probably have access to my records, so if I just make something up, they'll know I'm lying. I don't hang out with Brett too much, as I'm sure you can imagine. It'd be a little weird.

heather andruss

In the end things didn't work out as well as I would have hoped, I guess. But like they turned out pretty good. Kyle got seriously fucked over. I heard he was working at a video store or a movie theater or something. I mean that's pathetic. I got married to Brett, which could be better, but I'm still Mrs. Brett Keller and we got to have like an incredible wedding with like two hundred people and everything and Kyle didn't get invited. He and Brett don't really talk all that much anymore. Brett had an invitation for him, but I threw it in the trash when I mailed them all. Brett doesn't really want to, but I think his dad really wants us to like have a baby so we're going to start trying. I think he fucks other girls, but he has sex with me pretty regularly actually, so whatever. He works all day and I just mainly like decorate our house, which is so amazing. It's not like as big as his dad's or anything, but it's really nice in Plano and we have a pool and everything. I have pretty much everything that matters and I really like my life.

brett keller

In the beginning each day was akin to passing a kidney stone. The circumstances of my existence were so difficult for me to accept that I experienced headaches, had trouble sleeping, eating, et cetera. I hated my job. I despised my wife. I missed my best friend. As time wore on, these things became easier to accept, or more accurately the pain they caused me became easier to dismiss. The tedious and meaningless functions of my job became comfortable routine. The sharp hatred I maintained for my wife and all women like her drifted into general apathy that made me able to tolerate her. The memories I clung to of time spent with Kyle in our youth faded into emotionless mental abstraction. I found pleasure in the repetitive pattern that my life had become. My father has made his desire for a grandchild clear. Heather wants a child. I will more than likely oblige them both within a year's time and try to find somewhere in me that hope for my child that I once had for myself, that he will find some way to escape this all.

ALSO BY CHAD KULTGEN

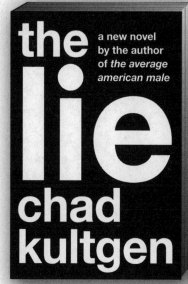

THE LIE
A Novel

ISBN 978-0-06-165730-6 (paperback)

From a writer whose unsettling, brutally honest, and undeniably riotous take on male inner life has rocked readers everywhere comes a dry and cynical tale of three college students who deserve each other.

THE AVERAGE AMERICAN MALE
A Novel

ISBN 978-0-06-123167-4 (paperback)

"It's so primal, so dangerous, it might be the most ingenious book I've ever read."
—Josh Kilmer-Purcell,
New York Times bestselling author of
I Am Not Myself These Days

"Buy Chad's book. It's a blueprint of how the mind—and penis—of a typical American male works."
—Maddox, author of
The Alphabet of Manliness

"An appalling book we couldn't put down."
—*Penthouse*